THE EARTHLING

The Earthling

Soldiers of Earthrise, Book I

Daniel Arenson

This novel is a work of fiction. Names, characters, places and incidents are either the product of the author's imagination, or, if real, used fictitiously.

Chapter One
Symphonica

Jon was waiting to join the war when his brother came home in a body bag.

At eighteen, Jon didn't want to fight. Like most boys his age, he was interested in girls, music, having fun. But he had graduated high school. His draft notice had come in the mail, folded inside a little brown envelope. In only a week, the army would take him. Break him. Train him. And send him into the fire.

His brother, Paul, had been only nineteen. Corporal Paul Taylor had not lasted long in the army. Not even a year. That meat grinder in deep space, that beast called the Colony War, had devoured another victim. Another kid who would never see twenty.

And still the beast was hungry.

I wonder how long I will last, Jon thought.

It rained during the funeral. They stood in the military cemetery—a sea of black umbrellas. They listened to the twenty-one gun salute. They watched Paul lowered underground.

The family was there, and they wept, and army officers were there, and they stood with solemn dignity. But Jon stood apart from them.

He stood with his friends. With the gang. The same gang Paul had belonged to. This group of misfits. This band of musicians, of poets, of dreamers. A band called Symphonica. A quartet cut down to a trio. They stood in the rain, scarcely believing, saying goodbye.

Him, Jon Taylor. Keyboardist and composer and leader of the losers. The rain in his long black hair.

George Williams, drummer. A giant, towering over the others, the largest boy in town, weeping like a child.

Kaelyn Williams, petite and pale, her red hair flowing. Soprano. Angel in the rain.

The three friends stood together. Survivors of Symphonica. They were the nerds, the outcasts, the lords of the suburbs. They grew up playing D&D and riding their bikes in the woods like stallions, dreaming of adventures in Middle Earth. They smoked weed in basements and listened to obscure symphonic metal bands from centuries ago. With their own band, they aped the ancient gods of metal. They themselves were but angels with clipped wings.

They shared secrets. They shared hopes. They wrote and played music, and they dreamed of stardom. As if there was no war. As if there was no meat grinder in space that tore boys and girls apart. As if the little brown envelopes had not come. Draft notices. Summonses to hell.

Symphonica. They were dreamers, and they were asleep.

And today, in this cemetery, they woke up.

Today they stood in the rain, saying goodbye to their guitarist, to their friend and brother, to their childhood.

The funeral ended.

The rain kept falling.

They walked home through mist and shadow.

"I still remember the day Paul left to war," Jon said later that day. "Only last year. And now he's gone."

And in a week, I will replace him, he thought, daring not speak of it. *I will stand on the front line, and I will face the enemy, and there will be nothing between me and them but a rifle in my shaking hands.*

And if I'm not strong enough, not brave enough, I will join Paul underground.

They were underground now too, though not yet in graves. The friends stood in Jon's basement—his little kingdom of music like the Phantom's lair. Posters of old symphonic bands hung on the walls, relics of better days, an era before the wars in space. Nightwish. Epica. Within Temptation. Holy names. The names of the old gods. Here in the basement was a temple. A keyboard stood like an altar, and a drum set rose like an orrery of planets. A purple guitar hung from the wall like a hallowed relic.

Paul's guitar. Silenced.

"We should play," Jon said. "For him."

The Williams siblings stared at him, silent.

George Williams was so tall he stood hunched over. Even so, his shaggy red hair brushed the ceiling. A tumor in George's brain, pressing on his pituitary gland, had caused him to sprout to a prodigious size. The doctors had removed the tumor two years ago. But they could not reverse his growth.

"I… I can't." George's voice was deep and rumbling like the drums he played. Tears flowed down his freckled cheeks. "Not without him."

His sister patted his back. Kaelyn William was nothing like her brother. She was short, slender, a third his size. But she had the same hair, red and wavy and beautiful. It was her eyes, however, that drew the most attention. Startling eyes. One blue, the other brown. Both intelligent and alert.

"Paul would want us to play," Kaelyn whispered. Even when she whispered, her voice was fair, angelic, a voice that could shatter hearts of iron.

Jon approached his keyboards. His sheets of notes were waiting for him, scribbled during bouts of frantic creativity. He had been working on his rock opera for a year now. Its name appeared atop every sheet. *Falling Like the Rain.* The story of a fallen soldier. Jon had never known death until today. Perhaps his muse had foreseen this loss, and as he began to play, his notes took on new meaning.

This was no longer about a fictional fallen soldier, a young man looking back upon his life as he rose to heaven.

It was now about Paul.

Jon played the bittersweet notes, a dirge in C minor, and George began to beat his drums—softly at first, almost hesitantly. Then faster and louder, faster and louder, and soon George was beating the drums like a blacksmith pounding hot steel. Beating the drums so madly Jon worried they would break. Beating the drums as if George could beat the enemy that had taken their friend and brother. The giant's eyes were mad, no longer wet but blazing with fury, and his beat shook the basement like artillery in the jungle.

And then Kaelyn began to sing.

She stood before the two boys, eyes closed, head raised, and she sang. It was a high keen, an aria, a prayer. Her voice was starlight. Her voice was angels weeping over the fallen. Her voice was beams of moonlight on the scattered pages of dead boys' poetry. It was a voice so pure that Jon could barely play his keyboards. He trembled. It was a voice that pierced him with a thousand crystal blades.

Paul wasn't here. But they had recordings of his guitar. Jon turned them on, and his brother's music filled the basement—distorted shredding at one moment, then clear and tragic the next, and it was like Paul was back. Playing with them.

And Jon had to stop playing, because tears filled his eyes. He could no longer see the keyboard.

And George let out a great howl, and slammed his drums so hard that they broke, and a cymbal crashed to the floor.

Kaelyn's voice trailed off. She stood still, pale, her eyes closed, a fallen angel.

Only Paul's guitars now sounded, a song from the afterworld. The living stood listening, silently letting the ghost of their loved one play his swan song.

The last guitar note played, then faded.

Silence filled the basement. The music had died. Perhaps forever.

"In a week, I'll be there, Paul," Jon whispered into the silence. "In a week, I'll be a soldier like you were. I will face the enemy." He clenched his fists. "I will make them pay. I will kill them! I will kill them for what they did!" His voice rose to a torn howl. "I will kill the bastards, and—"

He could say no more. He lowered his head. All the tears he could not shed at the funeral now came pouring out.

And Kaelyn was there, embracing him, stroking his hair and whispering soothing nothings. And George was there, wrapping them both in his massive arms, holding them against his chest, as comforting as a mother hen. The three stood together. The nerds. The weirdos. These lords of music and awkwardness. Symphonica broken. Friends in a war too big for them. Scared in the dark.

"Promise me something, Jon," Kaelyn whispered, stroking his hair. "Look into my eyes and promise."

He looked into her mismatched eyes. "What?"

She touched his cheek. "When you're there, Jon, don't hate the enemy. Don't seek revenge. Don't become a killer. Be a *survivor.* Nothing more. Promise me, Jon. Promise you'll be a survivor. That you'll come home. Promise me."

He admired her eyes in silence, the blue one and the brown one. The eyes of a girl he loved. Of a seventeen-year-old soprano he wrote his music for. Of his Christine, because he often felt like the Phantom. Of his beauty, because he often felt like the beast. The eyes of Kaelyn Williams, not only his singer, but his muse.

And in those eyes… he saw the war.

He saw fire and guns and enemies in the trees.

He saw rows of graves.

"I hate them," Jon whispered, voice shaking. "I hate them so much. For what they did to us. I hate those…" He could not stop himself. "Those *slits*."

Kaelyn gasped. She took a step back, and her eyes blazed. "Do not say that word. That's a slur."

"How can you defend them?" Jon said, voice rising. "They're the enemy! They're butchering us! They're barely even human. They have *aliens* helping them. Some say they themselves are part alien. Half breeds. Monsters. You see what they do." A tear fell. "What they did."

"They're not aliens!" she said. "They're just people. They don't even want this war. It's us Earthlings who started it, and—"

"How can you blame us?" Jon was nearly shouting now. "How can you talk like a traitor? After the funeral today! After they murdered Paul—my brother, your boyfriend—how—"

A roar.

A howl.

A torn cry filled the basement.

"Enough!"

Jon and Kaelyn spun around. The giant stood before them, hunched over, panting, face red.

"Enough," George repeated, voice shaking. "Please. No political debates. No fighting. Not today. Not so soon after he died. Please. *Please.*"

And suddenly the giant, so terrifying a moment ago, was crying, as meek as a kitten.

Jon patted him, then looked at Kaelyn.

"I'm sorry," he said to his singer.

She kissed his cheek. "Promise me, Jon. That you won't think like that. That you won't kill like that. Promise that you'll stay good. Do not come home a killer. Come back pure." She wiped her eyes. "Or come back dead."

A chill ran down his spine. He held her hand. "I promise, Kaelyn. I promise."

That night, after the Williams siblings went home, Jon could not sleep. He crept upstairs, careful not to creak the floorboards of this old bungalow on this little cul-de-sac. He tiptoed through the kitchen and past his parents' bedroom. They were asleep or grieving silently behind a closed door. The world was asleep. Only the crickets were awake, chirping outside like tiny armies fighting tiny wars. Jon walked past photos on the wall—captured memories of a smiling young man in a battlesuit. He walked through unbearable shadows and lingering silence.

Finally Jon climbed into the attic. A lightbulb swung from the rafters, casting yellow light. Jon opened a cardboard box, and he found a dress uniform amid mothballs, neatly folded. He found military dog tags. He reached under the uniform, and he pulled out a rifle.

Paul's things. Salvaged from the war and scrubbed of blood and ashes. Packed in a box like a cardboard coffin.

Now these artifacts would rot away in their box, and Paul would remain just a photo on the wall, and the house was silent. Jon's life was silent. And the silence only ended when he played his music.

And it wasn't only Paul. Because tens of thousands of soldiers were coming home in coffins. Because every day the starships came back from space, and the military hearses drove along the highways, bringing lost boys home.

Jon held his brother's rifle to his chest. He gripped the wooden stock, knuckles white. And that rage filled him. That hatred of the enemy. That desire to aim his gun and fire and hear the *boom* like a drum and watch the monsters die.

But Kaelyn had made him promise.

Promise me. Promise that you'll stay good.

"I promised," Jon said. "I will come back pure. Or I will come back dead."

He returned his brother's gun to the box, and he moved toward the window. He sat down. The crickets kept chirping, and a shooting star blazed outside like a burning starship. Jon pulled his knees to his chest, and he sat in the attic by the little window, gazing out at the stars. In a week, he would wear his own uniform, his own dog tags. He would fly up there to the stars. He would hold a gun of his own, and he would face them in the darkness.

The enemy.

But he would not be afraid, and he would not be a killer, because he would remember Kaelyn's mismatched eyes, and he would remember her pure voice. He would remember this night, and this falling star, and his friends. He would carry his music with him, and he would hear Kaelyn's voice even as the artillery boomed and the dying screamed.

He realized that he was holding a music sheet, the overture to *Falling Like the Rain*. He must have carried it from the basement without noticing. Kaelyn had signed her name on the top, and she had kissed the page, leaving a lipstick imprint. Jon remembered that day, that flight of whimsy, that signature of her lips on his newest work.

Paul got a little jealous, Jon remembered with a sad smile. *His girlfriend kissing my music! But then we all made music together and were laughing again.*

Jon stared at the sheet for a moment, then folded it and slipped it into his pocket. He would take it with him to war. His music and his muse would tether him to home like a rope of starlight.

This is my anchor, he thought. *Right here. This house, and this music, and her. I will be in darkness, but this strand of starlight will connect me home.*

He closed his eyes, and he slept, and he dreamed of his brother lost in the jungles of an alien world, fleeing shadows among the trees.

Chapter Two
Maria

Maria was toiling in the rice paddies when she saw the Earthling's plane, a wounded angel of death.

It was hurt, the hull perforated with bullet holes, one engine dead. A wake of crimson smoke trailed behind it like blood. Maria had seen flying machines before, rumbling overhead like mechanical demigods. Every day, these horrors from Earth flew on the hunt, bombing and killing, smiting the land. For the first time, Maria saw one bleed. She was a sparrow watching a dying eagle.

"Girls, run! To the village!"

Lola Mahalia was shouting, her wizened brown face raised toward the sky. She was the eldest of the farmers, indeed the eldest person in San Luna village. She waved a red handkerchief as if ringing an alarm.

"Girls, girls! Run! *Aswang, aswang*!"

Aswang. It meant demon in Tagalog, the ancestral language of the Philippines. For three hundred years now, Maria and her people had been living here on Bahay, this planet so far from Mother Earth. But the old stories remained. The old words. The old fears.

"It's not an *aswang*, Lola!" Maria said, using the Tagalog word for grandmother. "It's not an angel or a demon. It's just a machine. No different from a plow or seed thresher."

Her grandmother glowered. "Be silent, mouse. Your brain is full of such nonsense. Where do you learn these things?" The old woman pointed at the sputtering plane. "It brings the liquid fire! Run! Hide from the demon!"

Just a broken machine, Maria thought again.

The Bahayans didn't have advanced machines like planes or tanks, let alone starships. The Santelmos, the beloved spheres of light, had blessed the First Colonists long ago, flying them to Bahay in silver chariots. That had been centuries ago. Before Earth had learned to build such horrors of metal.

But I've learned so much about machines in this war, Maria thought. *I learned how cruel they are. I learned what wickedness they bring. And now I learn that they are mortal.*

Across the rice paddies, the farmers looked up, squinting in the sun, watching the plane. Old Mahalia was still shouting at them to flee, but they didn't heed her wisdom. They realized what Maria had realized. That this plane would not rain the napalm or poison that had slain so many. That this plane was dying.

It was circling overhead now, sputtering smoke. Perhaps seeking a place to land among the paddies. Perhaps seeking enemies below.

Maria could imagine the pilot's thoughts.

Is this village safe, or does the Kalayaan hide among the peasants? Should I crash land here? Or should I try to keep flying and fall into the sea?

One way or another, this plane was coming down.

"It must have come from the battles in the north," Maria whispered. "Why is it coming to our village? Did someone shoot it?"

Lola Mahalia groaned. "Always you are asking questions! How should I know?"

Maria looked around her. Where would this plane attempt its crash landing?

Several mountain peaks surrounded the village, draped with raiments of rainforest. Rice paddies covered the foothills—tier after tier of terraces like staircases for giants. The monsoon season had come and gone, flooding the paddies. It was now time to plant the seeds. In the valley below, alongside a river, nestled the village of San Luna, home to nearly a hundred families. And it was *her* home—Maria de la Cruz, rice farmer and official village troublemaker, seventeen-years-old and full of questions, her brain always bursting with what Lola Mahalia called nonsense.

It seemed the plane would overshoot the village. Perhaps it would glide into the sea beyond the mountain. Oddly, though these flying machines had slaughtered countless people, Maria pitied it. She wished this awkward metal bird could find its way home.

But then he emerged from the jungle.

Then Maria's heart shattered.

He was back. He had been away for a year, fighting the enemy in the wilderness, and she had hoped he would never return.

But here he was, returning into her life like an old illness.

Ernesto Santos. Her betrothed.

A year of war had changed him. Aged him. He stood on the far side of the terrace, but Maria had sharp eyes, and she saw him well. He was only in his twenties, but he looked older, wrinkles already tugging at his brown skin, gifts of years in his fishing boat, then a year of war. A new scar rifted his face, chin to forehead, destroying one eye. The eye was covered with a cataract like a ball of shattered glass, halving the scar.

He was like the plane above, cruel yet broken, a terror risen to shake Maria's life.

The Santos family owned three fishing boats, all built of sturdy reeds. Maria's family, the de la Cruzes, owned a rice terrace along the eastern hill. Both families had thought it a good alliance. Maria had been betrothed to this angry young warrior since age thirteen.

She dreaded the coming summer. She would be turning

eighteen, old enough to marry him.

She had asked her elders so many questions. *Why can't I choose my husband? What if I don't want to marry at all? What if I want to move to the city? What if I want to be a singer or writer or something other than a farmer?*

Question after question, and her parents would shake their heads sadly. Lola Mahalia would say that her mind was full of nonsense, and then threaten to thrash Maria like a clump of stubborn rice clinging to its husks. Lola grumbled a lot, but she never actually beat her. And nobody ever answered her questions.

Maria stared at the man now. Ernesto Santos. Pointing at the plane and shouting. And then aiming his rifle.

With a great *crack* that echoed between the mountains, the flintlock fired. Light sparked against the plane—a bullet hitting the hull.

Ernesto laughed in triumph, already reloading. More young men ran up beside him—fishermen and farmers from the village. They raised their own rifles, and *cracks* shook the air. Maria jumped with every one.

More bullets slammed into the plane. An engine caught fire. Clouds of smoke belched out.

And then the plane was no longer gliding, trying to find a landing spot.

It was falling like a comet.

A burst of movement, of color. The pilot—ejecting!

Maria caught her breath.

She stood in the rice paddy, her feet in the water, watching the plane pitch forward, become very silent, then plunge down.

It slammed into the foothills across the valley with a *boom* that shook the world. The hunk of mangled metal burst into flames. It had landed on another family's rice paddy, crushing several terraces, undoing so many hours of toil. At least the water contained the fire. Had it crashed just a short distance away, hitting the jungle, its flames might have spread for miles.

Maria stood in awe of the blooming fire, of the smoke unfurling like demons from slumber. She knew there was a war in the north. She had seen the bodies of fighters returned to the village, burnt and lacerated, faces gone. But she had never seen a blazing fire, this living being of fury.

This must be what the north looks like, she thought. *A sea of such fire spreading to the horizons.*

"There he is!" Ernesto ran uphill, pointing. "He's mine!"

Ernesto cocked and raised his rifle.

Maria looked upward, and she saw him there. The plane's ejected pilot.

An Earthling. A real, actual Earthling, here in San Luna!

He hung from a parachute, limp. If he had a gun, he was not firing. Maybe he was dead already.

A *crack.*

A sound wave pounded into Maria.

Ernesto lowered his smoking rifle. He squinted at his target. His bullet had punched a hole through the parachute but missed the pilot. Already Ernesto was reloading, and he raised his gun again.

"Ernesto, no!" Maria cried.

She ran toward him across the paddies, splashing through the water, scattering rice seed. Lola Mahalia was shouting at her to be still, that she was undoing all their work, but Maria ignored the old lady.

"Ernesto!" she shouted.

He fired again.

This time the bullet hit the Earthling. The man jerked in his harness. He cried out.

He was coming down fast now, air whistling through his perforated parachute. He was still flailing, still alive. The bullet had hit his leg, Maria thought.

She kept running. She reached Ernesto just as he was aiming again. She shoved the rifle, burning her hand against the hot barrel, not even caring.

"Stop!" she said. "Why are you doing this?"

Ernesto stared at her. At five foot seven, he was tall for a Bahayan, the tallest man in the village. Certainly he was taller than Maria's five feet. He was very thin, almost malnourished. That was not uncommon in these days of war. But there was a rawboned strength to Ernesto, a fire in his eyes, a coiled tension in his ropy muscles.

Now that tension sprung like a bowstring, and he backhanded Maria. Hard.

Not a hello. Not a kiss. Not even a nod after a year away at war. This was how her betrothed greeted her. With the back of his hand.

She stumbled backward, clutching her cheek. Before he had gone to war, he used to hit her sometimes. When she asked too many questions. When her brain was full of too much rubbish. But never this hard. And now his eyes burned with madness like that flame on the foothills.

"Don't worry, we'll get him, Ernesto," said one of his cousins, raising a pistol. He was a wiry man with a thin mustache.

"No, Miguel! Lower your gun." Ernesto stared at the parachuting pilot. "He's hurt. He can't get away. We'll take him alive."

Still clutching her cheek, Maria looked toward the Earthling. The wind had caught his parachute, carrying him northward over the village. His blood dripped onto the bamboo *nipa* huts.

"He's heading to the banana grove!" somebody cried out.

"He's mine!" Ernesto said.

"Let him go!" Maria cried. "Don't hurt him."

But the men were already running, storming across the

paddies toward the banana plantation.

Maria ran after them. Her *baro't saya*, the traditional dress of her people, woven of pineapple leaves, slapped against her thighs. Her straw hat flew off her head and tumbled across the paddies.

"Maria, get back here!" Lola Mahalia said. "Leave it to the boys. You come back here and mind the rice. Or I will thrash you!"

"Why don't you thrash the rice instead?" Maria shot back.

She kept running, feet splashing along the terraces, scattering rice seed. Some farmers shook their fists, but most were busy watching Ernesto and the boys, transfixed by the unfolding drama. The war had been raging for years, but San Luna had remained isolated, hidden in this valley between the mountains. Now the Great Freedom War had come here too, and Maria knew her home would never be the same.

The pilot fell into the banana grove. His parachute draped across the squat trees, entangled in the branches, and fluttered like a banner. The men kept running, entering the plantation, and Maria ran hot in pursuit.

She ran between the banana trees, her bare feet kicking up dirt. The trees were only slightly taller than she was, their fronds forming a canopy. It was cool here in the shade, a blessed relief from the heat of the day.

Tarsiers clung to the branches. The furry critters were no larger than Maria's fist, but their eyes were huge and round, as large as human eyes. Tarsiers lived in all the fruit trees in San Luna, guarding the banana, avocado, and mango groves. The tiny primates, originally from Earth, had been bred to eat the local Bahayan insects, protecting the precious harvest.

The bananas were still green and small. But in a few weeks, they would ripen, and the village would feast. Every family would boast that its own recipe was best. Some would fry bananas in honey and sprinkle them with coconut. Others would mush them with rice and bake sweet cakes. Some families roasted their bananas over a fire. It would be a time to gain some fat before the next monsoon season. The harvest was always joyous in San Luna, but now Maria wondered if more fire would burn. Did this Earthling bring with him just a single broken machine? Or a promise of devastation?

They found the Earthling among the trees.

He was lying on the ground, but Maria could tell he was big and tall. She could see how long those legs were, how wide the arms. He was probably even taller than Ernesto—and much heavier. Earth must have great harvests, and this pilot must have eaten many feasts. He was not fat. Maria had seen fat people before in picture books. No, this was not a fat man. But not rawboned either. Not small and slender like the villagers. Earthlings must be a race of giants.

And this particular giant was dying.

He lay on the dirt, clutching his leg. Blood dripped between his fingers. The bullet must have pierced him there. One of his arms seemed to be broken, and burns spread across his ribs. Blood and ash stained hair the color of straw. Strange hair. Maria had never seen hair any color but black. Never seen skin so pale, not brown like hers.

Maybe the elders are right, Maria thought. *Maybe the Earthlings aren't human at all but a race of demons. How could we Bahayans share a heritage with such creatures?*

The men ran toward the fallen pilot. Ernesto delivered the first blow—a hard kick to the ribs. The pilot cried out in pain. And soon all the men were kicking and punching, and one man lifted a branch and began thrashing the Earthling.

"Stop that!" Maria shoved her way between the men. "Leave him alone. Why are you doing this? We're not animals."

The men stopped brutalizing their victim and turned

toward Maria. For a moment, she thought they would turn their wrath upon her, beat her with as much vigor. Ernesto took a step closer, forming a fist. Maria's cheek still hurt from his earlier blow, but she refused to back down.

"Why are you trying to kill him?" she said.

"He's a *pute.*" Ernesto spat. "A demon of Earth."

"He's human like us!" Maria said. "And if you strike me again, Ernesto Santos, I will let the whole village know that you have a *titi* the size of a garden worm."

His face twisted with rage, and the men laughed, and when Maria stomped between them, they stepped aside. Already they were mocking Ernesto, asking to see the garden worm between his legs.

Ignoring them, Maria knelt by the Earthling. He was indeed a giant. His arms were almost the size of her body, his jaw was like a slab of stone. Beside him, Maria felt like a child.

Why are Earthlings so big? she thought. *What do they eat? Is the gravity different on Earth? Were we Bahayans bigger when we lived on Earth centuries ago, or were we always small?*

So many questions and nobody to ask.

The Earthling gazed at her, eyes pained. He spoke in a raspy voice.

"Water…"

She knew that word. He was speaking English. The village spoke Tagalog, an ancient language of the Philippines, their ancestral home on Earth, which they had not seen in centuries. But Maria knew a little English. She had some books and tapes an Earthling missionary had left here fifteen years ago, when she had only been a toddler. Maria had clung to her Catholic faith, rejecting the strange ways of Mormonism, but she had kept the books and tapes, and she had learned the language of the enemy.

"Here, drink." Maria opened her flask, formed from a hollow coconut with a bamboo spout. She poured green tea sweetened with honey into his mouth. The pilot drank, coughed, and finally managed to swallow a little.

"I… am I in the south?" he rasped. "I was flying along the northern border. Routine reconnaissance mission. One of the Kennys got me. Rocket launcher I think." He coughed. Blood speckled his lips. "I'm your friend. We're here to help you. Tell them." He glanced at the village men, wincing. "Tell them I'm a friend."

Maria turned toward Ernesto and the others.

"Does the *pute* beg for his life?" Ernesto said, speaking Tagalog, and his friends laughed.

"He's our friend, Ernesto!" Maria rose to her full height—not that it was particularly impressive—and placed her fists on her hips. "The Earthlings fight *with* South Bahay. *Against* the north. He's not here to hurt us, he—"

"You speak like a traitor!"

Face twisted with rage, Ernesto shoved her. Maria yelped, prepared to fight back this time. But Ernesto's cousins grabbed her, held her back, their hands like manacles around her wrists.

Ernesto was perhaps a southerner like her. Ostensibly, South Bahay was an ally of Earth—or at least a client state. But many, like Ernesto, considered this alliance treachery. They believed that Santiago, president of South Bahay, was nothing but a puppet who deserved the noose. Like many young South Bahayans, Ernesto had refused to bow before Earth. Full of youth's fervor, he had been fighting the Earthlings in the jungles. Maria wondered if Ernesto, lurking in the brush, had fired the rocket that had crippled the plane.

Maria didn't understand these politics well. Nobody in this village ever answered her questions. But one thing she knew: This Earthling was not a threat. He was in pain. And she wanted to save him.

"I speak however I want, Ernesto!" Maria said, struggling

in the men's grip. "Why do you fear my words?"

He glared at her. His good eye was narrowed and burning. The other eye was still wide, milky white, a sphere of broken glass. She could see herself reflected there a thousand times. Like looking into a broken mirror.

"When you're my wife, you will learn respect," Ernesto said.

"Why must I learn respect?" Maria said. "Why should I respect you?"

Ernesto spat on her. Maria cringed, shocked into silence.

Her betrothed turned toward the Earthling, and a mad smile twisted his lips.

"Hello, filthy *pute,*" Ernesto said to the wounded pilot. "I have a question for you."

"He doesn't speak Tagalog!" Maria said, struggling against the hands that clutched her. "Don't you know the Earthlings don't speak it?"

Ernesto smirked. "Then translate for me." He leaned down, gripped the Earthling, and shoved his finger into the bullet wound.

The Earthling howled. He thrashed, much larger than Ernesto, but weak with blood loss. Ernesto shoved his finger deeper. It entered the wound down to the knuckle.

"Look at me, *pute*," Ernesto said. "Look me in the eyes. And tell me. Do you know the name Roberto Santos?"

Maria froze. She remembered Roberto. She remembered the funeral.

"Translate!" Ernesto demanded, glaring at her.

Maria raised her chin, silent. But when Ernesto raised his fist, she begrudgingly translated his words.

The Earthling stared at Ernesto.

"I—" The pilot coughed more blood. "I won't tell you a goddamn thing, you fucking *slit.*"

Maria gasped. The word stabbed her like a bamboo knife. It was the most horrible word in English. A word that reduced Bahayans to mere animals. To something subhuman.

But Ernesto only grinned at the pilot, revealing a golden tooth. "Roberto was my brother. He joined the Kalayaan. What did you call them? The *Kennys*?"

The pilot's eyes flooded with fear. Just that one word. Three syllables. *Kalayaan*. To Bahayans, it meant freedom. To Earth, it meant terror. It made the giants tremble.

"Fuck you, you fucking gook," the Earthling growled. "We came here to help you. We're going to fucking—"

Ernesto raised his rifle, then brought it down hard.

The wooden stock slammed into the Earthling's face, shattering his teeth.

The man gave a gurgling red scream. Maria screamed too, trying to rush forward, but the village men held her back.

"You killed my brother." Ernesto slammed his rifle down again, cracking the pilot's jaw. "Roberto joined to fight for our planet. For our freedom. And you murdered him!"

He slammed his rifle down again and again, pulverizing the Earthling's face, still pummeling the man long after his screams had died. When finally Ernesto stepped back, there was little but red pulp where a face had been, and Ernesto laughed madly, blood on his hands.

The pilot gave a gasping, gurgling breath.

Still alive. Oh God, still alive.

Maria wept.

A shot rang out. Ernesto lowered his smoking rifle.

"See? I gave him mercy at the end." He looked at Maria. "I am a merciful man." He stroked her cheek, smearing it with blood. "I finally came back from the war to marry you, my beloved Maria. After the harvest, you will be my wife, and I will treat you with great mercy."

She stared into his eyes, refusing to look away. She spat on his face.

"Your brother was a fool. And so are you."

He raised his hand to strike her, his face twisting.

"A fool!" Maria repeated. "Roberto knew the risk when he joined the Kalayaan. When he began to kill Earthlings. Now you killed a man too! You murdered him! Not out in the jungle, but here in our home! Why? For what? You placed this whole village in danger, and—"

He did not strike her cheek this time.

He drove his fist into her belly.

Maria doubled over, coughing, gasping for air. He grabbed her hair, twisted it, and shoved her onto the dead Earthling.

"Look at him!" He held her face toward the bloody pulp. "Look at this *pute*. He's not a man. Just a demon." His voice rose to a shout. "Look at him, Maria! Look at the fate of those who would conquer our planet, who would subjugate our people. We fight for freedom. This is the cost. If you cannot pay it, you will always be a slave."

She tore free from him, and she ran.

She ran through the banana plantation, eyes damp.

She ran across the rice paddies, splashing through the water, ignoring the women who called after her.

She ran from the dead Earthling. From the mangled plane. From her betrothed. She ran but her world was so small—this valley, these terraces, and beyond them the mountains and the vastness of the jungle, sprawling toward the northern fire.

We should have let the plane fly on, she thought. *Let it cross the mountains and crash into the sea. We shot down a plane, and we brought the war to this oasis, and I will never forget what I saw today.*

Chapter Three
In the Maple Tree Shade

A day before they were drafted, before they flew into space to kill and maybe die, they decided to get tattoos.

"They're forever, you know." George shifted his considerable weight from side to side, hesitant. "Once you get a tattoo, it's for *life*."

Jon patted his giant friend on the shoulder. "George, old friend, we'll probably be dead within a year. Life ain't that long."

They were walking down a sunny street in Lindenville, New Jersey. Two boys. Jon—spindly like a beanstalk. George—like the giant the proverbial beanstalk led to. Two childhood friends. Best friends. Tomorrow the army would take them both.

Kaelyn walked with them, rolling her eyes. She was only seventeen, too young for the army. In a year, she would be drafted too. Maybe she would join them in the jungle. And maybe she would cry over their graves.

"You're an eternal fountain of optimism, Jon." Kaelyn brushed back strands of her long red hair. "You won't even have to shoot the enemy. Just talk to them, and you'll drive them to suicide."

"Or play them that first draft of *Falling Like the Rain*'s overture," George muttered.

Jon gasped at his giant friend. "*Et tu*, George? I thought you liked the original overture!"

"It had a horns section, dude," George said. "We're a metal band."

"A *symphonic* metal band," Jon said.

Kaelyn snickered. "The horns sounded more like an air raid siren than a symphony."

Jon raised his hands. "God, both of you! Get off my ass, Waldorf and Statler. The horns only sounded bad because I had to approximate the sound with my keyboards. I'm telling you, eventually we'll get real horn players, and—"

"Dude, we don't even have a bass player," George said. "And you're thinking of a horn section!"

No, we don't have a bass player, Jon thought. *Or a guitarist. Not anymore.*

The three fell silent. They were all thinking the same thing, Jon knew. They were all remembering Paul.

They kept walking the streets of Lindenville, their little hometown. They had been born here, grown up here, founded Symphonica here. And over the past few years, they had watched the town change. The war was raging in space, many light-years away, yet the grief was everywhere. Paper stars hung in house windows. Some were golden stars, symbolizing soldiers fighting on Bahay. Others were purple stars, symbolizing fallen heroes. Almost every house had a star in its window.

My house has a purple star for my brother, Jon thought. *Soon it will have a golden star for me. And maybe eventually two purple stars will hang in my window, and my parents will be alone, and people will hang their heads low as they walk by my home. But they will not drop in to comfort my parents. They will walk on by, too afraid, too hurt to face the grief.*

Jon tried to push that thought aside. To tell himself that he would survive. After all, many soldiers came home from the war. He saw them sometimes heading toward the veterans' legion down Petty Street. Some on crutches. Others in wheelchairs. Some still whole but staring ten thousand miles away. They came home alive. But nobody came home unchanged.

I made a promise to Kaelyn, Jon thought. *That I will stay pure.*

Stay who I am. If I ever come home, I must come home as the person I am now. As Jon Taylor the composer. The leader of Symphonica. The artist writing a rock opera. I must not change, must not come home a broken veteran like those who drink in the bars and sleep on the sidewalks. I must stay who I am. Or let that second purple star hang in the window.

The three friends walked by an old bakery, and they saw a veteran lying on a piece of cardboard. This was a middle class town, its houses large, its streets clean, but every day more veterans came. Not just veterans fresh from the battlefields but older veterans too. Many came from nearby New York City, haunted and broken and seeking a safe sidewalk to sleep on, a kind soul to toss them a coin, maybe to listen to their tale.

But the three friends walked by, silent, blushing, barely even glancing at the homeless veteran. Jon wondered if someday people would walk by him in the same awkward silence.

They walked onward. The tattoo parlor was only a few blocks away, but it felt like the longest walk of Jon's life.

They were downtown now. Cafes, shops, and other small businesses lined the street. Recruitment posters covered their walls.

"SMACK 'EM DOWN!" announced one poster. "JOIN THE LIGHT INFANTRY MARINES!"

The poster showed several brave marines leaping from a dropship, guns ablaze. Bahayans were drawn cowering between the trees, their eyes mere slits, their skin the color of mustard, their lips adorned with Fu Manchu mustaches. Caricatures. Barely human.

"TREAT 'EM TOUGH!" read another poster. "FIGHT WITH THE ARTILLERY!"

This poster featured Ensign Earth, an all-American folk hero, leaning against a cannon, smiling and giving the thumbs up.

Jon looked at another poster.

"BE A LEADER OF MEN. JOIN JULIUS MILITARY

ACADEMY. CADET LOANS AVAILABLE."

Jon didn't like any of those options. He didn't want to be infantry, or artillery, or an officer. Hopefully, they would let him serve in a marching band. Armies had marching bands, didn't they? It wouldn't be Symphonica, but it was still music. And more importantly, it seemed like a good way to survive. Jon had seen many war films, but he had never seen an army band march into battle.

"The army still has marching bands, right?" he asked.

George nodded. "Sure. Maybe they even have a horn section."

Jon punched the larger boy. "Shut up."

That broke a little bit of the tension. George smiled hesitantly. Kaelyn laughed. And for a moment, just a few breaths, they forgot about the stars in the windows, the veterans on the street, and the posters on the walls. And they were just friends again. Just Symphonica out for a stroll.

The fear came back, of course. It was never far. But for the briefest while, they had smiled. They had laughed. And that comforted Jon.

"Ah, here we are!" Jon pointed. "Our friendly neighborhood tattoo parlor."

George stopped on the street, blanching. "Do tattoos hurt?"

Jon snorted. "For God's sake, man, you're taller than an NBA player, weigh a metric ton, and give children nightmares. And you're scared of a tiny little needle?"

The giant gulped. "Yes. I'm pretty much scared of everything. I never asked to be this big, you know. It was a brain tumor that made me grow."

"Yeah, well, if you survived a brain tumor, a needle ain't shit," Jon said. "Come on, buddy. All three of us. We're doing this. We're getting Symphonica tattoos. Tomorrow…" He had to take a shaky breath. "Tomorrow we'll be separated from Kaelyn, you and I. And who knows what'll happen? Who knows where we'll end up? But with matching tattoos, well… Wherever we end up in the galaxy, we can look at them. And we'll know they link us together. We'll remember this place. Our music. Our friendship. We'll remember who we are." He smiled softly at Kaelyn. "We'll stay pure."

Her mismatched eyes shone, one brown and one blue, and both so kind. She gave him the slightest of nods and the warmest of smiles.

"All right, you talked me into it," George said. "You sentimental prick."

Jon grinned at his oversized friend. "Love ya too, you giant ginger jerk."

Kaelyn rolled her eyes.

They entered the tattoo parlor. They showed their design to the tattoo artist. The logo of their band. The word *Symphonica* written in stylized font, a clef forming the S. Kaelyn went first, handling the pain well, and Jon followed. While the other two went under the needle, George kept trembling. At one point he tried to flee the shop, only for them to drag him back. When finally George sat in the chair, barely squeezing in, he whimpered and cried out, "It hurts!"

"Oh for Chrissake, the needle hasn't even touched you yet," Jon said.

George clenched his jaw and gripped the armrests so tightly he cracked them, but he got through it somehow.

He'll have to toughen up, Jon thought, looking at his gargantuan friend. *We all will. Or we won't last long out there. The jungles of Bahay are cruel and dark, and the enemy wields more than needles.*

"I did it!" George beamed. "I did it, guys!" He flexed his enormous arm, showing off the tattoo. "Do I look tough?"

"You should have gotten a skull and bones if you wanted

to look tough," Kaelyn said.

Jon laughed. "George, a beast your size—you could get a winged pony tattoo and you'd look terrifying. Just don't let the enemy see you sniffle at the sight of a needle, and you'll be fine."

"Sorry." George lowered his eyes. "I couldn't help it. I hate needles."

For a moment, they were all silent. Images flashed through Jon's mind. Clips he had seen on the news. The enemy firing artillery shells. Booby traps in the jungle, filled with poisonous blades. Hailstorms of bullets and raging fire.

"George," he said softly, and he touched his friend's arm. "Up there, I'll look after you. I promise. I'm going to make sure you survive. That you come home with me."

George let out a huge sniffle. "Same to you, buddy. We'll look after each other. We'll come home."

The tattoo artist, who was trying to fix his cracked chair, looked up at them. "You two shipping off to Bahay?"

"We're being drafted tomorrow," Jon said. "Unless we shoot off a foot or hand by then, we're jungle meat."

The tattoo artist gave them a solemn salute. "Respect. I got two brothers on Bahay. One in the marines. The other flying junglers. I want to see you two back here in my shop, getting more tattoos after the war. These ones were on the house." He winked. "Kill some slits for me, huh?"

Kaelyn opened her mouth to object, but at a look from Jon, she closed it. They left the shop.

"*War no more!*"

The cry washed over them, coming from many voices at once.

"*War no more! War no more!*"

They came walking down Main Street, twenty-odd people holding placards. Jon read some of the signs.

BRING THE TROOPS HOME

END THE COLONY WAR
WHY DO WE DIE ON BAHAY?
PRESIDENT HALE BELONGS IN JAIL!

A man with dreadlocks, a vintage coat, and a long beard led the protest. He spoke into a megaphone.

"What is happening on Bahay is not a just war. It's a massacre! It's a war of conquest! When Ben-Ari was our president, we never fought other humans. Hale must stand trial for war crimes! War no more!"

The crowd behind kept the chant going, placards raised high. "War no more! War no more! Hale to jail! Hale to jail!"

Symphonica stood outside the tattoo parlor, watching the demonstrators walk by.

Jon couldn't help it. Anger rose through him, and he clenched his fists. "Look at them. Traitors."

George's cheeks flushed red. "They're defending Bahayans. Can you believe it? The bastards who killed Paul."

The bearded demonstrator raised his fist. "All youths of Lindenville, hear me! Reject the draft! Go to prison if you must. But do not fly to Bahay! Freedom for Bahay! Freedom for—"

"Hey, guy—shut up!" Jon said.

"Jon!" Kaelyn said, reaching for him.

But Jon dodged her hand and rushed onto the street. He stood before the demonstrators, blocking their way.

"Why don't you bastards shut the hell up?" Jon said, anger flowing through him, spinning his head. "You're talking like goddamn traitors."

The crowd began to boo. To toss things at Jon. A few raised their fists, seeming ready to fight.

But the bearded ringleader waved them down. "Enough! Let the boy speak." He turned toward Jon. "Did you receive a draft notice, son?"

"Yes, and I'm happy about it!" Jon lied. "Nobody likes

war. But we have to fight for Earth! To serve our planet!"

The bearded man raised an eyebrow. "Is that what your parents taught you?"

"My parents lost a son in the war!" Jon blurted out, eyes suddenly stinging. "My brother went to Bahay to help. To liberate the colony from the aliens. And the slits killed him. They…"

The street was suddenly swaying around him. Maybe it was the joint they had shared that morning before getting tattoos. Maybe it was the heat of the day. Maybe it was just the grief, the terror, and the shame.

Jon could say no more. His head swam. He turned and fled.

For a long time, he ran blindly, the town spinning around him.

His friends found him on Church Hill. He sat on the bench by the ancient stone church. The maple tree shaded him. It was the same tree where he and his brother used to play. The leaves rustled in the wind, and the robins sang, and it was beautiful, and it was music, and Jon knew that he would never see this beauty again.

I will return killed or killer, he thought. *I can't keep my promise.*

George was trying to run uphill toward him, cheeks red. Halfway up, the giant paused, doubled over, and wheezed.

Kaelyn climbed to the hilltop, her white dress and red hair fluttering in the breeze. Dapples of sunlight fell between the leaves, mottling her freckled skin. Kaelyn Williams. His soprano and muse. As she approached through beams of light, pollen glistening around her, she seemed to Jon an angel, welcoming him to the afterlife. Perhaps he was dead already.

She sat beside him and placed a hand on his thigh. He gazed in wonder into her mismatched eyes. In the sunlight, her brown eye turned hazel, flecked with green, like a forest in her soul. Her blue eye was a sea crested with foam, leading to distant lands of faerie.

"Jon," she whispered, and a tear fled her blue eye, a drop from her sea.

He reached up to caress her hair, and she leaned forward, and they kissed. Just a soft peck on the lips, mouths closed, but so soft and warm, and Jon knew he would always feel that kiss, always remember this moment. It was his first kiss.

She was Paul's girlfriend. *Had* been Paul's girlfriend. But now she was kissing him, and it was wrong, but tender and sweet, and Jon knew it would forever haunt him.

"Think of me up there," Kaelyn whispered. "In the darkness of space, or in the heat of the jungle, think of me. Remember today. I'll be here waiting for you."

George finally reached the hilltop, flushed and wheezing, sweat dampening his shirt. He spilled onto the bench beside them, nearly shattering it.

"Goddamn, what a climb." The giant wiped sweat off his brow. "They don't have hills on Bahay, do they?"

"Mostly mountains," Jon said. "You'll be fine."

"Just my luck," said George. "Can't we go to war on some flat planet instead? Ideally one with taco bars on every block."

"Next time I talk to President Hale, I'll ask," Jon said.

The sun began to set, shining in the stained glass windows of the nearby church. They went home.

Jon didn't expect to sleep much. Not tonight, his last night as a civilian. Yet as he lay in bed, he remembered Kaelyn kissing his lips, and he fell into a deep, dreamless sleep.

His alarm clock woke him at dawn.

It was time to rise.

Time to become a soldier.

Time for war.

Chapter Four
Saint Elmo's Fire

Maria only slowed down when she reached the village huts. Trembling, she walked down the dirt paths, and her heart pounded against her ribs. She forced herself to take deep breaths, to focus on the present moment, on her surroundings, to let the trauma fade. It was a technique she had invented during the long nights when she was so afraid. Just to breathe. To focus on her sensations. To live only in the now, a realm with no memory nor worries for the future. To calm down, because her insides often felt like a sea of warring serpents.

San Luna was a humble village. A hundred *nipa* huts rose here, sometimes known as *bahay kubo*—country houses. Each family built their own dwelling, inspired by the traditional huts of the Philippines, their ancestral homeland. The huts balanced atop wooden stilts, protecting them from floodwaters during the monsoon season, as well as rats and mice. The walls were bamboo, and fronds from the *nipa* tree formed the roofs, giving the huts their name. They were just crude dwellings. Sometimes the monsoons swept them away, stilts and all, and sometimes the typhoons knocked them down, but the villagers always rebuilt.

They were not helpless here. True, they did not have starships like Earthlings, but the Bahayans had some technology too. They had a generator in the village square, and the big rusty box kept humming and vibrating, pumping electricity to a network of cables that stretched over the village like cobwebs. The constant hum of electricity comforted Maria. It reminded her of many crickets chirping in the night, and she imagined a kingdom of them living, working, and singing inside the machine, generating sparks of electricity with their serrated little legs. It kept the village alive. The villagers could listen on the radio to reports on the war. They could power the rice threshers, rumbling machines that separated grains from husks. The wealthy Santos family even had an air conditioner, a rusty old machine that made an awful racket, and which Ernesto often boasted of. He had promised her an air conditioner in their future home. Maria would prefer the heat of hellfire.

From a plane flying above, it was probably hard to see the village—even with the crackling electric cables. There were a hundred trees for every hut. Papaya trees filled the air with their sweet scent. The fronds of palm trees hung heavy with fruit. Orange and coconut trees grew in yards. Tarsiers hung from the branches, feasting on insects, protecting the precious fruit. The animals' huge eyes, shockingly large in their furry little heads, peered curiously.

When the first Filipinos had come to this world, fleeing the wars on Earth, they had brought many seeds and animals with them. Over the centuries, the colonists had terraformed Bahay, spreading the life of Earth across the alien islands. And Bahay, in turn, had transformed the colonists.

Children ran about, climbing trees, playing ball, their skin bronzed by the sun. They had never known another world. Every generation was a little more native. They told stories of Bahayan folk heroes—of Miguel and the thousand colors of the night, of Alberto who conquered mountains, and of Lilibeth, the last rose of summer. They forgot the old stories from Earth. They sang new songs. Some had even begun to worship new gods, deities of the jungle and ocean. By now, few Bahayans remembered the homeworld. But Maria had her books and tapes. Maria remembered.

"Did you see the plane crash, Maria?" said a young boy. "Tito Ernesto is back from the war, and he shot it down!"

"Pow, pow!" shouted another boy, mimicking firing a gun at the sky. "When I grow up, I'm going to fight too."

"No you are not!" Maria placed her fists on her hips. "Don't you remember what happened to Tito Roberto? We're farmers and fisherman, not fighters! Go back to your mothers."

The children groaned. One blew her a raspberry. And then they ran off, chattering in awe of seeing the plane fall.

Some of these boys will grow up and join the Kalayaan, Maria thought. *They will rise in rebellion against Earth. And most will never come home.*

She lowered her head. She had been betrothed to Roberto once, a kind and honorable man. But he was dead, and Ernesto had inherited her, and Maria would soon have an air conditioner, a swelling belly, and a life of misery.

She walked around a guava tree, its fruit bending the branches, and approached her home. The nipa hut was small, balanced atop stilts. The walls were bamboo, the roof thatched with palm fronds. Some villagers built roofs from sheets of tarpaulin or corrugated steel, mimicking the fashions of the big city. Those were useful during monsoon season, but Maria's father called them an eyesore. He stuck to the old ways. His thatch roof leaked during the monsoon, but Father insisted it was worth it. The rice farmer feared technology, even something as simple as a metal sheet. It had taken years to convince him to allow electricity into the home. Only the baseball games on the radio, broadcast from the southern capital, had changed his mind.

Maria had to climb a wooden ladder to enter. When she stepped inside the humble dwelling, the scent of *arroz caldo* filled her nostrils—an intoxicating blend of ginger, lemon, and chicken. Her mother stood by the pot, adding garlic to the savory stew, while her father scooped rice onto banana leaves. It was a warm home. A loving home. Yet also a sad home, for Maria was an only child in a village where most huts contained many children.

Seeing her, her parents abandoned the cooking meal. They rushed toward Maria, arms outstretched.

"*Nini*!" Mother said, still addressing her as a little girl, even though Maria was already seventeen. "Are you all right? Did you know that a plane crashed?"

"Of course she knows!" Father said. "She's not blind, you know. The whole village saw it."

"Oh, be quiet," Mother said. "Maria, are you okay? What happened to your face?" She touched Maria's cheek. "Does it hurt? You're bruised!"

"I fell," Maria lied, still feeling the sting of Ernesto's hand. "When running to see the plane."

"Your head is in the clouds," Mother said.

Father rolled his eyes. "Leave the girl alone. Her head is perfectly fine."

"It's too big!" Mother insisted. "Too full of—"

"—questions and nonsense," Maria said. "I know. I've heard it many times."

Her mother's eyes softened, and she embraced her. "I'm glad you're okay, Nini. We saw the plane fall. We tried to find you in the paddies. They said you ran off."

"I'm fine, *Nanay*," Maria said to her mother. "Honestly. Nobody was hurt."

None of the villagers, at least, she thought, and an image of the Earthling's brutalized corpse flashed before her.

Mother sighed and brushed leaves out of Maria's hair. Kim de la Cruz was thirty-three, yet she had only one child. Most women her age had many children, often ten or more. A good Bahayan woman was expected to bless the village with many children—girls to plant seeds, boys to hunt and fish. Times of floods and plague took many village children. Every woman was expected to do her part to replenish the lost.

Yet Maria was an only child. She had broken something inside her mother's womb. Lola Mahalia liked to say it was Maria's big head, too full of questions.

"Come, *Nini*," Mother said. "Let me fry you some rice and fish, and then we'll return to the paddies together."

"But *Nanay*, why?" Maria said. "Why must I work every day? What if I want something else?"

Mother snickered. "Like what, silly girl?"

"To study the stars!" Maria said. "Or to travel south to Mindao, where they have libraries and schools, and I can learn things, and—"

"There's nothing to learn in libraries!" Father said. "You have everything you need here in San Luna. The cities are full of Earthlings these days. In the north, they kill. In the south, they steal and suck us dry."

"But why do they kill us?" she said. "Why are the Earthlings even here on Bahay?"

"Why, why, why?" Mother parroted. "Silly girl. Stop asking so many questions. Earthlings are evil, and the cities are dangerous, and good girls were not meant for such things. Good girls work in the fields, have many children, and—"

"But I don't want that!" Maria said. "I don't want to work in the paddies. I don't want to have children. I want to…"

Her voice trailed off.

"To what?" Mother said, tilting her head.

To fly away, Maria thought.

To fly far from this village. Far from this entire planet. Far from this war where men bashed skulls with rifles. Where planes crashed and burned. Far from the life that awaited her, of endless bruises and pregnancies and fire on the hillsides.

But she could say none of those things. Not to her parents. Despite it all, they loved her. They worked hard for her.

Dreamed for her to be happy, to be married into a family with an air conditioner and three reed boats.

Yes, Maria knew her parents meant well. But these were not *her* dreams. And she could not forgive them for arranging her marriage to a cruel man, no matter how wealthy he was. How could she tell them all this?

"I want to be more," Maria whispered.

Mother flinched, pain in her eyes. "More than I am? Is my life truly so pathetic?"

Maria let out a soft laugh. She hugged her mother. "I love you, *Nanay*. You're the best woman in the world."

Mother sighed. "And you're a silly little thing, but I love you too. Go escape to your room, and your books, and your dreams. You're special, Maria. You're my joy and light. I just want you to be happy."

"I don't know how to be happy," Maria said.

She left her parents and entered her room.

* * * * *

In San Luna, being an only child placed you somewhere between "poor soul" and "circus freak."

Behold! Lonesome Maria! The girl with a head so big it broke her mother's womb!

They said she was strange. That she must be lonely. That she must dream of having many children and filling her hut with laughter. They all dreamed their own dreams for her, and they laughed when she spoke of exploring the stars.

Yes, being an only child earned Maria much ridicule. But it also came with some perks.

She had her own private bedroom.

That was nothing to sneeze at. She was the only girl in San Luna with her own room. Her friends all shared their rooms with multiple siblings, even sharing beds. Let Ernesto brag of his air conditioner. Maria de la Cruz had *privacy*, a far greater treasure.

It was a humble room, barely large enough for her little bed with its little straw mattress. But it was her domain, her Lilliputian kingdom, her place to dream.

The sun was setting, and she looked out the window at the sky.

I dream of someday flying, she thought. *Not in a plane. Not in the blue sky. I dream to fly among the stars. To visit other worlds. Maybe even to visit Earth.*

Was it true that everyone on Earth lived in golden towers? That everyone owned a spaceship? That people could buy feasts in any local marketplace—true feasts for kings!—instead of toiling day after day in the paddies for a few grains?

She sighed. Silly questions. Silly fantasies. The dreams of a little girl. If she ever landed on Earth, they would kill her. She was only a slit. A gook. A yellowskin. All those horrible names they called her people. All the ways they demonized their enemy, made them subhuman, easier to kill.

I'm your friend, the pilot had said, his eyes kind.

And his teeth had shattered.

And Maria had stared at a bloody pulp where a face had been.

And—

Breathe, Maria. She took a shaky breath. *Do not succumb to fear.*

She turned toward the mirror and studied her reflection.

"My head is *not* too big!" she said to herself.

She was a slender girl, her skin tanned brown from long days in the sun. She wore a white *baro't saya*, the traditional dress of Bahayan girls. The *piña* fabric, made from pineapple leaves, was soft against her skin. Her black hair flowed down to her waist, just as smooth and silky. Her eyes were very black, the irises so dark one could barely see her pupils. Some said her eyes were too inquisitive, too piercing, too eager to stare and challenge. Whatever that meant. Mostly, Maria figured, it was just an excuse for people to berate her.

She touched her bruised cheek and winced. The gift of Ernesto's hand.

Her head was normal sized, perhaps. But there was something broken inside her. Something not like the other villagers, and it went deeper than her lack of siblings. It was the yearning to escape, to fly, to explore. A call she could barely understand, let alone articulate. She was different, had been different since birth, and everyone knew it.

She turned away from the mirror. What did her own life matter now as the war raged?

She knelt by her bed, reached underneath, and pulled out her decorative wooden box.

Inside she kept her greatest treasures. The books and tapes the missionary had left here years ago, giving her the precious gift of another language. A spiraling seashell she had once found on the beach where the river ended. An iridescent feather from a glimmerbird. A tooth from an ancient waterwhirl that had once washed onto the riverbank.

And most precious of all—little Crisanto. Her dearest friend.

He was sleeping now inside his jar, barely larger than a firefly, as delicate as dandelion fluff.

An alien intelligence.

A real live Santelmo.

"Wake up, Crisanto!" Maria said, speaking through holes in the jar's lid. "Why do you sleep for so long? I'm lonely."

Santelmos could live for centuries, she knew. There were

Santelmos today who had lived during the Exodus three centuries ago, who had shepherded the first Filipino refugees from Earth, and who still watched over the colony on Bahay. Those elderly Santelmos were large beings, some the size of watermelons, some even larger, perhaps even as large as the great boulder in the village square which nobody could move. They shone like Pilak Mata, the pale moon of the east, great orbs of luminosity and wisdom. They knew the secrets of the stars, flew in silver starships, and explored the galaxy.

These luminous beings had discovered Earth long ago, long before humans had built starships or even knew the secrets of metal. On Earth, humans had known them by many names. The English called them the wills-o'-the-wisp. The native Mexicans knew them as *brujas*, believing them witches. The Bengali called them the *ayelas*, thinking them the ghosts of drowned fishermen, while the Japanese called them *hitodama*, mistaking them for human souls. The Brazilians called them *boi-tatá*, thinking them the fiery eyes of hidden serpents. Throughout human history, they had been there. Every culture knew them—mysterious orbs of light, floating in marshlands and forests, watching over mankind.

In the Philippines, the ancestral homeland of Bahayans, these glowing orbs had been called *Santelmos*, the shortened form of Saint Elmo's Fire. And the Santelmos had chosen the Filipinos for salvation. With their silvery chariots, they had lifted refugees from the fires of war. They had brought them here to a distant planet. They had formed the nation of Bahay among the stars, most blessed of worlds.

But little Crisanto was a baby. He had done none of these great things. He was so small he could fit in Maria's pocket. Sometimes at night, he would wake up and fly around the hut, leaving trails of light. Maria had tried to teach him to spell luminous letters and numbers in the air—like a child might draw figure eights with a sparkler. But Crisanto never learned that skill. Perhaps he was too young. Or perhaps Santelmos simply did not have a mind for letters and numbers, despite their great wisdom.

Since he could not talk or write, Maria did not know how young Crisanto was. But she heard that Santelmos could remain babies for decades. Time flowed differently for them. Often Crisanto slept for days, even weeks, content to lurk in her pocket or box. For him, it was probably just a catnap.

To him, my life must seem as ephemeral as a flowerbug, shining for just a season, Maria thought.

Crisanto rose to hover before her, a shining marble. Suddenly he flitted left to right, up and down. His way of saying *good morning.*

"Good morning, sleepyhead." She tried to smile, but her tears flowed. "Oh, Crisanto! I'm scared. Something happened today, and an Earthling plane crashed, and a man died, and…"

She cried for a moment, overwhelmed, and then she told him everything. How the plane had burned. How the village men had murdered the pilot. How Maria thought that Earthlings weren't evil after all—at least not all of them. For long moments, she spilled her heart out.

Only one detail she did not reveal. She did not speak of Ernesto hitting her. It shamed her. And she feared his reprisal if she spoke up—even if it was just to a ball of light. So she spoke of Ernesto returning from the war, murdering the pilot, but not of his hand slapping her cheek. Not his fist in her belly.

While she talked, Crisanto rested on her palm, sometimes bobbing up in surprise, sometimes dimming in grief, then shining brighter in rage. When the tale was finished, the tiny orb of light rose off her palm, then flitted out the window.

Maria gasped. "Crisanto, where are you going?"

She leaned out the window, glimpsed him fluttering across the village.

She climbed out after him, wearing only her nightgown, and ran barefoot in pursuit.

"Crisanto, come back!"

She had found him as a little girl. He had been so tiny nobody else could see him, no larger than a period at the end of a sentence. She had nurtured him, tended to him, and he to her. But he had never flown away like this.

She chased him between the huts. The sun set quickly on Bahay, and by the time she reached the mango grove, it had dipped behind the mountains. Crisanto shone ahead in the darkness, fluttering between the trees. Maria slipped on a fallen mango and scraped her knees. She rose and kept running, limping now. Past the trees, she could glimpse lights on the river—the last few fishermen rowing home. They did not see her, and she ran onward, following the little light.

Soon she reached the jungle and froze.

A wall of trees rose before her.

The trees of San Luna were familiar to her. Mangoes, bananas, avocados, pineapple—trees her people had cultivated for thousands of years, trees grown from Earth seeds. But here, before her—here rose alien flora. Here rose the native rainforest of Bahay, a sprawling, breathing biosphere far older than the human colony.

The Santelmos had tried to find the First Colonists a familiar world, a planet similar to the Philippines. This world had come closest. Bahay was a planet of natural beauty—soaring mountains, verdant islands, glittering blue seas, an atmosphere rich with oxygen.

But it was still an alien world. Even now, three centuries after the Exodus, the alien jungles chilled Maria's blood.

She faced towering trees draped with vines like the hair of old men. Their leaves had little mouths, snatching up insects. Yellow eyes shone in the shadows, and grunts filled the darkness.

Ferns stirred, and curtains of moss swayed like ghosts. There were great predators in the jungle. The beasts respected the village territory, but they would gladly devour any human who entered their domain. There were worse than animals too. There were spirits in there. There were old gods and evil whispers.

Maria stood, watching Crisanto float into those alien shadows. His light grew smaller and smaller, and she only stood watching until it was gone.

She dared not follow. Not even to follow her best friend.

"Crisanto," she whispered. And the rainforest answered with whispers and rustling leaves and the deep breathing of hidden things.

Maria fell to her knees, feeling the weight of the war, of the entire sky, on her shoulders. She raised her damp eyes to the stars, but the lights seemed distant and cold, and her own precious light was gone.

He heard what we did, Maria thought. *He learned that we killed a man. And now my guardian angel has left me, and I'm in darkness.*

On the mountainside, the crashed airplane was still burning, and when Maria looked at the distant fire, she saw in the flames the pilot's battered, bloody face.

Chapter Five
A Little Off the Top

"Well, here we are!" Father said. "Fort Emery Recruitment Center. Sorry, son, I know I told you we're going to Disneyworld. But the army's just as fun!"

The jazz player looked into the Toyota's rear view mirror and winked. Jon, sitting in the back seat, did not laugh.

Many said they looked alike. Both father and son had long, shaggy hair. But Jon's was black, while Father's hair was grizzled. Both had stubbly beards, though Jon's was far thinner, barely more than fuzz, even at eighteen.

Soon we'll look different, Jon thought. *I'll have my hair sheared off. I won't look like Dad anymore. But I'll always have Mom's blue eyes. Paul had blue eyes too.*

"Oh, be quiet, Ronald," Mother said, slapping her husband. "Now's not the time for stupid jokes."

"Now's the best time for jokes!" Father said. "Jokes are what got me through the army, you know."

Mother didn't answer. Awkward silence filled the Toyota. They were all thinking the same thing.

They were thinking about Paul.

His grave was still fresh. And maybe, very soon, Jon would join him underground. And they were joking. Trying to maintain some sense of normalcy in a mad world of mourning. And in his father's eyes, Jon saw the terrible, crushing grief.

They drove into the recruitment center in silence. Soldiers stopped them at a checkpoint. Somebody searched their trunk.

Another soldier checked Jon's draft papers.

"Don't worry, sir," the wiry soldier said to Father. "We'll take good care of your son. We'll bring him back to you in one piece."

I wonder if my brother came back in one piece, Jon thought. *They never let us open the coffin.*

His parents pulled over by a concrete building. Other cars were stopping too, spilling out teenagers. Jon recognized many from school. All those who had turned eighteen this year. All those ready for the meat grinder.

Jon got out of the car. He stood on the asphalt, his long dark hair hanging past his shoulders, his Wolf Legion shirt faded with a hundred washes. You could barely see the band anymore. In his pocket, he carried the folded music sheet, the one Kaelyn had signed with a kiss.

Jon's parents stepped out too. But they left the engine running.

"Well, son." Father cleared his throat. "I suppose this is it. You'll be all right, huh?"

But the jazz player's eyes were red and damp. He had already lost one son. Now he was sending another into the fire. Two sacrifices on the altar of Earth's empire.

"I'll be all right," Jon said. "I promise."

Another promise he could not keep?

Mother burst into tears. She pulled him into her arms, and she wept, clinging to him, telling him to be good, to be careful, and that she loved him.

"Come on, Ma," Jon said. "You're embarrassing me in front of the guys."

She wiped her eyes. "Oh, you're just like your dad. Stupid jokes."

Jon kissed her cheek. "Love ya, Mom."

He shook Father's hand. Formally at first, almost coldly.

But then his dad pulled him into a crushing embrace, and they both shed tears.

And then the car was rumbling off. And another car replaced it, spilling out another child for the war. Another sacrifice to Moloch. Hundreds were gathering here.

Cannon fodder, Jon thought. *The jungle beast needs to eat, and we're fresh meat.*

*****

He spotted George in the crowd of teenagers. It wasn't hard. The ginger giant towered over everyone.

They say the Bahayans are smaller than Earthlings, Jon thought. *George will look even bigger there.*

"Georgie boy!" Jon called out, worming his way along the crowded sidewalk.

He didn't see Kaelyn anywhere. He had hoped she would come say goodbye. Maybe she had already driven off, and Jon had missed her. Or maybe coming here had been too difficult.

Jon kept elbowing between people. Hundreds of teenagers lined the sidewalk outside the recruitment center, clogging the entrance to the building. They were entering one by one through a security checkpoint. The bottleneck would probably last a while.

"George!" Jon cried again.

But his friend didn't seem to hear. The giant spun from side to side like a trapped animal.

"Stop it!" he said, then yelped.

Jon frowned. He shoved his way through the crowd, moving faster. And then he saw it.

Several teenagers surrounded the giant, jeering. A pasty boy with limp blond hair was poking George with a stick. A bucktoothed girl brayed with laughter, spraying spittle.

"Dance, giant!" said the pasty blond boy. "Dance like the bear you are."

"He must be retarded," said the bucktoothed girl. "Hey, giant! You retarded?"

Jon finally reached them. "Leave him alone!"

The thugs turned toward him and guffawed. There were five of them. Jon recognized their faces. High school dropouts and hooligans. He had seen them around town—smoking under bridges, robbing shops, even torturing stray cats and squirrels, constantly exploring the limits of juvenile delinquency.

The ringleader stepped toward Jon. It was the boy with limp blond hair. He wasn't as tall as George—nobody in town was—but he was burly, built like a refrigerator. His face was wide and fleshy, and his blue eyes were far set, giving him a strange alien look.

Jon knew him. Everyone in Lindenville knew this one, even the adults, and especially the police. Here stood Clay Hagen, infamous town thug.

With a wide callused finger like an old cigar, Clay jabbed Jon in the chest.

"Hey, you're the fucking ballerina, aren't you?"

"He's a *composer*," George said, not helping much.

The thugs burst out laughing.

"A composer, huh?" Clay said. "A composer of shit!"

The brute puffed out his chest, proud of his witticism. Nobody laughed until Clay glared at his fellow thugs. Taking the cue, the underlings laughed and patted Clay on the back.

"Good one, boss!" said the bucktoothed girl.

"Shut up, Bucky!" Clay shoved her, then spun back toward Jon. "You listen to me, you fucking ballerina. If I want to poke the bear, I will poke the bear!"

Madness filled those wide-set eyes. The boy's beefy fists

curled up. They looked like two roast hams. Jon decided it best to diffuse the situation.

"Ah, come on, the bear is harmless," Jon said. "He's just a big dumb ginger. Save your energy for the Bahayans."

But Clay flushed red. His lips twitched, and a vein throbbed on his neck.

"You think I'm scared of *slits*?" Clay said. "You think some yellowfaced gooks are too much for me? Do you know who I am, ballerina?"

Jon nodded. "Clay Hagen. I've heard of you."

In fact, Jon had more than *heard* of Clay. Years ago, Clay had bloodied his nose on Halloween—all to steal some candy. The brute had probably forgotten the encounter. Jon never would.

"Of course you fucking heard of me!" Clay said. "You know where I spent the past year?"

"In juvie," Jon said. Everyone in town knew about that.

"In fucking prison!" Clay said. "It was a real prison. With adult prisoners. I was there for a year for killing a man."

Jon remembered the newspaper stories. Clay had just gotten his driver's license. After a night of hard drinking, he ran over an elderly man, then drove off. Clay spent a year behind bars. Jon wished they had left him there.

"Well, then you shouldn't have any trouble killing slits," Jon said.

"You're goddamn right!" Clay grabbed Jon by the collar. "And if you ever talk shit to me again, I'll kill you too, I—"

A roar washed over his words.

George grabbed the blond brute with two gargantuan hands. He yanked the thug away from Jon, then hurled him aside. Clay stumbled, nearly falling onto the sidewalk. The bucktoothed girl had to catch him.

"I got you, boss!" she said.

Clay shoved her away. "Don't touch me!"

"And you don't touch my friend!" George roared. "You hear that, Clay Hagen? You don't hurt him!"

Clay straightened, scowled at the giant… then guffawed. Laughter seized him, and soon he was shaking with it. His henchmen glanced at one another nervously, then burst out laughing too.

"Look at those two fairies!" Clay said. "You a couple? Which one goes on top?"

Bucky brayed with laughter. "Good one, boss!"

Clay shoved her. "Shut up!"

The hooligans wandered off, roaring with laughter, poking one another in the ribs. Soon they vanished in the crowd.

George shook his fist after them. "Bunch of losers."

"Jesus, George, you're bigger than all of them combined," Jon said. "Why did you let them pick on you?"

George lowered his head. "I got scared."

"You didn't seem scared at the end. You seemed kind of terrifying, actually."

"Yeah, well…" George stared at his feet. "They were going to hurt you. And you're my best friend and all. I had to do something. Sorry if I made you look bad."

"Ah, fuck those guys," Jon said. "Assholes like Clay don't last long in the army anyway. I'm sure he'll find some way of getting his head blown off." He paused, looked around, then back at George. "Did Kaelyn…"

George lowered his head. "She didn't come. My parents dropped me off, but… It was hard for her. After Paul died, she…"

Jon understood. It hurt. He had wanted to see Kaelyn this morning. Maybe the last time forever. But he understood.

If I die in the war, my last memory of Kaelyn will be kissing her under the tree, he thought. *That's a good memory to die with.*

Buzzing filled the air. A little drone, no larger than a dinner plate, flew toward Jon and George. It was painted in military green and labeled "Human Defense Force Property." The machine hovered before the two friends, and a mechanical voice emerged from its innards.

"Recruits! Enter Fort Emery Recruitment Center for processing. Dallying will be punished."

"Oh yeah?" Jon said. "Big threat from a flying Frisbee. I bet I—Ow!"

The drone shot Jon with an electric bolt. He rubbed his arm, wincing. When he looked around, he noticed that only a few kids remained on the sidewalk. Everyone else had entered the concrete building.

"Enter Fort Emery Recruitment Center for processing," the drone droned on. "Dallying will be—"

"I know, I know!" Jon said, still rubbing his arm. "Goddammit, I heard ya the first time." He waved the drone away. "Now get lost."

The drone gave a mechanical huff, shocked Jon again for good measure, then flew off to harass another group of dallying recruits.

"Son of a bitch!" Jon rubbed his arm. "I think he got me in my new tattoo."

"We better go inside," George said, eying the drone nervously.

Jon patted George on the back. "All right, buddy. Let's step inside. It's time to be soldiers."

*****

The next few hours passed in a blur.

Countless teenagers filled Emery Recruitment Center, coming from across New Jersey. They flowed through a labyrinth of concrete. Drones kept buzzing everywhere, zapping recruits, herding them from room to room. Like cows in a slaughterhouse, the teenagers passed from station to station, poked and prodded and terrified. Like cattle—moving slowly toward death.

At one station—a medical exam. The recruits lined up and stripped down. A doctor checked their throats, their eyes, their ears. He weighed them, listened to their lungs, and he cupped and squeezed their balls.

"Sorry, kid, gotta check ya for hernias," the doctor said to Jon. "Promise you'll still love me in the morning."

A drone zapped Jon. "Proceed to next station. Dallying will be punished."

"Goddamn it!" Jon shouted as the drone shocked him. He scampered off, tugging up his pants.

At another station, they slapped an iron blanket over Jon, and they took x-rays of his teeth.

"See, kid, if the Bahayans blow you into hamburger meat, we can fish your teeth out of the pulp," the technician told him. "It's how we'll identify you. Hey, we can even send the teeth back to your mom."

"Do you brush them first?" Jon said. "My mom's always bugging me about that."

"Proceed to—" a drone began.

"I know, I know!" Jon said, waving the pesky machine away. He yelped as it shocked him.

At another station—an interview. They showed the recruits strange ink blots. They asked them to identify the stains. Jon didn't see anything but abstract shapes. He wondered if he was failing the test.

"This looks like a fucking slit," said Clay Hagen, taking the same test near Jon. The brute smirked at the ink blots. "And this one looks a fucking slit. And this one looks like a fucking slit. All slits to kill." He winked at Jon. "Maybe I'm gonna kill some ballerinas too."

Jon flipped him off. "Hey, what does this look like?"

Clay leaped from his seat and lunged to attack. It took two sergeants to pull him back.

"Assholes," George muttered, then returned his eyes to his own test. He gasped. "Hey, this inkblot looks like a taco! Great. Now I'm hungry."

At another station, they received their dog tags.

"Sweet, free jewelry!" George said, slipping the chain around his neck. The metal tags hung against his chest.

"Some jewelry." Jon slipped on his own tags. "If they can't even find teeth after the enemy blows you up, maybe they'll find these tags in the pile of ashes."

"That's actually pretty metal," George said.

Jon raised the devil horns. "Death Tags. There's the title of our next album."

They both laughed. Jon knew they were both terrified. Laughter helped. That was the meaning of humor, after all.

It's a coping mechanism, he thought. *Humor is a flower that grows from the ashes of fear and misery.*

But he couldn't suppress a shudder.

Scattered teeth, metal tags, and bad jokes. That's all that remains of some soldiers.

He thought back to his brother's funeral. It had been a closed casket. Jon wondered what had been inside that coffin. Maybe nothing but teeth, dog tags, and piles of ash. Maybe that's all that would remain of Jon too.

The day went on and on. More medical exams. More psychological tests. Interviews. Vaccines. More tests.

"Goddammit, are we soldiers or medical experiments?" Jon muttered.

They shuffled onward through the labyrinth, lost souls in the swarm. Finally they entered the fort's barbershop. Well, perhaps calling it *barbershop* was stretching it. It just was a concrete room where weary-eyed soldiers stood shearing recruits.

Jon settled down in a seat. He ran his hands through his long, shaggy hair. "Just a bit off the top."

A uniformed barber raised a buzzing razor. "Don't worry, kid, I'm sure you have a beautiful head in there. Somewhere."

Jon had been growing his hair for years. It flowed halfway down his back. After all, he was the composer, lyricist, and keyboard player of a symphonic metal band. He was a rock star in training. He needed to have long, luxurious hair, didn't he? Now he watched long, luxurious locks fall to the floor. The barber kept buzzing, shearing Jon like a sheep, hair and beard alike.

When the work was done, Jon stared at himself in a mirror.

He barely recognized himself.

His head seemed smaller. Without his beard, thin as it might have been, his chin seemed weaker. He looked younger. Just a skinny boy with a head of dark stubble.

George walked up beside him. "Bloody hell, bud. You look like a shaved alpaca."

Jon turned toward his friend. George's glorious red locks were gone, shaved down to stubble.

"And you look like somebody mowed a mountain," Jon said.

The giant touched the side of his head. "I don't like people seeing my scar."

Jon remembered that day. George undergoing brain surgery. The scar was still there, snaking around the skull.

Jon patted his friend on the shoulder. "If we emerge from this war with nothing but a few scars, we'll be lucky. Come on, bud. Let's become real soldiers."

* * * * *

They entered the next room, another station along the concrete path. It was a huge warehouse filled with uniforms, boots, and helmets.

Jon had to admit, this part was kind of cool.

He had seen photos, videos, paintings, even action figures of his heroes from the Alien Wars. Many kids on Earth grew up admiring Einav Ben-Ari, the Golden Lioness who had led fleets in battle; or Marco Emery, the War Poet, who fought aliens across the galaxy; or Addy Linden, the heroine with flowing blond hair, a crooked smile, and a smoking gun always in her hand. Those heroes had fought a century ago, members of the Great Generation, those who had rebuilt Earth from the ruins of alien invasions.

And to be honest, they all looked rather shabby.

In the photographs, those legendary heroes just wore tattered olive drab uniforms. Nothing fancier than what soldiers wore in the ancient photographs from World War II. After all, Earth had been dirt poor during the Alien Wars, barely surviving the devastating invasions from space. The military had operated on a shoestring.

Well, that was back in the twenty-second century. Today in the twenty-third century, Earth commanded a veritable empire. Human power stretched for light-years around, ruling many asteroids, moons, even planets, all rich with resources. And the army had upgraded its wardrobe.

Jon gazed around the warehouse with wide eyes. These looked less like army uniforms and more like, well, superhero outfits.

He picked one garment off a shelf. At a glance, it looked a little like a rubber diving suit. But on closer examination, the fabric was formed of millions of tiny scales, vaguely reptilian. And unlike a diving suit, armored plates covered these uniforms, navy blue and metallic. There were hooks to snap on various attachments—perhaps ammunition.

These were secondhand uniforms, Jon noticed. Somebody had polished the armored plates, smoothed out dents, and crudely painted over scratches and scars. But Jon could still see signs of old battles. A burn mark here. A scar there. He wondered if anyone had died in these suits, and a shudder ran through him.

"Whoa, these are cool!" George said. "You reckon they have one in my size?"

The shelves seemed to be sorted by size, small to large. Jon pointed. "Go all the way to the back. Top shelf. And suck in your gut."

Jon struggled to pull on his uniform. Other soldiers around him faced similar struggles. Finally Jon figured out there were buttons to loosen the armored plates, allowing him to wriggle into the suit. With a few juicy curses, he managed to pull it on. It fit snugly. Embarrassingly so. The armored plates stretched across his chest, back, and limbs, creating the illusion of gleaming metallic muscles.

He couldn't help but notice a few discolored circles on the left breastplate. Fixed bullet holes?

He picked a helmet from a rack. It too was used. There were a few scratches on the top, a burn mark on the back, and somebody had etched *WAR IS HELL* on the side. The helmet was the same color as the armored plates. The visor however was tinted yellow, the only part of the battlesuit that wasn't blue.

It seemed a bit odd to wear blue for a jungle war. Olive green or a camouflage pattern would be better choices. But hey, this was the mighty army of Earth, a galactic empire! An apex predator needed no camouflage! Or something like that. Maybe the army's fashion designer just loved ultramarine.

Ultramarine armor for the ultra marines, Jon thought wryly.

He put on the helmet and examined himself in a mirror. An armored suit, every muscle in the human body forged from deep blue graphene. A helmet with a yellow visor, disturbingly alien, like some insect with a single yellow eye. Jon didn't recognize the man who stared back.

I look like a superhero, he thought. *Or alien insect. Or both. Jon Taylor is… the Amazing Bugman!*

He smirked. But then he looked again at the buffed out bullet holes. At the etching on his helmet.

WAR IS HELL.

Somebody had fought in this suit. Maybe died in it. And soon Jon would be fighting in this armor too.

A shudder passed through him. The armored plates clanked. Great, so it was blue, *and* it clattered. What could go wrong?

George thumped toward him, wearing his own battlesuit. It clanked even louder than Jon's. The armored plates, meant to snap together like a puzzle, pulled apart across George's ample body like ice floes on a deep blue ocean, threatening to pop off. It was the biggest battlesuit in the warehouse, and it barely fit.

The two friends looked at each other.

"How do I look?" George said.

"Ridiculous," said Jon.

"Yeah, well, at least I'm not a shaved alpaca with a scrawny neck."

Jon snorted. "At least I'm not a giant ginger in tights."

George blinked, silent for a moment, then began to laugh. And then to cry. And then to laugh and cry at the same time.

Jon patted his friend on the back. And suddenly, bizarrely, he felt good. He had gotten through the morning. He was in the

Human Defense Force, and he was alive, and he was well, and he was with his best friend. Maybe, just maybe, he could survive this.

"Come on, buddy," Jon said. "Let's go win this war."

George nodded. "We got this."

They exited the warehouse into a sunlit courtyard. Only hours ago, they had been boys, sporting long hair and heavy metal shirts. Now, just like that, they were soldiers.

Chapter Six
The Songs of Bahay

Maria spent the night in the papaya grove, unable to return home, to face her empty room, to feel the walls closing in around her. Not without Crisanto. Not without her beloved friend. The luminous little alien had fled into the jungle, and her life was dark.

She lay on the crumbly earth among the trees. All night, the planet sang to her. The crickets chirped, a starlit choir. The leaves of the papaya trees rustled. Every once in a while, ripe fruit thudded onto the ground. Frogs trilled. Tarsiers cooed. Beyond the trees, reeds stirred along the riverside, and sleeping geese gave the odd snort.

Yet these were all Earth sounds, taken from the ancestral homeland, a song for a lost planet.

There was a deeper song too.

An alien song.

It came from the jungle. The strange, echoing cries of the glimmerbirds as they glided between the trees, sounds like water dripping into underground pools. A few times—the plaintive call of the mourning monks, furry animals that lived in the branches, shying away from the daylight. Creaking wood. Flowing water. The snapping jaws of *bibigpuno* leaves. Ancient whispers of spirits.

Two songs have become one, Maria thought. *The song of Earth and the song of Bahay, mingling together. Two lines of music braiding into one symphony. For centuries, we've lived in harmony. Now we're fraying apart.*

Now the Earthlings had come.

Now fire burned in the north.

Now her dearest companion, her connection to this new world, had fled her.

Finally the two songs lulled her to sleep, but Maria found little comfort in that murky realm. Dreams haunted Maria. Dreams of a man with no face, stomping toward her, his burnt feet scattering teeth like so many marbles. He reached out to her.

"My beloved," the faceless man hissed, but he spoke with Ernesto's voice.

The cock crowed at dawn, waking Maria.

She rose to her feet and brushed dirt off her white *baro't saya*. The papaya trees rose around her, dappled with sunlight.

Usually in the daylight, Bahay sang a new song, a medley of chirruping birds, laughing children, and singing farmers in the paddies. But this morning, the valley was quiet. The rooster crowed in a silent world like an angel of afterlife summoning forth the souls of the dead.

Maria clutched the cross that hung from her neck.

Something is wrong.

She padded through the grove, as silent as the world. She kept waiting to hear something, even a bird's song or an insect's chirp. Nothing. Nothing but the wind among the papaya trees.

Past the grove, she walked among the *nipa* huts.

Silence.

An old woman sat outside her bamboo home, weaving traditional *t'nalak* rugs, which her granddaughter would take downriver to sell in the cities. But the elderly weaver was not humming as usual. Two children sat in a doorway, huddling together, peering with wide eyes. They did not run around and play like on normal days. Young Anna Rodriguez, who normally fed her ducks in the morning, peered between the bamboo branches of her hut. On the hillsides, Maria could see farmers in the rice paddies, but they did not chat or sing as they toiled.

There is evil in the air, Maria thought.

When she reached the village square, she understood why.

She froze, and her heart nearly stopped.

They stood by the pineapple tree. Several strange men. Bahayans, yes, but not from this village. They wore plain white tunics, weathered clogs, and wide straw hats. They were thin, too thin, rawboned and wiry, but there was strength in their ropy limbs and a coldness in their eyes. Flintlock rifles hung across their backs. Their faces were hard. Faces likes stones. Like slabs of granite. Like cliffs. Faces of men who had seen the fire. Faces of killers.

They wore no insignia, no symbols, no uniforms. But Maria de la Cruz knew who they were.

Kalayaan, she thought.

Guerrillas. Freedom fighters. Spirits of the jungle.

A shiver ran through her.

Then she noticed that Ernesto stood among the men. Taller, stronger. Their leader. Blood still stained the wooden stock of his rifle—the dead pilot's blood. A clothing iron hung at his side like a satchel. A torture instrument. The Kalayaan sometimes used irons to burn their captives. Maria could practically smell the searing flesh.

Ernesto was from San Luna, had grown up with Maria, with everyone in this village. But seeing him like this, standing among the Kalayaan… it was like seeing a stranger.

Whoever you were, Ernesto—that man died in the jungle, she thought. *You've gone savage.*

Ernesto looked at her, one eye dark and shrewd, the other white and dead. He smiled at her, but it dripped wickedness.

He stepped onto a tree stump.

"People of San Luna!" he called out, voice ringing across the valley. "Proud Bahayans! A plague has come upon our land. The *banyagas* from Earth, cruel giants with metal machines, have invaded our beloved homeland. In the north, their planes and starships bomb and burn. In the south, they set up a puppet government, traitors to our world. Only the Kalayaan can defeat the *banyagas*! Only the Kalayaan can free Bahay! You've all heard of the dead Earthling, killed in this village. War is upon us all now. Join us, proud patriots! Join the Kalayaan!"

Maria shuddered. Every instinct in her body called upon her to flee. But she found herself stepping forward.

"We're not part of this war!" she said. "Why do you speak like this? San Luna is a peaceful village, nestled between the mountains. We're farmers and fishermen, not soldiers. Don't you know this? You're no longer one of us, Ernesto. What happened to you in the jungle? You became a different man. Return to your war. Leave us. And don't come back."

Ernesto glared at her. "Who are you to speak for this village? To give me orders?"

"I'm Maria Imelda de la Cruz," she said. "A farmer's daughter. That's all. Must I be more? I speak for myself, but I believe that others feel the same. Why must we fight? We've already lost two villagers to the war. Roberto came back in a coffin. You came back a monster."

Those words hurt to utter. With great sweetness, Maria remembered dear Roberto. Her first betrothed. A man she had loved. He had been kind and gentle—nothing like his younger brother. Both brothers had left San Luna to fight. But Roberto had fought because he loved Bahay. Ernesto fought because he hated Earth. To Maria, that made all the difference.

The kind brother died, she thought. *And the cruel one inherited three fishing boats, an air conditioner, and me.*

A smile twisted Ernesto's sharp face, and he stroked her cheek. The same cheek he had bruised.

"Yes, Maria. I'm a monster. A killer. The weak die in war. Monsters survive."

She refused to be cowed. "Is this why you came back to

San Luna? Not to marry me, but to recruit more soldiers. More flesh to feed the beast of war."

A fisherman's son stepped up, no older than fourteen.

"I'll join, Tito Ernesto!" he said.

Another boy ran forward, a rice farmer, thirteen years old, his voice still high. "I'll join too!"

A third boy. "I'll kill the *putes* likes you, Tito Ernesto! I'll join the Kalayaan."

More villagers approached, vowing to fight Earth. To kill or die for their world.

"You are farmers and fishermen's sons!" Maria said. "How would you fight the Earthlings? They have great machines that can fly among the stars. Huge boxes of metal that can crush trees beneath their treads. They even have strange automatons of metal and cables, no flesh to them at all, yet they walk on two legs like men. Don't you read? Don't you listen to the radio? Don't you know these things? If you fight them, you will die!"

The boys hesitated. They glanced at one another. One took a step back.

But Ernesto just laughed. "My betrothed is fearful! I understand. Her spirit is soft, her heart gentle. But we are strong men! We don't fear the *pute* machines. What is a machine next to the heart of a warrior, a patriot who fights for his home? I tell you, comrades—a noble heart can defeat ten thousand machines! I fought in this war. I slew enemies. You will too!"

The boys gathered around him, avoiding eye contact with Maria. After all, what did she know? She was just Maria the rice farmer. Just Maria the girl with too many questions. And Ernesto was a hero. A killer of Earthlings. A leader. She could say no more.

Ernesto snickered. "What's the matter, Maria? Are you frightened? Or did you finally learn to be silent when the men are speaking?" He laughed, but there was no mirth in it. "I see I finally taught you a thing or two."

Maria paused, licked her lips. Then she spoke carefully.

"Ernesto, I'm proud of you. You're very brave to return to the fight." She stepped closer and stared into his eyes. "I saw how bravely you fought the pilot."

He narrowed his eyes, scrutinizing her, perhaps seeking some mockery.

"And will you stay here like a coward?" Ernesto said. "There are some women who fight in the Kalayaan. Will you fight with us?"

Maria frowned. Was he serious? Or simply seeking to embarrass her?

"Me?" She shook her head. "No. I'm not nearly as brave as you. You're very courageous, Ernesto, to fight such a powerful enemy, to fight a war that slew so many." She narrowed her eyes, staring at him. "A war you might not survive."

Ernesto laughed and mussed her hair. "I'll return to you a hero, lovely Maria, with a chain of Earthling scalps around my neck. We'll hang it in our matrimonial home, and we'll celebrate Earth's downfall. Tend to my work while I'm gone. My parents will need help on their boats. And don't forget to pray for me."

"I'll pray for all Bahay," Maria said. "I'll pray for peace and freedom."

But not for you, she thought. *Because if you never return, I'll be happy.*

Guilt flooded her. What a horrible thought! How could she yearn for a man's death? Her betrothed no less? What kind of monster was she? Yes, Ernesto was a hothead, and he hit her sometimes, but she deserved it. She asked too many questions. Spoke too freely. And now—to wish a man dead! A man who loved her!

Am I a monster? she thought. *Maybe I'm no better than the Earthlings who bomb the north.*

Ernesto leaned forward, gripped her head, and kissed her on the lips. It was a hard, cold kiss, his mouth closed, his hand clasping her hair.

"I love you, Maria," he said. "I'll return a hero or a martyr. Your love will give me strength in the fight."

A handful of other villagers stepped forth. Farmers, fishermen, weavers. Men. Women. Boys. Girls. They followed the guerrillas out of the village. Some kept going, traveling with the Kalayaan toward the fire. Those who remained behind sang songs of freedom and patriotism.

Maria stood still for a long moment, even after the guerrillas were gone.

Then she ran through the village.

She raced by the bamboo huts, through the banana plantation, and up the rice paddy terraces. Her feet splashed through the water, her wet dress slapped against her thighs, and her eyes stung with tears, but she did not stop running until she reached the highest terrace. There she climbed a verdant mountainside and rose onto a jutting boulder. She stood in the sunlight high above the valley, so high she could see the glistening sea beyond the mountains. The rainforest spread below her, and distant sheets of rain swayed like curtains. The wind billowed her long black hair, scented of leaves and water and the distant hint of smoke.

She turned southward, and she saw the trees stir. A foreigner would see nothing but a rustling canopy, a green ripple in the wind, but Maria had been born and raised in these lands, and she knew the movement of every branch and leaf. That was the Kalayaan moving along the Freedom Trail. Heading to war.

"I'm sorry, Ernesto," she whispered, and a tear flowed down her cheek. "I'm sorry I hoped you would die. Live, Ernesto. I love you, despite everything that you are. I love all of you, my brothers and sisters. Live and come home."

A light flashed before her, whisked aside, fluttered toward the paddies.

"Crisanto!" she said.

She gazed with wide eyes at the ball of light. A tiny alien, no larger than a marble. He flew toward her, her old companion, then fluttered off again. Maria swayed on the boulder, nearly falling.

"Crisanto, don't be naughty! Come to me. Into my pocket. You like it in there."

He flew toward her again, then back, forward, and back. Finally he began fluttering toward the valley.

Something is wrong, Maria thought. *He wants me to follow.*

She climbed off the boulder and ran through the rice paddies, following the mote of light.

Chapter Seven
Dramatization

Thousands of recruits entered a gymnasium. Just that morning, standing outside on the sidewalk, they had all looked different. There were jocks, nerds, music geeks like Jon, rich kids, poor kids, juvenile delinquents, kids as American as baseball and apple pie, immigrant kids who barely spoke English, and every other type of kid known to mankind.

Here in this gym, only a few hours later, they were the same.

Thousands of kids in blue battlesuits, the armored plates bearing the scars of their previous owners. The boys with shaved heads and smooth cheeks. The girls with tight ponytails, not a strand out of place. They all carried duffel bags. They all wore leather boots. You couldn't tell who was rich, poor, popular, or a misfit.

"All cannon fodder looks the same," Jon muttered. He glanced at George. "All but you, that is. You still stand out. A giant ginger mountain."

"It's not my fault I'm so big," George said. He hunched over, ashamed, trying to shrink. "The biggest damn target in the army."

"And I'm standing next to ya," Jon said. "Perfect."

"You're just worried about yourself?" George said.

"Buddy, you could probably take ten bullets and stay standing. The slits will need a fucking nuclear bomb to take you down."

"Silence!" A drone hovered near them, and two sparks shot out, hitting the friends. "Eyes ahead. Backs straight. Face the white wall."

The drone flew away, shocking a few other recruits into silence. Soon everyone was facing the same blank white wall. The drone rose toward the gym's ceiling, then projected a beam of light. A crackling video appeared on the wall, showing the HDF flag fluttering in the wind. A golden phoenix reared on the fabric, symbolizing Earth's rise from the ruins of the Alien Wars a century ago.

"Imagine Symphonica playing for a crowd like this," Jon whispered.

"We'd probably need the drones to keep them around once your horn section starts playing," George whispered back.

Jon flipped him off.

"Welcome, new soldiers of the Human Defense Force!"

The voice boomed from the speakers, so loud Jon cringed.

An actor appeared on screen. He wore a gleaming blue battlesuit. Rather than navy blue like normal battlesuits, this outfit was azure like the sea meeting a summer sky. And it certainly wasn't scratched, dented, and perforated with old bullet holes. The man in the video carried a shield painted like planet Earth, America facing the viewer. He wasn't a real soldier. Jon recognized the square jaw, bad tan, and coiffed blond hair. He was a famous actor on Earth, appearing in many tabloids, though Jon couldn't remember his name. He knew more about dead symphonic metal stars than current celebrities.

"Hello, fellow soldiers!" The actor gave a sparkling smile. "This is Ensign Earth, reporting for duty!" He saluted briskly.

"Take off your top!" a girl shouted in the crowd.

"Strip, strip!" chanted somebody else.

The drones shocked them silent. On the film, Ensign Earth continued smiling, undisturbed.

"Gosh darn it, it's good to see you all. You've made a brave choice, joining the HDF." Ensign Earth placed his fist on his heart. "Thanks to your noble choice, your families can sleep well tonight, knowing that you defend them."

"Not exactly my choice," Jon muttered, remembering the day the little brown envelope had arrived. He wondered how many people here were volunteers, and how many—like him—had been drafted. Judging by the scowls and mutters, practically everyone was here against their will.

"Well, golly!" Ensign Earth checked his watch. "Looks like it's time to watch my favorite movie. I like to call it: *Why We Fight!*"

A few soldiers in the crowd booed.

"Porn, porn, porn!" one recruit chanted, earning scattered laughter and some groans.

On screen, the handsome actor became solemn. "As you know, twenty years ago, Earth made a startling discovery. We discovered Bahay, a planet three hundred light-years away, far beyond the borders of our empire. A planet with millions of humans!"

"Well, golly!" Jon said, feigning interest. A few soldiers around him snickered.

Hey, who says I can't heckle too? he thought.

Ensign Earth continued, oblivious. "How is this possible, you ask? Well, to find out, we'll have to go back in time. Come with me as we travel back through the ages. All the way… to the nineteenth century."

A cloud of mist obscured the video, and dreamy harp strings trilled.

When the mist cleared, Ensign Earth was gone. The video now showed jittery black and white footage, complete with scratching noises and the odd hair on the frame. Palm trees rustled on a tropical island. A few fishermen stood on the beach.

Letters appeared below the grainy video: DRAMATIZATION.

"Welcome to the peaceful islands of the Philippines!" rose Ensign Earth's disembodied voice. "In 1898, they are a tropical paradise, home to millions of friendly islanders."

The image showed a young Filipina picking papayas. She looked up at the camera and smiled brightly. Flowers bloomed in her hair.

"Show us your tits!" Clay shouted.

A few recruits laughed. Many rolled their eyes. Jon's hands itched to form fists and pummel the idiot. He forced himself to look back at the video.

Save your anger for the enemy, Jon, he told himself. *Clay is an asshole, but you gotta pick your battles.*

Ensign Earth continued to narrate the video, which now showed Filipinos emerging from bamboo huts, pointing at the sky, and crying out.

"And then, in 1899, evil came!" the film announced.

The video panned upward, showing luminous orbs descending toward the tropical islands.

"Santelmos!" somebody shouted in the crowd.

"Aliens!" shouted another recruit.

"Murderers!"

"Killers!"

Jon stared at the video, and he gritted his teeth. The Santelmos glided downward to the beaches. They were strange aliens with no physical forms, at least none that Jon could see. They appeared as blobs of light, nebulous, dimming and brightening, shrinking and expanding, as fickle as beads of sunlight on the waves.

Most aliens in the galaxy, to be blunt, were ugly fuckers. Jon had seen photographs, videos, and toys of space bugs, the kind of aliens who used to attack Earth a century ago. Those were nasty critters, all claws and fangs and scales. But the Santelmos were different. Not ugly. Even beautiful in a way.

But evil.

Perhaps more evil than any mindless space bug. Jon had grown up hearing tales of Santelmo malice.

Because of these bastards, Paul is dead, he thought.

The crowd booed. A few recruits rose and shouted at the screen. Clearly, Jon was not alone. So many had lost friends and family to these balls of light.

"The Santelmos!" announced Ensign Earth, speaking from off screen. "They're really nasty guys. Evildoers. Ancient aliens from a distant empire. For centuries, they studied Earth. Until one day, they recruited traitors from our very world."

"The slits!" somebody shouted hoarsely.

"Traitors!"

"Alien lovers!"

The voices in the crowd rang out. On the video, they all saw it happen. The Red Cardinal, leader of the exodus, guided a flock of Filipinos toward the slender silvery starships. The vessels rose, leaving Earth, and flashed toward the distant stars.

Jon clenched his jaw. He knew this wasn't an authentic historical video. It was a reenactment. But he couldn't stop the anger. How could humans do this? How could humans betray Earth, defect to an alien empire, and work with such evil creatures?

The video showed the alien starships travel toward a distant planet, an ocean world dotted with islands.

"Bahay!" came Ensign Earth's voice. "A planet three hundred light-years away, accessible only by wormhole. There the Santelmos bred the human defectors. There, over centuries, the traitors multiplied into a nation of millions. There the Santelmos trained their human pets to become killers."

Yes, Jon knew the stories. It wasn't Santelmos who had murdered his brother. Not directly, at least. It was the native

Bahayans. Human traitors who served the aliens.

"Twenty years ago," continued Ensign Earth's narration, "a brave explorer named Thomas Emery discovered Bahay. He learned about the missing human population. Earth sent a starship to liberate the Bahayans from their alien masters. But the aliens had turned the Bahayans against us! They built, brainwashed, and armed vast terrorist networks."

"Boo! Boo!" rose cries from the crowd. "Aliens suck!"

A few of those jeers sounded decidedly cynical. But most seemed full of true hatred.

Ensign Earth reappeared on screen, solemn. "Most Bahayans crave freedom. They loathe the terrorists who serve the aliens. And you know what heroes like me do? We fight evil-doers! And now, you're all heroes too. Together, we'll liberate Bahay! We'll banish the alien menace! We'll punish the Bahayan traitors! And gosh darn it, we'll bring Bahay into the embrace of the Human Commonwealth. Today Bahay is a rogue planet, overrun with aliens, and home to millions of hostages. But after our victory, it will become our most precious colony."

The phoenix banner returned—symbol of the Human Defense Force, billowing proudly.

"Boring!" somebody cried from the crowd.

"Play Freebird!" cried somebody else.

Ensign Earth smiled his huge toothy smile. "Woo! That was an exciting movie, wasn't it? Now how about we all stand up and sing my favorite song?"

The actor saluted the flag. Earth's anthem began to play.

Everyone in the gym rose and began to sing.

O Earth!
Our pale blue home
O Earth!
The world we love

Among all the stars
Your sun is brightest
Among all the worlds
You we call our home
In darkness we yearn for you
Under your sky we bless you
With all our courage we defend you
Forever you shall be
Our planet strong and free
O Earth!
Our pale blue home
O Earth!
The world we love

As he sang, Jon remembered the stories he learned at school, from books, and from his great-grandfather. Tales of the Alien Wars.

It was the twenty-third century now, an era of human might. The Human Commonwealth spread across multiple worlds, an empire centered around Earth. But the twenty-second century had been an era of terror. Earth had reached into space too soon, too weak, perhaps too curious. They had stirred the hornet's nest. Wave after wave of alien invasions had pummeled Earth, beating down this impudent young species that dared to reach for the stars.

Yes, last century had been an era of fear. But also of Earth's greatest heroes. Everyone knew their names. Marco Emery, the War Poet. Addy Linden, Queen of Fire, heroine of the Summer Uprising against the marauders. Lailani de la Rosa, the Heroine of the Rose, who had brought hope in humanity's darkest hour. And of course, Einav Ben-Ari, the Golden Lioness, her name etched alongside Alexander the Great, Caesar, and Napoleon. Einav Ben-Ari, a war heroine, a space explorer, a leader of humanity. She had built an empire among the stars.

History would forever remember these names.

But that was a century ago. Humanity had won. The aliens had retreated. The Age of Heroes was over.

Now is my generation's chance, Jon thought. *Now we can become heroes. Now we can fight for Earth like they did. Now we can write our own legends.*

His chest swelled with pride. He had grown up idolizing those heroes from the history books. They had fought against evil. They had sacrificed for humanity. And they had become legends.

I always dreamed of being a musician, Jon thought. *Of composing great music. But maybe, in the army, I can be great too. We can be heroes.*

Hatred filled him again. Hatred of the Santelmos, aliens who turned human against human. Hatred of the Bahayans, traitors, slits. Working together, the aliens and terrorists had murdered too many innocent people, ruined too many families.

I'm a soldier now, Bahay, Jon thought. *I don't have aliens helping me. I will show you human strength.*

Chapter Eight
The Toad

The mote of light flitted across the rice paddies, and Maria followed.

"Crisanto, come back here! Don't be bad!"

But the little Santelmo kept flying ahead, zooming over the terraces like a mad firefly.

Santelmos were strange creatures. She often spoke to her pet, and she swore he understood her language. Yet he rarely obeyed her, more like a stubborn cat than a dog.

Cat? Dog? No, those were not right comparisons. Even calling him a pet seemed unfair. Santelmos were intelligent. They flew starships. They ruled a galactic empire. But they could barely communicate with humans. Many times, Maria had tried to teach Crisanto how to spell letters in the air, if only figure eights. But the little blob of light would never learn—either too young, too alien, or simply too stubborn.

Now she wondered if he understood anything at all.

"Crisanto, come back to me!"

She paused for breath. She stood in a rice paddy, the water rising halfway up her shins. She leaned forward, placed her hands on her thighs, and took deep breaths. She had lost her straw hat somewhere during the run, and her hair clung to her cheeks, damp with sweat.

He fluttered up toward her, spun in mad circles, and flew onward.

"Fine, fine. I'm coming!"

Maria kept running.

She followed the luminous orb across the paddies, through the avocado grove, and there they reached it.

The jungle wall.

It loomed before them. The trees soared. Maria was used to Old World trees, those brought here from Earth. Trees like banana and papaya and guava, trees barely taller than her that gave sweet fruit.

But *these* trees, the native trees of Bahay, were different creatures entirely. They were taller than all the huts in San Luna stacked together. They bore no fruit, for they were not trees to give life but to harbor death. Their shade was not a welcome relief from the sun but a dark, pitiless abyss. She could see only a few steps ahead. Vines dangled in the mist. Yellow eyes peered from the shadows. A distant cry rang out—the call of a mourning monk, echoing and alien.

Crisanto paused as if to steel himself, then glided into the jungle.

Maria sighed.

"You're running off again?" She waved her hand dismissively. "Fine. Go then! I can't stop you."

The glowing orb paused among the trees. He hovered in the jungle, a speck of light in the shadows like a single eye, watching her.

Maria tilted her head. "What's wrong, Crisanto? Are you lonely in San Luna? Do you want to find your people? Your parents?" She lowered her head. "If you must leave me too, then leave. Everyone is leaving, and I feel so alone." Her eyes dampened. "I'm sorry. I should not just complain about myself. If you wish to seek another life, another family, I wish you well." Her tears flowed. "Goodbye, my friend."

She could not bear to say any more. She began walking back toward her village, blinded by tears.

Crisanto raced through the air, placed himself before her, and blocked her way.

"Crisanto!" She laughed and wiped her eyes.

He spun in rings around her. He thumped into her chest, weighing no more than a dandelion seed. He flew back into the jungle, then seemed to look at her. To beckon.

"You want me to follow?"

He bobbed up and down.

"I can't, Crisanto. I'm scared."

But he kept flying around her like a pesky mosquito, urging her into the jungle.

Maria bit her lip. Why was he doing this? Finally her curiosity overcame her fear.

Be brave, Maria. Two of your betrothed went off to war. Surely you can take a few steps into a forest.

She took one step.

Then another.

Then a third.

For the first time in her life, she walked through the rainforest.

Bibigpuno trees rose around her like cathedral columns. The Earthlings called them fangwoods, for their leaves were toothy and hungry like Venus flytraps. *Mamula* trees rose around them, their pollen glowing, while the *pagluna* trees seeped white sap valued in tribal medicine. Roots formed buttresses, rising taller than Maria's head, twisting, coiling, sprouting boles toward the lofty canopy. More roots coiled beneath her feet, braiding together, cradling puddles of water full of particolored fish. Mist floated among the boughs, and curtains of moss swayed like ghosts. Vines draped from the branches, and ivy and lichen crawled over boulders and fallen logs. Mushrooms grew from tree trunks, and flowerbugs scuttled everywhere, blue and green and chirruping. Every once in a while, a slender branch stretched out, and leafy jaws snapped shut, catching an insect.

Maria took another step. The trees creaked, grumbled, and groaned. They were speaking to Maria in a language she could not understand. She knew their names. And they knew her. In their strange wooden sounds she could hear her name. *Maria… Maria…*

The place chilled her. But there was beauty here too. It was an entire universe, a biosphere that covered the islands of Bahay, ancient beyond knowing. This rainforest had grown here for millions of years before humans arrived on Bahay. A place of antiquity and secrets. And suddenly it seemed to Maria that Bahay, the entire planet, was a single organism. And that it mourned.

This rainforest scares me, but it's precious, she thought. *And in the north, the Earthling are burning it. The rainforest weeps.*

Crisanto hovered over a fallen bole, peering like an eye. Many true eyes glowed among roots, inside trunks, and from burrows under outcrops of soil and moss. Whatever animals were watching remained hidden.

Crisanto flew deeper. And Maria followed.

"Crisanto, slow down! I can't run here. There are so many obstacles."

She wondered how the Kalayaan operated here. Every step was a struggle. She had to keep climbing over coiling roots, boulders, and fallen logs. Sometimes she had to wriggle between vines and bushes, even crawl under low roots. Animals hissed at her from burrows, and vines snagged at her dress with leafy fingers. A few times, she had to jump over gurgling rivulets. The tongues of submerged creatures rose from the water, lapping at her feet, perhaps mistaking her for a *jubatus* bat.

"Crisanto, where are we going?" Maria said. "We can get lost in here."

She stopped and looked around. Fear flooded her.

What am I doing?

She had been walking for only a few moments. Surely, the village was still near. But she was utterly lost. She might as well have been standing on an alien world.

Everywhere—the rainforest. Mist among the trees, and draping vines, and creaking roots that spread and coiled like tentacles. A howl rose above, maybe just a mourning monk. A glimmerbird shrieked and fluttered overhead, shedding iridescent feathers the length of Maria's arms.

She did not know north from south, east from west. The jungle was like the sea. Even just a few meters in you could drown. She could try to retrace her steps back home. But she was likely to stray the wrong way, to move deeper into the rainforest, to vanish in this world. A different reality. This was Bahay, the world her heart beat for, but suddenly the planet seemed so alien.

My people have been here for three centuries, she thought. *But that's nothing. These trees have lived here for millions of years. Maybe billions. And they're watching me. They have eyes.*

"Crisanto?" she whispered.

She could barely see him. He hovered ahead through the mist, going farther, deeper, becoming smaller. Maria remembered the stories she had heard. Back on Earth, people had called the Santelmo the wills-o'-the-wisp, thinking them magical creatures. And perhaps they were. This were not life as Maria understood it, yet here she was, following one through the murk.

A guttural sound, a sort of groan or croak, bubbled up from below. Maria paused. A strange toad sat at her feet. She had nearly stepped on it. Its skin was translucent, revealing glowing orbs among crystalline bones. At first, she worried that the toad had swallowed Crisanto, but no. Those glowing orbs were its organs, the heart red, the lungs glimmering white, the blood vessels blue and as intricate as the roots in the forest.

"A *panaginip palaka!*" she whispered.

She had heard of these beings. Dreamtoads. In the early

days of Bahay, the shamans would seek them in the rainforest. It was said that a *panaginip palaka* could reveal the future to those worthy.

Maria knelt and lifted the dreamtoad, and warmth spread through her. Her head spun, like it did sometimes when the village elders burned the holy *mamula* leaves.

The toad gazed into her eyes.

"It will be the only way to save her," the toad said. "You must use his knife."

Maria yelped and dropped the toad. It gave a deep croaking *ribbit*, then hopped off. Had she merely imagined its words?

She blinked and rubbed her eyes, still feeling dizzy.

A cry pierced the air.

At first, she thought it another mourning monk scuttling among the branches, or maybe another glimmerbird.

But the sound grew louder. Louder still. A rumbling. The bellowing howl of an ancient beast.

Briefly, Maria thought it a demonic god risen from the sea. But then she recognized the sound. She had heard this sound before.

"A machine," she whispered. "An engine." She shivered. "A plane. Maybe several planes."

The rumbles multiplied, came closer, louder. She stared up, but she could not see them. The rainforest canopy hid the sky. They were coming closer, they were over her now—directly over her! She ran, following the sound, leaping over roots. She gripped hanging ivy, swung over a stream, and there! Above the stream, where the canopy was thinner, she could glimpse shreds of sky. And she saw them.

Planes.

A squadron of planes, flying together, beasts of metal, leaving white trails.

Crisanto came to hover beside her. He seemed to gaze at the sky with her.

"They're flying to San Luna," she whispered.

Terror flooded her.

She stood frozen for an instant.

Then she began to run, screaming, calling for her parents, and—

A *boom* shook the rainforest.

Shock waves pounded into the trees, bending them, ripping off leaves and branches.

Maria fell.

Another boom.

Another.

The sound was so loud, and the forest shook, and branches fell onto her. Fire blazed in the distance. She could feel the heat. She could smell the smoke.

"*Nanay*!" she cried. "*Tatay*!"

Mother! Father!

She rose again, but more booms rattled the forest, and she fell, cowered, covered her head with her arms.

And then—the explosions ended.

And the forest was silent.

The song of Bahay was gone.

She heard no birds. No insects. Even the trees no longer creaked and moaned.

But she heard the fire. It crackled like laughing demons.

Maria stumbled through the rainforest, trying to reach her village, to find her parents, but her head kept whirling. She was so dizzy. So tired.

She found herself lying on a carpet of moss. She did not even remember falling. The forest spun around her, and the toad gazed into her eyes, and she slept.

Chapter Nine
Ride the Fire

The drones buzzed over the crowd of recruits, shooting electric bolts.

"Ow!"

"Dammit!"

"God!"

Soldiers winced, rubbing their wounds. The drones kept fluttering around, hurling shards of lightning.

"Into the courtyard!" the machines intoned.

A bolt hit Jon's chest. Pain radiated across his ribs.

"Goddammit!" he blurted.

The drones buzzed like the world's meanest wasps, herding the soldiers outside.

Hundreds of young soldiers spilled into a courtyard. Since parting from his parents, Jon had spent his time indoors, moving through the recruitment center. Medical tests. Interviews. Haircut. Shave. More tests. More doctors. More questions. Stop after stop in the concrete labyrinth.

Jon had no watch, but it felt like many hours had passed in that maze—at least a full day, probably half the night too. But here in the courtyard, the sun still shone. It was barely afternoon.

Time moves slowly in the army, he thought. *My God, has it really only been a few hours?*

Enlisted men served for three years at least. Many were kept longer. It would be a slow haul.

"Are those starships?" George pointed. "Goddamn, look

at those things."

"They're shuttles," Jon said. "Shuttles from a mothership."

George's eyes widened. "Are we going into space? I've never been to space."

"Me neither," Jon said.

It was 2223. Humanity had been operating in space for generations. Starting with a few humble spacecraft in the twentieth century, humanity had built an empire in space. They had colonized worlds. Explored the stars. Fought wars with alien species.

And yet, most humans had never left Earth. Unless you were a soldier, an asteroid miner, an ambitious colonist, or just a little crazy, you stayed home. Space was full of disease, darkness, and nasty alien bugs the size of bears.

"We're going up there *already*?" George said. "What, to fight the war now? We've only been soldiers for a few hours!"

"I don't know, George," Jon said. "But I doubt they'll hurl us at the slits today. We haven't even gone through basic training."

The shuttles parked across an asphalt spaceport, fifty or more. They were crude, boxy crafts, painted olive green, covered with armored plates. Their wings seemed squat, woefully undersized, like the fragile wings of chubby metal bumblebees. But the exhaust pipes on those shuttles were large enough for a man to crawl into. Their engines probably carried a serious punch.

And suddenly it hit Jon.

A crushing wave of homesickness.

He had only left home that morning, but it washed over him. He thought about his mom making him pancakes. His dad rustling music sheets, helping Jon craft his melodies. Kaelyn, beautiful Kaelyn in the shade of the maple tree, kissing him.

He didn't want to go to space.

Yes, Jon wanted to do the right thing. To fight for his planet. To be a hero like the old heroes from the stories. But so much fear now flooded him. Not just fear of the enemy, of the wily slits in the jungle. But the fear of never tasting those pancakes, never completing his music, never feeling Kaelyn's lips on his own again. It was all suddenly too much, and his eyes watered. He dried them quickly, hoping nobody saw.

If Clay sees me cry, I'll never hear the end of it, Jon thought.

But only George seemed to notice. The giant placed an overgrown hand on Jon's shoulder.

"It's all right, bud," George said. "We'll get through this. Together. It'll be an adventure."

Jon saw the same fear in George's eyes.

He's trying to cheer me up, Jon thought. *To be strong for me. But he's just as terrified.*

He nodded. "An adventure."

A shuttle's engines rumbled. The exhaust pipes glowed red, belching out smoke. The shuttle rose several meters, hovered toward the recruits, and slammed down. The crowd of recruits stumbled back, coughing, waving aside the smog.

A drone circled above the crowd.

"The following recruits will enter the shuttle!" the little machine announced. "Recruit Troy Murray, ID TY23437. Recruit Damian Smith, ID TY23438. Recruit…"

It kept reading out names and IDs. A few soldiers hesitated. They glanced at the shuttles, up at the sky, then back at the concrete building. A few drones buzzed low and fired electric bolts. Recruits yelped. One by one, soldiers entered the shuttle.

Jon checked his dog tags. He saw an ID written beneath his name. TY23439. That was him now. A serial number. One among thousands here at the recruitment center. One among millions in the Human Defense Force.

An image flashed through his mind. Himself—a puddle of

gore in the jungle. Somebody fishing this molten tag from the mess, unable to even read the number. Sending him home in a bag to the wrong family.

He shoved that thought aside. Some adventure.

Finally the shuttle was full. Jon had not counted, but he guessed that about fifty soldiers had entered. Most of the recruits still stood outside on the asphalt—including Jon and George, who had not been called.

The vessel rumbled, belched smoke, and rose to hover several meters above the courtyard. Engines growled. The world shook with waves of bass. Suddenly, with roaring heat and furious light, the shuttle's massive exhaust pipe spewed an inferno. Fire blazed with the wrath of gods. Standing below, everyone covered their ears and hunched over. The shuttle streaked upward, leaving a trail of fire.

Jon took a few steps back, coughing. He squinted, waved aside smoke, and watched the shuttle race across the sky. It blazed in a sphere of light, flying higher and higher, like a comet in reverse, rising from a ruined world. Within a few moments, it was just a distant speck in the afternoon sky.

Another shuttle taxied across the asphalt toward the crowd.

The drone began reading out more names. This time Jon counted. Forty-five names. The recruits entered the shuttle. This vessel too took off, roaring into space. Again, Jon and George remained below.

Shuttle after shuttle approached the crowd, picked up soldiers, and blasted into space. The crowd was seriously thinning out now. Only a handful of shuttles and recruits remained on the asphalt. The sun dipped below the horizon, and the stars emerged.

My first day in the army is ending, Jon thought.

His belly rumbled. He had not eaten all day. Not since his

mom's pancakes that morning, which he had only picked at, his belly a knot. Again he felt it—that homesickness, that sting of tears in his eyes. He buried the pain.

"Goddamn, this is taking forever!" rose a high-pitched voice from behind Jon. "I'll die of old age before the Bahayans kill me."

A few scattered laughs sounded. Jon turned toward the recruit who had spoken.

She was petite girl with light brown skin, black hair, and startlingly large green eyes. Jon had never seen eyes so big and bright. They seemed almost luminous in her dark face.

She's rather pretty, he couldn't help but think.

"Could be nice to sit out the war here on the tarmac," Jon said to her.

The girl snorted. "Not for me. I volunteered for this. I can't wait to go kill some bad guys." She winked, aimed her fingers like a pistol, and pretended to shoot Jon. "Pow!"

He clutched his chest. "Ow, you got me."

The girl stuck her tongue out. "Ah, come on, ya big baby. I only shot ya in the spleen, you'll be fine."

Jon held out his hand. "I'm Jon. And the ginger giant beside me is George."

The girl tilted her head. "You mean the giant who just ran off to hide?"

Jon sighed. Indeed, his friend had hurried away. George was now busy staring at an interesting rock.

"Sorry," Jon said. "He's scared of girls."

The girl shook his hand. Her hand was small but her grip was firm. "Etty Ettinger is the name. I know, I know, it's a dumb alliteration. Blame my parents. It makes me sound like a second-rate superhero. Peter Parker, Clark Kent, and the amazing Etty Ettinger!"

Jon laughed. "What's your superpower?"

"Being invisible in a crowd, apparently." She tossed an invisible cape. "Captain Etty to the rescue! Always chosen last for sports teams, group projects, and fighting space wars!"

Jon laughed again, already feeling a bit better.

A glint caught his eye. Etty was wearing a Star of David medallion. Jon looked back into her eyes.

She caressed the amulet, and her voice softened. "My lucky star. I was born in Israel. I bought this medallion there, and it brings me luck." Her eyes hardened, and her hands balled into fists. "You got a problem with that?"

"Of course not," Jon said. "Hey, you guys are tough fighters."

She preened. "Damn right! We Israelis keep getting back up on our feet. The Romans destroyed us. So we rebuilt. The Nazis butchered us. So we rebuilt again. Then the damn aliens bombed Israel to dust. So again… we rebuilt." She sighed. "To be honest, it gets a bit tedious, but hey, it's good exercise."

"The repetition must be boring you to death by now," Jon said.

Etty yawned theatrically. "I know, right? Genocide is so tiresome."

A deep voice rose from nearby, disturbing their conversation.

"Well, well, look at Jon Taylor! First he romances a giant fairy, and now he's consorting with Jews."

Clay Hagen came strutting toward them, smirking. His far-set blue eyes glittered in his wide, pasty face. Several of his lackeys walked behind him.

"What you say, you *ben zona*?" Etty sneered and raised her fists.

"Get lost, Clay," Jon said. "Go find a rock to crawl under."

The brute flushed red. His eyes bugged out. He snarled

like a wild animal. He lunged at them, barely human anymore. His fists swung.

Jon had not fought anyone since the third grade, but his instincts kicked in. He raised his arms, and protected his head. Clay's fist slammed into his shoulder instead. Even with the battlesuit, it *hurt*. The thug wasn't much taller than Jon, but he was far heavier. Clay had a chest like a gorilla, and his fists were like anvils. Jon stumbled a few steps back, pain pounding through him.

The remaining recruits formed a ring around the two combatants. Somebody began to chant: "Fight, fight, fight!"

Clay came at him again. Jon wanted to run. To hide. To seek help from George. But he knew: *If I run now, I'll be running forever.*

Against all instinct, he stood his ground. And he swung a fist of his own.

Clay raised his arms protectively. Jon's fist hit the brute's forearm. His knuckles crunched against the armored suit. Jon roared in pain.

I hurt myself more than him, he thought, wondering if he broke his knuckles. *Some fighter I am.*

"Kill him, boss!" shouted the bucktooth girl from earlier. She had been following Clay around all day.

"You're dead, Taylor!" Clay said. "You're fucking dead. You—"

"Leave him alone!" Etty screamed, lunging at Clay.

The Israeli was short and slender. Even in her battlesuit, she probably only weighed a hundred pounds. But she leaped onto Clay nonetheless, fists swinging. For a moment, she clung to his back, a honey badger attacking a bison.

"Get off, you whore!" Clay howled.

He grabbed Etty, ripped her off like a leech, and shoved her to ground. She hit the pavement, and Clay kicked her stomach. His boot thumped against her battlesuit, a sickening sound. Etty doubled over in pain.

Jon howled. Rage exploded through him, drowning his fear. He leaped at Clay, seeing red, ready to kill or be killed, and—

Electricity shocked him.

Jon screamed.

Another bolt hit him. Another.

He fell back, groaning. Through narrowed eyelids, he made out several drones. The little machines were bombarding the combatants, shocking him, Clay, and even Etty again and again. If the battlesuits offered some protection from punches and kicks, they did nothing for electric bolts. George raced toward them, only for drones to blast him too. The giant fell to the pavement, twitching.

"Into the last shuttle, recruits!" the drone buzzed. "Obey or be punished!"

Finally the drones ended their assault. Jon knelt on the asphalt, coughing. Smoke rose from his battlesuit.

He wanted to curl up and die, but Jon forced himself to limp toward Etty. She lay in a fetal position, moaning.

"Are you all right?" Jon said softly.

"Yeah." She groaned. "The bastard got me right in the ovaries. But I bloodied his nose, so we're even."

He helped her up. Etty stood swaying. She leaned against Jon, and he wrapped an arm around her waist, holding her steady. Woozy as she was, Etty managed to turn toward Clay and flip him off.

Clay struggled to his feet too. Blood dripped from his mouth and nose. He laughed maniacally, teeth red.

"You're dead, Taylor!" He pointed at Jon, cackling. "You're dead! You, the giant, and the Jew! Dead meat!"

Beside him, the bucktoothed girl brayed with laughter. "Good one, boss!"

Jon looked at the laughing girl.

What the hell is your story?

Her buck teeth were the least of her problems. The girl was gangly, her eyes peered from behind massive glasses, and her frizzy hair stuck every which way. In some cruel irony from above, her name was Becky, instantly leading everyone to call her Bucktoothed Becky or just Bucky. She herself had accepted the cruel nicknames, using them herself, often with a laugh, perhaps seeking to hide her pain behind humor.

"You sure showed him, Clay," the girl said. She let out another bray of laughter.

"Shut up, Bucky, shut up!" Clay said.

Only one shuttle remained on the tarmac. Its hatch opened, and the drones herded the recruits in.

Jon entered, grumbling and rubbing his sore knuckles. Whatever optimism had flickered in him now died. Especially when he realized he'd be sharing the shuttle with Clay and his lackeys.

The shuttle was roughly the size of school bus, maybe smaller. Forty-odd recruits shuffled in. The drones zapped a few of the stragglers.

There was nobody else inside. Not even a pilot. Just a drone hovering around the cabin.

"Goddamn, the last time I saw a living human, he squeezed my balls," Jon muttered.

"Hey, don't we recruits qualify?" George said.

Jon snorted. "We're not human anymore. We're grunts."

This wasn't anything like the stories Jon's father had told. The army today was far more mechanized. Jon had read all about the Alien Wars, including the autobiography of Marco Emery, the War Poet, one of the great heroes. Back then, few robots served in the army, and recruits trained on Earth. But that had been last century. Back then, Earth had been just a fledgling planet, plagued by alien invasions and crumbling technology.

Today Earth commanded an empire.

Here we are, the modern military, Jon thought. *A bunch of morons in a metal box.*

There were no seats, only harnesses along the walls.

George's shoulders slumped. "No way I'm fitting into one of those harnesses."

"Suck in your gut, buddy!" Jon said. "We'll strap you in."

George sucked his gut for all it was worth. He barely squeezed into the harness. Jon had to grab the straps, place his boot against the bulkhead, and tug with all his strength. Etty helped, tugging another strap. Finally George was strapped into place, looking like a trussed ham.

Jon slipped into the harness beside his friend. Etty took the harness at Jon's other side. She was far smaller than the boys, almost too small. With her, it was an effort to squeeze the harnesses tightly enough.

Clay and his thugs strapped themselves to the opposite bulkhead. Blood still covered Clay's face. He licked his lips and grinned at Jon.

"Asshole," Etty muttered under her breath. "Next time I'm gonna kick him in the—whoa!"

The engines roared.

The shuttle soared, riding a blaze of fire.

The recruits jerked in their harnesses. The g-force tugged on Jon so powerfully he nearly gagged. The straps dug into his chest, and blackness spread around his eyes. He struggled for air.

Across from him, Bucky passed out. She hung from her harness like a limp strip of meat.

Somebody else vomited.

George groaned, and then his head hit his chin. Unconscious.

The shuttle kept roaring, rattling, soaring higher and

higher. There was a little porthole above the harnesses, and Jon glimpsed blazing fire and smoke. He clenched his jaw, swallowed hard, and desperately clung to consciousness.

I guess this is why they didn't feed us today, he thought.

He was thankful for his helmet. His head banged against the wall again and again. The bones in his neck rattled. The shuttle jerked, and he bit his tongue and tasted blood.

They kept soaring.

Etty gripped his hand.

The g-force grew stronger, stronger, and Jon was blind, and everything was blackness and fire, and—

It ended.

The fire died.

The rattling eased.

The g-force released him.

The shuttle was flying through space. The narrow porthole revealed the stars. Jon slumped in his straps.

"I hate space already," he moaned.

Etty released his hand. "Sorry if I crushed every bone in your hand."

"It's okay," Jon said. "The ride up almost crushed every bone in my spine, so what's a hand?"

Those who had passed out were slowly coming to. Without gravity, only the harnesses kept the recruits in place. A pair of glasses, a wallet, and blob of vomit floated through the cabin.

"Well, would you look at that," Etty said, face pressed up against the porthole.

"Make room!" Jon said.

He looked out the porthole with her. And he couldn't help it. Even here, crammed into a metal can with thugs and floating vomit, every bone in his body aching, farther than he'd ever been from home… even here, he felt a moment of awe.

"A space station," he whispered. "It's an actual space station."

It was orbiting Earth—a metallic cylinder. It looked like a pipe floating in space, engines and antennae sticking out from its ends. Jon couldn't estimate its size. But he saw several other shuttles approaching the space station. They seemed like specks in comparison.

"It must be the size of a skyscraper," Jon said.

"Almost as big as George!" Etty said.

The cylinder was rolling along its axis, he realized. It was like a giant rolling pin in space. One side blazed with sunlight. The other was cloaked in shadows. As the station rotated, it revealed letters painted across the rounded hull, each letter larger than a house.

ROMA STATION: BASIC COMBAT TRAINING

"That's where we learn how to kill," George said. The giant shuddered.

"And how to die," Etty said softly.

The shuttle flew toward the station. Roma grew larger and larger ahead, soon blocking their view of the stars.

"My friends," Jon said, "welcome to hell."

Chapter Ten
Maria's Work

When Maria came to, the forest was full of smoke. Beams of red light fell through a charred canopy. She coughed, groaned, and pushed herself to feet. Smoke coiled around her like serpents, and ash rained from the sky, filling her hair.

"Crisanto?" she whispered, but her luminous friend wasn't there. "I must have fallen asleep."

She rubbed her eyes. How long had she been out? She had held a dreamtoad. He had done something to her mind. Maybe his glowing organs had cast a spell. The animal had given her a warning, perhaps a prophecy. She had forgotten his words.

She blinked, trying to remember, and suddenly it all flowed back.

The planes.

The explosions.

Maria's heart stopped in her chest.

"*Nanay! Tatay*!" she cried and burst into a run.

Mother! Father!

She had been lost before, but now it was easy to find her way. Many branches had burned away, allowing Maria to see far ahead. Blackened vines, once lush with leaves, now hung like knotted strands of hair. Maria ran over dead mourning monks, their claws still clasping fallen branches. A gust of wind blew charred feathers off dead birds. A shard of twisting metal lay among cracked roots, half sunken into the ground, radiating heat.

Finally Maria exited the forest. She stood atop a hill

looked toward the village in the valley.

San Luna was gone.

The huts. The trees. The people.

All had burned to ash.

She walked across the rice terraces. The water was gone. Her feet stepped on dry, burnt seeds. Bones lay around her. At first she thought them more animal bones. But then the realization sunk in.

They were her fellow farmers. Friends. Cousins. Nothing but bones in the dirt.

She walked among smoldering banana trees and into the village.

My parents.

"*Nanay*?" she whispered. "*Tatay*?"

Her feet scattered ashes. The wind billowed her hair, scented of burnt meat. Skulls gaped from the dirt, their eye sockets accusing. Wings fluttered and a black feather fell. A crow gave a sudden *caw*, landed on Maria's shoulder, then flew off, perhaps disappointed to find her still living. The carrion bird landed on a corpse and began to peck the blackened skin.

Maria kept walking. Feeing empty. Feeling hollow.

It was just a dream. Just a vision the toad was showing her. She was still asleep in the jungle. Had to be.

She walked toward an impact crater. Inside were shards of metal. The remains of bombs.

"Earthlings," Maria said. "Earthlings did this. Their flying machines did this. We killed one of theirs. So they butchered us all."

She walked between charred bamboo husks, and she saw it ahead.

Her home.

Her little bamboo house.

In her memory, it was beautiful, flowers blooming in the

windows, the wind rustling the thatch roof, and the palm tree shading the yard. Her parents stood outside, waving to her, welcoming her home.

But the memory faded. Before her rose a lump of burnt bamboo. Two corpses lay in the yard, black and red, their faces gone. An arm stretched out, hand open, trying to reach Maria even from beyond death. Maria didn't know if it was her mother or father.

And then she saw it.

On one of the skeletons. Hanging from loose strands of a belt.

The knife. Her father's knife.

And the toad's words bolted through her.

You must use his knife.

She did not know what destiny this knife had. But the toad had spoken. And her father lay dead before her. This was his last legacy. Everything was burnt and destroyed, but the knife was whole. A knife with an antler hilt.

Tend to my work while I'm gone, Ernesto had told her before leaving to join the Kalayaan. But now Maria had work of her own. And she toiled for hours, digging the graves. Burying her parents.

Finally she stood before two graves. She had made crude crosses from branches, and she had carved their names onto stones.

The only world I've ever known is gone, Maria thought. *The Earthlings took everything from me.* She clenched her hand around her knife. *So I will take everything from them.*

She left the village, the wind fluttering her hair and blowing ashes around her, kissing her with the remnants of the dead. She held her knife, and her heart lay shattered in her chest like the bones beneath her feet.

Chapter Eleven
Roma Station

The shuttle approached the space station. It was like a minnow swimming toward a barracuda.

Roma Station loomed ahead. It was massive, dwarfing the shuttle. The giant cylinder blinked with lights, slowly spinning like a rolling pin. Earth shone in the distance, painting the space station blue.

For a moment, watching from the shuttle, Jon felt disoriented. Which side of the station was up or down? Was this a towering structure like a skyscraper? Or maybe a horizontal structure like an oil tanker? He did not know. There was no up or down in space. It was all a matter of perspective.

One thing was certain. The station was huge, and his shuttle was small, and they were coming in *fast*. Jon cringed.

A hatch opened on the space station like a hungry mouth, surrounded by flashing white lights like teeth.

Jon winced as the shuttle flew into the gaping maw.

He couldn't see much through the narrow porthole. But the shuttle seemed to be floating down a white tunnel, perhaps an airlock. They passed through another set of doors, and Jon glimpsed a strange, dizzying view through the porthole. Soldiers stood far above him, covering the ceiling like moths. More soldiers stood along the space station walls. Jon tilted his head.

"What the hell?" His brain could not interpret the view. "Are you seeing this, George?"

The giant squinted through the porthole. "Why are they

upside down? What—"

With a thud, the space shuttle landed. Everyone jerked in their harnesses. Gravity once more was tugging them. The glasses, wallet, and blob of vomit hit the deck. The engines died. Scattered applause sounded throughout the shuttle.

"Hey, I never got my peanuts!" Etty said.

Nobody laughed. Maybe they were all too afraid.

The shuttle hatch opened. The recruits stepped outside.

Everyone tilted their heads back and gasped.

"Damn," Jon whispered.

They were standing inside an enormous tube. Jon felt like an ant inside a paper towel roll. He could barely make out the far end. There were no portholes. Just a metal cylinder as long as a city street, flooded with stark white light.

The walls were curved, and soldiers stood across the entire inner surface. Thousands, maybe tens of thousands. They stood on the walls. They stood on the ceiling. Wherever they stood, gravity pulled their feet down onto the surface.

Another shuttle entered, perhaps from another recruitment center. It landed far above him, all the way on the ceiling. Soldiers emerged, standing upside down. A few looked down at Jon and pointed. To them, *he* was on the ceiling.

"What the hell is going on?" George muttered.

Jon understood. "The entire space station is rotating. We're like a rolling pin."

"I don't feel us spinning," George said.

"You do, kind of," Jon said. "It's creating the illusion of gravity. The reason our feet are sticking to the surface? It's not actually gravity. It's centrifugal force. Ever try waving a bucket of water in circles around you?"

"Why would anyone do that?" George said.

"Well, imagine you did," Jon said. "The water wouldn't spill out. The centrifugal force would keep it stuck to the bottom of the bucket. Same principle here."

George nodded. "So we're inside a giant, rolling tube, sticking to the walls because it's spinning so fast." He frowned. "Hey, don't spaceships today have graviton plates anyway? My uncle worked on a mining ship once. He told me they had gravity. *Real* gravity. Something about the deck generating tiny gravity particles that pull your feet down."

"Graviton plates are expensive," Jon said. "They save those for the fancy starships. We're just cannon fodder."

A platoon of soldiers marched along the curving wall at their side. Their footfalls thudded through the station. Another platoon took formation on the ceiling. Their voices rang out. "Yes, Commander!"

Those platoons were quite far from Jon. It was an enormous space station, after all. The ceiling was distant, and the soldiers above seemed as small as ants. But every sound echoed in this gargantuan tube, eerily magnified.

"Listen up, maggots! Form rank now, or I'll blast your asses out the airlock!"

That voice was closer and louder. Jon started. He looked toward its source.

A young woman was sauntering toward the recruits. She was every inch a predator. Her golden braid swung like a lioness's tail. Her eyes shone with blue fire. An assault rifle hung across her back, and a whip hung from her hip, curled up like a serpent. Her skin tight battlesuit hugged feline curves. Three chevrons shone on the sleeves.

A sergeant, Jon realized. He recognized that insignia. *My brother was a sergeant when he died. He had three chevrons on his sleeves too.*

The sergeant halted before the recruits. Her right hand rested on her hip. Her left hand raised a cigar to her mouth.

Her hand is a prosthetic, Jon realized.

The fingers holding the cigar were metallic. Robotic

fingers, tipped with claws. Had she lost her real hand on Bahay?

The sergeant took a long, slow drag on her cigar, then puffed smoke at the recruits. A few of them coughed. The sergeant looked them over. Her lips curled into a crooked smile, and she snorted.

"Well, you maggots?" she suddenly shouted. "What the hell are you waiting for? Form rank!"

The recruits glanced at one another, uncertain what to do.

"Fifteen fireteams!" the sergeant shouted, raising a stopwatch. "Go, go!"

Jon glanced at his friends. "What—"

Etty grabbed him and George. "Come, we'll form a fireteam. Three soldiers standing single file. Basic military structure. Jon, you take the lead position. I'll take the rear. George? You play center."

Jon's brother had never taught him any of this. But Etty seemed to know her stuff.

All right then.

They stood single file—Jon, George, and Etty. A single fireteam.

At their sides, other recruits formed their own fireteams. The trios arranged themselves side by side, eventually forming a unit fifteen soldiers wide, three soldiers deep.

The one-armed sergeant lowered her stopwatch and spat. "Pathetic. Absolutely pathetic! I should blast you out the airlock. At attention! Backs straight, shoulders squared! Dammit, stand like soldiers!"

A few scattered voices rose from the platoon.

"Yes, ma'am!"

"Yes, sergeant!"

"Yes, sir!"

"It's *Commander*!" barked the sergeant. "Louder! Do you understand?"

"Yes, Commander!" they all shouted together. Even Jon.

The sergeant nodded. "Better. You're still losers, but maybe I'll delay your execution. Allow me to introduce myself. I am Sergeant Lizzy Pascal. My friends call me Sergeant Lizzy. To you, I am Commander. Never ma'am, never sir—I'm not an officer. *Commander*. Is that understood? Louder this time!"

"Yes, Commander!" they all shouted.

Sergeant Lizzy snorted. "I was told you're a platoon. But I see only a bunch of baby-faced morons. I'm supposed to train you. To turn you into killers. Are you killers, soldiers?"

"Yes, Commander!"

"Bullshit!" Lizzy spat. "You ain't killers. You're maggots who should be fed into the station's engines for fuel. You're worthless chunks of shit scraped off the surface of Earth. But when I'm done with you, ah…" She smiled and puffed her cigar. "Then you'll be killers."

It's a show, Jon thought. *The cursing, the shouting, the intimidation. Just a show. I've seen it in a million movies. In real life, she's probably a sweetheart.*

The sergeant walked among the troops. She stood before George. She was a tall woman, but George dwarfed her. Just to see his face, Lizzy had to tilt her head back.

"My, my, you're a big one." She nodded. "I bet your parents fed you goddamn steroids for breakfast, didn't they?"

"No, ma'am!" George said. Despite his size, his voice emerged meek and soft.

"Dammit, soldier, I'm not an officer!" Lizzy snarled. "You call me *Commander*, is that understood?"

"Yes, Commander!" He saluted her.

"Get your goddamn paw down, I'm not an officer."

"Yes, Comma—" George began.

"Louder!" Lizzy shouted.

"Yes, Co—"

"*Louder!*" the sergeant roared. "Dammit, soldier, a giant your size must have balls like watermelons. Let me hear that you got a pair!"

"Yes, Commander!" George shouted, cheeks flushed.

To be honest, even that attempt wasn't particularly loud, and George seemed close to tears.

Lizzy shook her head. "Pathetic." She turned toward Etty next. "And what do we have here? My God, your eyes are green and buggy. You look like a goddamn swamp creature."

The two women could not have looked more different. Etty Ettinger was short, slender, and dark. Sergeant Lizzy was tall, muscular, and blond. But the little Israeli recruit refused to cower before the Viking princess. She raised her chin high.

"Yes, Commander!" she howled. Far louder than George.

"You are?" Lizzy shouted. "A swamp creature?"

"No, Commander! I just look like one, Commander! If you say so, Commander!"

Lizzy snorted. "And if I say you're a good-for-nothing little bug who'll never kill a slit, will you agree with me then too, bug-eyes?"

"No, Commander!" Etty cried. "I'm a good soldier, Commander! My dad was infantry, and my mom was—"

"I don't give a shit who your parents are!" Lizzy said. With her metallic hand, the sergeant grasped Etty's neck. "I'm your mom now. I'm your dad now. I'm your god now. You have no family but me! You are nothing! You are worthless! You are a worm until I say you're anything else, is that understood!"

"Yes, Commander!" Etty cried hoarsely, her neck caught in the metal grip.

The sergeant nodded and released the girl. Etty coughed and rubbed her neck.

Lizzy moved on to Jon. She stood before him, sizing him up.

"You!" Lizzy barked. "Why are you here?"

Jon considered. "I was, um… drafted, Commander?"

Scattered laughter rose in the platoon.

The sergeant stepped closer. So close their noses almost touched. She narrowed her eyes, and her lip peeled back.

"If that's true," Lizzy said softly, "if you're only here because you were drafted, you're not going to last a day in the jungle."

A hush fell over the platoon. Jon felt everyone staring at him.

"So answer me again, recruit," Sergeant Lizzy continued, voice barely more than a whisper. "Why are you here?"

Jon raised his chin. "To fight, Commander. For Earth."

Her whisper became a scream. "Who are you going to fight?!"

"The slits!" he shouted.

"Who are you going to kill?" she shouted.

"The goddamn slits!" he cried.

"You're a killer, aren't you, recruit?"

"Yes, Commander!"

A snicker sounded in the platoon.

Sergeant Lizzy spun away from Jon, hissing. "Who's the cockroach who laughs about killing the enemy?"

Another snort. It was coming from Clay.

"I laughed, Sergeant!" the brute said. "That kid couldn't kill a mouse with a baseball bat."

Sergeant Lizzy marched toward Clay. She scowled at the beefy recruit. "You think you're a killer, recruit?"

Clay scoffed. "Hell yeah! I ain't no wuss like Taylor. I've killed before, you know. Spent time behind bars. I don't need no goddamn chick to teach me how to kill."

Lizzy arched an eyebrow. "Oh, you're hard, are you?"

"Goddamn right I am!" Clay gripped his crotch. "I'm hard

as hell. Wanna see, babe?"

Lizzy took a few steps back. Her eyebrow rose higher, and her mouth rose in a crooked smile.

Oh shit, Jon thought, watching the scene unfold. *This is not gonna end well.*

"Come on!" Lizzy beckoned Clay with her finger. "Come to me. Show me what you got."

Leaving the formation, Clay strutted toward the sergeant. He raised his fists, smirking. Sergeant Lizzy unslung her rifle and handed it to Jon.

"Hold this for me, will ya?"

Jon held the weapon. It reminded him of his brother's rifle.

Lizzy assumed a fighting stance, rocking on her heels, fists raised. Her prosthetic hand, when curled into a fist, formed a metal ball like a mace. Her smile vanished, and suddenly her face was all cold determination. Clay barked a laugh and lunged at her, fists flying.

It happened so fast Jon barely saw it.

Sergeant Lizzy sidestepped, dodged a fist, grabbed Clay, and flipped him over.

He hit the ground hard, tried to rise, and Lizzy's boot slammed down on his forearm.

They all heard the sickening *snap.*

Clay screamed.

"My arm!" he howled. "You broke my arm!"

Everyone stared in silent shock. Jon cringed. He could see the arm bent at a sickening angle.

Sergeant Lizzy pointed at Becky—or as everyone called her, Bucky. The bucktoothed recruit was trembling, her face pale.

"You! You're his friend, yes?" Lizzy said. "Take him to the infirmary." She whistled, and a drone flew toward the platoon. "This drone will show you the way. Go!"

Bucky helped Clay rise to his feet. He cradled his broken arm, grimacing. Bucky began leading him away, hand on his shoulder.

"You fought well, boss!"

"Don't touch me." Clay pulled himself free. "I can walk on my own. That psycho bitch broke my arm, not my legs."

Bucky brayed out laughter. "Good one, boss."

"Shut up, shut up!"

The pair walked away, following the buzzing drone.

"Ah, don't worry, Clay!" Etty called after him. "These days, doctors can grow you a new arm in no time. Not sure there's any hope for your micro-dick, though."

Jon returned the rifle to his sergeant. She slung it across her back.

So much for this all being an act, Jon thought.

Sergeant Lizzy looked at the platoon. "I bet some of you thought this was all a joke, right? Just a Hollywood drill sergeant, busting your balls for laughs. Let me make one thing absolutely clear. If you displease me—I will break every bone in your body! You will envy Recruit Clay Hagen. And that is nothing—*nothing*—compared to what the slits will do given half a chance. The slits won't just send you to an infirmary with a broken arm. They'll flay you alive, lock you in a bamboo cage, and leave you to rot in the sun. From now on, you obey me without question. If I say jump, you don't even ask me how high. You jump to the goddamn ceiling. I will train you to be hard. To be killers. Because if you are weak, we'll need mops to soak you up and send you home in a bucket. Is that understood?"

"Yes, Commander!" they all cried.

Sergeant Lizzy nodded. "Good. Welcome to boot camp, worms! Welcome to your first day as soldiers."

Chapter Twelve
A Thousand Little Lights

She walked through the jungle, a girl mourning, a girl alone.

Red smoke and ash hung behind her, curtains closing on the old story of her life. Before her spread the wilderness.

She was Maria Imelda de la Cruz of San Luna, Bahay, but here in the jungle, she was nobody. She was a lost soul. Her world had shattered. Her village had burned. Her family was dead. Her life had become like a rice seed husk fluttering in the wind, empty and forgotten.

She walked through the morning, and though her heart was full of grief, she found beauty in the rainforest.

A drizzle fell, pattering against the leafy canopy, whispering a song as soothing as the sea. Ferns rustled, rivulets trickled around mossy boulders, and roots and branches coiled, weaving a tapestry. Maria climbed and crawled, battling branches, roots, and rocks, every step a calculation.

There was so much life here. Glimmerbirds fluttered above, their long blue feathers trimmed with gold. They trilled for mates and hunted berries, iridescent spirits of the woods. Fangwoods snapped a million hungry jaws on a million hungry leaves, snatching up flowerbugs. Braids of moss dangled from curling boughs, filled with scurrying little mossballs, marble-sized animals some children kept as pets. *Gabi ahas* serpents dangled from the branches too, mimicking the braids of moss, indistinguishable until they opened their jaws to snatch prey.

I've always feared this forest, Maria thought. *But I should have feared home. Now I've become one of these creatures.*

She wondered if she would see the dreamtoad here. He had spoken to her. She remembered his words.

It will be the only way to save her. You must use his knife.

So Maria had taken the knife. She had peeled it off her father's burnt corpse. A knife with an antler hilt. It hung from her hip, forever tempting.

Draw me. Plunge me into your heart.

She walked onward in a daze, wandering through a misty dream. She climbed over roots, over branches, and the forest floor vanished beneath her. A mourning monk scurried along a tree, then paused to stare. The animal's eyes shone within a hood of dark brown fur, following her. A serpent coiled, a red fruit like a heart in its mouth.

She was lost here. She could no longer smell the burning village. No longer see the sky nor ground. The world was wood and moss, yellow eyes and fluttering feathers and the cries of strange birds in the shadows. The trees soared, twisting, braiding together, a cathedral the size of a planet, and Maria was like a mossball in a dangling vine, a single small being scurrying up and down, invisible.

And always in her hand—the knife.

The way out.

The path to her parents and her god.

She touched the cross that hung from her neck, and she wondered if God truly saw this strange forest on an alien world. She had been born here, her family had lived here for three centuries, yet Bahay had never seemed more strange.

The rainforest wrapped around her. Consuming her. Absorbing her.

Be one with us. Become one with ancient life.

And she realized that Bahay was alive. That here was a single super-organism, conscious, thinking, seeing, breathing. That it was digesting her.

The Bahayan people, even after so long, were still but parasites. But now she would truly become one with the world.

Draw me. Plunge me into your heart. Water the trees with your blood.

Shadows deepened.

Maria could not see the sky, could not see Bahay's twin moons nor suns. But she knew that Sargas, the larger sun that burned like a cauldron, was setting. Night would soon unfurl its dangerous cloak, and the shadows would advance, harboring whispered temptations.

Maria found a rug of moss between coiling roots and curtains of vines. Here she sat, but she would not sleep tonight. She would remain on guard. She would survive the night. She held her knife before her, waiting.

The light dimmed.

Creatures stirred and hissed around her.

Things creaked. Something breathed. Something raced by. She could smell them. The night predators of Bahay.

Maria held her knife firmly as the last light vanished.

The rainforest became a black pit, darker than the chasms between galaxies. A midnight symphony awoke, playing a song of creaking wood and rustling leaves and snorting beasts. The aromas filled her nostrils, a blend of moss, water, leaves, and the fur and feathers and scales of the night creatures. Maria could not see, but she thrummed with awareness of this world living, moving, breathing around her. This vast organism, this consciousness of a world. It scared her. And it was so beautiful.

I will be one with you, she thought. *I have no more village. No more family. I will be human no more. I will wet the moss with my blood, and mushrooms will rise from my body, and I will become one with the forest.*

She placed her knife against her chest.

She took a deep breath, prepared to plunge the blade.

And then she saw it.

A tiny orb of light, no larger than a star. It hovered before her like an anglerfish lure.

"Crisanto?" she whispered.

The orb of light floated ahead as if watching her. Its dim glow illuminated coiling roots and branches. A single light in the vast darkness. A single companion in the endless emptiness of existence.

And then, among the twisting trees—another light shone.

And another.

And another.

They rose from the forest. Dozens. Then hundreds.

The Santelmos.

They floated before her, around her, above her. Glowing white orbs like the stars. They were very young, most only the size of marbles. A few were even younger, barely more than dapples of light. Children. Youths. Like her.

They flowed around her, leaving trails of light, and when Maria raised her hands to touch them, she saw that she too seemed to glow. Her skin had become silvery like starlight. The Santelmos stroked her hair, tickled her, raced around her, and she laughed.

A thousand little lights watched her in the darkness. A thousand little lights would guide her. She tucked away her knife. She was not alone.

Chapter Thirteen
Basic Hell

War was hell.

Everyone knew that.

But hell had seven circles. And the first was called basic training.

Jon hated it. He hated it more than anything in the universe. He hated it more than he loved music. He hated every waking hour, and every aching, cold, miserable night.

Actual battle, he thought, *might actually be a relief.*

"Go! Faster, worms! Run!"

Sergeant Lizzy stood on a hovering platform, hands on hips, watching them run. Officially, she had named the platoon Lizzy's Lions. But the sergeant just referred to them as worms, maggots, cockroaches, and a host of other creepy crawlies. Never lions. They had definitely not earned their manes.

"Faster, dammit!" she shouted.

Her hoverform thrummed, blasted out smoke, and lifted her several feet in the air. In this hovering chariot, Lizzy followed the running recruits. She gazed down upon them from on high, a goddess of wrath.

And we are mere mortals, Jon thought.

"Faster!" Lizzy cried. "There's a freckled slit running away from you. Chase that bastard! Go, maggots!"

Jon ran, sweat dripping inside his battlesuit. The thing was damn hot and about as breathable as a plastic bag. The rest of his platoon ran at his sides, armored plates clanking. They were running a loop along the curving inner surface of Roma Station. Jon felt like a hamster in a wheel.

The platoon ran past an armory, a mess hall, and concrete barracks. The buildings all sprouted from the curving walls, facing inward like teeth in a lamprey mouth. As the platoon ran, the centrifugal force kept their feet on the curving wall. They told Jon that Roma was calibrated to simulate Earth gravity, but Jon felt sure they were sneaking in an extra g or two. He felt much heavier here than on Earth.

The tubular Roma Station had a large diameter. It felt like ages before Jon completed a loop.

The recruits ended up where they started. Jon was sweaty, shaky, and close to collapsing.

"Another loop!" Sergeant Lizzy barked. "Go!"

Jon nearly dropped dead then and there.

The sergeant approached him, snarling, and raised an electric whip. The lash hissed and crackled like a serpent woven of lightning.

"Go, Taylor! Run! You don't even stop if you die, soldier! *Go*!"

Jon kept running.

"Goddammit!" Etty said, jogging at his side. "She's a slave driver, ain't she? First my people had to suffer the Pharaoh, now Sergeant Lizzy. Kill me. Just kill me."

"Stop… wasting… breath on… talking." Jon panted, running at her side.

Etty was much smaller than him. Perhaps that gave her an advantage. The little Israeli complained, but she had barely broken a sweat. Her green eyes shone in her tanned face, and she flashed him a smile.

She's enjoying this, Jon realized. *The little bugger's actually enjoying this. She's mental.*

"I'm dying…" George huffed, face red. "I can't… I'm

dying…"

Etty grinned at the lumbering George. "Come on, ginger giant! You got this! We're only on the second loop."

George groaned. "You're on your *second* loop? I'm only on my first. I can't… I…"

The giant collapsed.

Jon tried to lift his buddy. But George weighed over three hundred pounds. Nobody was carrying him anywhere.

The platoon kept running, sans George.

More recruits dropped off, exhausted.

Jon ran onward.

He was not naturally athletic. At high school, he had usually skipped gym class, going home to compose music instead. Somehow, he managed three loops around the station. Barely.

Bayonets were stabbing his belly. Fire blazed in his lungs. Sergeant Lizzy was shouting at him, cracking her electric whip. The lash bit Jon like a snake. Electricity bolted through his battlesuit. But he could not physically take another step.

Jon collapsed, wheezing.

The last few soldiers fell around him.

Only one soldier kept running. Etty.

She completed one more loop, then rested, breathing heavily, hands on her thighs.

"Damn, that was a good workout!" She grinned at Jon and wiped sweat off her brow.

He could only moan.

And the day was only getting started.

* * * * *

It got worse.

They climbed an obstacle wall—an instrument of torture

from the depths of hell. The metal barricade towered, inlaid with blades, flashing lights, and nozzles that kept spurting fire. As the recruits climbed, the wall did its best to cut, blind, and burn them.

The recruits had no ropes. They climbed by gripping whatever they could—sometimes it was a rock, sometimes it was a blade. If they fell, they fell onto mattresses below. Very far below. And very thin mattresses.

Several soldiers plummeted down. One snapped a leg, and his screams echoed through the station. No, those mattresses weren't much help.

"Climb, go, faster!" Sergeant Lizzy screamed from below.

Jon climbed a hundred feet. His limbs shook with weakness. He grabbed a protuberance on the wall, thinking it a rock. It sliced his hand—a blade! It was designed to only cut skin deep, but it still hurt like hell.

Jon cursed. He stuck his fingers into a crevice instead. They were slippery with blood. He reached for another crack, hoping to find another fingerhold. Fire burst from the fissure.

Jon pulled his hand back. He tilted sideways, dodging the spurting fire. The heat singed his cheek. His head spun. He lost his grip and nearly fell.

Climbing nearby, Etty grabbed him. She pulled him back onto the wall.

"Hold on there, big boy!" she said.

"The big boy fell already," Jon muttered. George was moaning somewhere on the mattresses below. "Hopefully if I fall, it'll be onto him. He's softer than any mattress."

"Dammit, soldiers, the slits are almost here!" Sergeant Lizzy shouted from below the wall. "Stop chatting and climb!"

Something whistled. Something pinged against the wall beside Jon.

Again. Again. One soldier screamed and fell.

Jon gasped. "What the hell?" He looked down. "Sergeant

Lizzy is firing on us!"

The sergeant stood below, a crooked smile on her face, her blond braid tossed across her shoulder. She was holding her rifle, taking potshots at the wall.

A bullet slammed into the wall beside Jon.

Another soldier screamed and fell.

"Rubber bullets!" Jon said. "Dammit!"

Rubber bullets wouldn't kill him, perhaps. Definitely not in a battlesuit. But they would leave ugly bruises, maybe even break bones. And certainly knock him off this wall.

He and Etty kept climbing, faster now. Jon grabbed a round red stone. Hot! He hissed and pulled his hand back. The skin was charred. He tilted, nearly fell. Fire spurted from a hidden spout above, blinding him.

Etty scurried past him, but then a bullet hit her leg, and she screamed.

And she was falling.

Jon grabbed her. He tried to hold her up. But his wounded hand slipped, and they tumbled down together.

Etty thumped onto the mattress with a yelp.

Jon missed George, sadly. He landed hard beside the giant, knocking his breath out. For long moments, Jon could only lie there, gasping for air.

Nobody succeeded in cresting the wall that day.

And it got worse.

* * * * *

All day, Lizzy tortured them.

The recruits crawled under barbed wire. Over barbed wire. Through barbed wire. In their underwear—no battlesuits allowed.

They screamed as barbs tore their skin.

They sludged through pits of mud that rose to their armpits. Ravenous eels swarmed in the sludge, shocking them with electric bolts.

They ran through a forest of metal trees, each leaf a blade, as Lizzy zipped around them on her hoverform, firing her rifle. Her rubber bullets left nasty bruises. One even snapped a recruit's rib.

"Come on you worms, go, move, faster!" Lizzy screamed. "Do you want the slits to get you? Go!"

They ran through a forest of strip curtains, stumbling between the dangling plastic strands. Jon supposed the strips were meant to mimic jungle vines. It felt more like battling giant jellyfish tentacles. He panted, and a rubber bullet shrieked over his head.

"Goddammit!" he blurted out.

"Where did Sergeant Lizzy learn to train a platoon?" Etty said, panting beside him. "The Gestapo?"

George ran with them, barely able to breathe, let alone speak.

Jon found himself envious of Clay. Lizzy had broken the brute's arm. The lucky bastard was probably resting in an infirmary now, as comfortable as could be, while the others suffered.

"I hate this," Jon panted. "I really ha—"

"Run, worm!" rose Lizzy's voice from behind.

He spun around. The sergeant was charging on her hoverform. She seemed a goddess of fury in a chariot of fire. Her golden braid flailed like her whip. Her lips peeled back in a snarl, and her blue eyes shone like pitiless jewels. She raised her rifle, looked right into Jon's eyes, and gave a crooked smile.

Crap.

Jon spun away, ran, and—

Pain.

Pain bloomed on his back.

He pitched forward, stumbled through dangling plastic strands, and hit the ground.

She shot me, he realized. *She fucking shot me.*

"You're not dead yet, worm!" rose Lizzy's voice. "You can still suffer for me!"

Jon rose and ran. He winced in pain. The armored battlesuit helped a little. But just a little. It *hurt.* The rubber bullet had thankfully missed his spine, hitting him below the left shoulder blade. Jon had played paintball before, had taken some hits that left ugly green and yellow bruises. They seemed as gentle as caresses now. He missed that old pain.

* * * * *

Finally, after what seemed like ages, epochs, eternities—the first day of training ended.

Jon wanted nothing more than to collapse, sleep, and ideally die. But with more shouts, snarls, and shocks, Sergeant Lizzy herded them toward a mess hall.

"Yum, yum!" Etty licked her lips. "Chow time."

George's belly rumbled. "Finally! We've had nothing but stinkin' battle paste to eat all day. I ate ten of those tubes, and I'm still starving."

Etty frowned at the giant. "Dude, you do realize a single tube of battle paste contains enough concentrated calories to last a man a full day. You ate *ten*?"

"I was hungry!" The giant belched. "Still am."

Jon groaned and rubbed his aching shoulder. He couldn't see the bruises across his body, but he could feel every one.

"Guys. Please. Don't even talk. Everything hurts. I need silence and sleep."

George slung an arm around him. "Ah, a good meal will raise your spirits. Always works for me."

"Yes," Jon said, "but I'm not a ravenous monster who eats battle pastes like they're potato chips, and besides—ah!"

He shouted as an electric bolt hit him. Lizzy zoomed by, balancing on her hoverform like a surfer, electric whip in hand.

"Silence!" the sergeant barked. "Line up! Stand straight. Act like soldiers! You have ten minutes for chow, then I want you back here crawling at my feet. Go!"

The troops lined up outside the mess hall. Ahead, behind, and above them, spread a ring of concrete structures: barracks, armories, and garages full of armored vehicles. Even after a full day here in Roma Station, Jon couldn't get used to seeing buildings growing from the ceiling. He still felt like an ant stuck inside a pipe. His eyes were so weary the buildings blurred into gray smudges.

We're just ants in a pipe, surrounded by grout, he thought.

"What the hell crawled up her ass?" George muttered, glancing back toward Lizzy. The blond sergeant was now shouting at another group of recruits, shocking them into formation.

"She's just doing her job," Jon said.

George rubbed his arm. His battlesuit plates were dented, and the fabric beneath was torn at spots, revealing bruises and scrapes. "If her job is to turn us into beaten slabs of meat, give her the employee of the month award."

Etty rolled her eyes. "Come on, boys, it's not that bad."

Jon snorted. "Easy for you to say. You're the best runner and climber in the platoon. How the hell did you learn to—"

He fell silent as Lizzy floated back toward them, inspecting the lines. Under her watchful eye, they stepped forward one by one, entering the mess hall.

Lizzy's Lions lined up, forty-odd soldiers. Jon was starting to recognize some faces. The lanky kid with bad acne. The petite Chinese girl he thought was kind of cute. The twin boys with big ears. But mostly the other recruits were a blur. And he didn't know their names. Jon had spent the day with his fireteam: George the Ginger Giant and speedy little Etty. He was simply too exhausted and hurting to speak to the others.

A dour cook scooped slop onto their trays. The trays were dirty. The gruel looked like gray mud. George voiced a few objections, Etty grumbled, but Jon merely accepted his lot.

Many tables filled the mess hall, all crowded with chowing recruits. Several platoons were here. Everyone was stuffing their faces, scrambling to fill their bellies within their allotted ten minutes. Jon looked over the crowd, was surprised to see several familiar faces. Kids from his high school.

I'm in space, he thought, *trapped inside a giant metal cylinder, and I'm seeing kids from my little home town.* It made his head spin.

"Aww yeah!" George said, sliding down into a seat. It creaked dangerously beneath his weight. "I've been on my feet all day."

Jon sat beside the giant. "Dude, you can play drums for hours on end. This should be easy for you."

"I play drums sitting down." George tucked into his slop and spoke with his mouth full. "Besides, drums are fun. This is hell."

Etty squeezed in between them. She took a bite of gruel, winced, then forced it down. "Ah, come on, boys, it's not that bad. Sure, the food stinks, and Lizzy is a sadist, but that's the army for you. Hey, it's even kinda fun, amirite?"

"Fun?" Jon blinked. "*Fun*? Are you kidding me? It's torture! We've only been here for a day, and we've run loops around the station, climbed walls that spit fire, crawled through barbed wire, slogged through mud pits full of eels, got shot with rubber bullets, and—"

"I know, I know!" Etty said. "I was there, remember? And hey, I'm not complaining, right?"

Jon looked at the girl. She stared back. She narrowed her eyes, but they still seemed so large, unusually large, and brilliantly green, especially in contrast to her dark skin.

"Well, that's because you're a loony," Jon said.

He was just joking, of course. Busting her balls a bit, like he did with George.

But Etty stood up so suddenly her chair fell back. She glared at Jon.

"I'm not a loony!"

Jon winced. "I know. Geez, Etty. I'm only kidding." He reached out to her. "I—"

She shoved his hand back. "Don't touch me. Fuck. You soft American boys. What do you know of hardship?"

Jon stood up too. He wasn't a giant like George, but he was much taller than Etty, and he loomed above her.

He thought about losing his brother. About George in the hospital, getting his skull drilled into.

"I know plenty," Jon said.

Etty snorted. "Please. I'm from the Middle East, bitch. I grew up in a war zone. I was fighting as soon as I could walk. You think this is tough? Basic training? Wait until you see a real war. You need to toughen up, Americans, or the enemy will cut you down."

Jon couldn't help it now. Anger filled him. "Oh, so sorry for being American. I forgot that in America, it's all cupcakes, rainbows, and baby unicorns."

Etty glowered. "I didn't say that!"

"You just said that we're soft, that—"

"Guys, guys!" George said. "Please shut up. Your bickering is bad for my digestion. Etty, Jon is an idiot. Ignore him.

I ignore him most of the time, and it's done wonders to my stress levels. Sit down and eat with us, and save your fighting for Bahay."

Jon sat down.

But Etty spun away. She seemed to be wiping her eyes.

"I'm full," she said, voice choked, then ran out the mess hall.

"Hey, I'm finishing your gruel!" George shouted after her.

Jon wanted to run after her. What had he done? Why had he upset her? He must have touched a nerve. Maybe he had summoned a painful memory from her past. Maybe she had lost loved ones too. He liked Etty, even after this outburst. If he had hurt her, he wanted to fix it.

He took a step, meaning to follow, but Sergeant Lizzy burst into the mess hall.

"All right, worms! Chow time is over." She cracked her electric whip. "Out, now, go!"

The recruits rushed outside, swallowing last bites of food, and found Roma Station completely dark.

Only moments ago, bright lights had flooded the station. Now Jon could barely see a damn thing. A few lights shone along the curving walls, forming a ghostly tunnel. A memory flashed through Jon: sitting in the back seat of his parents' dented Toyota, taking a family trip, driving through a tunnel between New Jersey to New York. Paul was in the back seat, taller and stronger and smarter than Jon, playing video games and showing Jon all the tricks. It was still hard to believe he was gone.

Jon pulled himself back to the present. That old life was gone now. Paul wasn't coming back, and maybe Jon wasn't either. But least it was dark. At least after a day in hell, he could sleep.

The platoon took formation. Etty joined the fireteam, but she avoided eye contact with Jon, and her mouth was a hard line.

"Etty," he whispered.

She ignored him. Sergeant Lizzy walked by, whip in hand, and they stood still and silent.

"I considered letting you sleep tonight," Lizzy said. "I almost gave you a full six hours as a reward." Her voice rose to a shout. "But today you were a disgrace! Slow! Weak! Insolent! So you will spend the next hour on the obstacle course, and you will not sleep until you complete it! Is that understood!"

Nobody even groaned. They had learned quickly. A groan meant a lash. Rude words could mean a broken arm.

Jon was tempted, to be honest. A broken arm almost sounded better than another obstacle course. But Clay was in the infirmary, and Jon didn't feel like joining that asshole.

"Yes, Commander!" he shouted with his platoon.

For an hour, they suffered. They climbed over the spines of dead aliens, each the length of a city block, while monsters snapped their teeth in the pit below. They crawled through tunnels inside the station hull, and spiderlike robots chased them, shocking anyone they caught. They slid through a net of lasers, contorting, screaming whenever a beam touched their skin.

They suffered for an hour more, repeating the same obstacle course, then a third time until Lizzy decided they had suffered enough.

Bruised, bleeding, and burnt, the recruits finally stumbled toward their barracks.

Finally, after eras of torture, they could sleep.

Each squad of fifteen recruits got its own room. Jon limped into his squad's room—a concrete cell lined with cots. He barely spared the place a glance. He collapsed onto the first cot he found, closed his eyes, and—

"Up, you worm, guard duty! Go, go!"

Jon leaped up. He opened his eyes to see Sergeant Lizzy leaning over him, howling. Everyone else was asleep around him.

How long did I sleep for?

"Go, worm!" Lizzy cracked her whip, and an electric bolt drove Jon from his bed.

Guard duty. Perfect.

Jon exited the barracks. He marched around the concrete building several times, yawning, wincing with every step. The blisters howled on his feet, miniature goblins burrowing into his flesh.

Why the hell do I have to guard a barracks inside a space station? he wondered. *I don't even have a gun yet!*

Probably just to torture him a little bit more.

They said hell was underground. They were wrong. Hell was in space. Hell was Roma Station.

Finally Jon stumbled back into the barracks. His head swam, and his eyes were blurry, but he noticed something. He had missed it at first.

Etty had chosen the cot next to his.

He collapsed onto his bed and looked at her. The young Israeli was curled up, her back toward him. She seemed to be sleeping, even as Lizzy was shouting and shocking another soldier just a few cots down.

"Up, worm, up!" the sergeant screamed.

"Ow, ow!" cried a recruit. "Yes, Commander!"

Jon could barely form a coherent thought. Sleep was tugging him. But he forced himself to lean toward Etty.

"I'm sorry if I hurt you, Etty," he said softly. "I'm sorry if anyone hurt you. I…"

His eyes rolled back. He fell into a deep, black pit, and—

"Up, recruits, up! Enough beauty sleep. Time for another glorious day in the Human Defense Force!"

Jon opened his eyes. Fluorescent light streamed through the windows. How long had he slept? It couldn't have been more than a few moments.

"Up, damn it, faster!" Lizzy screamed. "Or do you want

more obstacle courses tonight too?"

That got everyone on their feet. They stumbled outside, took formation, and shouted "Yes Commander!" over and over.

Another day in hell began.

Chapter Fourteen
The Freedom Trail

Maria walked all morning, following Crisanto, until she found the Freedom Trail.

At first glance, she just saw more rainforest.

There was no paved road. Not even a dirt path. Not even any footprints. Just more jungle.

And yet—there were hints.

The branches did not thrust out too low to impede travelers. A few had been broken off, the stubs coated with moss like bandages. Boulders had been rolled aside. Maria could tell because their sides were covered in soil instead of moss. A fallen log spanned a stream, forming a natural bridge. Or perhaps not so natural.

An Earthling would have just seen more jungle. But Maria knew: somebody had carved this trail. And carefully hidden it.

The Earthling planes would never see it. A dense canopy hid the sky. Even Earthling soldiers, walking through the jungle, would miss this trail.

Maria would have missed it too. She only noticed because Crisanto had led her here.

"This is it, Crisanto, isn't it?" she said. "The Freedom Trail."

A shudder ran through her. Everyone knew about the Trail. Every harvest time, San Luna donated bags of rice to young women of the Kalayaan. The girls were slender, soft-spoken, their neat black braids hanging from under straw hats, their eyes shy.

Most were maidens under twenty, pure little angels. Yet guns hung from their belts, for they were angels of war. The girls loaded the rice into wheelbarrows, sometimes just into backpacks, and carried the precious grains down the Freedom Trail to the battlefields.

Maria had heard that the Freedom Trail delivered more than just rice. But also fighters. Also guns.

"Victory flows down the Freedom Trail!"

She had heard that phrase many times. When the older guerrillas came to her village for tribute, demanding men of fighting age along the bags of rice, they spoke that phrase. But Maria was skeptical.

Victory? She did not know about that. Certainly, the wealth of Bahay flowed south along the trail. The corpses flowed north.

Maria still remembered the day the Kalayaan had brought home dear Roberto, her betrothed. They had not even closed his eyes.

"Ernesto walked south along this trail," Maria said. "He can't be too far ahead. I know he's cruel, Crisanto. But he—and those who left with him—are the only other survivors of San Luna. He must learn what happened. And maybe he can help us. He loves me, you know."

Her cheek was still bruised. Yes, her betrothed could be cruel. But the Earthlings were worse. The Earthlings had burned her village to the ground. What was a man's fist next to the all-consuming fire of Earth's machines?

She walked south along the trail, seeking him.

As she traveled south, she marveled at the trail. It passed through water but not mud. Over stones but not moss. Over a ledge of dry earth in a beam of sunlight, avoiding moist soil below. Over hard wooden roots but not ferns that could be crushed. It was designed to minimize footprints. And where Maria did leave a mark, she covered it with dry leaves. She was careful not even to disturb the moss on trunks or boulders.

She did not travel here alone. Animal prints, tufts of fur, and feathers marked the trail. Once she saw a family of *ungoys*—native animals with many tails—trudge along the trail. The cubs clung to their mothers' underbellies, suckling on milk. Beetles scurried underfoot, feeding on the droppings. Spinning tailbugs buzzed above the *ungoys*, seeking the furriest tails, then descended to nest in these warm wagging homes. Yellow eyes peered from holes in trunks. Tongues shot out, grasped tailbugs, and pulled them into the shadows.

An ecosystem. Perhaps this was how the Freedom Trail began. Migratory routes for large animals and their smaller coteries. And perhaps Maria herself was now part of this ecosystem.

We cannot defeat the Earthlings with technology, Maria thought. *They have planes and starships and tanks, and we only have simple guns. They have suits of mechanical armor, and we only have homespun tunics. But we have the rainforest. We understand it. We are one with our world. They do not understand Bahay. They can only burn.*

The hatred rose in her.

Pure. Consuming. Blazing hatred for Earth.

Why did they do this?

"They're a race of cruel giants," Maria hissed. "They say we work with aliens, Crisanto. They hate your kind, so they hate us too. They say we're traitors to humanity. But they are barely human. I was sorry when the pilot died. But now I wish I could kill them all."

Crisanto fluttered around her, nuzzling her, and her fury abated. Shame filled her at these wicked thoughts.

"They killed my family," she said. "They also killed something inside me. I can no longer be that girl. Maria with the big head full of too many questions. There is a fire inside me now.

A fire they kindled. And it scares me like the fire that burned San Luna."

At night, she curled up inside a cage of roots, and she slept with Crisanto in her palm.

The next day, she traveled onward down the trail. She spied on glimmerbirds and found their trees of berries, and she ate. She plucked mossballs from vines and popped them into her mouth, shuddering as she swallowed the fuzzy little animals. Serpents coiled through a citrus tree, guarding their prize, but Maria banished them with rocks, and she ate the tangy oranges.

One time, along the trail, she noticed a coiling branch like a pig's tail, and it seemed unnatural to her. She approached and pulled it, and a wooden door swung open on the tree trunk. Inside she found packages of rice cakes, nuts, and *lechon*—crispy pig skin. A gift from the Kalayaan for hungry travelers. She ate two packages and left the rest.

On the third day from home, she was walking along a mountainside. At her left, the rainforest plunged down into a sea of mist. At her right, rocky slopes rose like a wall, draped with greenery. The path was narrow, and she nearly fell several times. The mist thickened, rose and fell, whispered around her feet like waves. The land was breathing.

The cry of a painted-moss owl pierced the forest. Maria froze and frowned. Owls only flew in the night, and it was noontime.

She stayed still for a long time, seeking the bird. But painted-moss owls had green, camouflaged feathers, appearing as mossy stones. If any were here, they remained well hidden. She shrugged and kept walking.

Another owl's cry.

In answer—a glimmerbird's song.

Leaves rustled behind her.

Maria spun around and gasped.

A figure leaped from the trees.

More figures burst from the rainforest and landed around her, blocking the path.

Maria's heart burst into a gallop. She spun from side to side, looking at the people.

They were slender, almost starving, wearing straw hats and ragged *piña* tunics made from pineapple leaves. Peasant clothes, yet she saw the bandannas around their arms.

Guerrillas.

And they raised rifles.

Maria raised her hands, heart thrashing. "I'm a friend of the Kalayaan!"

The men stared with cold, hard eyes, mouths like slits in leather.

"It's all right!" A tall man emerged from among the trees. "Comrades, she is Maria de la Cruz, my betrothed! It seems I have a little camp follower."

"Ernesto!" Maria cried, and tears leaped into her eyes.

She ran toward him, and he embraced her. And suddenly she was weeping. Suddenly all the tears she had kept inside spilled like a river. And she told him. What the Earthlings had done. How she had buried her parents. How a thousand little lights had guided her here.

Ernesto listened with hard eyes. His fists clenched. And when she spoke of everyone dying, of his family gone, Ernesto let out a howl that sent birds fleeing.

"Ernesto." Maria placed a hand on her shoulder. "I'm sorry. I—"

He grabbed her wrist. "Why are you here?"

"To join you," Maria said.

Ernesto laughed bitterly. "Join us? Back in the village, Maria, you objected to the war. Something about us being farmers and fishermen, not fighters. And now you come to beg and grovel?"

Maria glared at him. Across the trail, guerrillas muttered and lowered their eyes. Perhaps they feared Ernesto's wrath. Maria no longer feared anyone.

"That was before the Earthlings burned our village," she said. "Before they murdered our families. I was a rice farmer, yes. But now I'm a fighter. Now inside me burns a passion to kill the enemy."

Ernesto frowned at her, then laughed. A cruel laughter that did not reach his eyes.

"What do you know of fighting? When the fire rains. When men scream and die. When the forest burns, and your comrades die, and the fear sets in… will you turn and run? Or will you cower?"

"I saw all this already in San Luna. And I did not cower. I'm not afraid."

But that was a lie. She feared the planes that rumbled above. She feared the fire that burned the forests. She feared the fate of this living, breathing world.

But she no longer feared for her own life. And that made her strong.

She kept staring at Ernesto, chin raised. He stared back, his eyes boring, probing, seeking any sign of weakness.

"We do not fight like the *putes*," he said. "We do not drop bombs from the sky, nor lob rockets from afar. That is how cowards fight. We sneak through the forest. We come up close. We grab the enemy by the belt buckle. And we kill without hesitation. If I give you a gun, Maria who was once a rice farmer, can you pull the trigger? Can you kill a man?"

She took a step closer, so close they nearly touched.

"I will kill many," she said.

Ernesto smiled, revealing a golden tooth, and handed her a rifle.

Maria clutched it. It was nearly as long as she was tall. She was only a Bahayan, smaller than the mighty Earthlings, but with this gun, she felt ten times larger.

I will sneak through the forest, she told herself. *So close I could grab them by the belt buckle. They killed my parents, and with this gun, I will kill them.*

Chapter Fifteen
What Heroes Do

For days, the recruits suffered.

For days, they broke apart.

Before every dawn, they rose, marched, guarded their barracks. Tried to sneak in a few moments of sleep. Only for the electric whip to shock them. For the sergeant to kick them. For the torture to continue.

At nights, they cried. In stolen moments. Even the toughest of them shed tears into their pillows.

Ten thousand kilometers above earth. Trapped inside a rolling cylinder. Flesh inside a meat grinder. With blood, sweat, and tears, they tore apart.

They became less than human. And yet something more. Something greater.

They became soldiers.

And for several of these backbreaking, soul-shattering days, Etty ignored Jon.

She was still in his fireteam. She still joined him and George during exercises. But the little Israeli never made eye contact. If she had to say something, she spoke to George.

"Etty, can we talk?" Jon tried once in the mess hall.

But she looked away and ate her gruel in silence.

Great, Jon thought. *I managed to make one friend in an entire army, then messed it right up.*

For a week, the torture continued. Climbing walls. Crawling through mud. Push ups. Sit ups. Marching. Drilling.

Always the sergeant shouting. A week of hell… and then a miracle.

A blessing from heaven.

Sunday came to Roma Station, and the platoon was given a day of rest.

Sergeant Lizzy herded them into room full of plastic seats and a projector.

"Sit your asses down!" Lizzy said. "Today you rest your bodies and nourish your minds."

She turned off the lights and struggled with the projector, cursing as a tape jammed.

"Got any horror flicks?" Etty said from her seat. "I like horror."

"Your life will be a horror flick if you're not careful, Ettinger," Lizzy snapped.

She finally got the projector working. A movie began to play on screen.

Jon was exhausted. He had barely slept all week, only an hour here and there. He could hardly see the movie. His eyes were drooping. Soon they were closed, and sleep crept up on him. Dreams tugged him, full of dark claws and twisting vines.

"Taylor!" Lizzy barked. "If you can't sit without sleeping, you'll watch standing."

Jon opened his eyes wide and sat upright in his chair. "I'm awake, Commander!"

Several other recruits, after a sleepless week, were falling asleep in their seats too. Lizzy cracked her whip, spraying sparks onto the crowd. Recruits yelped. A few had no choice but to stand, blistered feet and all, in a desperate attempt to remain awake.

Jon alternated between standing and sitting. Each was a sort of torture. Standing hurt every muscle in his injured body. Sitting meant falling asleep and Lizzy shocking him. He rose and sat, rose and sat.

As days of rest went, this wasn't much. But it beat the obstacle courses. It was as close to a lazy Sunday morning as he'd get in Roma Station.

A familiar face appeared on screen—a chiseled jaw, fake tan, bright blond hair, a brighter smile. The man wore a sky-blue battlesuit, the armored plates shaped like muscles, and he carried a shield painted as planet Earth.

"Well, golly, it's good to see you again! This is Ensign Earth, reporting for duty!" The actor gave a brisk salute. "Welcome to another exciting installment of *Why We Fight*!"

"Boring!" Etty cried from the crowd.

"Ettinger!" Lizzy snapped.

On screen, Ensign Earth became solemn. "Last time we met, I told you about Bahay's history. How the Santelmos, evil aliens, kidnapped Filipinos three hundred years ago, transported them to a new planet, and bred them into monsters. But you might be wondering: How did the great Freedom War begin?"

"It's called the Colony War," Etty muttered, daring not speak louder lest Lizzy hear. "Only the fucking army calls it the Freedom War."

Ensign Earth walked along a moonlit beach, reflective. He looked up at the stars, then turned toward the camera.

"The stars. Beautiful, aren't they? It's hard to believe that only a few centuries ago, we couldn't reach them. We were trapped on Earth. But in the twenty-first century, brave astronauts began the Era of Exploration. Humanity established colonies on Mars, Titan, the asteroid belt, and finally…" Ensign Earth gestured with a wide sweep of his hand. "The stars. They're glorious, aren't they, folks?"

On the film, several stars grew larger and brighter. The names of colonies appeared above them.

Ensign Earth turned back toward the camera. "You are

gazing upon the Human Commonwealth. An empire of humanity spreading across the stars. Our empire is young yet ambitious. Our species is fledgling yet curious. The Human Commonwealth is a civilization of righteousness, benevolence, and my favorite—goodness."

"Those all mean the same thing," Etty muttered, slouching in her seat, arms crossed.

"Ettinger, shut it!" Lizzy warned, glaring from beside the projector.

Ensign Earth gazed back at the stars. "But one of those human worlds is not part of the Human Commonwealth. One of those worlds is lost from our civilization. Bahay!"

The camera zoomed in, streaming by many stars, finally displaying a green and blue planet. Oceans covered most of Bahay, but thousands of islands dotted it, lush with rainforest.

"Behold Bahay!" said Ensign Earth, now speaking from off screen. "Far and alone in the darkness. Home to millions of humans. Millions of hostages! You see, evil is at work on this beautiful world. When Earth offered to accept Bahay into its empire, that evil turned us away. Who is this evil, you ask? Well, let me tell you! It's time to… *meet our enemies*."

A caption appeared on screen: MEET OUR ENEMIES

Jon glanced at his side. "Hey, Etty," he whispered. "Can we talk?"

She looked away. "Not now."

"Etty, I'm sorry, okay?" He leaned closer to her. "Can we—"

"Taylor, eyes on the film!" Lizzy snapped.

Reluctantly, Jon looked back at the movie.

"On Bahay, we heroes will face three enemies," said Ensign Earth. "First, the Red Cardinal. This devious evil-doer rules the Luminous Army, a rogue military that roams across North Bahay. See, our brave Earthling troops control the southern hemisphere of Bahay. But in the north, the wicked Red Cardinal rules with an iron fist."

The film showed the Luminous Army—rows of Bahayan soldiers marching, rifles in hand. They wore armored black uniforms, and helmets hid their heads, the visors red. The design seemed inspired by Earth's battlesuits. Perhaps the Bahayans had captured a few Earthling battlesuits, reverse engineered them, and changed the colors.

As the Luminous Army marched, they chanted, "Death to Earth, death to Earth!"

Maybe they were actors, or at least dubbed, given that few Bahayans spoke English.

Behind them loomed a cardinal in a crimson robe, his arms spread wide, tipped with claws. He oversaw his troops like Lucifer leading the hosts of hell.

An animation showed Ensign Earth punching the Red Cardinal in the face. A caption appeared on screen: *KA-POW!*

Scattered applause sounded from the audience.

"Etty, did I offend you somehow?" Jon whispered to her. "If so, I'm sorry."

"Shh!" Etty scowled at him. "I'm watching."

At least she looked at him. That was progress.

"The second enemy," Ensign Earth continued, "is the Kalayaan. These are Bahayan terrorists who live in the south. They hide in the jungle like animals, ready to leap onto brave Earth heroes. If you find yourself in the southern hemisphere, Kalayaan Kenny is your enemy!"

The video now showed an image of the Kalayaan guerrillas. They were skinny Bahayans in homespun tunics, wearing straw hats, but their eyes were hard, and they carried rifles and machetes.

They're the ones who killed my brother, Jon thought, and sudden hatred blazed through him. *There are the bastards who took Paul.*

He wanted to be on Bahay now. To face them. To kill them. To avenge his brother and all the other dead. The purity of his hatred surprised him. Jon did not consider himself an angry man, yet now his fury surged.

A few others in the crowd were cursing at the video now. They too had lost loved ones to the dreaded Kalayaan.

Ensign Earth continued. "Finally, meet your third enemy. The Santelmos. These aliens run the show on Bahay. You won't fight Santelmos on the field. They're too cowardly to fight. They arm, train, and indoctrinate the Bahayan terrorists. If you do come across a Santelmo, shoot to kill. It's what good heroes do."

The video showed orbs of light floating in a swamp. It was probably just a special effect. Actually seeing real Santelmos was rare. Their planet was a thousand light-years away from Earth, and even on Bahay, they were just advisers, not fighters.

The camera panned toward Ensign Earth's face, then zoomed in. The actor shed a tear. A pan flute played a mournful note.

"My heart yearns to free Bahay from evil. My spirit craves to welcome Bahay into the embrace of the Human Commonwealth. So long as evil thrives on Bahay, its people cannot be free." His lips tightened, and he wiped away his tear. "But heroes like you and me still fight. We will defeat evil, and we will liberate Bahay. The planet will join the grand Human Commonwealth, free and strong." Ensign Earth saluted. "For Earth!"

The flag of Earth appeared on screen. The planetary anthem began to play.

In the room, a few recruits stood up and began to sing too.

But not Etty.

Etty Ettinger leaped onto her chair and shouted, "This is such bullshit!"

Lizzy snarled. The sergeant seemed ready to shout, even shock Etty with her whip. But the planetary anthem was playing. Out of respect for the flag, Lizzy remained still.

"Seriously!" Etty continued, standing on her chair. "This is just propaganda bullshit! The Bahayans aren't terrorists. I know terrorists, okay? I've been fighting them all my life." Her eyes were suddenly damp. "The Bahayans deserve to be free. If they don't want to join our empire, why should we force them?"

Jon reeled toward her, fuming. Maybe Sergeant Lizzy dared not act while the anthem was playing, but Jon had no such reserves.

"What are you talking about, Etty?" he said. "The Kalayaan is a terrorist organization! They murder people!" His voice caught. "How dare you defend them?"

Etty gave a mirthless laugh. "Really, Jon? The Bahayans have been living in peace for centuries. We show up on their world with armies. We bomb their villages. We burn their rice paddies. And you don't expect them to fight back, to—"

"They murdered my brother!" Jon shouted.

"And we murdered millions of them!" Etty cried, tears in her eyes.

Suddenly they realized how quiet the room had become. Earth's anthem had ended. The movie was over.

Everyone was staring at them.

Including Sergeant Lizzy.

The sergeant approached them, eyes flaming, and raised her electric whip.

Chapter Sixteen
Fire in the Sky

They spent weeks traveling the Freedom Trail before Maria's first battle.

Life in the Kalayaan was hard. The past few weeks had felt longer than Maria's years of toiling in the rice paddies.

During the days, they marched. They climbed cliffs. They crawled through mud. Sometimes they met other guerrilla units, exchanged intelligence, and marched on. Units broke apart and came together, always shifting. Thousands of patriots were moving through the jungles.

Sometimes Maria saw fighters without limbs. Sometimes she saw child soldiers, some younger than ten. Sometimes she saw smoldering craters where villages had been, fields of desolation where rice had once grown.

And they kept moving south.

Before every dawn, Ernesto woke them, and they trained. They fought one another with wooden sticks, fists, and stones. They listened to Ernesto as he read the Kalayaan manifesto again and again—every morning like clockwork—vowing freedom for Bahay and destruction for Earth. They chanted with him. Freedom for Bahay! Freedom for Bahay!

Maria was used to early mornings and hard labor, but nothing like this. Her fingers bled from climbing, her feet from so much walking. Insects bit her. A snake once bit her too, and the wound swelled and ached even after Ernesto sucked out the poison.

Worst of all, perhaps, was the hunger. There wasn't much food in the Kalayaan. They sometimes came across a distinctive curling branch, marking a place of storage. They opened a hidden hatch on a tree trunk, and inside they found rations of rice and crispy *lechon*. More often they foraged and hunted. Usually they were just hungry. Even when there was food, Maria was given the smallest portions, sometimes nothing at all. The older fighters horded most of the food.

The signs of war were everywhere. Planes rumbled overhead, and the Kalayaan hid under ferns and roots, waiting for them to pass by. Earthling troops rode armored trucks along distant roads. Guns often rattled in the distance, and explosions rocked the world. Sometimes they saw plumes of smoke on the horizon. Sometimes they found bullets among the trees.

There were many young guerrillas, and many were female. But Maria was still an innocent. She had never fought a battle, and they mocked her, called her a soft Mindao girl. Maria had never been to Mindao, the great city in the south. But apparently, Mindao girls were worthy of mockery.

But as hard as the days were, the nights were worse.

At nights, Ernesto came to her.

The guerrillas had no tents nor barracks like the Earthlings. Like the animals of the forest, they slept on moss and leaves. Every night, as Maria curled up, Ernesto lay beside her, stroked her hair, and cupped her breasts.

"No, Ernesto," she told him. "We must not. We're not married yet. It's a sin."

He would reach between her legs, trying to feel her, but she squirmed away.

"Maria, I love you," Ernesto said. "A fire burns inside me. For you, Maria. We might die tomorrow. Let us make love tonight."

Maria shook her head, for though the world burned, her

virginity was still sacred to her. It was not a gift she was willing to give him. When his hands became too persistent, she pleasured him in other ways. He spilled his seed inside her hand, then slept with his arms around her, and Maria felt trapped, and she lay like an animal in a hutch.

For weeks, this continued.

Marching.

Climbing.

Chanting.

Foraging.

Pleasing him.

And then it was time to fight.

* * * * *

Maria walked through the forest, wrapped in a ragged cloak, her long black hair billowing in the wind.

She emerged onto a burnt field, and her heart thudded so powerfully it banged against her ribs.

Please, God, be with me, she silently prayed. *Give me strength.*

Her cross hung between her breasts, exposed, cold against her skin even in the open sunlight. Her cloak fluttered in the hot wind. She took another step. Another. Ash fluttered around her bare feet. With every step away from the jungle, she felt more naked, more afraid. At any moment, a bullet could fly, could hit her.

She pulled her cloak open wider, revealing more of her breasts, hoping to kindle lust for flesh rather than blood.

Ahead she saw them. Still a hundred yards away.

Earthlings.

They had no idea how to live in nature. They had cut

down huge swaths of the forest. With the dead wood, they had built a crude camp in the field. It rose upon the land like a tumor. Palisades of sharpened logs formed walls. A guard tower rose above them. Between the wooden spikes, Maria could see olive-green tents spread across the camp. Several helicopters flew above, ferrying supplies to and from the base.

They desecrated our rainforest, Maria thought.

These wooden logs had once been trees, beautiful and mysterious and ancient. The Earthlings' great machines had crushed the land, shattering trees as holy as any cathedral. Maria walked around tree stumps and animal skeletons.

She took another step toward the fort.

She was alone.

She could barely even breathe, and the air smelled of smoke, oil, and gun powder.

"Oi!" A bearded man cried from the guard tower. "Oi, slit, stop where you are!"

Maria came to a stop, still a good distance from the fort. The guard was staring at her through binoculars. More Earthlings appeared above the wooden palisade. One man whistled.

"Nice tits, slit!" a man shouted. His friends laughed.

"Turn back!" said the bearded guard. "This ain't no slit hole."

He cocked his gun. The *click* sent chills down Maria's spine.

She wanted to turn. To run.

Instead, she stared at them defiantly.

"I'm hungry!" she said. "Will you feed me? I'll love you for food."

The Earthlings looked at one another, then burst out laughing.

"Ah, put down your gun!" an Earthling said to tower guard. "She's just a slit whore."

"She could be a fucking Kenny," said the bearded guard.

"She could be fucking *us*," said an Earthling on the wall, already undoing his belt. "Come here, slitty. Come into our little abode. We'll feed you. We've got plenty of baked beans. They're almost as big as your tits." He laughed at his own joke. Nobody else did.

Maria raised her chin. "I'm not coming in there! I'm scared. If you want me, meet me under my trees. Or are you scared of the jungle like little girls, you stinky *putes*?"

She ran back toward the rainforest.

A bullet whizzed.

Dust danced by her feet, and she realized the bullet had almost hit her.

She ran faster, heart thumping.

Back on the wall, some men laughed. Others cursed.

"Oi, don't shoot her!"

"She'd be more fun dead."

"You perv. Open the gates, damn it, she's getting away."

Maria kept running. Another bullet whistled overhead, and more men laughed.

"Run, slitty, run!"

They were toying with her. Maria snarled as she ran over the scorched Earth.

The giants were cruel and big and stupid. They had powerful machines, but mentally, emotionally—they were so weak.

She glanced over her shoulder and saw the gates open. An Earthling machine emerged from the fort—an armored jeep. Maria had seen such machines from a distance along the Freedom Trail. The jeeps were like their masters. Big, dumb, and loud. A squad of soldiers filled this jeep, and another jeep followed. Men hooted and hollered inside, sticking their tongues out at her, already pulling off their shirts.

Maria scoffed. Stupid *putes*. They had no brains under their helmets. They could only think with the little *titis* between their legs.

She reached the tree line and leaped into the rainforest.

She ran among the trees, leaping over roots, swinging from branches, as nimble as a greendeer. She heard the jeeps stop at the tree line, heard the giants open the doors, laughing, lumbering through the forest. They cracked branches. They smoked cigarettes one could smell from a distance. They snorted and spat and joked.

Stupid *putes*. Their only power was in machines. They had to leave those behind. Here in the jungle—this was her domain.

Only a few weeks ago, I was terrified of the jungle, Maria thought. *But now I'm a ghost among the trees.*

"Hey, sweet girl!" an Earthling cried.

She spun around, standing on a boulder, and stuck her tongue out at the Earthlings.

"Stinky *putes*!" she said.

She ran onward. They laughed and followed.

They stopped laughing when the first trap sprung.

Maria knew how to avoid it. She had seen the little stone—flipped over, its mossy side now facing the soil, its underbelly pointing at the canopy. To a Bahayan, it was as obvious as a flashing light. But the Earthlings could not read the forest.

The pit opened up, and the first Earthling in line fell.

Maria had spent that morning digging the pit, then filling it with poisoned bamboo spikes. A few weeks ago, she had dug graves for her parents. This morning she had dug graves for Earthlings.

She swung on a vine over the trap.

Behind her, the Earthling tumbled into the pit of spikes.

The sharpened bamboo tore through him. He screamed,

impaled but still alive. The spikes ended with fish hooks. They could enter flesh—but not exit.

Maria stared at the surviving Earthlings.

She made eye contact with one. The man who had shot at her.

He sucked in air and shouted, "It's a slit trap, ru—"

And then the wrath of Bahay burst from the trees.

The Kalayaan filled the branches, covered with cloaks of leaves and vines, camouflaged so perfectly even Maria could barely see them.

But she could hear their bullets.

She could see the Earthlings fall. The blood spill.

She scurried up a tree, raced along a branch, nearly fell, and grabbed a vine for support. *Ungoys* fled, their many tails flailing in terror.

There, among the branches, Maria found her rifle.

With the other guerrillas, she opened fire.

The Earthlings were screaming. More fell dead. Suddenly they seemed less like fearsome giants, more like boys. A few were trying to escape. From a branch nearby, Ernesto shot one in the back. The Earthling fell, screaming, still alive, only for more bullets to hammer him.

Maria's heart pounded, and she kept firing. She could barely see through the leaves. She didn't know if she was hitting anyone. But she fired again and again. For her parents. For San Luna. For all Bahay. She fired her gun, and she laughed at how easily the enemy died, and tears flowed down her cheeks.

"Hold your ground, dammit!" an Earthling shouted.

"Burn those trees!" shouted another.

The surviving Earthlings took cover behind boulders and logs. They raised their guns and fired back.

Their guns were a lot more powerful. The Bahayans fought with old flintlock rifles with wooden stocks. The

Earthlings wielded fearsome assault rifles.

A bullet whizzed by Maria.

Another slammed into the branch she stood on. The branch cracked. Maria swayed and nearly fell.

One guerrilla screamed and fell, a bullet in his chest. The assault rifle left a hole the size of a plum. More bullets pounded the man before he even hit the ground.

Maria grimaced. She had been too quick to gloat. She had underestimated them. The Earthlings were brutish, yes. They were big and dumb and noisy. But they were not cowards.

"Fire in the sky!" an Earthling howled and tossed something at the trees. It looked like a little metal pineapple.

The Earthlings ducked for cover.

"Watch ou—" Maria began.

An explosion shook the forest.

Maria's ears rang.

Shrapnel flew everywhere, embedding into trees. Three guerrillas fell, pierced with metal. The shock wave rattled the branches, and Maria nearly fell from her tree.

A grenade, she realized. She had heard of such monstrous weapons.

"Fire in the sky!" shouted another Earthling.

And another.

And a third.

And more grenades flew, and explosions filled the forest, and branches shattered, and trees caught fire.

And suddenly Maria was falling.

She fell through burning branches.

She tried to grab a vine, but she kept falling, and bullets whistled around her, and she hit the ground.

The forest blazed above. Bullets streaked above her. A man ran, screamed, fell at her side. Somewhere far above, helicopters rumbled. Burning leaves glided around Maria, a thousand little lights.

She stood up, coughing in the smoke, eyes stinging. Her leg was bleeding, and a bullet whistled by her head. A man ran, burning, a living torch. Another man ran through the brush, his arm ending in a stump. Somebody was shouting something in Tagalog. Maria's ears rang, and she could barely hear.

He emerged from the smoke before her.

The bearded Earthling. The guard who had fired on her.

He sneered, approaching her.

"You're gonna be mine, you little slit. I was going to kill you nice and easy. Now you're going to beg to die."

She spun and began running up a steep hillside.

He grabbed her leg. Painfully.

She yelped and pitched forward.

Her face hit the ground, and he was on top of her. He flipped her onto her back and pawed at her chest. She screamed, flailing and kicking. She might as well kick a boulder. The brute pinned her down. He grinned, drooling into his beard. He was so big. The biggest man Maria had ever seen, a veritable giant.

He gripped her throat.

"Oh, don't worry, slit. I won't kill you. Not yet. You're going to suffer first. You're going to suffer so much."

She couldn't breathe.

Darkness was closing in around her.

Above, the burning leaves still glided, and she imagined the thousand Santelmos in the night.

She saw the eyes of the dreamtoad.

She pulled her father's knife from her belt, and with a single fluid movement, she slit the Earthling's throat.

Blood sprayed her.

He gurgled, rose up, and clutched his neck, trying to hold in the blood.

Maria scurried away, and he fell down dead.

"Maria, come on!" Ernesto shouted in the distance. "Fall back! The helicopters are coming!"

The guerrillas were retreating into the forest. The mission was over. Maria could hear the helicopters roaring above. Through the burning trees, she saw more Earthlings approach, rolling forth machine guns.

Two Earthlings ran toward her.

She found her rifle on the forest floor.

She fired.

One Earthling fell dead, a bullet in his chest.

"Drop your gun!" she shouted at the second man.

"Maria, come on!" Ernesto cried from behind.

"Drop your gun!" Maria shouted at the Earthling.

He was a tall man. She looked like a child beside him. But he was young, his cheeks soft. He dropped his weapon.

"Move!" Maria jabbed him with her rifle. "Into the forest! Go! Faster!"

The Earthling raised his hands. This tall, powerful Earthling—trembling. Obeying her. She barely stood as tall as his belt buckle.

They moved deeper into the forest, fleeing the fire. An explosion bloomed behind them. Flames roared. They ran, and Maria kept poking the Earthling's back with her muzzle, herding him onward.

Ernesto approached her, cheeks singed. "Maria, what are you doing?"

"I took a prisoner," she said. "He's going to tell us who destroyed our village. And then—he'll lead us to the killers."

Chapter Seventeen
Etty's Secret

The door slammed shut, sealing Jon and Etty in the brig.

Dust flew, then settled over a small chamber, barely larger than a closet. There were two concrete bunks, a rusty sink and toilet, and a ventilation grate near the ceiling.

"Wonderful," Jon muttered. "My first week in the army, and I end up in jail."

"At least there's a lot of artwork to admire." Etty gestured at the walls, where a previous prisoner had scrawled dicks with wings and faces. "Hey, looks like self-portraits of Clay!"

"Sure, laugh about it," Jon said. "This is going on our permanent record, you know."

Etty gasped and placed her hands on her cheeks. "Oh no! Our permanent records! What ever shall we do?"

"Shut up. This is all your fault."

She snorted. "Oh please. You earned your own trip here."

Jon tried to pace, but he could only take three steps back and forth. There were little ventilation grates near the floor. Through them, he could dimly hear prisoners in other cells—talking, snoring, cursing. They would all be better company than Etty, but Jon was stuck here with her. Begrudgingly, he sat on one of the concrete slabs.

"You're the one who jumped on a chair and started ranting," Jon said. "Now we're stuck in the brig for twenty-four hours." He rubbed his arm, wincing. "Not to mention covered with marks from Lizzy's whip."

He expected Etty to get mad. Maybe to rant some more. But instead, the girl sat beside him. Her shoulders slumped. Strands of black hair fell across her face.

"I wish President Ben-Ari were still here," she said softly.

Jon rolled his eyes. "More politics."

She punched him. "Shut up! Things were better back then. I met her once, you know."

Jon raised an eyebrow. "You met President Ben-Ari, the Golden Lioness, the legendary heroine?"

Everyone knew the tales. A century ago, aliens had attacked Earth, slaughtered billions, and nearly destroyed the planet. It was Einav Ben-Ari, a young officer, who raised the broken, bleeding scraps of humanity, who defeated the aliens, and then built a human empire among the stars. Around the world, there were statues and murals of the Golden Lioness. Jon even had a poster of her in his bedroom back home. Many kids did. She was normally depicted young, golden hair billowing in the wind, charging into enemy lines. It was an iconic poster, hanging in millions of bedrooms.

For decades, the Golden Lioness had led humanity. But then, fifteen years ago, Ben-Ari disappeared.

At age eighty, the legendary leader of humanity decided not to run for re-election.

The day after announcing her decision, she vanished.

Some say she died. Others claimed she was exploring another galaxy.

Earth had a new president now. And some claimed the golden age was over.

"I was only an infant," Etty said. "Not even a year old. My parents took me to see her. Ben-Ari was Israeli, you know. Like me. On her last day on Earth, she gave a speech on the hills of Jerusalem. I was there. But I don't remember anything. I just know the stories. That the Golden Lioness stood on the holy mountain, spoke to her people one last time, blessed them… and then rose into the sky. Like an angel." Etty wiped her eyes. "She's still alive. I believe. But somewhere else. And now we're lost. If Ben-Ari were here, she would *never* fight a war against Bahay. Before she disappeared, she saw the seeds of the war, and she spoke out against it. She believed that humans should never fight other humans. I miss her so much."

Jon frowned. "Wait a minute. Your story doesn't add up. Ben-Ari disappeared in the year 2208. Fifteen years ago. You would have been a little kid. Not an infant."

Etty winced. "Um, yeah… about that. I'm sixteen. Actually, I just turned sixteen yesterday." She gave a shaky smile. "Happy Birthday to me!"

Jon blinked at her. "What?" He stood up. "You're *sixteen*? Dude! You have to be eighteen to join the army!"

Etty cringed. "I know, I know! I kinda… lied about my age." She stood up too and grabbed him. "Please don't tell anyone! *Please.* If they found out, they'd kick me out. Maybe even leave me in the brig forever. Promise you won't tell!"

He blinked at her, head spinning. His perspective of Etty completely changed. He was only two years older than her. But at eighteen, a soldier, he felt like an adult. Etty suddenly seemed like a child.

I was too hard on her, he thought. *She's sixteen and scared and confused. My God. I can't even imagine.*

"I won't tell," he said.

She hugged him. "Thank you."

He brushed back a strand of her hair. "Aren't your parents worried, Etty? Did they let you do this?"

A tear flowed. "My parents are dead. My whole family is dead."

Jon froze. He was silent for long seconds.

"God, Etty," he finally said. "I'm sorry. I don't know what

to say."

"You don't have to say anything. Jeez! Why do people always feel they have to say something?" Etty shrugged. "It sucks. It fucking sucks. What can you do."

But despite her flippant attitude, her eyes were watering, and she pulled her knees to her chest.

"Did the slits kill them?" Jon said.

"Nah." Etty shook her head. "It happened on Earth. I'm from Israel, you know. Lovely country! But not one known for peace. There's been a war going on there for…" She counted on her fingers. "Five thousand years now. Oh, the enemy changes. First it was the Philistines, the Hittites, the Amalek, the Babylonians, and a bunch of other ancient conquerors from the desert. Then it was the Europeans. The Greeks. The Romans. The Crusaders. Every time, we rebuilt. Over and over—genocide and rebirth. We were finally getting hopeful about a hundred years ago. So of course aliens had to attack. And wipe us out again."

"I remember that from the history books," Jon said. "The *Scolopendra titania*. The giant centipedes. They destroyed Israel."

"Yep, and again, like always, the survivors rebuilt. We never learn, do we?" Etty sighed. "The holy land is cursed. We recreated the country again, only for new wars to break out. Over tribes. Religions. Ethnicities. Same old bullshit. Humanity finally defeated the aliens, so in Israel, we humans went back to fighting one another."

"It sounds like a microcosm for Earth," Jon said. "Earth too is like that. Destruction and rebirth, over and over. Recovering from the first world war, then fighting another one. Recovering from the second world war, then launching right into the cold war. Ending the cold war, then fighting the aliens. Recovering from the aliens, and now Earth is fighting Bahay."

"We humans seem to need a fight," Etty said. "Maybe it's evolutionary. Millions of years ago, we fought wild animals. It made us strong. We need competition. An enemy to cull the weak. If we can't find wild animals or aliens, we fight one another."

"That's a cynical view of humanity," Jon said. "I like to think I'm in the army to fight for justice. To defeat evil."

Etty snorted. "Everyone thinks they're the hero. Even the goddamn Nazis thought they were the heroes."

"I don't know if I'm a hero," Jon said. "My brother was a hero."

Etty placed a hand on his knee. "I'm sorry for your loss, Jon."

Jon placed his hand atop hers. "Do you want to tell me how your family died?"

"Terrorist attack," Etty said. "We were in the market. Just out shopping in Jerusalem's old city. I ran off to play. A second later, I heard the blast. The suicide bomber killed twenty-three people. My father died right away. My mother clung on to life for a week, but her wounds were…" Etty lowered her heads, tears falling. "She died too."

"Oh, Etty." Jon hugged her. "I'm sorry."

She sniffed. "I was just a kid. They sent me to America. To live with my aunt. I lived with her for three years, and then she died too. Cancer. I was almost sixteen and homeless and scared. I didn't know where to go. What to do. So I went to the recruitment center that day. The same one you went to. And I lied about my age, told them I'm eighteen. And I joined the army. I'm not a hero. I don't really want to fight Bahay. I just… needed somewhere to go."

Jon held her close. "You have a new family now, Etty. You have us. This platoon." He thought for a moment. "Okay, maybe not that asshole Clay, and probably not Bucky either. But me, and George, and the rest of us. We love you. We'll look after you."

A smile broke through her tears. "Thanks, buddy."

He mussed her hair. "No problem, kiddo."

The rest of their prison time passed easily enough—aside from using the toilet, which was very public and very uncomfortable, and involved one person turning around and singing loudly. Mostly they talked. With George, Jon would joke around a lot, talk shit, never get into anything too deep. But with Etty, he talked about history, art, the stars. During this day in the brig, he got to know her. Her soul. Her secrets.

They became friends. It felt like they had been friends for years.

Finally keys turned in the lock.

A robotic jailer pulled the cell door open.

Jon and Etty stumbled out, blinking in the pitiless white light that filled Roma Station.

The robot stared at them with black eyes. He was a cheap unit, really just a metal chassis vaguely shaped like a skeleton. On Earth these days, you sometimes saw androids that were remarkably lifelike, practically indistinguishable from humans. They served as maids, teachers, caregivers, romantic companions. The military didn't bother spending money on expensive skins. Its robots just needed to be efficient, not pretty.

I just wish they sent robots to die in battlefields instead of humans, Jon thought. *But even the dumbest robots are expensive. Human life is cheap.*

"I hope you have been rehabilitated," the robot intoned in a mechanical voice. "Next time, I will keep you locked for a week. Then a month. Understood?"

Etty saluted. "Aye, aye, Captain!"

The robot ignored her. Gears creaking, it approached the next prison cell. It unlocked the door.

"I hope you have been rehabilitated," the robot said, speaking into the other cell. "Step out, human."

A shadow fell.

Jon's belly churned.

Out of that cell, his arm in a cast, stepped Clay Hagen.

Crap, Jon thought.

His heart sank into his pelvis.

"Thank you, my good man." Clay tipped an imaginary hat at the robot. "I'm now fully rehabilitated."

Jon could only stare with dread. He hadn't realized that Clay had been imprisoned in the neighboring cell. He remembered hearing snoring, some muttering through the wall, but Jon had never imagined it was his nemesis.

Etty and I spent the whole day talking, Jon thought. *Sharing our dreams and secrets. Did Clay hear?*

Etty was staring at Clay too, face pale.

"What's a matter, Ettinger?" Clay asked. "You look like you saw a ghost. You're not scared of ghosts, are you? I mean, you *are* an adult now. Not a kid. Right?"

He winked, and his smile was cruel.

"Clay!" Etty said, going pale. "You can't tell anyone. Please."

The brute laughed. "What, me tell?" He grinned, arms outstretched. "I didn't hear nothing! Of course, if *somebody* heard *something*, and if *somebody* told Sergeant Lizzy, and if *somebody* happens to be underage, well…" He barked a laugh. "But that'll never happen."

Etty cringed. "Clay, I get it. Look, I'm sorry I said you have a micro-dick. I'm sure it's enormous. And I'm sorry that I laughed when Lizzy kicked your ass, it's just that—"

"That bitch didn't kick my ass!" Clay roared. "First of all, Sergeant Lizzy has a bionic hand, and that's cheating. Second, I let her win, because she's a girl."

Jon stepped forward. "Dude, calm down. Look, let's just forget what happened and move on, alright? We—"

"Fuck you, ballerina." Clay shoved him. "You and the Jew.

You both watch out. You fuck with me, I'll make your lives a living—"

The robotic jailer approached. "Do not engage in rowdy behavior. Depart the premises!"

Clay snorted. He walked away, whistling, a bounce to his step.

Jon and Etty looked at each other.

"Fuck," they said together.

Chapter Eighteen
Iron

He must have stood over six feet tall, the tallest man Maria had ever seen, a true giant from another world.

An Earthling.

An invader.

A monster.

And little Maria, shorter than his shoulders, marched him through the forest.

"Go!" she said. "Move!"

She walked a step behind, aiming her rifle at the Earthling. He shuffled forward, wrists bound behind his back.

The other guerrillas walked ahead, navigating through the rainforest. They carried their guns, their wounded, and their dead. In battle, they were victorious. They had killed a few Earthlings, taken one captive.

But many of the Kalayaan had fallen. Far more than the Earthling losses. It felt to Maria like a Pyrrhic victory.

Ernesto was carrying one dead man. The corpse hung across his back, gazing at Maria with accusing eyes. Half the dead man's jaw was gone. Other guerrillas carried more of their fallen.

I killed two men.

Maria's arms trembled.

I slit a man's throat. I shot another.

Her breath shook.

Who am I? What have I done?

The Earthling turned toward her. Tears filled his eyes.

"Please," he said. "Please, I'm just a private, I don't know anything. I want to go home. My mom must be worried. Please, I—"

"Move!" Maria shouted, and jabbed him with her rifle.

Because she was afraid.

Because he terrified her.

Because he appeared as just a scared boy, but he was a monster who had murdered so many.

The Earthling shuffled onward through the jungle, crying softly.

They bomb us. They butcher us. They kill like monsters. Peel back their metal machines, and they cry like boys.

Pity filled Maria's heart. She couldn't help it. But she thought of her village, of the corpses of her parents, of the ruins of her life. Of the millions of dead Bahayans in the burning north.

And she hardened her heart. And she jabbed the Earthling in the back, shoving him onward. He obeyed. He did not fight. The dreaded giant who towered over everyone, even over Ernesto—he cried and begged.

But he walked on.

Maria clutched her rifle, and she noticed that blood still stained her hands.

The images flashed before her.

Slitting a man's throat.

Her gun booming. A man falling.

Her parents in the ashes, their faces gone.

Just a few weeks ago, I was Maria the rice farmer, the girl with the big head full of questions, she thought. *Who am I now?*

It was a long, hard march to the camp. The helicopters and planes always rumbled above. Bombs exploded in the distance. Every second—another *boom* like a dying man's heartbeat. The smell of smoke and gunpowder filled the rainforest. One time, a plane flew so low that the canopy bent, and a great explosion bloomed only a hundred yards away, tearing down trees.

Trudging ahead, Ernesto looked over his shoulder. Sweat soaked his face and hair. The fire painted him red. He grinned at the captive Earthling. A cruel grin. A predator's grin.

"Your stupid *pute* friends are looking for you, little boy," Ernesto said to the prisoner. "I think they want to take you home in a bucket."

He tossed back his head and laughed.

Maria remained solemn.

"Quiet, Ernesto, and hurry!" she said.

Fire spread across the sky. They ran.

For hours, they pushed through the jungle, leaving the fire behind, but the threat of planes forever hovered above.

At night, they slept in the mud, a dozen men and a dozen corpses, and Maria dared not sleep, because sleep brought visions. Sleep brought memories. Sleep brought parents without faces, strange toads, and her knife in a man's throat. She guarded the camp, knuckles white around her rifle. Blood still stained her hands, dark brown under her fingernails. The prisoner slept tied to a fangwood, weeping softly all night.

In the morning, they found that bugs had laid eggs in their skin. Maria worked with a knife, digging into her arm, plucking the eggs out one by one. Nobody helped the prisoner, and when Maria tried to remove the eggs from him, Ernesto shoved her back.

"Let him suffer." He laughed. "*Putes* are only good for breeding bugs."

The corpses, which they had carried since the battle, were rotting. So they buried them. They did not mark their graves.

"I should put up crosses," Maria said. "And their names. So their families can visit someday."

But Ernesto shook his head. "No. The Earthlings would find the bodies, add them to their kill tally. They would gloat and celebrate our losses. Let the bodies be hidden."

"But they will not be forgotten," Maria said. "I will remember each name."

As they trudged through the jungle that day, she repeated the names of the dead over and over. Farmers. Fishermen. Villagers like her who had lost their families, who had joined the Kalayaan, who had given their lives for freedom.

I will remember you. Always. I will remember you all.

On the third day, another man died, succumbing to a bullet wound.

On the fourth day, a woman fell ill after drinking from a pond, and they carried her, but she died on the fifth day, a rot inside her. Maria wondered if anyone here would survive the jungle's crushing embrace.

That night, for the first time, the Earthling did not cry. As Maria stood guarding him, he looked at her.

"You speak English, don't you?" he said.

She pointed her rifle at him. "Be quiet!"

He gave her a hesitant, shaky smile. "I know some Tagalog. Just a few words."

She jabbed the muzzle into his chest. "Don't talk, *pute*."

"Your name is Maria, isn't it?" he said. "I'm David. I'm eighteen years old. I'm from Oklahoma. That's in America. On Earth. Maria, I just want to go home. To my parents. I was drafted. I didn't ask to be here. You understand, right? Maybe I can pull strings, bring you to Earth with me. Whatever you want."

She sneered. "Earth? Why would I want to go there? Earth bombed my village. Killed everyone I know. Earth murdered millions of my people."

David lost his shaky smile. Tears flowed down his cheeks. "Maria, I'm scared. Please. I'm so scared." He trembled. "I just want to go home."

Maria couldn't help it. A tear flowed down her own cheek.

As the other guerrillas slept, she cleaned David's wounds, plucking out the insect eggs one by one. She fed him, and she even loosened his ropes, letting more blood flow through his limbs.

But she did not release him.

Because she was one of the Kalayaan. She was a woman mourning. She had to stop the bombings. She had to sacrifice one scared, crying boy to save her world. She had killed two men, and her soul could never be cleansed.

* * * * *

Finally, after a week, they reached the Kalayaan camp.

A village! It was a village! So much like San Luna!

A handful of bamboo huts. Rice paddies. Groves of papaya, banana, and pineapple trees. Chickens roamed freely, pecking for seeds. It reminded Maria so much of her home. Her tears fell.

Yet as they entered the village, she realized: This was nothing like San Luna.

This village was just a front.

Kalayaan fighters huddled in the huts, not families. More guerrillas worked in the fields, disguised as peasants.

Maria wandered around with wide eyes. For the first time in weeks, she was not in the jungle, and her head spun. She inhaled deeply, savoring the scent of the rice paddies, and approached a papaya grove.

"Maria!" Ernesto grabbed her. "Watch out!"

She froze. Ernesto leaned down, rolled back a sheet of grass like a carpet, and revealed a pit full of spikes.

Maria winced.

I was a second away from falling to my death.

Ernesto snickered. "The village is full of booby traps. Be careful. Don't walk anywhere without me."

He took a few steps away, knelt, and pulled back another sheet of grass. This one revealed a tunnel.

"Come, Maria. We go underground. Bring our Earthling guest. In the shadows, we'll ask him some questions."

The tall, young Earthling was ashen, his eyes sunken. They had barely fed him all week. His wounds were infected and bloated, and maggots had invaded them. His wrists were still tied behind his back, and a rope was tied around his neck. Ernesto tugged the rope, yanking the prisoner down. David knelt by the tunnel, trembling.

"Don't treat David so roughly," Maria said. "He'll answer our questions."

Ernesto snorted. "*David*? He's nothing but a filthy *pute*." He kicked the prisoner and laughed.

Shame filled Maria. She hated seeing this violence. Hated seeing the terror in David's eyes.

But she had to know. Who had bombed San Luna? Who had killed her parents? She had to prevent more massacres. David was a scared boy, yes. But he was also a soldier of Earth. An enemy. And he held the answers.

They entered the darkness.

Maria crawled through the tunnels, still aiming her gun at David's back. She could barely squeeze through, and she was so small. Normally, an Earthling would never fit, but David had lost much weight over the journey. Ernesto pulled the rope, dragging the prisoner, and Maria pushed him, and they moved through the tunnels like moles.

The tunnel system was larger than the village. They wormed left and right, down and down. It was like a great ant colony. The tunnels took them by several earthen chambers: some filled with guerrillas sleeping on hammocks, others with ammunitions. Some were storerooms full of bags of rice. One room was an infirmary, and several men lay here, bandaged and moaning. These were barely more than burrows. The walls were just crumbly soil reinforced with wooden slats, threatening to cave in at any moment.

At one point, Maria looked down a narrow tunnel, smelled delicious cakes, and her stomach growled. She made to crawl down there, unable to resist. But Ernesto stopped her.

"Maria! Don't go that way. That's a false tunnel." He grinned. "If Earthlings invade our tunnels, they will go that way. *Boom!*"

Maria peered down the tunnel and squinted. She noticed cables along the ceiling. She shuddered.

Deep underground, they reached a cold, dark burrow.

Old blood stained the walls. Chains were attached to a rafter.

A few other guerrillas entered the chamber, eyes hard. All had lost loved ones to Earth's fire. They hung David from the rafter. The Earthling trembled, eyes closed, and whispered prayers.

"Please, Maria, please…"

And she realized: He wasn't praying to God, Jesus, or Mary. He was praying to her. Hoping she could save him.

Ernesto pulled a clothing iron from his pack. He hefted it and approached David.

He spoke in English, his accent thick. "I interrogated an Earthling once, you know. A bitch called Lizzy Pascal. She didn't speak at first. After I took her hand, she spoke." He laughed. "What should I take from you?"

"Please," David whispered.

Maria stepped forward. "You don't need to hurt him! He'll talk. I'll interrogate him."

Ernesto shoved her back, barely acknowledging her. He plugged his clothing iron into a generator. It buzzed and began to heat up.

"Do you know what they call me, *pute*?" he said. "They call me Ernesto Iron Cortes. Not only because I'm hard like iron. But also because of my favorite tool."

"No!" Maria cried.

Several guerrillas dragged her out of the chamber. She screamed and kicked, but they pulled her through the tunnels.

She could no longer see David. But she could hear him scream. She could smell his sizzling flesh. She could hear him call her name.

The guerrillas pulled her aboveground, and Maria collapsed onto the grass, trembling, weeping. Her cross dangled on its chain, accusing.

"What have I done?" she whispered.

Chapter Nineteen
Ambush

"We have a problem," Jon whispered.

George sat beside him in the mess hall, stuffing his face with gruel. "Not now. Eating."

Jon didn't know how his friend could enjoy the slop. The military changed it up sometimes. At breakfast, it was oatmeal slop. At lunch, it was bean slop. At dinner, meat slop. Last Friday it was fish stew—code word for slop with bits of tuna in it. It was always awful. But George always polished his plate. And he often ate other recruits' leftovers too.

"George!" Jon rolled his eyes. "This is serious."

"What?" George scooped more of the glop into his mouth.

Jon leaned toward his giant friend and whispered, "Etty is sixteen."

George glanced at him. "No shit!" He returned to his food.

"George." Jon pulled him closer. "Clay knows. And we think he's gonna tell."

That finally made George lose his appetite. The giant pushed his tray away. "Damn."

Jon had spent all that day worrying. Since early that morning, the platoon had been training. Climbing walls and ropes. Racing through obstacle courses. Watching propaganda reels. Running, climbing, swimming, hurting. Throughout the day, Jon kept glancing toward Clay. Would the beefy recruit tell on Etty?

Every once in a while, Clay looked at them. And hatred burned in his pale, wide-set eyes.

"Clay has known since last night," Jon said. "Etty told me in the brig. We didn't know Clay was in the cell next door. He heard us. If he tells the sergeant, Etty is toast. She'll be kicked out of the army. Maybe even tossed into prison for lying."

He spent a while describing Etty's tale. How she had grown up in a war zone. How a suicide bombing had killed her family. How she had nowhere else to go.

George listened carefully. "Maybe we'll be okay. Clay hasn't told Lizzy yet, right?"

"He hasn't had a chance," Jon said. "The sergeant's been drilling us all day. But tonight…"

Every night before bed, Sergeant Lizzy gave her platoon an hour off. They called it PH. Personal Hour. Most soldiers used PH to shower, change, refill their canteens, bond with one another, or sometimes—even the toughest recruits—find a quiet place to cry.

During PH, Lizzy sat in her trailer, accepting visits from recruits like a queen granting an audience to peasants. During this hour, you could approach Lizzy with personal problems. Maybe you needed fresh socks, sanitary pads, or a certain medication. Maybe you had a sick relative at home, and you wanted permission to call them. Maybe you felt suicidal. Whatever help you needed, Lizzy would listen, and her whip remained hanging on the wall.

It was a standard feature of basic training. All sergeants gave their platoons personal guidance during this hour, a chance to talk one on one. After all, a sergeant wasn't just a slave driver, despite how it seemed. A sergeant had to keep her platoon running smoothly, and personal attention was part of that.

Some sergeants helped many recruits during this hour. Some sergeants considered it the best part of their job.

But not Lizzy.

Few recruits dared approach Lizzy Pascal's trailer at night. With her steel claw and fiery temper, she was just too damn terrifying. Nobody could forget the *snap* of Clay's arm, the sting of her whip, or the agony of her rubber bullets. The sergeant probably spent PH bored in her trailer, torturing little animals to pass the time.

But during PH tonight, Jon feared, Clay Hagen would approach the sergeant's trailer.

And he would rat on Etty.

"Fuck me," George said. "What do we do? We gotta protect Etty. I mean, I know the army is shit and all. But hell, it beats homelessness." He thought for a moment. "Okay, maybe not boot camp. And maybe not war. But… ah well, I don't care what's worse! I ain't letting Etty get in trouble."

Jon nodded. "I was going to spend PH tonight having a long shower. I haven't showered in three days. I smell like a wet dog who just swam through the sewer. Instead, I'm going to make sure nobody tells Lizzy our fireteam's little secret."

"Good evening, gentlemen!" Etty plopped down beside them, holding a tray of slop. "Sorry I'm late. Long line at the ladies' latrine. What are you boys up to?"

They said nothing. Perhaps the plan was best kept between them.

Training continued. They marched around the base. They practiced Krav Maga, fighting robots who flailed from side to side, swinging padded fists. They crawled through tunnels, dodging stinging drones the size of bees.

Finally the lights across the station dimmed.

Personal Hour began.

* * * * *

Jon and George huddled in the shadows, waiting.

Sergeant Lizzy's trailer was a hundred yards away. An alleyway between armories and warehouses led toward it. If Clay was going to rat on Etty, he had to take this path.

And we'll be ready, Jon thought.

It was night in Roma Station. There was no true night or day on the space station, of course. But the lights dimmed and shone and dimmed again, enforcing a circadian cycle. Half the time, Roma Station was in darkness.

Of course, the recruits only got three hours of sleep a night. Four if they were lucky. Jon supposed dimming the lights for a full twelve hours was less about mimicking Earth, more about saving energy.

The station was spinning lazily. Joe knelt behind a concrete barricade, gazing at the distant wall. It sloped upward, then curved along the ceiling. Dim lights from barrack windows shone far above. It almost looked like the stars. Jon knew that they were orbiting Earth, that home was just a short flight away. But he had not seen the blue planet, nor the stars, nor the moon, since entering this base.

He wondered if he would ever see Earth again. Would the next planet he saw be Bahay? And would that be the last place he saw?

In the shadows, he found himself thinking of Kaelyn. Remembering her kiss. Her beautiful mismatched eyes. Her brave soul.

He thought about his parents. His dad jamming with him in the basement, playing bass while Jon played keyboards. His mom so proud, telling her friends that her son was a composer, was in a real band, would someday be a rock star.

And suddenly tears were flowing down Jon's cheeks.

During the days, he would never cry. He would never let his platoon see. Here in the darkness, they flowed.

He heard a choked sound beside him. George was crying too.

"You all right, buddy?" Jon said.

George nodded. "Yeah. I just miss home. And I hate always being so scared."

Both boys were cut, bruised, and exhausted, but the pain inside was worse. The homesickness. The fear of the war ahead. Jon suddenly missed the obstacle courses, even missed Lizzy's whip. It was impossible to think during the craziness of training. Impossible to miss home. There was only pain, and that was easier.

In many ways, Personal Hour, the time when the demons and memories rose, was the worst time of basic.

Footsteps sounded in the shadows.

Jon stiffened.

George and him knelt, very still, and peered around the concrete barrier.

"Here he comes," Jon whispered. "We were right. That bastard."

The burly figure came walking through the shadows. A passing drone flew overhead, briefly illuminating stubbly yellow hair, a wide face, and wide-set blue eyes.

"Now!" Jon said.

He and George leaped from cover, lunged at Clay, and grabbed him.

Clay tried to scream, but George slapped a heavy fist across his mouth. Jon grabbed Clay's left arm, pinned it back. George struggled to control the right arm.

The thug fought like a madman, and goddamn, Clay was strong. Not unusually tall, not like George, but all bulging muscle. Jon wished they had brought backup. Even little Etty would have been helpful now.

Thankfully, George was the size of two men. With great effort, they dragged Clay behind the concrete barrier, where they knocked him to the ground. George literally sat on him, pinning him down.

Clay knew he was beat. He glared at them, eyes bulging. His face, normally so pasty, was turning red. He could barely breathe with George's hand pressed against his face.

"Why, fancy meeting you here, Clay," Jon said. "I suppose I should tell my giant to let you breathe. But you must promise to be quiet. Can you promise that, Clay? Because if you make noise, George will get angry. And you don't want to make the Giant Ginger angry."

Clay just lay there, crushed under the giant. Glaring.

Jon nodded at George, who pulled back his hand.

Clay took a deep breath, and he didn't scream.

"I'm going to flay you," Clay said, speaking calmly, as if discussing the weather. "Do you know what flaying is, Taylor? It's removing the skin. *Peeling* it. I've done it to animals before. While they were alive. That's what I'll do to you."

George growled. "You won't dare, because I'll kill you first!"

He pressed his knee against Clay's chest. Clay gasped for air.

"Listen to me, Clay," Jon said. "And listen good. We saw you heading toward Lizzy's trailer. Maybe you were planning to rat on Etty. To get her discharged. Well, you could do that. But I want you to know the consequences."

"We have footage of you," George said.

Clay coughed, struggling, unable to shove the giant off. "You ain't got nothing on me."

Jon raised an eyebrow. "Oh, but we do. Remember when Sergeant Lizzy challenged you to a fight? And she kicked your ass? I remember how ashamed you were. Hell, when Etty mentioned it this morning, you flew off the handle. How would you like everyone in America to know a girl beat you?"

"My uncle is a journalist," George said. "He writes for the Sol Chronicles. One call from me, and he'll print the story. Earth might like to know that sergeants are breaking recruits' arms. That a *girl* broke your *arm*."

"You can't prove a damn thing!" Clay said.

"Sure we can!" George said. "There are security cameras everywhere in Roma Station. They were filming you when Lizzy kicked your ass. It ain't classified. My uncle can pull strings, get the footage, no worries. The army has to comply with journalists. The public's right to know. It's the *law*."

"Hey, George," Jon said, "you reckon it'll end up on the front page? With a picture of Clay crying at a girl's feet?"

"I reckon it will," George said. "Sergeants ain't meant to break bones. It'll be a scandal."

Jon gasped. "Hear that, Clay? You're going to be famous!"

"The video will definitely end up online," George said.

"Millions of views!" Jon said.

"We can add the Benny Hill song," George suggested.

Clay fumed. His face was red again, and this time not from lack of air.

"All right, I got it." He spat, nearly hitting Jon. "Call your giant off. I wasn't going to rat on the Jew."

"Her name is Etty." George drove his knee deeper into Clay's stomach.

Clay groaned in pain. "Whatever the hell she's called! I ain't a rat. Get off."

George looked at Jon, who nodded.

Grimacing, Clay rose to his feet and rubbed his torso. "Goddamn, you nearly cracked my bones, you fatass hippo."

"Remember what happened here tonight," Jon said. "If we

ever learn you told on Etty, we'll—"

"I was going to the sergeant to talk about my mother," Clay said. "She's in the hospital. She has cancer."

"Yeah right," George said. "We're not buying your sob story."

"It's not a sob story." Clay's voice was suddenly solemn, and he lowered his head. "She's dying. I'm going to ask Sergeant Lizzy if I can head down to Earth. Just for a weekend. To be with her. My dad's in prison, and I don't want my mom to die alone."

Head low, Clay kept walking toward Sergeant Lizzy's trailer.

Jon and George remained behind in the shadows.

"Well, I suddenly feel like shit," Jon said.

"He's lying," said George. "The bastard is a damn liar. Don't believe him for a second."

Jon wondered. Had they truly saved Etty? Or had they started a vendetta they could not stop?

As he returned to his barracks, he wondered if Clay was truly a lost, hurting boy, dealing with tragedy at home. And how swift and horrible his revenge would be.

Chapter Twenty
Pin-Ups

Maria lay in bed, jaw clenched, tears falling.

I slit a man's throat.

She rolled over, tightened the blanket around her.

I shot a man.

She pulled a pillow over her head.

I marched a prisoner through the jungle.

She wept in the darkness.

I smelled hot iron on human flesh.

She curled up.

I found my parents dead.

In the darkness, the visions came. Bloodied faces, dead faces, all dancing around her. Finally Maria could not stand it. She rose from bed.

She shared a bamboo hut with several Kalayaan women, all fighters. The others were asleep, sprawled across straw mattresses. Some had gray hair, others were barely teens. Nobody spoke of their past. Maria wondered how many had once been farmers like her. How many had lost their families. Whoever they had been—those old lives were gone. They were Kalayaan now, and they slept with rifles in their arms.

Maria crept outside the bamboo hut. Darkness cloaked the Kalayaan village, and the palm trees rustled in the night. The chirps of insects rose in a jungle symphony.

A stern guard met Maria outside the hut. The woman wore a homespun tunic, sandals, and a straw hat—peasant clothes—but she carried a large flintlock, and her eyes were stones.

"Where are you going?" the guard asked.

"Rosa, I have to pee," Maria said.

The guard glared at her. "Not now. It's night. The *putes* are out."

"Tell that to my bladder!" Maria said.

Rosa scrutinized her, eyes hard, then nodded. "Fine. Go pee. Be quick."

Maria leaned closer, cheeks heating. "Rosa, I might have to poo poo too, so it might take a while."

"Fine, fine! Just go! Don't tell me your life story."

Maria hurried off, leaving the guards and huts behind. Her feet bent the wet grass. She almost stepped on a trapdoor and plunged onto poisoned spikes. At the last moment, she remembered to turn left at the mossy stone.

The village had a generator and a few electric lamps, but the power was off tonight, and Bahay's two moons were thin crescents. She could barely see a thing. She pulled Crisanto from her pocket. The little Santelmo glowed, illuminating her path. If not for him, she would surely have fallen into the next booby trap.

Nice of Rosa to warn me to be quick but not careful, Maria thought. *What a shrew!*

She reached the spot by the papaya trees. She paused, looked around. She saw only one guard patrolling the village perimeter, another standing in the rice paddies. They were facing the wilderness, watching for Earthlings, not sneaky little girls with heads full of questions.

Maria reached down, rolled back the grass, and exposed a hole. The entrance to the tunnels.

She crawled through the narrow tunnels, holding Crisanto. The alien shone, lighting the underground. Even with illumination, Maria could not remember the way. She made a wrong turn once, finding herself in a cistern. She climbed another tunnel, took another wrong turn, and almost activated a booby trap. She had noticed the wire just in time.

She felt trapped here underground. The walls were closing in. She could feel the weight of the world above her, and for a moment, Maria panted, struggling to calm herself. Her heart galloped. Noticing her distress, Crisanto nuzzled her cheek. She took a few deep breaths, calming down.

Slowly, she found her bearings. She passed by familiar chambers: storerooms, armories, the infirmary. In one chamber, several Kalayaan slept in hammocks, and Maria closed her hand around Crisanto, hiding his light. She crawled by quietly, not even daring to breathe.

Finally she made it there.

The interrogation room.

A guard was stationed at the door—a wiry man named Oscar, a boxer in his former life. The tunnel was a bit taller here, allowing him to stand. He grunted at Maria and gripped his rifle more tightly.

"What are you doing here, girl?"

Maria stood before him, panting. "Oscar, Oscar! It's urgent! You must go now!"

He frowned. "What? Do the Earthlings attack?"

She shook her head. "Worse! Your wife is running around, all upset! She found the dirty *banyaga* magazines you hide. The ones that show *pute* women with blond hair and no clothes."

Oscar inhaled sharply. "What? I don't have any—"

"She's telling everyone, and she says she's going to leave you, Oscar, because you are a dirty man who likes looking at naked *dibdibs*, and—"

Oscar groaned. "Dammit! Maria, here." He shoved the rifle into her hands. "Guard the prisoner. I must go to my wife."

He ran off.

Maria took a deep breath, then approached the door. It

was just a crude slat of metal, perhaps salvaged from a downed plane, bolted into the tunnel. Ragged breathing sounded behind it.

A lock dangled from a chain.

"Crisanto?" Maria said, pulling him from his pocket.

The glowing orb rose, swirled around her, and whipped back and forth, agitated.

"Crisanto…" Maria rolled her eyes and jangled the lock. "I know you can do it. Stop complaining."

The Santelmo hovered, then bobbed and squeezed into the lock. The tunnel dimmed. Crisanto's light beamed from the keyhole.

The lock clicked.

Crisanto emerged.

Maria kissed the little orb. It felt like kissing a feather. "Thank you, my dear friend."

She hesitated for a moment, fearing what she would find inside. But she had to hurry. Before Rosa and Oscar and the others discovered her ruse.

She entered the room.

He was there. David. The Earthling.

Maria gasped, covered her mouth, and tears leaped into her eyes.

She could barely believe he was alive. He still hung from the rafters, shirtless, his toes grazing the floor.

The clothing iron's marks covered him. Three ugly red scars across the chest. Another across the side of his face. He looked up at her, one eye burned shut.

"Maria," he whispered. "I didn't know. What they asked me. I didn't know…"

Her heart trembled in her chest. Fingers shaking, she drew her father's knife and cut the ropes. David fell to the floor, moaning.

"Can you walk? How about crawl?"

He nodded. "To get out of here, I can fly."

"Hurry! They don't know I'm here."

He was wounded, could barely move his arms. Perhaps they were dislocated. But he managed to crawl, the fear driving him on. Maria crawled ahead, leading the way.

"Hurry!" she whispered. "Faster! And be quiet. Don't even breathe."

They passed by the chamber of sleeping men. They crawled in darkness, not breathing. They made it by the sleepers. They passed the infirmary, the armory, the storehouse, and—

Grunting sounded behind her.

A voice echoed.

"Who goes there? Oscar, is that you?"

Maria's heart froze.

She kept crawling.

Another voice cried out. "The *pute* is gone!"

Dammit!

David gave a strangled cry. Maria grabbed his hand. "Come on, faster! Crawl!"

He was wounded, maybe dying, terrified, but David crawled onward. No, these Earthlings were not weak, not dependent on machines. That was the lie the Kalayaan told. Peel back the metal, the guerrillas said, and you find only soft baby flesh. But the Earthlings were strong. Just as strong as the Bahayans.

David pushed onward, dragging his wounded body through the tunnels. Sweat beaded on his brow, and his jaw clenched. He winced with every moment, swaying with pain, but kept crawling.

Strong, yes. But David was still very large and slow.

And the guerrillas were crawling in pursuit.

Maria inhaled sharply, fleeing as fast as she could, and David followed, and there she saw it.

The false tunnel.

Maria winced and shoved David ahead of her.

"Go, go!"

He dragged himself ahead, leaving a trail of blood. Maria glanced behind her. The guerrillas were crawling closer.

One reached for his gun.

Maria took off her shoe, hurled it into the false tunnel, and crawled after David at top speed.

A *pop*.

A blast so loud the tunnels shook.

Fire and dust raged behind her. Light washed across her. A shock wave pounded her like hammers.

She fell, and a siren rang, louder and louder, an air raid siren filling the tunnels, and she realized it was her ears ringing.

She could not move.

"Maria!"

A voice from beyond the ringing. Barely audible. Somebody grabbed her hand.

It was David. He pulled her along.

They emerged from the tunnels into a village in chaos.

"Run!" Maria whispered, clinging to his hand. She could not even hear herself. Only the ringing. "Before they get the generator going!"

They ran in darkness, crouched over. People were emerging from the huts. Shouting. Somebody was trying to kick-start the generator.

Lamps flickered on, casting yellow light across the village.

Maria and David leaped into the papaya grove.

They rushed between the fruit trees and vanished into the jungle.

For a long time, they traveled in darkness. Maria dared not even take Crisanto from her pocket. The Kalayaan would see the light, know to follow. She and David moved blindly, hitting trees, boulders, stumbling, rising and moving onward.

Maria banged her head against a branch.

She fell. She hit a stone.

She tried to run onward, stumbled again. She shivered. The trees coiled all around her, and branches grabbed her like cruel hands, and shouts rose in the distance. The Kalayaan was following.

I can't escape. It's too dark. I'm too afraid.

Crisanto burst from her pocket and shone.

"Crisanto, no!" she whispered.

He whisked away, and Maria dared not breathe, sure that the Kalayaan would see.

And then they rose.

A dozen or more.

Orbs of light.

Dim. Barely glowing at all. But enough for the Kalayaan to detect.

"Santelmos!" the men shouted. "Santelmos will show us the way to the traitor."

The orbs of light scattered, each flying in a different direction. And the Kalayaan followed.

Maria understood. "Our friends are drawing them off."

David's eyes widened. "Are those… the aliens? Saint Elmo's Fire?" His eyes shone. "The army told us they were evil. But they're beautiful. They're so beautiful."

Crisanto dimmed. He became so dim Maria could barely discern him. A mere hint of gray in the night. The Kalayaan would not see him this way. He hovered forward, and Maria and David followed.

Crisanto shone too dimly to illuminate the trees, but enough to guide them around trunks, over roots, and under branches. The rainforest, which Maria had always feared, became almost beautiful in the darkness, and she could hear music in the rustling leaves, the creaking branches, and the scattering soil beneath her feet.

The rainforest was always different, she reflected. Sometimes imposing and alien, a den for monsters. Sometimes a torturous bog full of insects and weariness and hunger. And sometimes, like tonight, it was like a dark ocean, beautiful and full of secrets.

The jungle seemed so vast, so eternal, that it was easy to forget: Bahay was a world of islands.

And Maria reached the sea.

She emerged from the trees onto a sandy shore. Bahay's two moons shone above, one deep blue, the other white. Both were narrow crescents, barely visible from inland, but above the sea they shone brightly. Beads of light danced on the waves. The smell of salt filled her nostrils, and a breeze tousled her hair. A memory filled her: going to the beach with her parents as a little girl. And this time she did not cry at the memory. She smiled and wiggled her toes in the sand. She was still missing one shoe.

David walked across the sand, fell to his knees, and wept.

Maria knelt beside him and embraced him. He flinched. His wounds still hurt. Maria wished she could heal him.

"I'm sorry, David," she whispered. "I'm so sorry. I was so afraid."

He looked at her with one eye. The iron had ravaged half his face, sealing one eye shut. "And I'm sorry too."

"For what?" she said.

"For what happened to your village. For what we did. For coming to your world. Maria, I… I killed people. I don't know how many."

She studied him. Just a boy, scared, missing home. But yes, also an Earthling. A killer. An enemy.

Terror filled Maria.

And I freed him. I threw everything away, and I freed a killer.

What have I done?

"David, walk north along the beach. Walk all night, and you'll reach it. An Earthling base. We've seen it from the mountains. And when you get there, David, tell them about me. Tell them that a village girl saved you. That we're not evil. That we just want to be free. And if you ever return to Earth, tell them of Maria de la Cruz. Tell them that a slit showed you mercy."

He reached out to touch her cheek. "You're not a slit. And I'm not a *pute*. We're both human. Goodbye, Maria de la Cruz."

He limped along the beach, leaving her behind.

Maria knew she could never return to the Kalayaan. They would kill her for what she had done. Nor could she go with David. The Earthlings would treat her no better.

She held out her hand, and Crisanto landed there.

"It's just me and you, old friend," she said. "The north is burning. Our village is gone. We're alone."

Crisanto bobbed on her hand, glowing bright, comforting her. Maria sat on the sand, her feet in the water, gazing up at the twin moons.

Chapter Twenty-One
Plastic Jungle

"Behold, troops!" Sergeant Lizzy smiled crookedly. "Oakeshott Mark 3s. The best damn assault rifles in the galaxy. And your new best friends."

The recruits stood in an asphalt courtyard. Other troops ran along the curving walls to their left and right, singing marching songs. Along the ceiling far above, troops were racing through an obstacle course. Every platoon here was in a different circle of hell.

"Sweet gun!" Etty said, eying the assault rifles. Her large green eyes grew even larger. "Beauties."

George winced. "I don't like guns. They scare me."

Jon looked at the pile of weapons. He wasn't scared of guns like George. Nor did he find them beautiful. Mostly, he thought about his brother's gun back home. Paul's name was engraved in the stock.

Will my rifle someday rest beside his? Jon wondered. *All that remains of two brothers?*

"Yes, ladies and gentlemen, the Oakeshott Mark 3!" Lizzy continued. "Named after Ewart Oakeshott, an ancient weapons expert. And what a weapon this is! She's a sweet bullpup assault rifle, selecting between semi-automatic and full automatic mode. Bullpup means your magazine of bullets go in behind the trigger. That gives the Oaky an extra-long barrel for increased accuracy."

"What, a magazine?" rose a voice from the platoon. It was Bucky, the girl with buckteeth. "You mean *bullets*? Like from last century? Don't she shoot plasma bolts? My brother is a lieutenant, and he always shoots plasma."

Lizzy raised her eyebrow. "Oh, is that so, your brother's a fancy officer? La dee da." The sergeant's face flushed red, and her voice rose to a shout. "Well, I ain't no blue-blooded officer, and neither are you sorry lot! So shut the hell up, recruit, before I jam this rifle up your ass, pull the trigger, and show you how mean bullets can be."

Bucky gulped. "Yes, Commander! Sorry, Commander."

Lizzy turned away from her. She swept her eyes across the platoon.

"Yes, bullets! The Oakeshott fires good old classic bullets! No plasma charges, no lasers, none of that junk. Good old bullets, just like grandma used to make. They won the Alien Wars a century ago, and they sure as hell will beat the slits today."

Clay whooped and rushed toward the guns. "That's right! We're going to slaughter those fucking slits!" He puffed out his broad chest. "I used to fire Oakys all the time at home." He scoffed at Jon. "When you fire a gun for the first time, ballerina, try not to piss yourself."

"All right, enough!" Lizzy barked. "Get into formation, Hagen. Don't make me break your dick this time."

Clay snorted. "It would take a sledgehammer."

Lizzy raised her whip. "Want to test that hypothesis?"

Clay recoiled.

A few recruits laughed. Clay grew very pale and very silent. His eye twitched, and a vein bulged on his neck. He glared at Lizzy, opened his mouth, but she stared him down. He turned away, muttered a curse, and stepped in line. He formed a fireteam with Bucky and Ugly Hank, a hulking kid with a scar across his head and bad acne.

"Good one, boss!" Bucky said. She grinned, and the fluorescent lights flashed across her thick glasses. "You sure showed her."

"Shut up, shut up!" Clay hissed at her.

"Hey, Clay!" Etty said, leaning toward the other fireteam. "You don't have to worry. Your dick is safe from Sergeant Lizzy. It's much too small for anyone to find."

Clay growled and prepared to attack. But then Lizzy swung her whip overhead like a lasso. Electric bolts rained onto the platoon. Even Jon took a hit and grunted. His battlesuit could perhaps protect him from bullets, but it didn't do much to stop electricity. Soon Lizzy had the entire platoon giving her thirty push-ups. Etty also earned latrine duty for the night.

"All right, worms!" Sergeant Lizzy said. "Come up and get your guns. It's time to learn how to kill."

They stepped up to grab their Oakeshotts. They weren't the most elegant weapons. Not graceful like the plasma rifles you saw on military parades or in action movies. Oakys were crude weapons, bulky, with squat stocks. They were also clearly second hand, scratched, the muzzled charred.

Jon knelt and reached for an Oakeshott that looked in decent shape.

"Out of the way, ballerina." A boot kicked him down. "That one's mine."

Jon leaped to his feet and found himself facing Clay. The brute lifted the rifle, smirked at Jon, and turned the muzzle toward him.

For a split second, Clay was pointing the gun right at Jon's chest.

"Boom!" Clay said, then laughed. "Pissed your pants?"

Jon glanced toward Sergeant Lizzy, but she had her back to them.

Clay snorted. "Gonna tell on me to your mommy?"

But he lowered the gun. And Jon remained silent. He didn't feel like involving the sergeant. That could result in more push-ups, runs around the base, or even broken bones. Lizzy's wrath was like a wildfire. It was likely to burn anyone who got close.

During the brief altercation, the other recruits had grabbed their own assault rifles. That left only one for Jon to choose. It was the worst gun, the barrel scratched, the handle cracked, and the stock engraved with a certain part of the male anatomy.

Jon tried to hide the rude etching, but Clay noticed and snickered.

"You enjoy holding dick, don't you?" the brute said.

"It's bigger than yours!" Etty said.

George approached the group. The Oakeshotts were large, heavy guns, but George made his seem as small as a pistol.

"Here, have mine, Jon." The giant handed him his rifle, which looked relatively new. "I'll take yours."

Jon patted his friend's arm. "Thanks, buddy, but it's all right." He hefted his dented and defaced weapon. "I bet this girl killed the most slits in the jungle. All worked in. She's perfect."

He clutched the gun, and a sudden feeling of power surged through him. Jon imagined himself in the jungle, fighting the enemy. Firing his assault rifle. Roaring. Filling the bastards with bullets.

For what you did to Paul.

His grip tightened, and Jon sneered. He would not be weak. He would not be a victim. He would not die like Paul.

I'll kill you all.

The daydream changed, and he remembered mismatched eyes. One blue, one brown. He remembered soft lips.

Come home pure or come home dead, Kaelyn had told him.

I can't, Jon thought. *Because the pure die. The weak die. The artists die. I must become a killer. Because I refuse to die.*

And he wondered if that was not another sort of death. The death of the artist inside him. Of the musician. The boy he had been.

Then let the boy die, Jon thought. *Let me become a killer. I'm sorry, Kaelyn. I'm sorry.*

"Hey, Jon, you all right, buddy?" George said. "Come on! Lizzy will be pissed if you straggle behind."

Jon blinked, returning to the present. Sergeant Lizzy was leading the platoon across the base. The soldiers were marching in single file. Etty was marching with them, gesturing madly for Jon and George. They hurried to catch up.

Lizzy's Lions marched through the base, following their sergeant. Bucky walked in front, holding the platoon's banner. The gangly girl marched briskly, knees rising to her chest, her frizzy hair flying every which way. She chanted: "Left, right, left, right!"

Jon wasn't surprised that Bucky had become the flagbearer. The girl seemed to love authority, never missing a chance to kiss up to Clay, Lizzy, even the damn cooks in the mess hall.

We should be called Lizzy's Loonies, Jon thought. *We're all crazy here.*

* * * * *

The platoon marched by an armory, a few barracks, a yard where soldiers trained in Krav Maga, and an obstacle course. As they were walking along Roma's inner curve, Jon noticed an airlock opening at the cylinder's end. Shuttles flew in, and new recruits emerged into the station. They blinked, stumbling around like newly-hatched chicks, trying to form rank as their new sergeant shouted and shocked them.

"Fresh meat," George muttered.

"That was us not long ago," Jon said. "But it seems like forever. We're old hands now."

"A day in the army lasts a year. That's just science." George pulled out another tube of battle paste. "That's why I'm always hungry."

They approached a concrete building, the largest Jon had seen inside Roma so far. It was a crude edifice, rust leaking down its craggy walls. A sign hung above a gateway: ROMA FIREARMS TRAINING.

Jon had been to a firing range a few years ago. His uncle had taken him and Paul. He was looking forward to the exercise. He wasn't much of a marksman or gun nut. But a nice, quiet firing range sure as hell beat obstacle courses, runs around the base, or endless push ups and sit ups. Okay, it probably wouldn't be *quiet*. But beggars couldn't be choosers.

"All right, platoon!" Lizzy shouted. "Form rank!"

The platoon formed into fireteams. They stood at attention, three by three.

Only days ago, we stumbled and tripped over our own feet, Jon thought. *Now we can form rank like pros. Goddamn. Lizzy broke us into a million pieces. And now she's putting us together.*

He found himself wondering about the sergeant. How had she lost her hand? Had she seen battle? Fought slits in the jungle? When she wasn't brutalizing recruits, was she as mean? Or was this all an act? Did she have hobbies, loved ones, a personality beyond always shouting and whipping?

Jon would never know. Whoever they had been outside? Those people were dead. He was no longer Jon the musician. He was Jon the soldier now. They all had sob stories, he supposed. Jon had lost his brother. George had suffered his brain tumor and grown to prodigious size. Etty had grown up in a war zone. Clay had been to prison. Bucky, no doubt, struggled with low self-esteem. Every soldier here, Jon realized, had fought some battle on the outside. Had likes, dislikes, loved ones, enemies, a real personality.

But not in here. In here they weren't human. In here they were machines. Killers. That was all.

Come home pure or come home dead.

Maybe there was no more home. Jon had only been here for a day, and he already felt like a different man. If he ever went back to Lindenville, perhaps that town would no longer feel like home. Because he was not the same person.

If basic training broke me so bad, I can only imagine what actual war does to a man, he thought.

"Platoon!" Lizzy barked, tearing Jon away from his thoughts. The sergeant marched past the platoon, cracking her whip. "You will now train to use your assault rifles. I will hand every recruit three magazines of rubber bullets. This is your last day using rubber! Tomorrow you will train with live ammo. For now, I'm going easy on you. Every fireteam, in turn—step up, take your bullets, and go kill some fucking slits!"

Jon frowned. Kill slits? This was just a training base orbiting Earth. What was she talking about?

"Taylor!" the sergeant barked. "Lead your fireteam inside. Then make your way to the back door. Go!"

On the march here, Jon's team had been last in line. He supposed this was the punishment.

"Yes, Commander!" he barked.

He approached the concrete building. George and Etty walked behind him.

He stepped through the doorway, expecting to find an old-fashioned firing range… and found himself in the jungle.

The door slammed shut behind him.

Jon felt the blood drain from his face.

Here, inside the concrete box, the army had recreated Bahay.

Trees rose everywhere, branches coiling, hiding the ceiling. Roots spread across the floor like serpents. Ivy hung from the branches and curtains of moss swayed. A bird cawed, and what sounded like a monkey shrieked among the branches. Lightning flashed, thunder boomed, and rain fell.

There was only one thing missing. The smell.

They're fake, Jon realized. *Just props. A plastic jungle.*

It was hyper-realistic. Jon had to pause for a moment, to admire the artistry.

Then figures rose among the branches and opened fire.

A bullet pinged off Jon's helmet, ringing his head like a bell. He ran, leaped behind a tree. Etty and George ran with him. The girl dived for cover, as fast as a gazelle fleeing a predator. The giant was slower. A bullet slammed into him, knocking off an armored plate. George howled and dived for cover.

Jon crouched behind a tree and peeked around the trunk.

Bahayans!

They wore green tunics and straw hats, blending into the jungle. They were hideous creatures. The faces were grotesque, the skin sallow. They barely had eyes, just narrow slits. Their mouths were locked in animal snarls. Fung Shu mustaches hung down past their chins. Humans? No, they could not be humans. Clearly these were more goblins than men.

"Die, bastards!" Etty shouted and opened fire. Her bullets slammed into the figures above.

One of them crashed down beside Jon. The dead Bahayan stared up at him.

A doll. Nothing but a doll with glass eyes.

Etty kept firing, taking out two more Bahayans, and the barrage from the trees died.

The fireteam regrouped. George was limping and mewling, holding onto his wounded leg. Etty beamed.

"I got three!" She grinned and raised three fingers. "Three

kills for me! How many for you guys?"

Jon grumbled, "None yet. Come on. Lizzy said we need to reach the end of the building. It's a long way."

Etty's grin widened. "I *like* it here."

They kept advancing among the trees. Ferns rustled around them. A waterfall cascaded nearby. The plastic brush was so thick every step was a struggle. A bird fluttered overhead, a doll on a wire.

"See any more slits?" Jon said.

"I can barely see a meter ahead," George said. "The brush is so thick."

Jon took another step, and—

He was falling.

He screamed and reached up, but there was nothing to grab.

He landed in a pit, crushing dry bones. A skull rolled.

Eyes flashed. Teeth shone. Somebody was here with Jon—in the pit!

A demonic figure lashed a knife, eyes ablaze.

Jon sidestepped, swung his rifle, and knocked his assailant down. He shoved his muzzle at his enemy and pulled the trigger.

A *boom* filled the pit. Jon's ears rang and his head spun.

A doll. He forced a deep breath. Just another doll.

He heard more bullets above. More screams.

"George!" Jon shouted from the pit. "Etty!"

They were screaming. Firing their guns.

"They're in the trees!" George shouted above.

"I'll take care of 'em!" came Etty's voice. "Get Jon out!"

Gunfire kept rattling. George leaned over the pit. It was a deep chasm, too deep for Jon to climb out of. But George had long arms, and he gripped Jon mightily and yanked him out.

Jon stumbled into the forest, breathing raggedly. Everything hurt, and his ears kept ringing.

More bullets flew from the trees.

One slammed into Jon's shoulder, denting the battlesuit, nearly knocking him back into the pit. He screamed.

He looked up, saw them there. Two snipers among the branches. He opened fire, roaring, knocking them down. Etty was firing nearby, sweeping her bullets in an arc of suppressive fire.

"Come on!" Jon shouted. "Run!"

Behind them, they heard more fireteams enter the gauntlet. More screams rose and bullets shrieked.

Jon and his fireteam ran.

The enemy was everywhere.

They fired from the trees. They swung on vines. Their bullets streaked. Another bullet hit Jon, this time on the thigh. Without a battlesuit, it probably would have broken his femur. It still hurt like a bitch, and it left an ugly dent in the suit's armored plate. He limped onward, firing, shouting. Another doll dropped down. George and Etty charged at his sides, screaming, spraying bullets into the jungle. The rest of the platoon ran behind, several meters separating each fireteam.

The dolls' faces spun around Jon, grotesque creatures, buck teeth jutting out, narrow eyes inhumanly thin. Jon was running through some nightmare forest from the darkest of fairy tales, and the goblins danced all around.

Here they were. The monsters who had killed his brother. The creatures who had murdered tens of thousands of Earthlings and counting. Traitors. Alien-lovers. Slits.

Sub-humans.

Jon screamed as he fired his gun, emptying magazine after magazine, and he was no longer just firing on dolls. He was firing on the bastards who took Paul.

"Fuck you, slits!" Jon screamed, tears falling, rage pulsing. "I'll kill you all! I'll kill every last fucking one of y—"

"Jon!"

A slit leaped up before him, a creature with shining green eyes, and Jon fired his gun.

His bullet slammed into the slit's chest.

The creature stared at him, eyes wide, frozen for a second.

Etty.

It was Etty.

"Etty!" he cried.

She gasped for air, seemed to be choking. He had hit her right in the sternum.

Rubber bullets wouldn't kill you—not if you wore a battlesuit. But they left bad bruises, could even crack bones. A blow to the solar plexus, right between two armored plates, was the worst place to hit.

Etty collapsed, mouth open, finding no air.

Jon knelt beside her.

"Etty! Oh God. Etty, can you breathe?"

She finally managed to draw in some air. Jon held her in his arms. His hands shook. Had he broken her sternum or ribs? Would she die in his arms?

"Jon," she whispered. "Fuck… you…"

Jon couldn't help it. He laughed. And Etty managed to laugh too. And Jon noticed that they had reached the end of the gauntlet. The back door was just beyond a few more trees, and—

A boot slammed into Jon's side.

He fell onto his back.

A shadow loomed over him. A soldier.

Far-set blue eyes gleamed with hatred.

Clay aimed his rifle at Jon's chest.

It was set to automatic.

"Tried to blackmail me, didn't you?" Clay said.

"Clay, wait—" Jon began.

"Die, slit." Clay opened fire.

A stream of rubber bullets slammed into Jon's chest.

They dented his battlesuit's armored plates. Then cracked them. The pain was so bad Jon couldn't even scream. And the bullets wouldn't stop.

The agony plowed through him. A magazine of furious pain crashed through his body, and there was nothing but darkness, ringing in his ears, diabolic laughter… and then silence.

Chapter Twenty-Two
A Slow Death

She fled him.

His betrothed. The woman he loved. Sweet Maria.

She betrayed him!

Ernesto stood in the village, tossed back his head, and howled.

"Maria!" he shouted. "Maria!"

Birds fled and the sky itself shook.

She had freed the *pute* prisoner. She had killed a man in the tunnels, activating the booby trap. She had betrayed him and her people.

"I will find you, Maria," Ernesto vowed, fists shaking. "I will break you."

"Sir." One of his guerrillas approached him. She was a young woman, not yet twenty, named Floribeth. "Sir Ernesto, maybe you should let her go. Maria will probably die in the jungle. She can't survive there alone. Why waste time chasing her when we have Earthlings to kill?"

Ernesto spun toward the woman.

He sneered, reached out, and grabbed her.

Floribeth winced, tried to escape. He held her fast.

"You're her friend, aren't you?" he said.

Floribeth struggled in his grip. "Sir! No, sir. I'm friend only to the cause!"

"Liar!" Ernesto shook her. "I saw you two skulking together in the jungle. Claiming you're going off to pee together?

To connive! To plan your betrayal!"

Floribeth's eyes flashed. "I'm no traitor! I fight for Bahay. I've killed for Bahay! I—"

She gasped as Ernesto's knife entered her belly.

He dragged the blade across her, carving her open like a roast pig.

She tried to scream. But blood filled her mouth. She could only gurgle.

Ernesto released her, and she fell to the ground. Her entrails were slipping through her cut. She gasped for air, placed her hands on her wounds, and trembled. Pathetic traitor.

The other guerrillas were watching. All across the village, they watched. Ernesto spun in a circle, bloody knife in hand.

"Anyone who dares give her a mercy death will suffer the same fate!" Ernesto shouted. "Anyone who tries to heal her will burn! Leave her here. Leave her to die."

It could take all day, Ernesto knew. Maybe even two days. And every moment would be an eternity of agony. Good. Traitors deserved to suffer.

As the traitor lay bleeding, praying, dying, Ernesto gathered his warriors. Fifteen soldiers, battle-hardened, eager for blood.

They left the village. They entered the jungle. Maria had learned how to hide her tracks. But Ernesto knew he could find her.

"You will be mine again, Maria," he whispered between clenched teeth. "I love you. You are mine. You will be my wife. Or you will envy Floribeth."

Chapter Twenty-Three
War Stinks

Jon floated in a void.

There was no pain here. There was no sound. There was barely any self. He was consciousness in the abyss.

Yet as he floated, he beheld coiling vines in the darkness. Branches. Twisting boughs. Little crawling things. There was no forest floor, and no canopy, merely an eternity of twisting, braiding strands of wood, black and deep purple and shimmering dark green. Luminous beings clung to the branches like mold, and pollen floated, guiding his way.

He traveled deeper into the abyss, floating past ancient pines, their needles poking him a thousand times. Branches hit his chest. Again and again. Pounding him. Breaking him. And the luminous mold stared at him with a billion, billion microscopic faces.

Jon.

A wind through the void. A moan.

Jon, I'm here.

"Paul?" Jon whispered.

Jon.

"Paul! I'm here! Where are you?"

Jon found no ground for his feet. He tried to fly through the forest, to navigate among the coiling branches, to find his brother. But he could only move slowly. And every pine he passed led to an eternity of more trees.

Jon.

"I'm trying to find you!"

He beat his arms, swimming through the glimmering pollen, seeking his brother, seeing nothing but the forest. He was trapped. Lost. A prisoner in the labyrinth of old things.

"Jon. I'm here."

Branches wrapped around his arms with wooden fingers. The trees were holding him. Speaking to him.

"Jon?"

The pollen brightened like a thousand chandelier lights, and Jon opened his eyes, and he gasped for air.

A face materialized before him. A wide, honest face, freckled and topped with red hair.

"George?" Jon whispered, blinking in confusion. "What happened? I was dreaming…"

"Oh, we know," George said. "You were talking in your sleep. Waving your arms around like a maniac too. Almost knocked over the nightstand."

Jon looked around him. He was lying in an infirmary, a cluttered little room. Several wounded recruits shared the room with him, lying on cots. A poster hung on a concrete wall, showing a cat with a bandaged leg and thermometer in its mouth. Through the window, Jon could see the distant curving wall of Roma Station. Troops were running across it. Jon thought he'd never get used to living inside a tube where people walked on walls and ceilings.

He propped himself onto his elbows and groaned. He looked down at his chest, found it wrapped in bandages. "Ow. I feel like an elephant stomped on my chest. And you were riding it, you giant ginger."

"Well, you *should* feel that way," George said. "The doc says you cracked three ribs. And cracked your sternum. Not to mention a ton of bruises. Doctor says you were lucky. Your broken ribs could have pierced your organs. They patched it all up while you were sleeping. You should be fine in a few days. Ain't modern medicine great?"

Jon rubbed his eyes. "The last thing I remember was a deranged troglodyte in the forest, firing his gun at me. No, wait." He blinked and tilted his head. "More is coming back. Medics carrying me here. A doctor with round glasses. It's all fuzzy." He bolted up. "Etty! I shot her with a rubber bullet! How is—"

"Out of my way, out of my way!"

Etty's voice boomed from the hallway. Clattering and curses followed. Etty came barreling down the hallway, elbowing nurses and medics aside, overturning their trays of medical supplies.

"Move it, my friend is up!" Etty said, shoving her way forward, and barged into the room.

The young Israeli ran toward the bed, bumping into another patient's IV stand, nearly overturning it.

"Sorry, sorry!" she said.

"Etty, try not to destroy the entire space station on your way to my bed," Jon said.

"But I want to destroy it all!" Etty leaped onto his bed and gave him a crushing hug. "Because you got hurt here. How are you? Feeling any better?"

Jon croaked. "Etty! Etty, you maniac! You're crushing me. Ease up!"

She released him. "Sorry! I'm an aggressive hugger. I was worried about you. I thought that jerk Clay had *killed* you."

"Forget about Clay," Jon said. "Etty, I'm so sorry. For shooting you. How are you?"

She waved dismissively. "I'm fine. Your measly little rubber bullet couldn't hurt me." She cupped her breast. "Luckily I got natural padding." She winced. "The bruise is ugly, though. Purple and yellow. Looks a bit like a Rothko."

Sitting beside them, George gasped. "You shot her in the

tit!"

Jon felt his cheeks flush. "I'm sorry."

The girl only laughed and mussed his hair. "Forget about it, dumbass." She slammed her fist into his chest—right where Clay had cracked his ribs.

"Ow!" Jon cried out.

Etty grinned and kissed his cheek. "Sorry. Needed some payback."

"You lunatic!" Jon groaned and fell back onto the bed. "At least I got the day off from boot camp. Clay hammering my chest with bullets is only slightly more painful than Lizzy's whip."

He expected his friends to laugh. But George and Etty went dead serious.

"Jon…" George twisted his fingers.

Jon frowned. "What is it? Tell me, buddy."

The giant winced. "Lizzy said that… Ah, hell. You and Clay both."

"*What?*" Jon rose onto his elbows again.

"I know it's not fair, but…" George wiped sweat off his brow. "After what happened in the plastic jungle, you both have to stand court martial. Today. And Jon… they might even toss you both out of the army."

Those words hit Jon harder than Etty's fist.

* * * * *

Jon shuffled down the corridor, still in lots of pain. The doctors had injected his ribs with InstaHeal foam, using his own stem cells to regrow the bones. It was cutting-edge technology, unavailable during the horrible Alien Wars, marketed as a miracle cure. Jon doubted it worked quite as well as advertised. Every breath was a saw inside him.

"Come on, Taylor," Sergeant Lizzy said. "Fuck the pain and walk faster. We haven't got all day."

Amazingly, the sergeant wasn't screaming, kicking, or whipping him. She was speaking almost normally.

Jon looked at her. Lizzy was accompanying him down the corridor. It was only the two of them here. It was almost jarring to see the sergeant in a normal environment, not hovering over a suffering platoon, meting out punishment. Lizzy still wore her battlesuit, an assault rifle hung across her back, and her prosthetic hand looked as mean as ever, each finger a claw. But Jon could see her as a person now. A young woman. Only a few years older than him.

She's an actual human.

She was tall, as tall as him, and her braid was golden and long. He noticed freckles on her nose. She was quite pretty, actually.

What's your story, Lizzy? How did an All-American girl become a one-handed drill sergeant who breaks the bones of her recruits?

"Problem, Taylor?" Lizzy said.

Jon realized he was staring. He hurriedly looked away. "Sorry, Commander."

He should worry less about her, more about himself now. He was heading toward his court martial.

Goddammit, I've been in the army for just a few weeks, and I'm already being court martialed, Jon thought. *Some war hero I'm turning out to be.*

He imagined being dishonorably discharged. Sent back home in disgrace. He thought of his father, silent, disappointed. Jon had never wanted to join the army. He had been drafted. But dammit, Paul was dead, and Jon was here now, and he would avenge his brother. He would defend his planet. He would see this through.

Those were his desires now. And they could all be broken like his ribs.

The greatest heroes never wanted to go on their journeys, Jon thought. *The call to adventure summoned them. They simply had the courage to accept the call. But my own journey might be ending before it barely began.*

It was a long walk down the corridor. The longest walk of his life.

Finally they reached a door and stopped.

Lizzy turned toward him.

"Taylor, you're about to meet Lieutenant Carter, your platoon's commanding officer."

"Our platoon has a commanding officer?" Jon frowned. "I thought you were our commander, Sergeant."

"I'm not an officer, recruit. I'm your drill sergeant. My job is to turn you into warriors. *His* job is to lead you. Normally, recruits don't meet their commanding officer this early. Not before I've broken them in a bit. We're going to make an exception in your case. When you face Lieutenant Carter, stand at attention and salute. Address him as sir, and answer all his questions truthfully. Understood?"

Jon nodded. "Yes, Commander."

The different ranks still confused Jon. But he was slowly learning. There were two military branches in the Human Defense Force, he understood. Most soldiers were like him. Enlisted men and women. Some had volunteered. Most had received draft notices in little brown envelopes. They went through boot camp, became privates, then corporals, and some—like Lizzy—even became sergeants. They served as grunts, bombers, gunners, drill instructors, and a host of other jobs, some rising high in the NCO ranks. They were the backbone of the Human Defense Force.

But officers were different. Officers were a class above. They went to military academies, sometimes for years, where they studied military history, tactics, and leadership. In the army, they began as ensigns, could then become lieutenants, captains, majors, even colonels. The most successful officers could even become generals. Jon had no officers in his family. Nobody he knew had ever gone to a prestigious military academy, ever commanded troops in battle. In fact, Jon had never even seen an officer up close. To him, they were as alien as the Santelmos.

We're the grunts, even Lizzy, Jon thought. *Trained to kill and be killed. The officers are the masters of life and death.*

Lizzy knocked on the door. "Sergeant Lizzy Pascal reporting!"

For a moment—silence.

Then, from inside, a voice answered, "Come in, Sergeant."

Lizzy opened the door, stepped into an office, stood at attention, and saluted. Jon entered behind her, snapped his heels together, and saluted too.

First salute and first court martial on the same day, he thought. *And maybe it's my last day.*

An officer stood behind a desk, gazing out a window. His back was turned to Jon, but Jon could see the insignia on his shoulders. Two golden bars on each shoulder strap. A lieutenant.

The officer spoke again, still facing the window. "I've always thought the plastic jungle is a bad exercise. It's nothing like real warfare. It's missing the smell."

"The smell of the forest, sir," Jon said. "I noticed that too."

Lizzy glared at him. "Soldier! The lieutenant did not ask your opinion."

The officer stood still for a moment. Slowly, he turned to face Jon. He was of average height, average build, graceful and neat. His skin was dark brown, and his black hair was buzzed down to stubble. At first glance, he seemed almost mild, harmless. The face of your friendly neighborhood mailman or pharmacist, not a warrior.

But then Jon noticed his eyes.

There was deep strength in Lieutenant Carter's eyes. There were old ghosts. There was determination, honor, and quiet courage.

"I don't mean the smell of the forest," Carter said softly. "I mean the stench of battle. The coppery blood. The stench of men shitting themselves in fear. Of entrails spilling. The stench of *death.* The plastic jungle is just that. Plastic. Sanitized. War stinks, recruit. On Bahay…" Carter stared out the window again. "At Bahay the stench of death never leaves."

Jon couldn't help but shudder.

Cheery fellow, he thought.

"Sir, I'm sorry for what happened," Jon said. "For shooting Etty. I was all riled up, and thought she was a slit, and…"

He gulped, unable to say more.

Lieutenant Carter turned back toward him. "Taylor, all platoons have accidents in the plastic jungle. That's why you use rubber bullets until you're used to the terrain. Some incidents of friendly fire are expected. And they're designed to hurt. Even to break bones. Pain is the best teacher. I'm disappointed that you shot Etty from point blank, but not surprised. I'm more concerned about what happened with Recruit Hagen."

"Clay Hagen is a maniac!" Jon blurted out, unable to stop himself. "Sir. With all due respect. We're from the same small town. I know him. He killed a man on Earth, spent time in prison, and he's always hated me, even back on Earth, and—"

"Recruit!" Lizzy barked. "The lieutenant did not ask for your life story."

Jon fell silent. He stiffened, facing his officer. "Sorry, sir."

Carter stepped around his desk and approached Jon. Again, Jon was struck by how phlegmatic he seemed. Carter didn't shout. Didn't get mad. Wasn't any taller or stronger than Jon. At a glance—a perfectly normal, mild-mannered man. But when those eyes fixed on Jon, he saw deep chasms of fire.

"Taylor, what if you must serve with Clay in the jungle? The real jungle. What if his life depended on you? And yours on him? What if you fought side by side with the enemy closing in? Can I trust you then, Taylor? I must know now. If you cannot resolve your feud with Recruit Hagen, you could put my entire platoon at risk."

Jon stiffened. "Sir, I will do whatever I can to defeat the enemy. I *will* defeat the enemy. That is my only objective. Will Clay Hagen and I ever be friends? No. But we're both Earthlings. We're both on the same side. I understand that. You can count on me, sir. Don't discharge me from the army. I can do this. I…" He hesitated, then plowed on. "My brother died on Bahay, sir. Corporal Paul Taylor." His eyes dampened. "I will finish what he started."

The lieutenant's eyes softened just the slightest. He placed a hand on Jon's shoulder. "Paul was a good man."

Jon blinked. "You knew him, sir?"

"He was the best man in my platoon. And a good friend." The lieutenant nodded. "You aren't in any trouble, Jon Taylor. I'll mention this on your record, of course. And I'll be watching you closely. Now get out there, rejoin your platoon, and continue your training."

Jon's head spun. The lieutenant knew his brother? Carter had fought with Paul? Had Carter seen him die? Questions wheeled through his mind, all jamming in his throat.

"Recruit!" Lizzy barked. "Dismissed!"

Jon blinked, gulped, and saluted his officer. He stumbled out of the office, feeling dizzy. And it wasn't his injuries this time.

In a daze, he stepped outside and approached his platoon. They were sitting in a circle, cleaning their Oakeshotts. George was grumbling, struggling with his thick fingers to separate the components of his rifle. Etty was singing a jaunty tune in Hebrew, bobbing her head, and oiling her gun's components.

"Hey, George, want me to clean your gun for you?" Etty said, slamming her gun pieces together. "I'm done with mine."

"No, I can do it. I just… need to…" The firing pin slipped from George's fingers and flew across the courtyard. "Dammit! These pieces are so tiny. Why don't they—oh hi, Jon."

Etty spun around, her eyes widened, and she leaped up. "Jon, you're back! Are you still in the army?"

He blinked at his friends, still feeling dazed.

My lieutenant knew my brother. They fought together. Paul was here along this very path before me.

He nodded. "Yes. I'm still in the army."

I'm still alive. And his ghost is with me. And I saw countless ghosts in Carter's eyes.

"Excellent!" Etty said. "We missed you, Jon Jon. Just don't shoot me again."

Jon sat between them. George, his oldest friend. Etty, his newest friend. Both dear to him. Both people he loved.

And soon, we'll be there, he thought. *In the real jungle. We'll smell the stench of war. We'll fight where Paul died.*

A shiver ran through him, and that night, he was in that dark forest again, hovering with no ground beneath his feet, lost in the mist.

Chapter Twenty-Four
Carter's War

Sergeant Lizzy Pascal stood in the office, fists clenched.

"Carter." She had to force in a breath, to keep her voice calm. "I can understand keeping Jon Taylor. But the other one? Clay Hagen? I can't believe you just gave him a slap on the wrist." She shook her head in disgust. "With all due respect, Hagan deserves time behind bars, then a dishonorable discharge."

The brutish recruit had just left the office moments ago, grinning in triumph. Lizzy was still reeling. She had been sure—sure!—that the psychopath would end up in prison. Shooting Jon like that in the chest? A full magazine? And with Jon already down? Lizzy was tempted to run outside, catch Clay, and break his other arm. Then his spine.

She took another deep breath, forcing herself to calm down. It was the anger. The same damn anger again. Not the show she put on for her recruits, screaming insults at them. No, that was only theater. Lizzy was now feeling the *real* anger. The deep, simmering, horrible kind that burned you from within. That demon had been coiling inside her since Bahay.

Her commanding officer was gazing through the window at the platoon. The recruits were sitting in the yard, polishing their guns. For a long moment, Lieutenant Carter was still and silent.

Finally he spoke, voice soft, as if speaking to some spirit only he could see. "Do you remember Corporal Campbell?"

Lizzy nodded. "Of course. He commanded Second Squad on Bahay."

"He came from a rough background," Carter said. "His dad would beat him. His uncle would molest him. The kid ended up burglarizing shops, stealing cars, dealing drugs… total mess. Hopeless. Probably never belonged in the army," His voice dropped even lower. "Yet one day, in the jungle, he saved my life. Your life too. He kept going back into the fire, pulling soldiers out. On Earth, he'd have ended up in prison. In the jungle, he became a hero."

Lizzy rolled her eyes. "I seriously doubt Clay Fucking Hagen is built of the same material. Hagen isn't just a troubled youth who needs a hug. He's rotten through and through. And you treated him with silk gloves." She sneered. "He shot Taylor in the chest, Cart. With a full magazine of rubber bullets. On purpose. He could have killed him. Hell, it's a miracle Jon survived."

Carter sighed. He poured himself a cup of coffee, held the thermos out to Lizzy, but she shook her head. Carter took a sip, still standing by the window.

"Mmm. It's good coffee." He lowered the steaming cup. "Lizzy, what is our job here at Roma Station?"

"Cart, please—" Lizzy began.

"Humor me, Lizzy."

She sighed. "To train recruits for war."

"And we do that, Lizzy, by taking in boys and girls, breaking them, and rebuilding them into soldiers. Some of the kids we take are soft. Artists. Thinkers. Even cowards. Some of the kids we take are hard. They come from broken homes. From gangs. They're angry and scared. Lizzy, my father is a general. Your father is a colonel. War is woven through our DNA. But we're rare. The HDF isn't a volunteer force. These are normal kids we pulled from homes across America. Every one is an individual, dealing with his or her own struggles. Our job is to shatter these kids into a million pieces. Shatter them until nothing of their old self remains. Then, Lizzy… then we can rebuild them. Stronger than before."

Lizzy curled her prosthetic fist. The metal creaked. She didn't like it when Carter brought up their parents. Yes, his father was a general. A general who had abandoned him, leaving him to grow up in the slums. Yes, her father was a colonel. And she had flunked out of military academy, ended up an enlisted grunt, and broke his heart. Who cared about famous parentage? A last name did not define a soldier. A soldier was only as good as his gun and grit.

But she let it slide. For now, Lizzy had other grievances to air.

"And you think we can rebuild Clay Hagen? Really? Even the best chef can't make a burger from rotten beef."

Carter placed down his mug. "Clay came to us already broken. You've read his file. His father beat him. Savagely. Throughout his childhood. He came to us broken, and you broke him some more—literally and figuratively. If I sent Clay to prison, or banished him to Earth, I would be sending a million shattered pieces in a bag of skin. A broken soul. A dangerous soul. On Earth, he would kill again. He would destroy and hurt others. He would end up in prison again and again, eventually for good. And he would leave a trail of victims. But in the army, Lizzy, maybe we can save him. Maybe we can turn him into… not a good man. But a worthy man. We'd not only save society from Clay Hagen. We'd also save his soul."

Lizzy snorted. "I thought our job was to win the war, not save civilization."

"Civilization," Carter said softly, as if tasting the word. "There is nothing civilized about war. There is no civilization in the killing fields. That is where civilization falls apart, revealing the bleeding, pulsing organs within. But there is civilization behind us. We soldiers stand with our back to civilization, and we face chaos.

We charge, and we bleed, and we die in fields of fire, so that civilization can continue. So that our people, our friends, and our family can live in green lands which we remember but no longer see. We are agents of death, and we are the pillars of life."

"Lovely speech," Lizzy said. "But Clay's still a dick."

"Lizzy." Carter stepped closer. "I know this isn't just about Clay. You can talk to me, you know."

Suddenly tears filled her eyes.

Her goddamn fucking tears.

She turned away from her officer.

"I know," she whispered.

Carter placed a hand on her shoulder. "It's strange, I know. To see Jon Taylor. He looks so much like his brother."

Lizzy lowered her head. A tear splashed onto the floor.

Yes, she had noticed that the first day. Jon Taylor was younger, softer, not yet a hardened warrior. But the black hair, the blue eyes, the somber features…

Yes, he looked like Paul. Like the man both Lizzy and Carter had loved. The man who died in their arms.

Lizzy closed her eyes, and images flashed before her. The fire blooming in the trees. The screams. The smell of blood. Paul holding back the enemy, shouting at her to run, and bullets flying, and the hands grabbing her. The march through the jungle, and the bamboo cage, and the blades and whips, and—

No.

Lizzy took a deep, shaky breath.

No. Not now. Don't remember now.

"Lizzy." Carter's voice was soft, and he brushed her hair. "I'm here for you."

She reeled toward him. "But you weren't here for me then! When the jungle burned, and the Kennys bound me, you—" She closed her mouth and trembled. "I'm sorry, Cart." Her tears flowed. "I'm sorry."

Carter's eyes hardened for just an instant, then softened again. "Lizzy, I love you. And I know it was hard for you. You went through months of hell I can't even imagine. I promise you, I spent those months searching for you. Every day. Every night. I fought through the forest, and—"

"Cart." Lizzy's voice shook. "Please. *Please.*"

He held her hands. "We've never talked about it. About Paul. And about what happened to you in the camp."

"We just did," Lizzy snapped. "And we'll never talk about it again. Promise me, Cart. I love you too. But I can't talk to you about this. Not yet. Maybe not ever."

"All right, Lizzy. All right."

He held her closely. And she felt safe in his arms.

She looked into his eyes. Her commanding officer. Her secret lover. The only other man to survive that day. And she wondered if Carter was being strong for her… or if he needed her strength. Whether he wanted to hear her talk… or needed to talk himself. Gazing into his eyes, she saw the war. And she realized that Carter was still fighting that war every day.

She turned to leave, then looked back at him.

"Cart," she said softly. "We can stay here. On Roma Station. Or even transfer down to Earth. We don't have to go back to Bahay. We don't have to fight again. We've done our share."

Carter's eyes hardened. So did his voice. "Our platoon was wiped out that day. Paul died that day. I cannot let their deaths be in vain. I must go back. I know the army wants me here. They think I suffer from shell shock, that I need to sit out the rest of the war. But I'm going back. I'm going to finish what we started. I'm going to win this war. For Earth. And for Paul."

Fresh tears rolled down her cheeks. "Then I'm going with you."

"You don't have to."

She wept. "Yes I do." She saluted. "Sir."

He returned the salute, eyes haunted.

Lizzy left his office. She stood for a moment in the corridor, wiped her eyes, and composed herself.

Then she stepped outside to her platoon of recruits.

"All right, you stinkin' maggots!" she shouted. "Your guns are cleaner than a nun's diary. Up, worms! *Run*!"

Training continued. Lizzy kept breaking these soldiers, shattering them into smaller and smaller pieces… like the enemy had shattered her. She would eventually rebuild her recruits, but Sergeant Lizzy Pascal didn't know if she herself could ever be whole.

Chapter Twenty-Five
Hell to Hell

The recruits ran the plastic jungle again.

This time with live ammo.

On their final day of basic training, they fought plastic soldiers with bullets of lead.

This was a different plastic jungle. Not the one where Clay had shot Jon with rubber bullets. That had been easy. *This* plastic jungle filled a quarter of Roma Station—a vast labyrinth of darkness, coiling trees, and hidden enemies.

Jon ran among the trees, shouting. George and Etty ran at his sides.

The enemy was everywhere. Robotic Bahayans filled the trees, firing electric bolts designed to hurt like real bullets. One hit Jon's arm, and he screamed, but he ran on.

The enemy was everywhere.

A soldier fell, an electric bolt buzzing across her chest.

A pit opened up. Another soldier fell in, landed on electric shockers, and screamed.

The survivors ran onward.

The enemy fire, while painful, could not kill them. But the recruits' own guns could. Jon knelt behind a fallen log, aimed his Oakeshott, and fired live bullets at a tree. A Bahayan robot fell, plastic face twisted in anguish.

"Go!" Jon shouted to his fireteam. "I'll cover you! Cross the river!"

His friends ran through water and mud. Fire blazed above.

Electric bolts streaked from the trees.

Several pounded into George, and he screamed and fell.

"George!" Jon shouted.

He emptied a magazine into the trees. Branches snapped and enemies fell into the water.

Jon slogged through the mud, fell, rose and ran again. Etty was trying to pull George out from the water. The enemy bolts clung to the giant like little spiders, shocking him again and again, mimicking the agony of real wounds.

"Go on without me," George moaned.

Jon shook his head. "Not a chance, buddy."

Somehow, Jon and Etty managed to pull him up. The bastard weighed three hundred pounds, but they pulled him from the water. They ran, holding George between them, limping through the forest, firing on snipers in the trees.

The plastic jungle seemed to spread forever. Jon knew it was fake. Just a set. An obstacle course. But it felt so real. And he realized this was the place from his dreams, that dark forest without ground or sky, that endless labyrinth he became lost in every night. He was living his nightmare.

And it was Bahay.

And it was the place where Paul had died.

It was the place where Jon was going.

It was the place that haunted him. The place he had to face—and overcome.

So he ran onward, carrying his friend, and he kept going even as another bolt hit his shoulder, and then one hit his leg. He ran through the pain, pulling his friends with him.

He would not die here.

He had made a promise.

He had to come home and see Kaelyn again.

He had to escape the nightmare.

Buzzing with half a dozen bolts, panting, barely able to

move at all, Jon made his way to the other side.

Etty walked with him, drenched in sweat. The little spider-like bolts clung to her arm, buzzing, shocking her again and again. George limped between them, breathing raggedly, covered with the crackling little machines.

The three of them stepped out from the darkness into the light.

The bolts fell off.

The recruits collapsed onto concrete that felt as soft as a princess's mattress.

Sergeant Lizzy was waiting there, smiling.

"Good job, soldiers," she said.

Jon gave her a weak smile and thumbs up, then closed his eyes. He fell asleep, right there and then. And for the first time in many days, he did not dream.

* * * * *

After ten weeks in hell, the day was here.

It was over.

It was done.

The last day of boot camp.

Jon was both relieved and terrified. One hell was ending. Would another begin?

The plastic jungle had broken them—their bodies and souls. But they had passed through the gauntlet. And that night, they celebrated.

Normally, the recruits slept in concrete rooms, a squad of fifteen soldiers in each cell. Tonight, the entire platoon spilled into the hallway, wearing pajamas or just underwear. They caroused, and soon more platoons emerged from their bunks, joining the fun.

Somebody had lugged candies all the way from Earth, hiding them throughout ten weeks of boot camp. Etty, meanwhile, had pilfered several bags of potato chips from the mess kitchen—snacks normally reserved for the higher ranks. George had even smuggled a harmonica from Earth, and he played, and soon everyone was singing old songs, even Jon.

"Hey, boys!" Etty said through a mouthful of potato chips. "Do a Symphonica song!"

Jon's cheeks flushed. "No thanks."

"What's Symphonica?" somebody asked.

"It's a heavy metal band!" Etty said. "Jon and George are in it."

"*Symphonic* metal," Jon said. "It's a genre that combines metal with classical music, and I don't really have the right instruments here, so—"

But a chant rose in the crowd. "Symphonica, Symphonica!"

Jon's cheeks burned even hotter. He was probably red like a tomato. He had never played before an audience. But the chanting grew louder, and Etty was leading it.

"Fine, fine!" Jon tossed his hands into the air in resignation.

"Falling Like the Rain?" George said. "I'll drum."

He began to tap a beat, using two spoons and a bowl.

Kaelyn, their lead singer, was back on Earth. So Jon sang instead.

He wasn't a particularly good singer. He hated singing in public. Absolutely hated it, and his knees shook, but after the first verse, a calmness fell upon him. He sang softly, and he was back in his basement at home. He was with Paul, his brother and guitarist. With Kaelyn, his soprano and muse.

He sang the music that he wrote. His poem about a dead

soldier looking back upon his life. Jon had written the song about a fictional soldier, but he realized that the song had changed. It was now about Paul.

As he sang, silence fell across the company. Everyone was listening, silent. Etty had tears on her cheeks.

Jon reached the last verse, stopped, and cleared his throat. "Um… there should be a horn section here."

"Thank God you don't have horns," George said.

The spell was broken. Everyone laughed. Etty wiped her eyes and hugged him.

"It's beautiful." She kissed his cheek. "You're brilliant, maestro."

George grinned. "Hey, that should be his nickname from now on. Maestro."

"Please don't call me that," Jon said.

Etty hopped around him, laughing. "Maestro is getting angry!"

A few soldiers began singing, arms slung around one another. They performed a rowdy version of "Falling Like the Rain," complete with dirty lyrics they invented on the spot. Other soldiers were wrestling, some eating, a few sharing photos of girlfriends back home. They were all exhausted. They all had to wake up again in a few hours. Nobody cared. They were partying tonight.

Tomorrow we'll be shipped out, Jon thought. *Earth or her colonies for the lucky, Bahay for the doomed. So let's party one last night. Let's laugh with friends.*

He reached for a bag of potato chips when the barracks doors banged open.

Sergeant Lizzy stomped into the corridor.

She growled, eyes burning, and cracked her electric whip.

At once, everyone stood at attention. Bags of potato chips rolled across the floor.

The sergeant glowered. "What the fuck is going on here?"

Jon gulped. "Commander, it's just—"

"Is this a party?" Sergeant Lizzy shouted.

"Yes, Commander, but—"

Lizzy sliced the air with her whip, silencing him. "Tell me, soldiers. What kind of party doesn't have beer?" She whistled. "Drones!"

They flew in from behind her.

A fleet of drones, each carrying a case of beer.

Cheers filled the corridor, so loud they shook the barracks.

"Yeah, boys!" Etty said. "I knew it! I fucking knew it! Lizzy is a party animal!"

Amazingly, Lizzy actually smiled. Then laughed. Recruits gathered around her. For ten weeks, Lizzy had tortured them, broken their bodies and souls. Now they were toasting her, slapping her on the back, and a few soldiers even lifted her overhead, cheering.

She's human after all. Jon gazed at his sergeant in wonder. *She's an actual human being, not a demon from hell.*

But even as Lizzy laughed, even as the soldiers carried her across the corridor, he thought he saw sadness in her eyes. He wondered how she had lost her hand. How she had gathered those ghosts that haunted her eyes.

A drone flew toward Jon. A robotic voice emerged. "Brewski, soldier?"

Jon pushed aside thoughts of the war, of Lizzy's eyes, of the loss and pain.

"Don't mind if I do."

He took a beer and drank.

* * * * *

The next morning, they gathered in a courtyard in the center of Roma Station. Earth's banners flew. The planetary anthem played. Thousands of recruits stood in companies, platoons, squads, and finally fireteams.

This morning, after ten weeks of hell, they were graduating basic training.

Not everyone was here today. Not everyone had survived boot camp. Jon had no actual data. But he heard the whispers. He saw the dwindling numbers.

Many recruits had flunked the grueling gauntlet. Obstacle courses, robotic enemies, barbed wire, walls that spurted fire—they had culled the weak. Those failed soldiers flew down to Earth in shame. Back on the homeworld, they would serve in noncombat roles.

A few recruits had died in Roma Station. Friendly fire had killed some in the plastic jungle. Other recruits, they whispered, had committed suicide.

Yes, the culling had been ruthless. Only half the recruits were graduating today.

Today, the survivors became warriors.

Jon was proud to stand among them. He stood tall, chin raised, singing his planet's anthem.

He didn't have to be here. He could have given up. Could have purposefully failed the obstacle course, taken the flight of shame down to Earth, and spent the war in an office. He could have bitten a bullet.

But he had worked hard. He had bled for this. Cried for this. Fought for this.

He was graduating.

No, this wasn't a fancy military academy. Not even Officer Candidate School. Not training for some elite unit. It was good old-fashioned boot camp. As basic as could be. A rite of passage for millions of boys and girls throughout the ages. He was not unique.

But today, Jon felt prouder than he'd ever felt.

During the training, the recruits had not seen much of Lieutenant Carter. Sometimes the officer would observe the exercises. Sometimes even speak a word or two. Mostly, the recruits had suffered under Lizzy's heel. She had tortured them like an angel of wrath, while Carter had watched from on high, a god on Mount Olympus.

But today, Lieutenant Carter faced his platoon, and more officers stood across the square, facing their own units.

When the anthem ended, Sergeant Lizzy approached the lieutenant, snapped her heels together, and saluted.

"Sir!" she said. "May I present to you—the graduating soldiers of Lizzy's Lions!"

They stepped up one by one. Recruit after recruit. Boys and girls turning into men and women.

Jon approached his lieutenant and saluted.

"Sir!"

Lieutenant Carter turned toward him. There was old pain in his eyes. But also the hint of a smile on his lips.

"Hello, Taylor," the officer said.

They exchanged a look. Just for a second or two. But it spoke of years of pain, of war, of loss. Of understanding.

Lieutenant Carter pinned insignia onto Jon's sleeves. One chevron on each.

"Congratulations, Private Jon Taylor," the officer said. "You are now an official soldier of the Human Defense Force. I'm proud of you."

Canned words, perhaps. The lieutenant probably said the same thing to every graduating recruit. But there was deeper honestly in Carter's eyes.

Jon hesitated, knowing he should return to his platoon, to

let another soldier approach and receive their insignia.

He looked back at his platoon. They were standing in formation, stiff and still, but George gave him the slightest of nods, and Etty winked. If Sergeant Lizzy noticed the breach of protocol, she ignored it.

Jon turned back toward his officer. He took a deep breath.

"Sir, you commanded my brother," Jon said. "And you were his friend. You were with him when he died. I don't know if I can fill his shoes, sir. He was always taller, stronger, faster, braver. But sir, whatever I have, for whatever it's worth, I will give."

Carter placed a hand on his shoulder. "You're a good soldier, Jon Taylor. You have a lot to give. To me and to your friends. I'm proud to be your officer. And I know that Paul is watching us now, and that he's proud of you too."

Jon couldn't stop his eyes from dampening. He saluted. "Thank you, sir."

Carter returned the salute.

I will follow you, Jon thought. *Together, we will make Paul proud.*

He returned to his platoon. He stood with his fireteam. George and Etty smiled at him, both already wearing their new insignia. He was among friends. More than friends. He had lost Paul, but he had a platoon of brothers and sisters.

He had come here a scared boy. Today he was a soldier.

The platoon marched toward the end of Roma Station—the far side of this massive cylinder in space. Over ten backbreaking, soul-crushing weeks, they had passed through the gauntlet.

The hell of boot camp was over.

The hell of war was about to begin.

Chapter Twenty-Six
Children of Poison

The world was aflame.

Maria stood on a mountaintop, the wind in her hair, gazing upon the devastation of Bahay.

Red smoke covered the north like a blanket. Distant fires blazed. The Red Cardinal still fought there, leading the Luminous Army, the great military of North Bahay.

And so Earth punished that hemisphere. Relentlessly. With endless wrath and horrible firepower.

Standing here, Maria could hear it. Bomb after bomb. She could see the distant planes. See the missiles like comets slicing the sky, hurled from the starships above like lightning bolts from the hands of vengeful gods. She could smell the death. She shed a tear for the millions dying in that inferno.

She turned toward the south.

The Earthlings had conquered the south with ease. Twenty years ago, their starships had arrived. Within a single year, their troops had captured the southern hemisphere. Bahay had been unprepared. Shocked. Awed. Half the planet had fallen so quickly.

The rainforest still covered much of the south. The Earthlings were less likely to burn lands they controlled. But even here, south of the equator, there was so much suffering. The Kalayaan fought in jungles, ports, and villages—a great peasant uprising that terrified even the mighty Earthlings. The Earthling machines rumbled across the sky, tore through the jungle, and polluted the water.

Farmers and fishermen fought great machines from space. Farmers and fishermen died by the millions. Maria's generation had been born into this war. And now they were taking up the fight. Millions had died. Millions of new warriors picked up arms.

Two hemispheres. One a hell of war and genocide. Another crushed under conquest, rising in rebellion. Two faces to the great Freedom War. Two nightmares. One world.

A world where Maria was all alone.

"Where should we go, Crisanto?" She held him on her palm. "To the north, to fight and die in the fire? Or to the south, where the cruel Earthlings rule over us?"

A tear fell. She wished she could go home. To her village. To her family. She just wanted to go home.

But home is gone, she told herself. *My family is dead. I must shed no more tears. Only with strength can I survive now.*

She stared south again. Beyond the horizon it lay.

Mindao. The great city of the south. Home to two million people, the greatest city on Bahay.

Maria had never been there. She could not even imagine two thousand people in one place, let alone two million. But everyone had heard of the city. If your harvest failed, and you faced starvation, you traveled south to find work in Mindao. If the Earthlings polluted your river, and all the fish died, you went to Mindao. If you were sick, and no herbs could drive away the illness, you traveled to seek healers in Mindao.

If you were lost, you went to Mindao.

And Maria was lost.

And Maria was hungry.

Mindao—city of lost souls. Of the wretched and unwanted. A city under the heel of Earth.

She would go there.

"We tried to fight the Earthlings, Crisanto," she said. "But

I cannot fight anymore. I cannot kill again. I cannot hear more screams or smell more blood. I cannot stand the nightmares. So let us walk into the lion's den. Because we have nowhere else to go."

*****

She walked south through the jungle.

She did not take the Freedom Trail, for the Kalayaan still moved there, streaming fighters and weapons toward the Earthling strongholds.

She did not walk along the coast, for Earth's machines moved in the water, flew overhead, and spied from above the sky.

Maria walked in the deep jungle, hidden inside the breathing lungs of the world.

But after a day, the cover of the rainforest thinned. The trees grew fewer leaves, then none. Ferns wilted. No moss or lichen covered the boulders and fallen logs. The forest was sick, and a foul smell filled Maria's nostrils.

She walked onward, and the ground became hot and dry. She only had one shoe, and her sole burned. The trees rose naked and thin, reaching toward the sky like skeleton fingers. Bugs scurried underfoot and buzzed over bones. No birds sang.

Animal corpses covered the ground. Sometimes human corpses too. But it was hard to tell. They were twisted corpses. Deformed. People with multiple rib cages sprouting from their spines. Children with two heads. Creatures with many human limbs but no torsos.

Maria came across a metal barrel on the forest floor. It was painted with a skull, and English words were printed across the barrel: DEFOREST HERBICIDE.

"Poison," Maria whispered to Crisanto.

She had heard of this poison. Deforest Herbicide—it was created to wilt the rainforest, leaving the Kalayaan no place to hide. The deformities were incidental. In the villages, they called the poison Mister Weird.

Rumbling sounded in the distance.

Maria gasped. A plane!

There was no cover here. She ran among the naked trees, seeking shelter. She climbed a hill between skeletons, heading toward a cluster of trees that still had a few leaves.

Atop the hill, she beheld a swath of living rainforest in the east. There would be shelter there. Clean air. Food to forage.

The plane flew over the forest and began to spray sizzling orange liquid. It gushed out in a mighty torrent, drenching the canopy.

Where the spray landed, the forest wilted.

The plane flew eastward. When it passed over farmlands, it sprayed the rice paddies too. And the huts and barns. It flew until it disappeared in the distance.

Maria walked onward, passing by more empty barrels of herbicide. Past more dead trees, dead animals.

In the evening, she reached a village. The rice paddies were dry, and the fruit groves had wilted. But people still moved among the nipa huts, and Maria saw no guerrillas nor Earthlings.

She entered the village, hoping for a kind soul to feed her. She had not eaten all day. People peered from their bamboo huts, eyes dark and suspicious. A rooster moved across the dirt, pecking at pebbles. It had no feathers.

"Hello?" Maria said. "I come from San Luna in the north. My name is Maria de la Cruz."

Wind rustled through the naked guava trees, and dead leaves scuttled across the ground, whirled around a well, and blew through the ribcage of a skeleton.

"Why have you not buried your dead?" Maria said.

A woman emerged from a hut. She was naked, starving, her skin draped across jutting ribs. She looked like another skeleton. She held something, and it took Maria a moment to realize it was a baby. The child had a long, pointy head, bulging eyes, and clusters of fingers that grew directly from the shoulders. No arms.

"Leave this place," the skeletal mother said. "There is death here."

Maria took a step back. "What happened?"

A man approached her, his skin bright red, a mass of glowing scars. He had no clothes, no hair, and a chemical stench rose from him.

"They bathed our village with Deforest," he said. "Most of us died. The rest of us changed."

Another mother emerged, bald and starving. She held conjoined twins without faces. Their heads were just smooth balls of skin with slits for mouths.

"Leave," the mother said.

Maria ran.

She fled the village, heart pounding, not sure if she felt more pity or horror.

Am I infected? Will I too change?

She ran east through the charred landscape, over corpses, a rusty bicycle, a stroller with a dead baby inside, and she did not stop running until she reached the sea.

She plunged into the water and scrubbed herself with sand, and salt filled her eyes, and she wept.

She wept for what she had seen.

She wept for her own tragedy.

She wept for her sundering world.

Maria did not know why this was happening. Why the Earthlings had invaded. Why the Bahayans fought. She would surrender if she could, reject the Santelmos, and join the Human Commonwealth. Or she would knock the Earthling starships from the sky, slay every Earthling soldier on Bahay, and even strike them on their own distant world. But she could do neither. Not surrender or win. She was powerless. She was just Maria de la Cruz, seventeen years old, a girl with too many questions, with too much fear in her heart. She could do nothing but try to survive.

Come deeper.

The ocean whispered.

Come into the embrace of the waves.

She stood, the water up to her waist, gazing at the ocean. There was a world under the waves. There was a secret kingdom of life. A kingdom the Earthlings could not deform. A place of fish and mermaids and castles, where no babies were born without faces, where no parents burned, where she could become a mermaid and feel no pain.

Come to us.

Come deeper.

Come into our embrace.

But Maria could not. Because the toad had spoken to her. The toad had said she could save someone. With her knife. It was the only way. She could not go into the sea because the Santelmos had glowed around her, a thousand little lights, delivering her from death. She had survived when so many had died, and she had a mission she did not understand.

So she turned away from the waves.

She walked away from that promise of wonder and forgetfulness.

Cleansed of poison, she kept walking south. A girl with one shoe. A girl in rags. Hungry, maybe starving, maybe infected. A girl who had slit a man's throat and shot another. Maybe a girl who could still be redeemed.

She walked the longest walk of her life. Through death.

Past craters dug by Earthling shells. Past enemy bases. When helicopters roared overhead, she hid under fallen logs, cringing as bullets peppered the trees around her. She walked through dying rainforest. Through villages of living skeletons and the children of poison. She stood as jeeps rumbled by, as Earthlings hooted and hollered and shouted at her to show her breasts. She walked onward.

Closer to the city, others joined her. Refugees from the burning north. Some were families. Many were alone. Many were burnt, missing limbs. Some carried deformed babies kissed by Mister Weird. They traveled the roads and trails, they sailed rafts down the rivers. They headed to the same place. Toward the city. Toward hope.

Maria walked with them, but she kept to herself. Her demons were company enough, and she felt ashamed of her sins. She walked until she saw the city in the distance.

Mindao. Home of Lost Souls.

A city of Bahayans under the banners of Earth.

Purgatory.

Her ragged dress fluttered in the ashy wind, and she stumbled along a cracked highway, heading to her new home.

Chapter Twenty-Seven
The Garden Path

"Where do you think they'll send us?" George wrung his hands. "Oh goddammit, I can't take this tension."

"They'll probably drop your fat ass on Bahay," Etty said. "Boom! Instant victory."

George flipped her off. "No need. They'll just drop you down on Bahay, and you'll annoy the enemy to death."

"Damn right!" Etty raised her Oakeshott and mimicked firing. "I'm gonna annoy them with bullets. Pew pew pew!"

Jon grumbled at his two friends. "Will you two knock it off? Etty, lower your gun, dammit, you're a private now, not some dumbass recruit. And George? Stop biting your fingernails. You're making me nervous."

They were still in Roma Station, but standing at the far end of the cylinder. Over the past ten weeks, they had gradually moved through the station, airlock to airlock, each level a battle. They had reached the end. Now they gathered before a concrete building, waiting for their names to be called. Waiting to be sorted.

"We're all nervous!" George said, raising his hands in dismay. "How could we not be? They're gonna sort us soon! In just minutes, we'll know how we'll spend our entire army service. The next *five years*. Some of us will be sent down to Earth to defend the home front. Some of us will be sent to guard Mars, Titan, or the asteroid belt. And some of us to Bahay."

Jon lowered his head. "And some of us won't come

home."

George groaned. "Oh, *that* makes me feel better. Thanks!"

"Hey, you reckon they'll recommend some of us for officer school?" Etty said. "I think I'd make a great officer. Just as good as Lieutenant Carter."

"You ain't gonna become an officer," George said. "None of us. Because we're dumbasses. We're cannon fodder. I know it! We're doomed to be sent to Bahay. Doomed!"

"Guys, calm down!" Jon said. "First of all, the sorting officer listens to requests. If you don't like where you're sorted, you can argue, change the army's mind. My brother did that. He was sorted to Earth. He insisted to go to Bahay. To fight."

Suddenly everyone was silent. Even the rest of the platoon overheard and hushed.

The unspoken words hung in the air.

And he never came home.

They all stared at their feet for a while.

"Hey!" Etty broke the silence. "You reckon they have a sorting hat in there?"

George tilted his head. "A what?"

"A sorting hat!" Etty said. "You know, like in that old movie with the wizards! You put a hat on your head, it reads your brain, and it announces your destiny." She spoke with a baritone English accent. "You—to mop latrines! You—to a desk! You—yes, you, you giant ginger idiot, to Bahay!"

"He'll sort you to the loony bin," George muttered.

More names were being called. One by one, the privates stepped into the concrete building. They left by the back door, entered shuttles, and flew off into space.

Some down to Earth.

Some to the colonies.

Some to the fire.

The line moved quickly, and soon Jon was only a few

steps away. Cold sweat began to drip down his back.

I want to be sent to Bahay, he thought. *I want to fight. Like my brother fought. But I'm scared. If they station me on Earth, will I dare ask to fight? Or will the fear overwhelm me?*

"Private Taylor!"

A voice from behind.

Jon spun around to see Sergeant Lizzy approaching.

"Commander?"

She beckoned to him. "With me, Private Taylor. *Now.*"

Jon glanced at his friends. They stared back, pale. Etty gulped.

"*Taylor!*" the sergeant barked.

Jon hurried toward her. "Yes, Commander."

The sergeant began walking across the station. Jon followed. They walked along the curving wall, moving upward, like hamsters in a huge wheel. Finally they stood at right angles to the other privates.

Amazingly, here inside this space station, they found a little yard. Actual trees grew from pots of soil—not even plastic. Jon could smell them, and a bird sang on a branch. Among the trees stood a trailer, hidden from the bustle of Roma Station, a sanctuary among the chaos.

Lizzy walked around an oak tree and toward a garden. A gardener knelt in the dirt, his back facing them, tending to cherry tomato plants.

Lizzy slammed her heels together and saluted.

"Sergeant Lizzy Pascal reporting!"

Jon too saluted. "Recruit T—I mean, Private Taylor reporting!"

The gardener stood up, faced them, and returned the salute.

It was Lieutenant Carter.

"My little sanctuary," the officer said, gesturing at the

garden and trees. "A last comfort. What do you think, Jon?"

Jon admired the garden, trees, and chirping birds.

"I would have preferred training here than in the plastic jungle, sir."

Carter did not even crack a smile. "The plastic jungle is easy, Private. Compared to what's out there. To the true jungle."

Jon nodded. "Yes, sir. Sorry, sir."

"Jon." The lieutenant's voice softened. "Come, sit down. Let's talk."

They sat on a bench under the oak tree, and Carter handed Jon a bottle of beer. He cracked open a bottle of his own, and they both drank. It was good beer. Cold and dark. Lizzy remained standing, ever vigilant, her gun in her hands. Between the trees, Jon could see the rest of the space station, but sitting in this garden, it was easy to imagine that he was back on Earth, just sitting on a porch, enjoying a cold one.

Jon didn't know much about the military. But he sensed this was unusual. Privates normally didn't sit on benches with their commanding officers, enjoying a beer. He said nothing, waiting.

Carter took a slow sip, then lowered his bottle. He spoke softly. "Jon, your brother was a good friend of mine. You know that, right?"

Jon nodded. "Yes, sir. He was a squad leader in your platoon."

"He was more than that," Carter said. "Paul was like a brother to me. I know I'm not his real brother. You are. But together in the war, we became that close. I was with him when he died. And I remember who killed him."

Jon felt a chill. "Paul died in an explosion," he whispered. "A roadside bomb."

"That's what the official report said," Carter said. "Only Lizzy and I know the truth. We were there. We saw it happen.

Jon, what I'm about the tell you is highly classified. You must never speak of it to anyone. Understood?"

"Perfectly."

Carter looked into his eyes. "Your brother was executed."

Jon felt the blood drain from his face. His heart beat madly. His hands shook.

"Who executed him?" Jon whispered.

"A Bahayan. A Kalayaan terrorist. A man named Ernesto Santos. He's nicknamed Iron because he tortures his victims with a clothing iron."

Carter pulled from his pocket a photograph. It depicted a Bahayan standing in the jungle. A scar rifted his face, and a cataract covered one eye. The man was smirking, revealing a golden tooth. Blood covered his hands.

Nearby, Lizzy winced. Just the slightest movement. But Jon noticed.

"My God," Jon whispered.

"There was no God in the jungle," Carter said. "There was just us and the Kalayaan. We fought them in the darkness. We fought them hard. They knew the jungle and we did not. They knew every branch and stone. They could vanish among the trees like ghosts. They picked us out one by one. Until only three of us remained. Me, Lizzy, and Paul."

"And they killed him," Jon said. "But you got away." He stood up. "How did you get away? How are you alive while he's dead?"

Blood drummed in his ears. Lizzy took a step toward him, but then she looked away, face hard.

Carter remained seated. He gazed ahead at the oak tree, as if gazing back at the jungle. "Paul tried to fight. Tried to kill Iron. He was the bravest man I knew. The Kalayaan held him down, disarmed him, bound his arms. They asked him a question or two. And then Iron put a bullet through his head."

Jon slumped back onto the bench. He placed his head in his hands. "I wish I could have been there. Could have stopped it. Could have saved him."

Carter placed a hand on Jon's back. "Paul gave his life for me. With the time he bought me, I was able to escape that day."

Finally Lizzy spoke. "I was not."

Jon turned toward his sergeant. Lizzy was staring ahead, face expressionless, but her eyes were damp.

"Lizzy, I'm sorry," Jon whispered.

The sergeant didn't look at him. She spoke to the distance. To an old memory. "For weeks, Ernesto kept me in a cage. For weeks, he beat me. Raped me. Tortured me." She pulled up her shirt, revealing scars across her torso—shaped like irons. "He burned me, and when I still would not speak, he took my hand." She clenched her metal fist. "Carter came back to me. He came back with a company of soldiers and freed me."

"And Ernesto Santos?" Jon said. "The man in the photograph? Did you kill him?"

"Not yet," Carter said. "But we will."

"We will," Lizzy vowed.

"You're going back there, aren't you?" Jon whispered. "Back to Bahay."

The lieutenant nodded. "After our ordeal, we stepped away from the war. But the war never left us. We have to go back. To finish what we started. Lizzy and I came to Roma Station to train new soldiers. To find true warriors. We're going back, Jon Taylor, and you deserve to come with us. To help us kill Ernesto and avenge your brother."

Lizzy finally let down her guard. She joined the men on the bench, put a hand on Jon's shoulder, and spoke softly. "You don't have to come with us, Jon. We won't force you. If you ask us, we'll get you a job on Earth, far from the fight. You're a musician, right? We can recommend you for a military band. We'll keep you safe."

Jon stood up. He walked toward the oak tree, lowered his head. For a long moment, he stood there. Overcome.

I miss you, Paul. We all do. We miss you so much.

Jon tightened his lips, wiped his eyes, and turned toward his commanders.

Lieutenant Carter and Sergeant Lizzy stood and faced him.

Jon raised his chin. "I never wanted to join the army. I never wanted to be a soldier, only a musician. But a war broke out. And a little brown envelope came in the mail. And I lost a brother. Even now, I'm tempted. To go home to Earth. To wait out the war. But I can't go back. I can't turn away from what happened. I've been dreaming about the jungle, and in my dreams, I'm lost in that darkness, trapped in the labyrinth. And if I go back to Earth now, I'll be lost forever. I'll go with you. To Bahay. To war. To avenge my brother. To serve my planet. And to finally find my way out of the darkness."

"And we're going with you!" rose a cry from behind.

Etty ran between the trees and burst into the garden, panting.

"And me too!" George stumbled after her, cheeks red, gasping and heaving.

"You can't get rid of us!" Etty added. She jabbed Jon in the chest. "We're your best friends, buster. And if you're going to war, we're right behind ya."

Lieutenant Carter cleared his throat. "Privates, are you aware of the penalty for eavesdropping on an officer of Earth?"

Etty and George turned toward the officer and paled.

George gulped. "You won't toss us out the airlock, will you, sir?"

Etty snorted. "Oh, don't worry, your fat ass won't fit."

"Shut up, pipsqueak!" George curled his fists.

The lieutenant cleared his throat again. "Privates!"

They all fell silent. The three privates faced their officer.

"Seems like we're all going, sir," Jon said. "If you'll have us." He glanced at his friends, then back at Carter. "We're not the bravest soldiers. Or the strongest."

"Or the brightest," Etty said.

"But if you lead us," Jon continued, "we won't let you down. We'll find Ernesto Santos. We'll finish the job."

He saluted his officer. His friends did too.

For a moment, sadness filled Carter's eyes—an old sadness, haunted and cold.

But then the young officer returned the salutes. "We leave today. Your training is over. Your war begins."

Chapter Twenty-Eight
Concrete Jungle

With one shoe, ragged and dusty, Maria entered the city of lost souls.

Mindao.

Home of the damned.

It seemed a place risen from hell.

She walked along hot asphalt streets, eyes wide. This seemed an alien world. A world of cement and metal. Of crackling electricity and buzzing lights.

There were no trees here. Mindao seemed as barren as Mister Weird's fields of poison. But this was another kind of life. The city itself seemed a jungle, growing, coiling, decaying, its own ecosystem, as mighty as the rainforests in the north.

Concrete buildings grew like trees, lined with balconies like branches. Their paint was peeling, rough like bark, and rivulets of rust dripped from barred windows like sap. Electric cables stretched across the narrow streets like vines, braiding together, all knotted and crackling. More electric cables bundled atop poles, hopelessly tangled, looking like some deranged spider's cobwebs or the cocoons of monsters.

Lower in the concrete jungle rose the underbrush. Huts. Thousands of huts. But these were not bamboo *nipa* huts with thatched roofs. Nothing like the bucolic dwellings of Maria's village. They were shanties, constructed haphazardly from scraps of plywood, sheets of corrugated iron, and tarpaulin. No two were alike. They were all crooked, rotting, some of them piled up three or four high. They balanced atop stilts like mad mushrooms on slender stems.

Finally there was the concrete forest floor. Garbage rolled in the wind, whipped around Maria's legs, and piled up in corners. It flowed down gutters, completely hiding the water. Train tracks carved through the slums like riverbeds, lined with shanties like reeds. Cars rattled down cracked asphalt like lumbering beasts on a hunt. Mopeds and rickshaws whipped back and forth like frightened prey. Jeepneys rattled everywhere—old military jeeps, given to the Bahayans, painted with psychedelic colors, scuttling like mad beetles.

Mindao—a jungle. An ecosystem.

And the people. So many people.

"I never knew so many people existed in the world," Maria whispered, head spinning.

They crowded every layer of the jungle. They peeked from windows and balconies, scrawny people with bare chests and sun-browned skin. They huddled inside the shanties, peering between rotting slats and sheets of tarpaulin. They lined the train tracks, thousands of squatters in rags, entire families, generations, bartering and begging. They clogged the streets. Thousands and thousands of them. Rushing back and forth. Begging. Dying.

Young people, clean and well-dressed, hurried to work, heels clacking. Orphans huddled on the roadsides, naked and filthy, crying and begging. Two toddlers hugged themselves on the road, leaning against the curb, as cars rushed by, splashing them with mud. A child sat on a concrete staircase outside a brothel, trying to get his younger brother to breathe again, both boys so skinny, so ravaged with disease. Schoolgirls skipped to school, dressed as little sailors, while naked children ran between barrels, chasing bugs. Some women sat in corners, sticking needles into their wrists, while others stood on street corners, dressed in fishnet stockings, miniskirts, and bruises.

Maria walked by a landfill, a towering mountain within the city, as large as the mountains back home. Garbage trucks trundled up the landfill and spilled their rancid treasures. Hundreds of scavengers raced toward the trucks, fished through the garbage, found chicken bones, rotting peels, scraps to eat. They were filthy, rummaging like animals, but humanity shone in their eyes. They returned to their homes—burrows on the landfill where they were born, lived, and died. Children lay on piles of trash, covered with flies. Young women cradled babies and swelling bellies. The landfill too was an ecosystem, feeding and sustaining its human parasites—just long enough for them to breed, and then devouring them, pulling them down into the rotting depths. Maria wondered how many generations had lived and died upon the trash heap.

Maria saw this all. The panoply of her people. Policeman and prostitutes, priests and madmen, urchins and orphans—a tapestry of human suffering.

But more than the squatters, or the trash people, or the starving orphans on the roadsides, it was the Earthlings who scared her.

Many Earthlings filled Mindao.

They were soldiers.

They sat in roadside kiosks, drinking beer. They guarded checkpoints, guns in hand, and patrolled the streets. They catcalled at passing women, and they kicked dogs, and they knelt to give food or coins to orphans. They beat a man, shouting "Kenny slit!" as his blood splattered the street. They pulled prostitutes into alleys, and one Earthling pulled a blanket over a homeless old man, and another fed a stray cat from a bottle. They were cruel and kind, old and young, men and women, and they too formed a panoply of humanity.

But they were all soldiers.

They all wore navy-blue battlesuits, the armored plates like muscles, the yellow visors like strange insect eyes.

They were all tall, standing head and shoulders above the local Bahayans, and even their women seemed a race of giants. At five feet tall, Maria was an inch or two taller than the average Bahayan woman. But she felt like a child whenever an Earthling walked by her.

"Hey, baby." An Earthling approached her, visor raised, beer bottle in hand. He whistled. "I bet you're sugary sweet under that filth. What say we take a shower and find out?"

His friends snorted and elbowed him. Maria hurried away.

"Slit-slut!" the soldier cried after her. He tossed his beer bottle, and it shattered by her feet. His friends laughed.

Maria walked along a roadway lined with kiosks of rusty corrugated steel. She noticed that some Earthling men were walking with Bahayan girls, their beefy arms slung around slender waists. The girls were dolled up, wearing high heels, miniskirts, too much makeup. Some were laughing. Some had sad eyes. Some had black eyes.

A jeepney rumbled by. The repurposed army jeep was painted with yellow sunflowers, garish rainbows, and dancing blue butterflies. It splashed Maria with mud. She kept walking. She stepped over an orphaned toddler sleeping in the gutter, and her heart broke. But she walked on, dazed, because she could not save them all, and there were millions here who needed saving. Girls in bruises and miniskirts, dying children on concrete staircases, toddlers huddling on the street as rickshaws raced by, girls addicted to drugs, and girls dying from STDs, and the thousands crawling across the trash heaps.

Mindao. City of refugees, of hunger, of freedom.

A city with no glowing orbs of light, no wise Santelmos to guide its hordes of humanity.

A city of Earth.

I am lost, Maria thought. *And among the lost, I find my home.* She walked the streets, hungry and hollow. *I am home.*

Chapter Twenty-Nine
The Goddess of Safe Return

On his last hour at Roma Station, Jon called home.

He stood by a porthole, gazing down at the blue planet, as the line rang.

Earth. It was so close. Right there outside.

This might be the last time I see it.

Finally home answered. His family appeared on the payphone's little monitor.

"Jon!" his mother cried.

"How are you, buddy?" his dad said, beaming.

Jon watched them on the grainy little screen, and for a moment he could not speak. All he could do was struggle not to cry. So many thoughts and feelings filled him. Memories of a loved childhood. Of his brother. Fear of the war ahead. Visions of his death, his parents grieving the loss of both sons. Past and present and future, all clogging his throat.

"Mom, Dad," he finally managed in a choked voice, and he told them.

That he was going to Bahay.

That he promised to stay safe.

That he promised to come back.

His parents wept, but then laughed through their tears, told stupid jokes, struggled through the terror to keep their spirits up.

It was hard to say goodbye.

His mother wept, and even his dad shed tears. Jon had

only seen him cry twice. Once when Paul died. And now.

"Goodbye," Jon said softly. "I'll call back soon. Once I'm there."

His parents nodded, unable to say more.

The call ended.

And Jon didn't know if he'd ever talk to them again.

He made another call.

He called Kaelyn.

After four rings, she appeared on screen. The same freckled face, wavy red hair, and mismatched eyes, one brown and one blue. His beautiful soprano. His muse. The girl Paul had wanted to marry, his high school sweetheart. The girl who sang in Symphonica, giving life to his music. Kaelyn Williams.

She grinned at him. "Jon!"

And he told her too.

And she wept.

"I'm going to get him, Kaelyn," he whispered, tears on his cheeks. "I'm going to find the bastard who killed Paul."

"You don't have to avenge him!" Kaelyn said. "You can come back. You don't have to fight. Don't go! Come home to me, Jon. You don't have to—"

"I do—"

"Jon!"

"Kaelyn, I have to. I have to. Goodbye. Goodbye…"

She wept, but she nodded, and she kissed the camera. And she could say no more.

The call ended.

And it was time to go.

* * * * *

The privates gathered in the hangar.

A thousand soldiers.

A full battalion.

From those at Roma Station, they had been chosen. They were the strongest. The toughest. The meanest.

Or perhaps just the most expendable. They were the soldiers chosen to kill or die.

Not everyone who graduated Roma was going to war today. All day, shuttles had been departing the space station, carrying privates to Earth and her colonies. They would serve in hangars, warehouses, checkpoints, or behind desks. They would guard mines on asteroids, defend starships, transport cargo among the worlds.

They would maintain the empire. But they would not fight.

But *this* battalion. These thousand soldiers. Jon and his brothers and sisters. They were going to war.

As Jon stood in his platoon, he glanced to his side. Clay Hagen was standing a few rows away. The beefy private gave him a cruel smile. Death shone in his wide-set eyes. He ran his finger across his neck.

"You're dead meat," he mouthed.

Of course they chose Clay, Jon thought, heart sinking. *The bastard is crazy. Born for the jungle.*

With any luck, Clay would get his head blown off on the first day. Jon would not celebrate such a death. But he wouldn't mourn either.

They entered shuttles, and for the first time in ten weeks, they left Roma Station.

Jon sat with his friends, gazing out the shuttle porthole. Roma Station became smaller and smaller, a metallic cylinder rolling around its axis, orbiting Earth.

The blue planet seemed so fragile from up here. The

Western hemisphere faced Jon. He looked at America, his home. Just there, just outside the window—everyone he had ever known and loved. A delicate sphere wrapped in a thin blue blanket of air. Jon had never seen the entire planet like this, a full blue circle. He had never been so far from home. He gazed in silence, awed by how small the world really was, how beautiful and precious.

This humble blue planet, he thought. *The center of an empire. And it's nothing more than a marble floating in the vast emptiness. It's so small.*

"Only a century ago," Jon said softly, "Earth was burning, and alien fleets bombarded us, butchered us, brutalized us. Now from this world spreads an empire. The Human Commonwealth, the great civilization heroes built. From this shore of the cosmic ocean, we spread across the stars."

"Now *we* get to brutalize small worlds," Etty muttered.

George snorted. "Dude, nobody forced you to fight."

"Yeah, well, I happen to be a loyal friend," Etty said. "And I ain't letting you two dumbasses get yourselves killed."

"Shut up, both of you," Jon said. "Look."

He pointed to a porthole.

The entire squad crowded around.

"Well, would you look at that," George said, eyes widening in wonder. "Now that's a pretty sight."

Jon placed his hand on his friend's back. It was the first time since joining the army that George didn't seem miserable.

A starship floated ahead.

Not a shuttle. Not a crude space station. An actual interstellar warp-class starship.

"She's beautiful," Etty whispered, the starlight in her eyes.

She was shaped like a sailing ship of old, missing only the masts and sails. A figurehead thrust out from her prow, shaped like a golden goddess. Her hull was painted blue and white, and silver letters shone on the starboard side: HDFS *ADIONA*

"Adiona," Jon said. "The ancient Greek goddess of safe return."

"Ironic," Etty said. "Given that half of us will probably return in body bags."

"Exactly why we need *Adiona*'s blessings," George said. "She is absolutely my favorite goddess."

Etty poked his belly. "Your favorite is the goddess of food."

George pushed her away. "You could use some food, pipsqueak. You weigh less than my left butt cheek."

"Dude, Manhattan weighs less than your left butt cheek," Etty said.

Jon rolled his eyes. "Goddammit, you two, must you ruin every moment?"

An airlock opened, and the shuttles entered the starship. They thumped down in a cavernous hangar.

The troops emerged. Jon looked around him with wide eyes. The hangar was vast. It probably spanned the entire lower deck of the *Adiona*.

The battalion formed rank—companies, platoons, squads, and finally fireteams. Jon joined his familiar fireteam. Him, Etty, and George. In this strange place, in this crazy war, his friends gave him comfort.

If I must fly with anyone to war, it's these people, Jon thought.

George had been his friend since childhood. But in just ten weeks, he and Etty had become just as close. Indeed, everyone in the platoon were like siblings to him now.

Well, maybe not Clay.

Lieutenant Carter was here too, standing at the head of the platoon. Jon looked at the officer, trying to catch his eye. But Carter stared ahead, face blank.

Finally, when everyone was getting restless, a door opened. A man entered the hangar, coming from deeper in the starship. He stepped onto a stage.

Only by sheer discipline did Jon not gasp.

"It's him!" Etty whispered. "It's actually him! Ensign Earth!"

"It's just an actor," George whispered.

"Both of you hush!" Jon said. Sergeant Lizzy was already glancing their way, and even with basic training over, she still carried her electric whip.

Ensign Earth—or at least, the actor playing the character—raised his chin and saluted. A screen behind him came to life, featuring a billowing flag of Earth. The planet itself was painted on his shield.

"Welcome, brave soldiers, to the *Adiona*!" said Ensign Earth. "This state-of-the-art starship will take you on your first journey across the gal—"

The handsome officer flickered, then vanished.

A sergeant cursed, stepped onto the stage, and kicked a projector. Ensign Earth returned in full holographic glory. A few soldiers had to stifle laughter, earning glares from their sergeants.

"So much for visits from celebrities," Jon muttered.

"… transport you all the way to Bahay!" the hologram continued. "First, our cutting-edge azoth crystals, embedded deep in *Adiona*'s engines, will actually bend spacetime. The very fabric of the universe! Did you know? Only azoth, a crystal mined on a distant moon, can bend spacetime, making faster-than-light travel possible. Discovered in the twenty-first century, azoth crystals were embedded in engines during the First Alien War, when—"

"Hey, Jon!" Etty leaned toward him. "I had an idea for your song. Maybe instead of horns, you can—"

"Etty, I'm trying to listen."

He returned his attention to the hologram.

"… and in a week, we'll reach our first wormhole!" Ensign Earth was saying. "Did you know there are over *four hundred* known wormholes in the Orion Arm of the Milky Way Galaxy? That's right! And did you know they're over *a million* years old? An ancient species built them long ago. The ancients are extinct, but thanks to their wormholes, we can travel to the most distant stars. With a combination of azoth crystal and wormholes, we will reach Bahay within—"

"Seriously, dude," Etty said. "You need a pan flute instead of horns. Just a single pan flute! I played one as a kid. Can I join your band?"

"Etty, hush!"

He tried to focus on the lecture. He knew a little about wormholes. As a child, he had studied plastic models of the Tree of Light, also known as Wormhole Road. This ancient transportation network spanned the galaxy. Even with warp drives, journeys between the stars could take months, even years. But reach a system with a wormhole, and you could travel anywhere instantly. Without them Bahay would be much too distant to fight, or even to care about. It was three-hundred light-years away, far outside Earth's dominion.

But it also happened to be near a wormhole.

Jon knew that Earth's leaders wanted to liberate Bahay, to kick out the Santelmo aliens and welcome the Bahayans into the Human Commonwealth. But there were more than ideals of unity at work here. So close to a wormhole, Bahay could become an important gateway to the distant stars, perhaps the most important planet in the empire. Bahay would give Earth a foothold in the depths.

Right now, Jon didn't really care about that. What was empire building to him?

All I care about is finding you, Ernesto, he thought. *You killed my brother. So I will kill you.*

"Dude?" Etty whispered. "You okay? You're shaking."

Jon forced a deep breath. "I'm fine. Yes, flutes. Good

idea."

Ensign Earth ended his lecture with a proud salute. "Godspeed, soldiers of Earth. Now let's sing my favorite song: Earth's planetary anthem!"

The song filled the hangar. The flags billowed on the screens. Ensign Earth's hologram vanished halfway through, and the sergeant cursed and kicked the projector.

Chapter Thirty
City of Lost Souls

Maria walked through the city, so hungry, maybe starving.

She had no family. No roof over her head. No man aside from the cruel Ernesto, whom she had fled. Maybe no hope.

But right now, all of that faded.

Right now, she had no food. And her hunger consumed her.

"Please, *Tita*, food."

A toddler lay in a puddle, leaning against a cement curb, naked. He reached out a hand to Maria.

"Please, *Tita*, I'm hungry."

It was hard to tell his age. He was as small as a baby.

"I have no food," she whispered and walked on.

The toddler slumped into the puddle. A few steps away, older children were rummaging through a trash bin. They found chicken bones, let out cries of joy, and began nibbling on pieces of fat and skin, not even minding the flies.

Around the street rose concrete walls—cliffs of peeling paint, trickling rust, and billboards. On one billboard, a glamorous woman modeled a diamond necklace. Prostitutes leaned against the wall beneath her, boys and girls barely into their teens, smoking cigarettes. Another billboard advertised perfume. Naked children ran beneath it, covered in mud. A third billboard entreated Maria to *BUY HER CHOCOLATES*. A junkie sat beneath the sign on a cardboard throne, snorting *shabu*, the drug of lost souls.

Maria walked onward, leaving the concrete canyon, and

entering a shantytown. She did not know if the ground here was soil or cement. Garbage covered it, rising halfway up her shins. A sea of plastic, paper, and rot. The shanties rolled across the hills, stacked three and four high. The squatters built them, collecting plywood, scraps of iron, and sheets of tarpaulin, constructing crude shelters. The metal was rusting. The wood was rotting. It was hard to distinguish the shanties from the trash; both were equally decayed.

When Maria passed by a river, she saw a towering figure walking along the bank, moving between the shanties. The figure seemed humanoid, but it was as tall as a tree, even taller than Earthlings. Its limbs were like poles, long and black, and its blank face swung from side to side, a single white eye in its center, bobbing and shining like an anglerfish lure. It was an alien, Maria realized. Life from beyond Bahay or Earth. Along with Earthlings, other life must have landed here. Perhaps this alien was a galactic scavenger or beggar, washed up in Mindao with the rest of the refugees. Maria paused for a moment, watching the slender giant as it waded through the river, then vanished behind a landfill. A shudder ran through her.

She continued to explore the city, hoping to see more aliens, to ask them of the worlds beyond, of the magical realms among the stars. But she saw no more. Only humans. Millions of humans, crammed together in the crucible.

A little girl in a red dress waded through the garbage, laughing, chasing a cat without a tail. Three toddlers sat on a tin roof, naked, nibbling on bones. A young woman in a pink dress was dancing, a ballerina of the slums. Perhaps in her mind, she danced on a stage in a grand concert hall. Another young woman, probably younger than Maria, was nursing a baby. Two of her older children sat beside her, crying, hungry, covered in flies.

There were few men.

The men were in the Kalayaan. Or in the Southern

Bahayan Military, the force that served Earth. Or they were dead.

Most likely they were dead already.

"Was the city always like this?" Maria wondered aloud. "Or was this once a grand metropolis, clean and peaceful and prosperous, and the war broke it?"

Just more questions. Same old Maria with the big head.

Another question filled her mind.

"Will I be like this? Like the squatters and the trash people? Am I like this already?"

A voice boomed in the distance.

"Yeah, that one. No, no, not her! Oi—the little one, what with the long hair. Yeah, yeah, you. Come here."

Maria frowned. A voice speaking English, one of the common Earth languages.

She waded through the trash. Train tracks ran alongside a landfill, lined with squatters. Maria found the man there. An Earthling soldier with a blond mustache. He faced a mother with eight or nine children, all younger than Maria.

"Yeah, that one!" the Earthling said, pointing at a girl. "She's a pretty one. I'll give you a nice shiny Earth dollar for her. Oh, don't worry, I'm not buying her. Just renting her for the night." He licked his lips, scratched his crotch, and held up a coin.

The mother scrutinized him. All her children were hungry. They were naked. Desperate.

Finally the mother nodded and reached for the coin.

"Hey, stop that!" Maria ran toward them.

The Earthling turned toward her. His eyes widened, and he laughed. "Well, would you look at that. Another rat slit crawled out from the trash." He squeezed his crotch. His armored suit clanked. "You want some too, slitty?"

She drew her knife. "Get back!" She stabbed the air. "Back, back! The girl is not for sale. Nor am I."

The Earthling growled. "Everything's for sale here. You

slits are fucking rats who sell your own kids for a dollar." He tossed the coin at Maria. "Go on, pick it up, slit. Bend down, pick it up, and then suck my—"

Maria stabbed him.

Right in the thigh. Right below the crotch where two armored plates came together.

The Earthling screamed. He clutched his wound, and blood gushed between his fingers.

"You fucking whore!" he shouted.

She waved the bloody knife. "I was aiming for your *titi*, but it was so little I missed. Go! Go away, or I'll try again!"

Cursing and spitting, the Earthling limped away.

Maria turned toward the mother. Her children huddled around her—including the girl the Earthling had favored. She was probably only eleven or twelve, her hair tangled and caked with mud, her limbs stick thin.

"Are you all right?" Maria said. "I—"

"Why did you scare him away?" the mother cried. "What business is it of yours? Are you a priest's daughter? No! You're just a squatter like us. No better! Go away! Go!" She began pelting Maria with trash. "Go, go!"

Maria winced. "But—"

The mother hurled more garbage at her. Maria fled.

But on her way, she picked up the dollar.

She wandered through the shantytown, seeking a place to wash. She had not bathed in weeks. The urge for clean water became as mighty as the hunger. There was plenty of water in Mindao. Gutters overflowed with it. Streams coursed through the city. But Maria could not even see the water, just the film of trash floating on it, rippling and undulating like the skin on a slithering snake.

A train chugged by, carving its way through the slums. Squatters ran alongside, begging. A few passengers tossed out scraps, and the squatters scrambled to catch them. But there wasn't enough for everyone, and soon fights broke out.

Maria walked along the tracks, this vein through the shantytown, home to thousands. She listened to snippets of conversation. Some people were refugees from North Bahay. But many had been born and raised here by the tracks. Children washed in plastic buckets. Women hung laundry from ropes that stretched between shanties. Everywhere, like barnacles, grew crude huts of rusting corrugated steel and crumbling plywood, stacked together, as many as four or five shanties high, swaying, sometimes collapsing in the breeze, being rebuilt, rising again and again like a child repairing his sandcastle after the waves.

There was an economy here, Maria realized. Some sold their flesh to Earthling soldiers. But they also bartered. A can of rainwater for an old chicken bone with some meat still clinging to it. A pinch of *shabu* for an old cabbage, the inner leaves barely rotten at all. A battery for a turn with the lice comb.

Food. Water. Sex. Drugs. They powered this city.

Back home, we had groves of papaya, banana, and mango trees, Maria reflected. *We had rice paddies that covered the hillsides. We had humble homes, but they were comfortable and warm. That world is gone. It feels like a dream.*

"Pagpag?" An old woman approached her, carrying plastic bags. "Pagpag? Do you want to buy pagpag, girl?"

Maria frowned. "What's pagpag?"

The old woman held out a plastic bag. It was full of some kind of stew. Maria's stomach grumbled.

She held out her dollar. "Give me all this will buy."

The woman's eyes widened. She snatched the dollar, tossed Maria a bag, and hurried off. Soon the old woman was wandering across the tracks, chanting, "Pagpag, fresh pagpag for sale!"

Maria opened the bag. It was a sticky stew of meat,

carrots, some cabbage. She devoured it. It tasted divine. It was the best meal she had ever eaten.

Her belly full, Maria wandered on, seeking shelter for the night. In an alleyway, she came across the pagpag vendor again. The old woman was kneeling over, fishing garbage from bins and gutters. When she came across chicken bones, the old woman plucked bits of meat off. She found a few rotten vegetables too. With wrinkly, stiff hands, the old woman set up a portable grill and began cooking the garbage.

A few children ran toward the cooking meal. "Mmm, pagpag!"

"Back, back!" The old woman swung a ladle at them. "Back!"

Maria's stomach churned. She covered her mouth.

I ate garbage, she realized. *Cooked garbage.*

She spent that night near the train tracks, but she did not sleep. All night, commotion rolled across the shantytown. Junkies danced and fought and shouted, eyes rolling back in euphoria. Prostitutes prowled, mostly young women, but children too, boys and girls, selling their diseased bodies for food, water, or drugs. A thief rummaged through bins, and a woman shouted, and mopeds roared by, and gunshots echoed in the night. Rats scurried everywhere.

Maria huddled against a wall of rusty iron, holding her knife before her. The Earthlings were gone, sleeping in their barracks, but new dangers filled the city, demons of drugs and disease, and blood spilled across the night, and the tears of Bahay flowed like a river along the train tracks.

An old man reached for Maria once, licking his lips, pawing at her breast, and she sliced his fingers. A boy tried to steal her only shoe, and she gave it to him. A crazed, drugged woman screamed at Maria, pointing at her, shouting, "Aswang, aswang!" *Demon, demon!* People laughed. The woman tried to stab Maria with a sharp stick, and Maria ran, her tail between her legs.

Finally she found shelter in an alleyway far from the tracks. She huddled between shanties, amid orphans, stray cats, and a snoring addict. Maria fell into a deep sleep, and in her dreams, she was trapped in a dark labyrinth, and there were no lights to guide her home.

"Give me, give me, give me…"

A voice rasped in her ears.

Claws clutched her leg.

Maria's eyes snapped open, and she scuttled back. An old man was pawing at her legs. His mouth opened in a lurid grin, revealing one brown tooth. Sores oozed across his face.

"Give me, give me…" He reached out, hand shaking. "Shabu, shabu, just a taste… Give me, give me."

"I have no drugs," Maria said.

The old man screeched and clawed at her, and Maria fled. She dared not sleep again, but stayed standing against a wall, knife held before her, until dawn.

Chapter Thirty-One
Welcome to Bahay

It was a long journey from Earth to Bahay.

For two weeks, Jon prowled the starship, feeling like a tiger in a cage. After the busy chaos of boot camp, it felt strange to have so much free time. Time to think. To worry. To miss home.

This was a military starship, and there was a strict routine. They woke up early in the morning. They sang the planetary anthem and saluted the flag. They exercised, and there was even a firing range on board, which they visited every day. They all had kitchen duty, cleaning duty, and laundry duty.

But most of the time, they just waited.

Every soldier found a way to spend the time. Many stayed in their bunks, where they could watch television or read books. Others spent hours in the ship's gym, while some socialized in the lounge.

Jon spent most of his time on the upper deck, a narrow observatory away from the crowd. Up here, in the shadows, he could hear the ship—the vibrating decks, the humming engines, the million moving metal parts. Wide viewports gave him a grand view of space all around. For hours, he would stand, listening, watching.

They were flying at warp speed, weaving spacetime into a bubble around them. The stars stretched into thin lines, delicate trails of light all around. Everyone else thought the view boring. But Jon found that he could stare into space for hours, lost in thought.

Music came to him—inspired by the starship's sounds and the beauty of the starlines. He bought a notebook in the commissary, and he wrote a song every day. He had no musical instruments. He could not play what he composed. But he wrote the notes, and he sang softly under his breath.

It was a reason to return home someday. To go into the basement with George and Kaelyn. To play this music of space on Earth.

He even wrote a flute part for Etty.

In some ways, it was nice to have this time to think, to compose, to return to himself. To become Jon the musician again, not just the exhausted, bruised, weary recruit.

But in many ways, this was harder than boot camp. On Roma Station, he could focus on nothing but pain and exhaustion. Here, aboard the starship *Adiona*? Here he had time to think. To remember home. To miss his parents. To miss Paul. Here there was no pain. Worse—there was grief. There was fear. And it made him miss the thoughtless agony of basic training.

At night, he lay in his bunk, along with the rest of his squad. As the others slept, Jon would gaze up at the dark ceiling, and Lieutenant Carter's words echoed.

Your brother was executed.

Every night, Jon conjured new images of his brother's killer. Sometimes Ernesto appeared like the Bahayan robots in the plastic jungle—a caricature, a wily slit, Fu Manchu mustache and all. Sometimes he appeared to Jon as demonic, one eye blinded by a cataract, mouth full of fangs, fingers sprouting claws, laughing as he killed. In his dreams, Jon found himself trapped in the labyrinth again, that strange realm of coiling branches and shadows, and Ernesto chased him, swiping with his claws, his fangs bright, a primordial vampire.

Two weeks after leaving Earth, a voice emerged from

every speaker, filling the starship.

"All soldiers report to Lounge 13 in preparation for wormhole jump."

Jon was sitting in his bunk, scribbling notes on a music sheet. He glanced at his friends. Etty and George looked back. Nobody said anything. They didn't need to.

We're almost there, Jon thought.

This brief daze, this solace from violence—it was ending.

Wordlessly, they made their way to the lounge. It spread across the front of the ship, built above the bridge. The soldiers took formation in their units. Viewports stretched across the prow, forming a semicircle, affording a view of space. They were still flying at warp speed. The stars stretched in countless lines.

The voice emerged again from the speakers.

"Prepare for drop from warp. Entering normal spacetime."

Jon's head spun. He nearly fell. The lounge seemed to bend around him, to sway. He felt ten feet tall, then as small as a child. Everyone around him stretched out, shrank, stretched again, like reflections in fun house mirrors.

Jon was suddenly in his basement at home, playing music, and Paul was there.

He was a toddler, running in the yard, playing with his dog.

He was in a dirty little room, holding a woman in his arms, a young woman with brown skin and silky black hair—a Bahayan.

And then he was back in the lounge. He groaned.

"Whoa." Etty rubbed her temples. "What the hell just happened?"

"Spacetime bent around us," Jon said. "Not just the three spacial dimensions, but time too. I think we just saw the past." He shuddered, remembering the dirty room and dark-eyed girl. "And the future."

Etty shivered. "I didn't see a future. Does that mean that…" She gulped.

"I saw you in *my* future," George said. "We were together among palm trees. I don't know where. Maybe Bahay." He groaned. "What a trip."

The starlines had vanished, becoming points again. The Milky Way spread across the viewpoint, a glimmering vista. Slowly the starship's prow rose, and there above…

Jon pointed. "The wormhole."

It appeared as a sphere of light, almost like a luminous moon. When Jon had been a child, his parents had bought him a plastic model of the Tree of Light, the galaxy's network of wormholes. He had connected dozens of wormhole portals, represented as yellow spheres, using blue tubes. When constructed, the model seemed like a tree with many branches, each node another part of the galaxy.

Nobody knew who had built the Wormhole Road. Jon was about to fly along a million-year-old highway.

The starship approached the wormhole. Across the lounge, everyone stared in awe. The wormhole grew larger and larger, soon taking over half the viewpoint. It swirled and shone like a star.

"I imagined it as a ring," George said.

"It's three-dimensional," Jon said. "Like a black hole. It's a type of black hole, in fact. A tear through spacetime."

"Hold on tight, boys!" Etty said. She grinned, but her grin was nervous, and she clutched Jon's hand. Hard.

The *Adiona* flew closer, closer, and the wormhole covered the entire viewport, and then—

Jon wobbled on shaky legs. A few soldiers swayed, and one crashed onto the deck.

The starship plunged down a tunnel of light.

"Woo!" Etty cried.

Jon winced. They raced forward, faster, faster, and walls of light streamed at their sides.

And then—it was over.

All at once, they were back in regular spacetime.

They had completed the jump. Within a single moment, they had leaped hundreds of light-years.

"That," Etty said, "was awesome."

George gulped. "I'm gonna throw up."

"Ugh, George, move away from me!" Etty said. "You already threw up on me once."

"That was me *drooling* on you," George said.

Etty placed her hands on her hips. "Why are you drooling over me anyway? Can't stand the sight of a beautiful woman?"

"Etty, I was sleeping!" George said. "And you were trying to steal my chocolate bar."

She rolled her eyes. "Well, if you didn't sleep on a pillow of chocolates…"

"Guys," Jon said. "*Guys*. Look."

"I wouldn't *have* to sleep on my chocolates if *somebody* didn't try to steal them all day," George continued, "and—"

Jon grabbed his friends and pointed out the viewport.

A planet floated ahead.

It was mostly water—in all three states. Vast oceans. Swirling clouds. Frozen poles. But through the clouds, one could make out many islands. Thousands of islands and archipelagos, green and lush.

"There it is," Jon said softly. "Bahay."

"It's beautiful," George said. "I don't know what I expected. A ball of fire? It's a world at war, but it's beautiful."

Etty lowered her head. "Typical humans. We find a beautiful world, so we have to fuck it up."

"Maybe that's why Earth is fighting so hard to liberate Bahay," Jon said. "Because it's such a great planet."

Etty snorted. "Liberate? Or conquer?"

Jon groaned. "You're talking like the enemy."

"No." Etty shook her head. "I'm talking like somebody who thinks for herself, not somebody who just listen to Ensign Earth's propaganda."

"I don't just listen to Ensign Earth!" Jon said. "I—"

I lost a brother, he was going to say. *And I know who killed him. I saw him—Ernesto Iron Santos. And that's all I care about. Not empires, not conquest, not liberation—but revenge.*

But he could say none of that. Would Etty understand? Would anyone understand? Even Jon did not understand it. The anger he always felt. That all-consuming fury. The hatred of the enemy and the never-ending mourning. The emotions confused him, controlled him. Etty was wrong. He didn't let Ensign Earth think for him. It was his own emotions, confused as they were, that led him. That controlled him.

There's a reason why generals throughout history drafted teenagers to fight their wars, he thought. *Teenagers are confused, emotional, and stupid, and when hurt enough, they will willingly go kill and die.*

As the starship flew closer to Bahay, Jon felt a sudden, overwhelming urge to flee. To fly back to Earth. To step away from it all. To drown in his music and misery.

But he could not change his path now. The starship entered Bahay's orbit, and orders came through the speakers.

"All soldiers—report to your shuttles. Welcome to Bahay."

Chapter Thirty-Two
Under Two Moons

Mindao was not all poverty. Not all despair. When Maria climbed onto the landfills, she could see them in the distance.

Buildings.

Actual buildings. Not shanties of plywood and plastic, but real buildings of real concrete.

"Maybe there is hope there, Crisanto," she said. "Maybe we can find work. Live in an apartment. Still find a life."

She kept her pet Santelmo hidden in her pocket. The Earthlings hated the aliens more than anything. If anyone saw Crisanto, if anyone told, they would kill him. And probably kill Maria too.

But sometimes Maria still whispered to her hidden friend. So softly nobody else could hear. She knew he could hear.

She began to walk down the landfill, heading toward that distant promised land of concrete and light.

It was only a day's walk from the shantytown. But it felt like the distance between stars.

By the time she emerged from the slums, the suns were setting—both Sargas, which burned like a great oven, and Konting Liwanag, its smaller, dimmer companion which glowed like a candle. Even as night fell, Maria could not see Asul Mata or Pilak Mata, Bahay's two moons. Too much smog hid the sky. Even without the smog, she doubted one could see the moons from Mindao. Neon lights shone across the city, advertising bars, brothels, and opium dens. Skyscrapers soared beyond them, some ten or twenty stories tall. That probably wasn't very tall for Earthlings, but to Maria these seemed like the tower of Babylon. There was no sky on Bahay. No more than there was sky in the jungle.

The streets buzzed and rattled. Countless mopeds, psychedelic jeepneys, and rickshaws bustled back and forth, ferrying the locals home from work—or to the countless pubs and bars that lined the roadsides. Maria also saw jeeps and armored trucks painted with the phoenix of Earth's army. Earthlings filled them, some already drunk, many catcalling at women.

The Earthlings were everywhere here in the city center. They prowled the streets, whistling at girls, and smacking them on their behinds. They sat at roadside bars, nursing bottles of beer. They spilled out of brothels, pretty Bahayan girls on their arms, taking their hired dates out for a night of dancing and drinking.

The Blue Boulevard. It was a place of light and laughter. Yet even here, in the bright center of Mindao, sadness lurked.

Beggars sprawled on every street corner, reaching out shaky hands. Many of the bargirls had arms scarred from years of *shabu* use, and their eyes were dim and vacant. Urchins scuttled underfoot, begged, or slept in alleys. Most were Bahayan orphans, their skin brown, their hair black. But some children had blond hair, blue eyes, black skin, and a variety of other colorings.

They were *mestizos*, Maria realized. Half Earthling, half Bahayan. The sons of Bahayan women and Earthling soldiers. Homeless. Forgotten. Scurrying through alleyways or begging for scraps. Children of the war. The *mestizos* seemed the lowest on the rungs of beggars, hiding in the darkest alleys, eating the poorest of scraps. The downtrodden among the downtrodden. Maria wondered how many of their fathers were carousing with bargirls as their children from previous pleasures starved only feet away.

A group of soldiers stumbled down the road, leaning on

one another, arms slung around shoulders. They held bottles of beer, and they sang a drunken song until they saw Maria.

"Hey, look what washed up from the slums," said one.

Another soldier wrinkled his nose. "Fuck me, she stinks."

"Pretty for one of the urchins, though," said a third soldier. "Wash her, put her in a nice dress, she'd be a snack." He smacked his lips and stepped toward Maria. "What's your name? Are you hungry?"

Maria stared at the soldiers.

And she heard the planes rumbling overhead.

She felt the fire.

She saw her parents' burnt corpses.

She fled down the road, heart pounding, and the Earthlings laughed.

I killed two of these giants, she thought. *But they still terrify me.*

She took a deep breath. Right now, she had no time for fear. She needed food. She had eaten nothing since the *pagpag* last night, and already she was dizzy with hunger.

She walked a few more blocks, moving away from the larger cluster of Earthlings, and along narrower streets. She approached a kiosk. Its walls were made from plywood, and its roof was a loose sheet of corrugated steel, rusty and dented, held down with old rubber tires. A flower shop, she realized when she stepped inside. Hundreds of plants grew from clay pots, filling the shanty with a sweet scent.

"Hello, I'm Maria de la Cruz," she said to the owner.

"No urchins here!" the old man said. "Go, go!"

"I'm looking for work."

The old man snorted. "So are a million refugees. Go, leave! Your stench will make my flowers wilt."

She left the flower shop. She walked down the cracked asphalt, passing under tangled bundles of crackling electric wires, strings of laundry, and a stained concrete overpass. A stray cat hissed at her, fur bristling, one eye puckered by scars, then turned and ran. A little neighborhood of shops had sprung up around the overpass's pylons, reminding Maria of barnacles under a fishing boat. People had stretched out plywood and sheets of plastic, forming crude shops and dwellings. The air hung hot and humid like a soup, filled with the odors of the city.

Maria walked toward another shanty, a place that sold knockoff watches, healing crystals, and prayer beads supposedly carved from the cross Christ himself had died on.

"I'm looking for work," she said.

But the lady who worked there tossed her away. "No urchins!"

Maria emerged from under the overpass, walked down a street, and leaped back to avoid a racing rickshaw. She walked between crumbling apartment buildings, their paint gone, their concrete stained, their barred windows leaking rust. The buildings looked barely habitable, so decayed and filthy Maria kept expecting them to fall. But people lived here. Rusty air conditioners rattled in windows, and laundry hung between them, and orphans gathered around their doorways, begging as people came and went. Countless electric cables draped across the alleyways like the cobwebs of mechanical spiders, tangled up, buzzing and shedding sparks.

Maria stepped toward a building covered with graffiti and smog stains. A rusty sign swayed from hinges: HOTEL PARADISO.

She entered. She found a corridor that reeked of mold, and she approached a front desk. A pretty young woman sat there, dressed in ironed livery, her makeup meticulous. She seemed out of place amid such decay.

"I'm looking for work," Maria said.

"Are you a virgin?" the pretty woman said.

"I… What?"

The pretty woman nodded. "Men pay extra for virgins. Can you dance? Show me your breasts. Let me see what I'm working with."

Maria ran from the hotel. As she stumbled outside, she nearly bumped into soldiers. The Earthlings were returning to the hotel. Scantily clad girls—and a few boys—hung on their arms.

Night was falling again. More urchins emerged, battling for scraps. Maria, desperate with hunger, tried to rummage through trash bins, but the urchins had a pecking order, and they shooed her away.

The human body can survive for weeks without food, she reminded herself. But she had barely eaten for weeks already, and she began to worry that she would starve to death here. Perhaps it would have been kinder to burn with her parents.

She spent the night in an alleyway between a bar and brothel. She wanted to stay awake, fearful of rats, junkies, and rapists. But her exhaustion was too great, and she slept deeply. When she woke up, it was dawn, and a soldier was pissing into the gutter beside her. Droplets sprinkled her leg.

Her stomach growled. She was so dizzy. She stumbled down the street, delirious with hunger, and smelled frying pancakes. Her eyes rolled back. The smell practically grabbed her nostrils like hooks and tugged. Following her nose, she found a little shop where an old man was frying batter, wrapping the pancakes in newspaper, then serving them to customers. Maria had no money, but she entered the alleyway behind the bakery and opened the trash bin.

Two children and a cat were inside, licking crumbs off crumpled newspapers. Maria reached inside, and a child bit her. She fought. She was stronger. She managed to pull out some newspapers and collect a few precious crumbs.

At lunch, she found a place selling fried chicken. Earthlings queued up for lunch, joking around and swapping stories of battles in the north. Maria had to fight the urchins again, fighting her way toward a garbage bin, and she managed to score a chicken thigh. Somebody had eaten most of it, but there were still precious shreds of meat to be found. She revelled in her triumph, even as the hungry children wept, and she hated herself for it.

I should return to the rainforest, she thought. *I could live like an animal, hunting, foraging.*

But so much of the rainforest had burned. Mister Weird had wilted the rest. Maria feared those lands. Feared the villages of deformed babies. No, she dared not pass through that wasteland again. Even if virginal rainforest still existed on Bahay, it grew beyond her reach.

She tried to find work. She entered shop after shop.

"I can cook pancakes."

"I'm a good cleaner."

"I can sell anything, I can sell these rosaries for sure! I'm a good Catholic girl, you know."

But the shopkeeps all tossed her out. No urchins! No refugees! Half the city, it seemed, was like her. Refugees of the war, come to find work, finding only slow death.

She explored more neighborhoods, and she found more shantytowns. So much of Mindao was a slum. And the farther you went from the Earthling streets, the worse it became.

Maria traveled miles of slums, of misery, of teenage girls with so many children, of starving babies, of toddlers fighting dogs for scraps. This seemed barely a city at all, more like an asylum, a hellscape that never seemed to end.

She walked through throngs of starving people, over mountains of garbage, through shantytowns constructed of the trash they grew on. The landfills had come alive, sprouting cities of their own. From a hilltop, she saw the slums rolling in all directions, a sea of despair, of hungry eyes peering through decaying flotsam, rotting away, and the rivers of filth flowed.

And in the middle of these slums, she beheld light.

Beauty.

A beacon of hope.

Maria shuffled through the crowds, through the decay, heading toward that light. Barefoot and in rags, so filthy, a sinner by the glory of god. It towered before her, taller even than the barracks where Earthlings lived. A cathedral. A grand miracle of architecture, painted azure, its spires reaching toward heaven. Maria shed tears, for she had never seen anything more beautiful.

Many of the poor shuffled toward the cathedral, to worship in its light. But gates held them back. An iron fence would not let them in. A priest emerged to bless them, but he gave them no food. There was beauty and wealth here, there was a palace of glory, but Maria now saw it as a place of greed and false hope.

She slept outside the gates of the Azure Cathedral that night, and in the morning, she collected scraps of food from the landfill, and she sold them to those too weak to rise. All day, she moved back and forth, collecting edible garbage, selling it for pennies, until at night she had earned twenty pesos.

She spent them on an *empanada*—a pastry full of potatoes and beef, the outside hot and crispy, the inside soft and heavenly. It was the best meal she had ever eaten. And after she ate it, she threw it up, and she trembled all night, vomiting, feverish. Perhaps the potatoes and beef had come from the landfill, and perhaps the poison from the countryside had filled her. In the morning, she thought that she was dying.

She sat under a cluster of buzzing electric wires, and she drew her father's knife.

She sat in a city of decay, of concrete and rust and vomit and tears, but in her mind, she was back in San Luna. The papaya trees were blooming, and the rice was growing in the terraces, and her mother was cooking *arroz caldo,* tangy rice gruel rich with ginger and chicken, garnished with roasted garlic and scallions. The rooster was crowing, and in the evening when the air cooled off, she would run among the mango trees, picking sweet fruit.

She placed the knife against her wrist, trying to slice her veins. But she was so weak her hand couldn't tighten around the hilt, and she dropped it.

Crisanto emerged from her pocket, and the ball of light nuzzled her. It was a little light in the darkness of her soul. It kept her alive. She sheathed her blade.

So let hunger kill me, she thought. *Or disease or a broken heart. But it will not be despair.*

She stumbled onward, barefoot, heading toward flashing neon lights.

It was there that she found the Magic Man.

It was there that he changed her life.

Chapter Thirty-Three
Bugs

It was hot.

That was the first thing Jon noticed about Bahay.

It was damn hot.

He walked across the base, drenched in sweat, blinking in the sunlight.

"Goddammit, my balls are swimming in a pool of sweat," George muttered, walking beside him.

"Gross!" said Etty.

"Hey, you were just talking about boob sweat earlier today!" George said.

Etty snorted. "Yes, but my boobs are things of beauty, and your balls are… Well, let's just say I don't want to walk in on you in the shower again."

"Dude, my balls are bigger than your boobs," George said.

Etty rolled her eyes. "Ooh, good one. You got me."

Jon sighed. "Are you two going to bicker the whole war? Focus on finding shade, not flirting."

"We're not flirting!" they both said together.

Jon rolled his eyes. "Suuure."

Etty flipped him off. "Fuck you, Maestro."

They had been on Bahay for several hours now, free to explore the base. Fort Miguel was a sprawling base located in South Bahay, fifty miles north of Mindao. Named after Miguel Lopez de Legazpi, the European conqueror of the Philippines, the fort was home to an HDF brigade. Thousands of Earthling soldiers bivouacked here.

The three friends kept walking through the base, exploring it.

This was nothing like boot camp. Back there, you'd end up in deep shit if your boots weren't perfectly polished, or your shirt not perfectly tucked in. Here, soldiers ambled around in wife beaters, rifles slung casually across their backs, smoking cigarettes. A few soldiers were playing soccer in a dusty yard. Others lounged under a Eucalyptus tree, listening to classic rock from an old-fashioned boom box.

The guitars were shredding, but Jon could barely hear them. Fort Miguel was *loud*. Gunfire rattled from the firing range. A tank squadron rumbled by, and Jon and his friends stood, waiting for the gargantuan machines to pass. Helicopters roared overhead, and far above them, Jon could make out a starship in orbit, a pale smudge in the sky.

Even the sky seemed alien here. This was a binary star system. Two suns lit Bahay. The largest one was named Theta Scorpii A, also known as Sargas. It was far too bright and hot for Jon's liking. Bahay orbited this star. Theta Scorpii B, known to the locals as Konting Liwanag, was smaller and dimmer. It wasn't much larger than Venus viewed from Earth, but it shone for all it was worth—just to add a little heat and make Jon a little more miserable. Twin moons hovered in the sky between the suns. Asul Mata was pale blue, while Pilak Mata was white. Both were crescent-shaped today, pale in the daylight. They would not reveal their true glory until Sargas set in the east. Yes, the sun set in the east here on Bahay.

We're definitely not in Kansas anymore, Jon thought. *I miss Earth's sky. I—*

He started.

"Hey, hey, let go!" Jon kicked wildly. "What the hell is that?"

A furry little creature clung to his pant leg. It stared at Jon with huge eyes. The eyes were almost comically large for such a small creature. It was no larger than a hamster, but it had human-sized eyes.

"Aww, it's a tarsier!" Etty said.

"It's got my pants!" Jon said.

Etty knelt and fed the animal some crumbs. "Here, buddy."

The tarsier snatched her phone from her pocket, stuck out its tongue, and climbed a palm tree.

"Little fucker!" Etty cried and aimed her rifle. Jon had to push the barrel down.

"Save it for the enemy, Ettinger. Don't waste bullets on the local wildlife. They're harmless! A few little animals never killed any—ow!"

A giant insect landed on Jon's arm and bit him.

Etty burst out laughing.

"Bastard!" Jon shook the bug off—it was the size of a pigeon—and aimed his gun.

"Hey now, no firing on helpless animals!" Etty pulled his gun down.

"That wasn't harmless," Jon muttered. "That was a goddamn incubus."

They kept walking. Many palm trees rustled around them. Many more had been cut down to make room for Fort Miguel. One couldn't take a step without stumbling over a tree trunk. But outside the camp, the jungle was everywhere. It grew beyond the fort's outer fence, looming like green cliffs. It draped across the mountains. It coated a hundred islands that rose from the eastern sea.

Heat. Engines. Bugs. That was Jon's first morning on Bahay.

He was about to find a place to sit, close his eyes, and

relax when a flash of light caught his eye.

He looked up. Sergeant Lizzy was walking through the base, her golden braid hanging across her shoulder. Her prosthetic fist was reflecting the sunlight, flashing like a beacon. Her electric whip hung from her hip. Thankfully, it was turned off. Now that boot camp was over, hopefully that whip would see less action.

A tall, burly man walked beside the sergeant. His wide chest compensated for an ample gut. His hair was thick and white, his face pudgy, but Jon saw the resemblance to Lizzy.

He's her father, Jon realized. *Yes, they have the same face, only his is male, older, and gone to fat.*

Three stars gleamed on the man's shoulder straps. Jon gasped. A colonel! An actual colonel! It was the most senior officer Jon had ever seen.

Jon snapped his heels together and saluted. A second later, George and Etty followed suit.

Walking by, Lizzy raised an eyebrow. "Well, well, if it isn't the Three Stooges." She turned toward the colonel. "Dad, meet Larry, Curly, and Moe. I trained these clowns at Roma Station."

The colonel looked them over, nodded, and returned the salute. "At ease, soldiers. My god, you look like proper misfits." He squinted at Jon. "Goddamn, son, your arms are skinnier than my granddaughter's wrists. Get yourself a sandwich." He turned toward George. "Holy Mother of God, you're a giant. You're going to attract enemy fire from miles around." He finally noticed Etty. "Dear lord, and this one is tarsier-sized. In fact, you look like a tarsier with those buggy green eyes." The colonel sighed. "No wonder they sent you to my brigade. You're perfect cannon fodder."

Lizzy glowered at the trio. "You better prove Colonel Pascal wrong. You will show him you're warriors!"

"Yes, Commander!" they said.

Lizzy nodded. She and her father walked onward.

After the sergeant and colonel departed, the friends looked at one another, silent for a moment.

George shuddered. "What did he mean by cannon fodder?"

Jon sighed. "We've been assigned to Apollo Brigade. That was Colonel Joe 'Crazy Horse' Pascal. He's the brigade's commander. I've heard of him. My brother served here." He watched the heavyset colonel trundle toward the mess hall. "I didn't realize he's Lizzy's dad until now."

Etty's eyes widened. "Hey, I've heard of Apollo Brigade too! It's on the news back on Earth a lot. They say it's the worst brigade in the army."

"That's us," Jon said. "If you barely passed boot camp, they send you here. A place for misfits and troublemakers. Apollo Brigade is notorious. It gets sent on the most dangerous missions."

"Because… we're the best soldiers?" George said hopefully, though he was already looking queasy.

Jon laughed. "Because we're expendable. As the colonel said—we're cannon fodder." He slapped George on the shoulder. "But hey, it ain't all bad. Lizzy is still our platoon sergeant. And her dad commands the entire brigade! We might get some preferential treatment."

Etty groaned. "And attract every goddamn Kenny in the jungle who wants to destroy the colonel's favorite platoon."

"Yes, well, pros and cons," Jon said. "Come on, guys, let's not think about blowing up just yet. Let's find a commissary. I'm so thirsty I could drink tarsier piss."

They walked a while longer through the hot, dusty base. They found a commissary among eucalyptus trees, and soon all three were drinking cold Cokes, lounging in the shade. The commissary radio was playing a country song, and tarsiers scuttled between the branches.

"All right, boys, you gotta admit." Etty leaned against the tree and took a long gulp. "Bahay ain't as bad as we thought."

"It's horrible!" George said. "So much heat and bugs! And the music stinks. Where's all the heavy metal?"

But the giant was only joking. Jon knew that. He had to admit: perhaps his fears had been overblown. Jon had imagined something like from the old war movies. Like the trenches of the Somme or the slaughterhouse of Corpus. This, well… this wasn't half bad. Some cold drinks, some tunes on the radio… Jon could see himself passing the time here at Fort Miguel, sipping Cokes, shooting the shit with his friends, and hopefully never facing a bomb or bullet.

"Ya know," Etty said, "our fireteam needs a name."

"Oh yeah?" George said.

"Sure!" said Etty. "Our platoon has a name. We're Lizzy's Lions. Our company has a name. Cronus Company. Our battalion has a name. Horus Battalion. Our brigade has a name. Apollo Brigade. And our division—"

"We get it, Ettinger," George said.

She placed her hands on her hips. "My point is—what about us three?"

"Fireteams don't have names, pipsqueak," George said. "They're just three soldiers. Too small."

Etty poked his belly. "With you, big boy, nothing about us is small. How about… Fireteam JEG?"

George tilted his head. "Why JEG?"

"Jon, Etty, and George!" she said. "Duh."

"That sounds stupid," George said. "The army has enough acronyms."

Etty thought for a moment. "How about… The Little Rascals?

"I'm not little!" George said.

Etty tapped her chin. "The Little Rascals Plus One."

George groaned. "No. God no." He tilted his head, lost in thought. "How about Fireteam Symphonica? On account of our band."

Etty snorted. "I ain't part of Symphonica."

"You are now, pipsqueak," George said. He looked at Jon. "Tell her. About the flute part you wrote for her."

Jon felt his cheeks flush. He hadn't meant to tell Etty about that. Ever. It was just something he had done one lonely night. "Um, I…"

"He wrote you a flute section!" George said. "On the song 'Falling Like the Rain.' Great tune. Flute will sound much better than a damn horn section."

Etty's eyes widened. "I'm honored!" She kissed Jon's cheek. "Fireteam Symphonica!"

Jon wasn't sure about this. Symphonica was something deeply personal to him. The band he had created with his brother and Kaelyn. Neither of whom were here.

But maybe he needed that connection to home. To who he had been.

Kaelyn's words echoed. *Come back pure, or come back dead.*

"All right," Jon said. "We're Fireteam Symphonica. Not that it matters anyway, since fireteams don't even have official names."

But it did matter. And it felt right. And for a moment, the three sat in silence, knowing that something profound had just happened, that they had forged a link to home and identity. That they had tied themselves to art in a world of war. They could not articulate it. But they held hands. And they understood.

* * * * *

Boots thumped, and a shadow fell.

"Hey there!" A young captain in a jumpsuit came walking toward the fireteam, interrupting the deep moment. "You fellas are fresh meat from Earth, right? Horus battalion?"

"That's right!" Etty said. "Best damn battalion in the army." She placed her hands on her hips. "If you need dumb cannon fodder who don't know what's best for 'em, we're your guys! Especially Fireteam Symphonica, being us three."

Jon saluted. "Sir, yes, sir."

"Welcome to Bahay, fellas. And hey, no need to salute officers nonstop here, this ain't boot camp." The captain winked. "Unless you see a general with phoenixes on his shoulders, we're pretty casual here. The name's Pete. No need to sir me either. As I said, we're laid back here. How you guys acclimating so far?"

"All right, sir!" Jon said. "I mean—all right, Captain Pete. It's not as bad as we thought."

Pete laughed. "Well, it's a quiet day. Just last week, we had the goddamn Kalayaan raining missiles on our base. The week before, half our force rolled into the jungle. A bunch never came back. That's why they shipped you in. You guys are replacing the dead." He barked a laugh. "Ah, you should see your faces! Don't worry. It ain't that bad. You use common sense, obey orders, and you'll fly home to mama in one piece."

Jon wasn't sure if the captain was joking or not. So he just nodded and said, "Thank you, sir. I mean—Pete."

Pete gestured at a helicopter on a nearby patch of grass. "That's my bird. We're giving new soldiers tours of the island. Care to go for a scenic flight?"

"Hell yeah!" Etty said. "It's boring down here."

"I like boring," George said. "I don't like helicopters."

Etty snorted. "Jesus, dude, you flew in a starship through a wormhole. You can handle a helicopter."

"Starships in wormholes aren't flying over enemy

territory," George muttered. Yet as the others began following Pete toward the helicopter, the giant joined them.

It was a Pelican-class transport helicopter, a large machine with two rotors, a fat hull, and a front hatch that lowered like a beak. A dozen or so soldiers were already inside—familiar faces from Roma Station.

Fireteam Symphonica took seats, balancing their rifles between their knees. Jon tightened the straps on his helmet.

"I just hope the helicopter can take off with your fat ass in here," Etty said, poking George.

"I swear I'm going to throw you out!" George said.

"Ettinger, leave the ginger giant alone," Jon said.

"Aww, he knows it's cuz I love him." She ruffled George's hair and kissed his cheek.

George blushed.

"Well, well, would you look at that. A tarsier kissing a hippopotamus."

They turned in their seats.

Jon's heart sank.

Clay Hagen entered the helicopter and took a seat across from them.

"Perfect," Etty muttered. "We're three hundred light-years from home, and we still gotta deal with Private Putz here."

"Jon and I also had to grow up with him," George said. "He's from the same town."

"My condolences," said Etty.

Jon remembered those days. Clay tormented them throughout their childhoods. One time he had dragged George by the hair across a street. That had been before the brain tumor, before George had grown to monstrous size. But Jon knew his friend had never gotten over the pain.

"What's that, dickheads?" Clay rose from his seat and gripped his rifle. "You wanna say something, you say it to my face."

"Soldiers!" Captain Pete marched across the helicopter. "There a problem here?"

Clay snorted. "We got a bug infestation."

"Sit your ass down, Private," Pete said. "You're itching for a fight, I get it. You been stuck in boot camp, then a starship, then here on base, and you gotta blow off steam. Well, save it for the enemy. You'll get your chance soon enough. Now sit down cuz we're about to take off for the royal tour. I'm flying." The captain glanced at George. "That is, if we can take off with you on board, big boy."

"It'll take a miracle!" Etty said, chipper.

But the helicopter managed to rise, carrying the squad of soldiers. After so long in space stations, shuttles, and starships, Jon figured he'd be used to flying. But the helicopter was worse. His belly roiled and he clung to his seat.

It didn't help that the helicopter's side doors were open, exposing them to the sky. And the ground. And that there were no parachutes.

The helicopter rose higher, and mustering his courage, Jon leaned toward the open hatch. He could see the entire base from here. Thousands of soldiers. Hundreds of tanks and armacars. Artillery cannons. Row after row of tents. Squat concrete armories. It was a little world carved from the jungle.

The helicopter flew along the coast, leaving Fort Miguel behind. To one side spread the sparkling sea. To the other—the rainforest.

"All you see here is South Bahay!" Captain Pete shouted from the cockpit. "The southern slits are our allies. At least most of the poor fuckers. These here jungles? They're full of Kalayaan Kennys. Those are the bad slits. Those are the slits you kill. Those are the slits who turned down our generous offer of liberation, and who chose to rise up against Mother Earth. For that sin, we will smite them down with the fury of gods."

Several miles up the coast, they came across a village.

A Bahayan village. The first one Jon had ever seen.

Hell, he had never even seen a Bahayan *person* before. Just the robotic ones in the plastic jungle, the little goblins with the Fu Manchu mustaches and buckteeth. He looked with interest at the village below.

It was a small village, only twenty or thirty bamboo huts. Several reed fishing boats floated on the water. Villagers sat in the grassy commons, rowed the boats, and stood along docks, fishing rods in hands. More moved amid groves of fruit trees and gardens, while some worked in a rice paddy. They wore straw hats and simple tunics.

"My God," Etty said, voice so soft Jon barely heard over the rumbling helicopter. "It's like something out of ancient history."

Jon nodded. "Remember your history lessons? The Santelmo aliens brought a group of Filipinos here in the nineteenth century, hoping to save them from the Philippine-American War. Their technology advanced a little. Since arriving here, the Bahayans figured out radio communication, electricity, and combustion engines. They're about where Earth was in the early twentieth century."

"Why did they advance so slowly compared to Earth?" George asked. "In that time, Earth invented the internet, starships, warp drives, and hot dog flavored Bugles."

"Still no flying cars, though," Etty muttered.

"Well, they started with only a few thousand colonists," Jon said. "Considering their humble beginning, they've made remarkable progress in three hundred years. They've colonized a world."

Clay Hagen rose from his seat. "They're just a bunch of retarded slits." He leaned out the helicopter. "Hey, slitties!"

Several villagers below were watching the helicopter. One pointed.

"Yeah, you, slits!" Clay shouted. "You ain't nothing but bugs!"

Clay aimed his rifle and opened fire.

A gunshot echoed through the cabin.

Below, a Bahayan fisherman fell down dead.

Clay hooted. "Woo! Yeah! Take that, fucker!" He laughed hysterically and fired again. Another Bahayan fell dead. "Two dead slits, yeah! Come on, stop running away, slits! Woo!"

Clay aimed his rifle again, prepared to kill a third villager.

Jon grabbed him and pulled him back.

"Stop that!" Jon shouted. "What the hell are you doing?"

But Clay just laughed, head tossed back. A deranged, high-pitched laugh.

"Winning the war, asshole!" He wrestled himself free and aimed at a fishing boat. "One by one, we'll kill the slits!"

Clay fired again.

But this time, Jon pulled him back, and the bullet flew wide.

The villagers below were fleeing. Fishermen were rowing back to the shore.

"Dammit, Taylor, you slit-lover!" Clay spun toward him, gun hot and smoking. "I should put a bullet in your brain."

"You should save your bullets for the enemy!" Jon said.

"I was killing the enemy!" Clay said. "You traitor."

"You were murdering villagers!" Jon said. "The Bahayan civilians aren't our enemies."

"They're all fucking slits!" Clay said. He grabbed Jon. "If you love them so much, go down and fight for them."

He shoved Jon toward the open hatch.

Jon's heart burst into a gallop. With one hand, he caught the doorframe and clung for dear life. Clay pushed again, trying to shove Jon to his death.

And then George was there, howling, wrapping Clay in his massive arms, and Etty was screaming, pulling Jon back into the helicopter. Everyone was shouting. A few soldiers were laughing.

"Fight, fight, fight!" a corporal began to chant.

Still flying the helicopter, Captain Pete looked over his shoulder. "Goddammit, soldiers, stop acting like kids. Sit your asses down! All of you!"

"Sir!" Jon said. "I must report that Private Clay Hagen was firing on civilians, violating the HDF's code of conduct, and—"

"And he tried to murder Jon!" Etty burst in.

"Soldiers, I said sit down!" Captain Pete said.

"Sir!" Jon said. "With all due respect, this is serious. He—"

"Private, this ain't Earth no more," the pilot said. "This is the jungle. There ain't no code of conduct here. We fight the slits here. And we *do not* rat on fellow soldiers."

Jon sat down, stunned. Etty and George looked at him, shocked into silence.

Clay only smirked. He pointed at Jon.

"You know what happens to rats, Taylor?" Clay swiped his finger across his neck, then burst out laughing.

The helicopter continued the tour, flying over jungles, mountains, rice paddies, and several HDF outposts.

Jon spent the rest of the trip silently, barely looking at the view. For the first time in his life, he had seen death. Not just a closed coffin, but men and women dying.

He felt empty.

And it was only his first day on Bahay.

That evening, he walked through Fort Miguel, heading toward his tent. Etty and George walked beside him. They were all silent. A few soldiers laughed nearby, kicked a ball around, and music played. But Jon could still hear the bullets.

Jon lay on his cot that night. More cots filled the tent; an entire squad bunked here. Clay was awake, bragging about his kills. He was pretending to fire his gun, making sound effects of bullets and dying villagers. Other soldiers listened in rapt attention. When Clay imitated Jon complaining, his voice rising to a whine, the soldiers laughed.

"Asshole," Etty muttered, lying on her cot beside Jon. It was the first word she had spoken since the helicopter ride.

Sergeant Lizzy appeared at the tent door, shouted at them to lay down and sleep, and they killed the lights.

But Jon lay awake for a long time in the darkness, and when he finally slept, he dreamed that he was falling from a helicopter, falling and falling into a dark pit and never finding the ground.

Chapter Thirty-Four
Revenge Is a Hot Bullet

Bahay had broken her. Taken her arm. Shattered her soul. And now Lizzy Pascal was back, and she felt like shards of glass rattling inside a suit of armor. An illusion of strength. A broken warrior.

Back in the Lions. Her lover's platoon.

Back in the Apollo Brigade. Her father's brigade.

Back on Bahay. Her people's war.

I'm strong, but I could not fight them, Lizzy thought. *They dragged me back. And now I'm broken.*

"We should never have come back," she whispered, staring out the trailer window at the jungle. "We should have forgiven."

Carter rose from his desk, leaving his maps of the jungle, enemy camps marked with red pins.

"Forgiven?" His face was a tense mask, hiding his rage. "Forgiven that monster? After what he did to you?"

Lizzy nodded, eyes damp. "Yes. They say the best revenge is living well. We are not living well."

Carter walked around the desk. There was tension in his steps. In his shoulders. He forced air in. "It's been said that revenge is a dish best served cold. What a contemptible lie! Revenge is a hot bullet in your enemy's heart. How can you forgive Ernesto for…" His jaw clenched. He could say no more.

"For raping me," Lizzy said softly. "For burning me with his iron. For cutting off my hand. The pain still fills me. The nightmares still haunt me. Now more than ever. Cart, we should have stayed away."

She gazed out the window again. She was in a small trailer at the edge of Fort Miguel. From here, she could see the security fence, a guard tower, and beyond it—the sprawling jungle. That hell where she had fought the enemy for two years. Where she had languished in a bamboo cage for weeks. The jungle she would soon enter again.

Yes, her lover commanded her platoon. And her father commanded her brigade. And both men were brave warriors. But Lizzy felt so alone here. Her lover, her father, and all the soldiers here could not protect her. Not from what was out there.

"Lizzy." Carter hugged her from behind. "We'll do this together. And it'll be over soon. It—"

She wriggled free. "Stop touching me. It will never be over!" She spun toward him, tears in her eyes. "And if we kill Ernesto, what of his men? The men who helped him? And if we kill them, what of the whole Kalayaan? Then what of this whole world? It will never end for you, Cart! You'll always keep fighting, because…" She hung her head. "Because that's all you know."

He took her hands. "I was born the son of a general. A general who abandoned me and my mother, leaving us to the slums. But I escaped! I proved I'm my father's son. I went to Julius Military Academy, an honor denied to most. I served, and I fought, and I killed, and I watched friends die. I saw my entire platoon wiped out, and I kept fighting. Because I'm a soldier, Lizzy. That's what I was born for. What I trained for. What I vowed to always be. But it's not all I know." His voice softened, and he stroked her cheek. "I know how to love you."

She wept. "You don't—"

"I do—"

"You don't know how to love me!" Lizzy said. "You want to protect me. To avenge me. I'm just an excuse for your war! This? Love?" She laughed bitterly. "There is no love here. Not on this planet. Only hatred. Only pain."

"Lizzy." He gripped her hands, refused to release her. "I love you. Do you hear? I love you! I would burn down the galaxy for you."

"I never asked you to burn anything for me," she whispered. "Maybe sometimes just try to hold me. To be here for me. Not for your war. Not for your revenge. Just for me."

He pulled her into his embrace. Lizzy lay her head on his shoulder, tears silently falling, and he kissed the top of her head.

"I'm here for you," Carter whispered. "Just for you. Always."

Lizzy touched his cheek. "You're a good man, Lieutenant Michael Carter. You're honorable, and kind, and brave. But you're broken. You're more broken than I am."

"We will heal," he said. "I promise. But I can only heal the way I know how. Not with forgiveness, but with lead and fire."

Lizzy took a step back. "You scare me."

Carter caressed her prosthetic hand, silent for a long moment.

"I scare myself," he whispered. "I'm scared of losing more soldiers. I'm scared of losing Jon so soon after we lost Paul. I can't let my troops see. I can't let my superiors know. But I'm always scared, Lizzy."

She hugged him, kissed his lips, and her tears fell.

"I love you," she whispered. "And I'm with you. If this is the path you must take, if you must walk again into the heart of darkness, into the jungle where we broke… I'll walk with you. Always. To the end of the universe."

That night, they shared his bed, and they made love in the hot, humid darkness. Lizzy straddled him, head tossed back, his hands on her breasts, and her skin glistened in the light of Bahay's twin moons. Her skin was pale, silvery, while his was black as the space between stars. They were darkness and light, love and fire, and as Lizzy rode him, she felt like she was in the jungle again. Running. Fleeing monsters in the shadows. Lost forever in the nightmare. And when she climaxed, she cried out so loudly Carter had to cover her mouth.

She collapsed into his arms, crying softly, so afraid. He smoothed her hair, kissed her tears away, and held her until the dawn.

Chapter Thirty-Five
Fortunate Son

For the first time in his life, Lieutenant Michael Carter was going to meet his father.

It frightened him more than battle.

He walked through Little Earth, the finest military base on Bahay. This was nothing like Fort Miguel, the crude outpost where Carter spent most of his days. The Old Mig, as they called it, was a mere swath of scorched soil carved from the rainforest, peppered with trailers and tents. That place was rough. But here? Little Earth, where the generals lived? Here was a piece of paradise.

Little Earth was right outside Mindao, the sprawling capital of South Bahay. Walking here, it was hard to believe that shantytowns, shabu dens, and despair could lurk just a short distance away—just beyond the white walls that surrounded this compound. Here, within the walls of heaven, grassy lawns rustled in the wind. Flowerbeds bloomed with color and sweet scents, attracting butterflies. Rather than tents or shanties, the buildings here looked like ancient Greek temples, boasting marble columns, glimmering white under the sun.

Carter was wearing a dusty, dented battlesuit. The scars of war marred the armor plates: burn marks, bullet holes, a crack from an enemy's machete. He felt woefully underdressed. A few other officers were present, strolling along the pebbly paths, wearing dress uniforms. The white fabric sported golden cuff links and buttons. They looked more like Disney princes than soldiers, if you asked Carter.

He sighed. Even after three years at Julius Military Academy, he still felt out of place among these people. He felt like a crude vagabond walking among royalty. Like an impostor.

You always carry your childhood with you, Carter thought. *Even the wealthiest, most powerful men are just broken boys inside. I might be an officer now. A graduate of Julius Military Academy, the most prestigious school on Earth. But I'll always be that fatherless kid from the streets of New York.*

He winced, his childhood returning like waves, beating against him. The grassy lawns, blooming flowerbeds, and marble columns disappeared. And once more Michael Carter was only a child, racing barefoot through the concrete canyons of New York City, lord of the slums. The public housing apartment blocks soared around him, draped with fire escape staircases like braces on the stone teeth of titans. Graffiti-coated brick walls, forming forests of color, the artwork of the city. A beggar reached out a shaky palm, and a junkie hid in an alley, staring from under a ragged hood. A gunshot echoed in the distance, and somebody screamed.

But young Carter knew no other world. He did not fear the pimps, nor the drug dealers, nor the crossfire of battling gangs. He feared monsters under his bed. He feared vampires and wolves in the alleyways. Every day, people died around him, this battlefield far from any war in space. And Carter dreamed up monsters and ghosts in the shadows.

He would spend his days on the streets, returning home after midnight. There was such sadness in his home, a concrete box on the sixth floor, overlooking an alley full of dumpsters. When his mother was away, working two jobs to survive, the apartment seemed so empty, lonely, like a prison cell. When she was home, it was worse. Even as a boy, Carter saw the hunger in her eyes, her nervous mouth. She always cooked him two full meals every night, even when she herself went hungry.

Men came and went. A string of Mother's boyfriends. A few beat her. A few beat Carter. They stayed for a while, spent more money than they earned, then wandered off. But young Carter and his mother remained, scars deepening.

"Your father is a powerful general," Mother told him many nights, stroking his hair. "And someday he'll come back to us."

"I want to see his picture again!" the boy said. "I want to see Daddy!"

That always made Mother seem so sad. But she showed him the photograph.

"Here he is, son."

Cart stared at the man in the photograph. A white man in a military uniform, his face hard and craggy like a boulder, his blond hair streaked with silver. The boy had inherited his mother's darker skin, wise brown eyes, and black hair. It was hard to believe this officer was truly his father.

"Why did he leave?" the boy asked so many times.

Mother smiled and wiped a tear from her eye. "It's time to sleep, Jimmy. No more questions tonight."

And now, twenty years later, Michael Carter was walking here through Little Earth, a wealthy military base hundreds of light-years from home. He wore the insignia of an officer on his shoulders. His path had been long. And it had led him to here. To this planet. To this war. To finally meeting his father.

He approached a neoclassical building, climbed an elegant staircase, and stepped between marble columns. Two guards greeted him, both men resplendent in dress uniforms. Carter showed them his tablet.

"Here, signed by Colonel Joe Pascal," he said. "There's a holographic vidature too. I have a meeting with General Ward today."

The guards gaped.

"*You* have a meeting with General Ward." A guard rubbed his eyes. "*You.*"

Carter smiled thinly. "Yes, this young lieutenant in the beat-up battlesuit has a meeting with General Ward, high commander of all HDF forces on Bahay. I know it seems crazy. Which is why I have this tablet, signed by a colonel. You can view the attached hologram to confirm."

A guard raised a minicom, a small portable computer, and scanned the barcode on Carter's tablet. A small hologram of Colonel Pascal, commander of the Apollo Brigade, appeared and confirmed the meeting. Vidatures were becoming more and more common in the military, harder to fake than mere signatures in ink.

The guards exchanged glances, then shrugged and let Carter in.

He walked through the building, his boots thumping against the polished tiles. People crowded the building, Earth's headquarters on Bahay. Most were senior officers. They wore dress uniforms and displayed stars and phoenixes on their shoulders, not butterbars like Carter's insignia. There were also Bahayans here—servants in livery. They were cleaning. Pouring coffee. Typing notes. Carter didn't know how trustworthy they were—after all, Earth had conquered half their planet—but the top brass considered the South Bahayans loyal allies in this war against the Red Cardinal.

The South Bahayans hate the Red Cardinal just as much as we do, Ensign Earth had vowed in a recent video. Carter found that hard to believe.

But right now, he had other things on his mind.

He passed several more guards, checkpoints, and interrogations. He was patted down. The vidature was scanned again and again. He stood in line to speak to a small army of clerks. He spent a lot of time in waiting rooms.

Finally, long after entering Little Earth, Carter entered the office of General Charles "Chuck" Ward.

And there he sat. The supreme commander of the Bahayan War. The highest ranking officer on Bahay, answering directly to the president on Earth. The hero of Titan who had suppressed the rebellion with his iron will and flaming warships. The famed Granite General himself, his face and heart both said to be as hard as stone.

My father, Carter thought.

He instantly recognized the officer from the photograph. Ward had aged. After all, that photograph was a quarter century old. The hair was fully silver now, cropped close. The face was even harder, craggier, a face like a granite boulder, the mouth like a crack in stone. But the eyes were the same. Cold eyes, blue like frozen seas, like death. Eyes like a winter that never ends.

Those eyes chilled Carter. And they weren't even looking at him. The general was busy riffling through papers on his desk.

Carter found it odd that Ward still used actual physical paper. Carter had never touched paper. In an era of holograms, augmented reality, and even direct-to-brain video feeds, paper seemed quaint.

But Ward was clearly a man from another era. Carter glanced at the books on the general's shelf. *The Art of War* by Sun Tzu. *De re militari* by Vegetius. *De Bello Africo* by Julius Caesar. *The Memoirs of Napoleon Bonaparte* by Louis de Bourrienne. Hundreds more leather-bound books of ancient warfare, most of them written centuries or millennia ago. *The Chronicles of the Alien Wars* by Einav Ben-Ari was the only modern title, and even that was a good fifty years old. Several maps hung on the walls, but they depicted ancient Earth during the Roman Empire, the British Empire, and the United Hegemony following the Cataclysm of 2093. Again, nothing from this century.

Ward had risen to command the Bahayan Garrison, so

clearly he was a capable man. But it was the year 2223. At least judging by his office, Ward was far behind the times.

He's my father, Carter thought. *The man I saw in the photograph so many times. The man I've wanted to see since I was a child. But he looks like a stranger.*

Carter stood at attention and saluted.

"Sir, Lieutenant Michael Carter reporting!"

For an agonizingly long time, the general ignored him. Ward kept looking through his notebooks and maps. He raised a pen, flipped a page, and wrote a note. A thick ring, set with the jewel of Julius Military Academy, gleamed on his finger. That and the phoenixes on his shoulders, denoting his rank, were his only ornamentations. Some senior officers wore medals and pins like a portable trophy case across their chests. Ward did not need to peacock his honors. Everyone on Bahay recognized his authority.

Finally Ward spoke, though he did not raise his eyes from his work.

"Yes, the young infantryman from Apollo Brigade. Colonel Pascal was quite adamant that I see you." The general wrote something in a leather-bound notebook. "Normally lieutenants don't step into my office. Especially not wearing dusty battlesuits." He licked his fingertips and flipped the page. "This must be *quite* important."

Carter took a deep breath. It was just the moment he had been waiting for since childhood. No pressure.

"Sir, I won't beat around the bush," Carter said. "I'm your son."

That got the general to raise his eyes.

He stared at Carter for a long, piercing moment.

Then Ward returned to his notebooks and kept writing.

"I don't believe it. Dismissed, Lieutenant."

Carter did not leave.

"Sir," he tried again, "I know we don't look alike. I look

like my mother, Abigail Carter." He raised a photograph, showing his mother smiling on their balcony. "You met her twenty-five years ago. She was working as a maid in the Palaye Hotel. You spent a night there in 2198, and you had dinner together. Fried octopus, she said. And—"

"Ah yes." General Ward put down his pen, scrutinized Carter, and nodded. "Yes, yes. I see it on your face. I remember her now. A young African-American maid. Bit skinny, but she made her uniform look good enough. Her name was Anabelle, you say?" He cleared his throat, flipped a page in his notebook, and returned to work. "Dismissed, Lieutenant."

Carter blinked. "But—" He was lost for words. "Sir, I—I'm your son. I thought that…"

His voice trailed off. He had never imagined their reunion like this. He had not imagined warm hugs, per se, but at least… a discussion.

General Ward looked up again from his work. His face hardened. "Lieutenant, I've got a war to run. I can't be the father you want. *Dismissed*."

"Sir!" Carter took a step closer to the desk. "I've been waiting all my life to meet you! Do I mean nothing to you? Does my mother mean nothing? She told me you loved her, that—"

"Your mother was a distraction for a night. That was all. She means nothing to me. I haven't thought about her since that night twenty-five years ago. I know you want a father, Lieutenant, but right now, I need you to focus on your duties as a soldier. *You are dismissed*. Leave now, or I'll have security drag you out."

Carter was a decorated officer. He had led men in battle. He had gone deep into the jungle, had killed enemy soldiers, had held his dying friends in his arms. He was a scarred, battle-hardened warrior. But right now, his eyes dampened, and pain stabbed his chest like a dagger.

He saluted. "Sir."

He turned to leave.

As he was stepping through the door, General Ward spoke again. "Lieutenant?"

Carter froze. "Sir?"

"One more thing, Lieutenant." The general stared at him. "Don't come back here. Ever again."

Carter tightened his lips, fighting back the damn tears. He nodded, closed the door, and walked down the corridor with a cold, hard lump in his chest.

He left Little Earth. He returned to his base, and he rejoined his platoon.

Lizzy was there. The love of his life. The tall woman looked at him, her golden braid hanging across her shoulder, sadness in her eyes.

She knew what happened. She read it on his face. She understood.

I'm sorry, her eyes said, damp and full of love.

I love you, Lizzy, Carter thought. *You're the only good thing in this whole damn galaxy.*

She could read his thoughts. He saw that in her eyes, in her hint of a smile.

That silent communication lasted only a few seconds. Then Lizzy's face hardened. She pressed her heels together, saluted, and shouted, "Attention!"

The platoon snapped to attention.

Carter looked at them. Young privates and corporals. Green boys and girls from Earth. Jon. George. Etty. All the rest of them. They stood stiffly, rifles in hands, and he saw the fear in their eyes.

Tomorrow I will lead them to battle. Many of them will never come home.

A hollowness filled Carter. This war suddenly seemed so meaningless. His life—so purposeless.

But no.

There was still one task to complete on Bahay.

He had failed to connect with his father. But there was a more important goal.

I will find Ernesto. He clenched his fists, fury washing over him, hotter than ever. *I will find the man who hurt Lizzy. And then my life will have meaning again.*

Chapter Thirty-Six
Eyes in the Dark

After a week in Fort Miguel, Jon was almost grateful to be out in the jungle.

Almost.

His week at the Old Mig had passed slowly, full of quiet tension. It was easier than boot camp. There was less drilling, more free time. But with that time came worrying. Thinking. Missing home. Sometimes when nobody was watching, the tears would come, and a hard lump would fill his chest. By the week's end, Jon had been climbing the walls.

Having Clay in his squad didn't help matters.

And now, it had come. His first mission. A journey into the wilderness.

The platoon walked through the brush, rifles locked and loaded. In the green jungle, they wore navy blue battlesuits. Whoever had chosen this color deserved a court martial, if you asked Jon. To send troops in blue into a green jungle was a colossal blunder or, more likely, an act of supreme arrogance. Jon could imagine the generals chortling around a table somewhere on Earth.

Redesign our battlesuits that worked so well on Ganymede? Ah, hell, screw that. Who needs camouflage anyway when you're an apex predator? Hell, maybe we want the slits to see our boys! Strike terror into their wily little hearts!

Jon grumbled under his breath. Thankfully, the troops on the ground had improvised. They had covered their battlesuits with mud, leaves, and branches, creating crude camouflage. Where the high command blundered, the grunts adapted. This tradition went back throughout the history of warfare.

Still, Jon suspected the camouflage wouldn't fool too many Kennys. The troops' boots snapped every fallen branch and twig, and they were breathing like pigs. Greendeer watched them curiously from the trees, strange beings with luminous white antlers and leafy fur, while iridescent glimmerbirds fled from their advance. Braided serpents hung from branches, nearly indistinguishable from dangling strings of moss. Only their watchful eyes revealed their sentience. If there were any Kalayaan guerrillas among the branches, they were undoubtedly watching too.

"A Kenny!" George suddenly cried out, pointing at a tree.

At once, the platoon leaped for cover and aimed their guns. But it was only a mourning monk—a furry critter, apelike, its brown fur vaguely resembling a monk's habit. The animal watched them lazily. Clearly, it had never evolved fear of humans.

Clay shot it. It thumped down dead. It would have to evolve that instinct soon.

Clay smacked George on the back of his head. "Dumbass."

They were fifty soldiers in the Lions platoon. Some were fresh from Roma Station. Others had been on Bahay for a year or two now, were already battle-tested. Jon tried and failed to hide his nerves. Every hooting bird, every scuttling animal, every rustling leaf—it made Jon jump and aim his gun. The more experienced soldiers smirked.

One corporal patted Jon's helmet. "Nervous virgin."

Jon took a deep breath. He tried to calm down, to focus on the nature surrounding him.

Bahay was, despite being a war zone, beautiful.

Moss coated boulders and fallen logs, and rivulets

streamed over particolored stones. Creatures filled the water, covered in scales of different colors, blending perfectly among the river stones whenever they froze. Curtains of ivy and lichen swayed, and mist hovered like ghosts.

The trees soared, taller than any trees on Earth, their boles like the columns of cathedrals. Branches intertwined overhead, forming vaulted ceilings rustling with countless leaves. Fangwoods sprouted millions of hungry leaves like Venus flytraps. Their branches moved, and their jaws snapped, capturing furry little insects. Jon *loved* those trees. The bugs on Bahay were a constant pain in his backside—sometimes literally. The buggers got everywhere, sneaking under armor and undergarments, and their bites hurt like hell. Sometimes they laid eggs under the skin. Extracting them involved big knives and searing iodine. Yes, Jon decided that bug-eating trees were his best friends on his planet. After the war, he vowed to personally plant a hundred more.

Some of the plants and animals on Bahay, mostly those found in local villages and army bases, had come from Earth. Rice. Fruit trees. Tarsiers. All familiar. But here in the jungle? Here was an alien ecosystem.

"It's beautiful here," Jon said. "Say what you like about Bahay, the nature is gorgeous."

George was waving bugs away. "It's awful."

"If you think this is beautiful, you should see the deserts of Israel," Etty said. "Rolling dunes, limestone mountains, sprawling plains of sand…"

"There she goes again," George said. "Blabbering on about sand."

Etty glowered. "Sand is beautiful!"

"Sand is what cats shit in," George said.

"George, I swear, I—"

"Soldiers!"

At the head of the column, Sergeant Lizzy looked back at

them. She held a finger to her lips. They all shut up.

Jon needed a break from the bickering giant and girl. He walked ahead along the trail, leaving his fireteam, and passed by several squads. He reached the head of the platoon.

Lieutenant Carter was walking here, staring ahead, rifle in hand. He moved with the deadly grace of a prowling tiger. War paint covered his face, and leaves stuck out from his helmet, hiding the insignia of an officer. Ferns and trees rustled around them, insects buzzed, and the sun bathed the trail with searing yellow light.

"Sir," Jon said. "I was hoping to speak to you."

"You should address any concerns to your squad leader, Private," the officer said. "Don't go over his head."

Jon lowered his voice. "Sir, I had to come directly to you. It's about what we discussed." He dropped his voice to a whisper. "Our secret mission on Bahay."

"All right," Carter said. "Talk to me."

Jon swallowed. "Back at camp, sir, you told us we need to secure a hilltop in the jungle. Sir, is that truly our mission? Or is there more to it?" He glanced behind him, made sure nobody was listening, and looked back at Carter. "Are we still tracking Ernesto Santos?"

For a long time, Lieutenant Carter was silent. They walked on through the rainforest. Finally, Carter nodded.

Jon's heart hammered. "So we *are* tracking him. We *are* going to face him. The man who killed my brother. Sir, if we find him, I…" Jon hesitated, then the words spilled out. "I should be the one who does it, sir. I've never killed a man." His voice shook. "I never wanted to kill a man. But Paul was my brother, sir, and if we can find his killer, we—"

"Private Taylor?" Carter said.

Jon swallowed. "Sir?"

"Right now, I need you to return to your position in my

platoon, and to obey orders without question, and *not* to get emotional. Is that understood?"

Jon nodded. "Yes, sir."

He fell back and rejoined his squad.

They walked all day. It began to rain, mist hovered, and mud flowed around their boots. The battlesuits made the heat even worse. Bugs kept biting their exposed necks and faces, thunder boomed, and shadows filled the forest. By evening, Jon wondered how he had ever found the rainforest beautiful.

There was nowhere good to make camp. They slept in the mud. The rain pounded their tents, leaking through to soak them. Rivulets flowed everywhere, ready to steal a man's boots or canteen with watery fingers. Leeches clung to any exposed skin, and some even wriggled under men's armor. Thunder boomed throughout the night. When it was Jon's turn to guard the camp, he felt useless. Blackness cloaked the trees. If there were enemies in the rainforest, they could sneak right up without Jon ever seeing.

You're out here somewhere, Ernesto, he thought, shivering in the darkness, rain pouring down his face. *You're close. We're aliens here. We don't know the rainforest like you do. But we're strong. We're Earthlings. We're going to find you and kill you.*

In the darkness, he saw Kaelyn's face. He heard her voice.

Come home pure.

Tears flowed down Jon's cheeks along with the rain.

"But I'm no longer pure, Kaelyn," Jon whispered. "I'm no longer that boy who wrote those songs for you. Something broke inside me when Paul died. The army broke whatever remained. I've never killed before. But I have a killer's heart. I was filled with music, but now I'm filled with hatred."

It scared him. It scared him more than ten thousand guerrillas in the shadows.

Morning dawned cold and wet, and the platoon kept

traveling.

It kept raining all day. The bugs kept biting.

"I hate the rain," George said, soaking and miserable.

"I'm telling ya, buddy," Etty said. "The desert is where it's at."

"Fuck jungles, and fuck the desert, and fuck space, and fuck the army," George said. "I wish I was home."

Etty lowered her head. "I wish I had a home. I have nothing waiting for me back on Earth."

George opened his mouth, perhaps preparing a scathing retort. But then he placed his hand on Etty's shoulder. "You do, Etty. *My* home. Once we're back on Earth, you have a place to live. With me and my sister."

Etty leaned against him. The top of her helmet only came halfway up his chest. She looked like a child beside George.

"Thanks, Ginger Giant," she said, and she had to wipe away tears.

They walked all day, and still no sign of the enemy. Jon approached his officer again, but Carter remained tight-lipped. The lieutenant kept to himself, rarely even speaking to Lizzy, walking at the head of the troops. He drove them on at a punishing pace.

Walking through the brush, Jon looked at his lieutenant and sergeant. He couldn't help but shudder.

Ernesto hurt you too, Jon thought. *He wiped out your last platoon, Carter. He brutalized and mutilated you, Lizzy. He hurt you even more than he hurt me.*

It was no wonder the pair kept marching onward, even as everyone else was nearing exhaustion. This was not just a military mission, Jon knew. It was a personal vendetta.

* * * * *

Night fell again.

Jon lay down in the mud. He was so exhausted he fell asleep at once. But he slept fitfully. The rain kept pattering against him, and squirming creatures in the mud kept biting him. Everything hurt.

In his dreams, he lay in a filthy room, a shadowy girl in his arms. He remembered her. The girl he had seen during the warp jump aboard the *Adiona*. Warp engines bent spacetime. They said they could provide glimpses into the future. But Jon's glimpse was blurry at best, a mere hint of soft skin, moldy walls, a whispering voice.

"Wake up, dumbass."

A foot jabbed Jon. He opened his eyes, groaning, and found himself back in the mud.

"Up, Maestro!" Etty said. "Guard duty."

"For fuck's sake, Etty." Jon pushed her boot away. "Do you really have to kick me awake?"

"What were you expecting, a kiss and breakfast in bed? Get to guarding!" She yawned. "I'm exhausted. Time to crawl into my nice warm puddle of mud."

She was snoring by the time Jon rose and loaded his gun.

He stood in the darkness, guarding blind, staring at shadows. He had nothing but his flashlight, for all the good the damn thing did. He could barely see more than one leaf at a time.

After two days and nights in the jungle, with no sign of the enemy, boredom had begun to replace his fear. Jon swept his flashlight from side to side, drawing figure eights on the trees. He yawned, checked his watch, yawned again. In fifteen minutes, George would relieve him, and Jon could collapse again.

To stay awake, he kept moving his flashlight, drawing letters of light, spelling out his name. Finally he pretended to be a conductor, facing an orchestra performing his symphonies.

He was conducting a silent version of "Falling Like the Rain," which he felt appropriate given the weather, when his beam of light swept across two gleaming eyes.

Jon froze.

He moved the beam of light back.

The eyes were gone.

Jon's heart galloped. He forced a deep breath.

Only a mourning monk, he thought. *Or a glimmerbird.* He had begun to recognize some of the local wildlife.

He moved the beam again, side to side, seeking the eyes. The beam was trembling. The fear was back.

Nothing.

"Just a bird," he whispered to himself. "Just a stupid bird in the trees, and—"

His hackles rose.

Somebody was watching him. He could feel it.

He raised the flashlight, and—

A figure in the trees!

Somebody in the branches!

Time froze.

Jon couldn't breathe. Couldn't make a sound.

A bullet shrieked.

The flashlight exploded in Jon's hand. Shards of glass stung him.

He screamed, aimed his gun at the darkness, and opened fire.

"Kalayaan!" he shouted, squeezing his trigger.

And he realized that his gun wasn't even firing. He had forgotten to switch off the safety.

More bullets whistled around him.

He ran. Something seared his leg, and he ran another step, fell, leaped behind a log. His hands shook. He fumbled for the safety, cursing himself.

I trained for this. Don't fuck up now! Come on!

Bullets slammed into the log, ripping out chunks of wood, and moss flew, and—

George burst from the tent, howling, his assault rifle roaring at the trees.

"You leave him alone, you Kenny bastards!" the giant bellowed, his muzzle flaring, lighting the night.

Finally Jon managed to flick off the safety, aim his rifle, and fire. His muzzle burst with light, and he glimpsed figures among the branches, and—

Ringing.

Searing light.

His head exploded with pain and sound.

A bullet hit me, he thought. *I'm shot, I'm shot—*

But it had only grazed his helmet. He touched his head, felt no blood.

Etty burst from her tent too, gun firing, and more soldiers joined her, and soon the platoon was roaring and firing into the darkness, and gunfire lit the night.

"Fire in the sky!" somebody shouted.

Jon realized it was Lizzy. He glimpsed the sergeant hurling something at the trees, and—

An explosion roared across the jungle.

A grenade!

"Fire in the sky!" George howled and threw his own grenade.

Another boom rocked the trees.

"Die, slits!" Clay was shouting, laughing hysterically, firing on automatic.

"Jon!" George cried, running toward him. "Jon, are you okay? Are—"

A bullet slammed into his leg. The giant howled and fell.

"George!" Jon cried.

Not even hesitating, he leaped from cover and ran toward his friend. Bullets whistled around him. Jon ran through the fire.

"Jon, get back!" George shouted, lying on the forest floor. "Get to cover!"

Jon raced toward his friend as bullets flew everywhere, streaking through the night, slamming into trees.

A soldier fell beside him, clutching his chest. The bullets had cracked through his armored suit.

Another soldier fell, visor shattered, head blown open.

Etty was shouting somewhere behind, firing at the trees, and a grenade burst above.

Jon ran through it all, reached his fallen friend, and grabbed him by the shoulders.

"Come on, George, get up!" he shouted, tugging the giant.

George was so much larger. Jon was not a small man, but George was twice his size. The giant tried to rise, winced, fell back down.

Etty ran up toward them, firing at the trees.

"Get to cover, assholes!" she howled.

Her gun clicked. A bullet scraped across her arm, and blood sprayed, but Etty loaded another magazine and kept firing.

With strength Jon had not known was in him, he lifted George.

He carried his friend across the forest. George's feet scraped across the ground. Jon strained under the weight, ground his teeth, and kept going.

Another soldier fell.

A tent burst into flame.

Everywhere in the night—blood and fire, and figures in the trees, and laughter.

"I see him!" Lizzy shouted. "It's him! It's Ernesto! He's in the trees!"

And Jon was back in the labyrinth, back in the shadowy realm of his dreams, lost in darkness. And the demons danced all around.

And he kept going.

He dropped George behind the fallen log, then rose and fought again.

Later, Jon would learn that the battle had raged for only minutes. A quick raid and retreat.

But standing here in the fire, it seemed to last for eras. A lifetime of fire and blood.

And when it ended, when the guerrillas pulled back, the sun rose above a canopy of shattered branches and burnt leaves. Its light fell upon a scene of death and sacrifice.

They laid the dead side by side.

Private Dave Roberts, eighteen years old.

Corporal Denise Kummerow, nineteen years old.

Private Troy Lisboa, eighteen years old.

All three had stood before the enemy, laying down suppressive fire, never thinking to take cover, never thinking of anything but saving their friends.

All three could have survived. All three gave their lives.

Jon knelt before them, head lowered, tears falling. He closed their hands, and he covered them with blankets, and he collected their dog tags. He would always remember their names.

The platoon medic worked for hours, pulling bullets from the wounded, stitching wounds. Three soldiers were too hurt to continue. One was dying, three bullets in his stomach.

Jon approached his officer in the pale morning light.

"Sir, what do we do?" Jon said. "Do we go back to camp?"

Lieutenant Carter turned to stare at him. The officer's eyes were hard. Those eyes were boulders that would not fall before a storm.

"It was him, Private Taylor," the officer said. "The enemy who killed them. It was Ernesto. We must go on."

Jon licked his dry lips. "Sir, with all due respect, it was dark. They were wearing face paint. We couldn't see them, and—"

"It was him, Private. I would recognize the Iron Terror anywhere." Carter knelt and lifted his backpack. "We keep going! Until we find his camp. Up, platoon! On your feet!"

"But sir, the wounded—" Jon began.

"We'll put in a call for a helicopter. We'll leave a man behind to guard the wounded until evac." Carter stepped closer to Jon and softened his voice. "Do you want to stay with the wounded, Jon?"

Jon shook his head. "No, sir. If we keep going, I'm with you."

George limped toward them. "Me too!"

Jon shook his head. "George, no! You took a bullet to the leg."

"It ain't nothing, Jon," George said. "The medic pulled it right out. Thankfully I got a lot of fat on me. Was only a flesh wound. And those Insta-Stitch strips the medics use? Wonderful stuff! I'm as good as new."

But the giant was pale, fighting back the pain.

"George—" Jon began.

"I'm not leaving you." George clasped Jon's shoulder. "Not ever. Not even a tank could hold me back."

Jon hugged his friend, and tears stung his eyes. "Thank you, George."

Etty ran up toward them. "Hey, don't you dare hug without the entire Fireteam Symphonica!"

She laughed, but tears flowed down her cheeks, and the three friends stood together, crying as the dead lay beside them.

The platoon kept moving through the rainforest, heading deeper into the wild.

Chapter Thirty-Seven
Magic Man

Night cloaked the city of Mindao, draping the shantytowns with black sin, but the inner city shone like a heart. Neon lights hid the rotting concrete, filling the dark sky with blazing luminescence like the trails of psychedelic fireflies. Mindao was a rotting corpse, buzzing with insects, but the heart still beat with the pulse of a cosmos.

Maria walked among these lights, mottled with green, red, blue, and gold. A thousand little lights had once guided her through the rainforest, but here shone a million neon faces, selling vice.

GIRLS! GIRLS! GIRLS!
CHEAP BEER CHEAPER GIRLS
MEET YOUR BAHAY PRINCESS
SHABU PARADISE
BOYS NIGHT
MIDGET DANCERS

Maria walked in a daze. There were countless Earthlings in this city, all thirsty for beer, all hungry for flesh, all scared and homesick and desperate for forgetfulness. Thousands of bars lined the roads, luring them in, like angler fish luring their prey. And Maria knew these were traps. She knew that the bargirls of Bahay were like little spiders, trapping Earthling men in their nets, clinging to their arms, sucking their money like liquefied flesh from an ossified husk. The men of Bahay were fighting in the jungles or lay dead among ashes, but Bahay's daughters fought a different war, and inner Mindao was a neon battlefield.

Barefoot, dressed in rags, her body damp with landfill juices, Maria stepped onto a bright street corner, and she gazed upon a dizzying array of mottled lights in the night. People moved back and forth, smudges in the kaleidoscope, and Earthlings and Bahayans seemed almost as one, ghosts in the glowing forest.

And Maria began to sing.

She sang old songs. Songs her mother used to sing. Songs that had filled her village for generations, that had been sung even in the Philippines, the ancestral homeland of the Bahayans.

They were songs of golden beaches and swaying palm fronds. Songs of reed boats exploring blue seas. Songs of harvest. Songs of family and joy and love. They were songs alien to this neon underworld, but the music still beat in the heart of every Bahayan, from the bargirls in their fishnet stockings to the begging toddlers on the roadsides. Songs that perhaps even warmed the hearts of Earthlings, for these were songs that whispered of Earth.

As Maria sang, it began to drizzle, washing the filth off, purifying her, and the raindrops became part of her song.

A *tuk tuk* passed by—a brightly colored rickshaw with a rattling motor. The driver tossed her a coin. It clattered at Maria's feet. A few toddlers raced up, and she let them have it. She kept singing.

An Earthling soldier walked by, a bargirl on his arm. He stopped for a moment, listened, and tears filled his eyes. He placed a coin in her hand.

"Go, go!"

Several Bahayan women ran toward Maria on high heels, miniskirts swishing. Their fishnet stockings could not hide the bruises.

Prostitutes, Maria realized.

She stopped singing.

"This is our corner!" one of the girls said. "Go, go!"

"No!" Maria said. "It doesn't belong to you. Let me sing!"

One of the prostitutes drew a knife. "Don't fuck with me and my brothers, bitch!"

Maria frowned. Brothers?

They're boys, she realized. This was a dreamland, so different from the world she had known.

The boys began to beat Maria with their purses. She fled, splashing through puddles.

She reached another street corner, and she stood under neon lights, and she began to sing.

A passing soldier tossed her a coin.

But soon beggars approached her, beards long, teeth crooked and orange, eyes bloodshot—the telltale signs of shabu addiction.

"This is our spot!" they hissed, clawing at her. "Leave!"

They tried to bite, and Maria fled, fearing their diseased gums.

She sang for a moment here, a moment there, fleeing prostitutes and beggars, urchins and policemen. That night, she was the proud owner of three Earth dollars. That was worth over fifty Bahayan pesos. It was the richest she had ever been.

That night, Maria feasted.

She approached a roadside stall where a merchant sold *adobong baboy*—a traditional pork stew, simmered in vinegar and soy sauce, sprinkled with garlic and peppercorns that crunched between her teeth. It was real meat. Not even pulled from the landfills. It was Maria's best meal since leaving San Luna. For dessert, she ordered *halo halo*, a treat of crushed ice topped with syrup, sweet beans, and purple taro potatoes.

At the end of her feast, she felt stronger. Maybe even hopeful.

She even had a dollar left. It would buy her breakfast tomorrow. She planned to have pancakes.

Yes, this was a city of decay, but also of such carnal pleasures.

That night, she found an alleyway, and she lay down to sleep.

In her dreams, she was trapped in the labyrinth again, but this time she was pulling a rickshaw. An unseen figure kept whipping her, shouting to go faster, faster! Maria ran, pulling her burden, but she could not find her way, and she plunged ever deeper into the neon maze, like a fly only further ensnaring itself in the web.

"Give me, give me, give me."

Claws grabbed her.

Maria opened her eyes and screamed.

It was the old man from before. He was pawing at her legs. He grinned at her, his one rotten tooth sticking out from black gums. He stared with one eye. The other was blinded, covered with cataracts, and his wispy hair fluttered like a corpse's hair.

Maria screamed.

"Leave me alone!"

"Need shabu, need shabu, give me, give me, give me…"

His fingers were gnarled but strong, and he pawed at her, reached into her pocket, and found her coin.

Maria lashed her knife.

She sliced off one of those knobby fingers.

The man screamed and fled. He kept the coin. He left the finger.

The next night, she walked the neon streets again. She passed bar after bar, the haunts of soldiers. Girls stood behind panes of glass, lining up onstage, parading their slender, underfed bodies, while Earthlings hooted and tossed money and bid on their favorites. Maria walked as pimps rumbled on mopeds, circling in closer and closer, louder and louder, herding more and more soldiers toward the bars. The Earthlings stumbled into the honey traps, not even aware they were being puppeteered.

Maria stood outside a whiskey bar, and she began to sing, and somebody tossed her a coin. But the owner emerged, shouting and waving a broken bottle.

"Stop stealing my customers' money!" he cried. "Go, go, *puta*! Go back to whatever bar you're from!"

"I'm not a bargirl," she said. "I come from a village far away."

The bartender burst out laughing. "They all do. Go, get lost!" He tossed the bottle at her. "You stray bitch."

She fled.

She made another dollar singing in an alleyway, but several Bahayan men circled her, wielding knifes. One was missing an eye, another the leg. War cripples. Unwanted. Starving and hungry and willing to kill for money. They circled her, closing in, and Maria knew she was beaten. She surrendered her coins.

Another night, she was forced to sing in shadows, driven here by competing buskers, beggars, and bargirls. A big Earthling approached her, and he ripped her clothes, shoved her down, and reached between her legs. She stabbed him in the belly and fled, screaming, but everyone around her just laughed. Their eyes shone with drugs and shell shock and lust.

She didn't eat that day.

Most days she didn't eat more than scraps.

Here in the city center was another type of landfill, this one of human garbage, and life here was just as hard. And just as ephemeral. Maria was turning eighteen tomorrow, but she did know if she'd even live that long.

Her birthday dawned gray and cold, and a hard rain fell all morning. News came in from the radios, leaking from kiosks across the streets. More bombings in the north. More villages wiped out. The Earthlings were on a rampage, a beast that could not be sated, unable to conquer the north, but able to inflict so much pain. So much death. The death toll kept climbing. Higher and higher. A hundred thousand dead Earthlings in the jungles. Millions of dead Bahayans across a sundering world. And here in Mindao, this southern sanctuary—a hive of rotting life.

Often, Maria thought that death would be kinder. Often, she envied her parents. Often, she drew her knife, contemplating.

It was on that gray rainy day, her eighteenth birthday, that the Magic Man came to her.

* * * * *

She was standing on a street corner between Pinoy Pleasure and The Manic Monkey, two nightclubs that were closed until evening. She sang for passersby. Traffic was light, but at night, when the neon lights hummed, this same corner became a battleground where bargirls, pimps, buskers, and beggars all battled for territory.

Right now, in the daylight, Maria stood alone. A three-legged cat curled around her feet, keeping her company. She had collected only a few pesos, not even enough to buy a bowl of *adobo*. If business did not soon improve, she would be eating from trash bins tonight, fighting the cats and urchins.

One passerby seemed a promising prospect. Maria perked up and sang louder. He was a Bahayan man, one of few who remained in the city. He seemed to be about fifty, perhaps too old to fight. But nothing about him seemed frail. He was muscular, and his goatee could not hide his square jaw. He wore a purple leisure suit, a frilly white collar, and gator-skin shoes. His black hair was slicked back and smelled like roses. Gemstone rings, golden chains, and dazzling earrings glittered across him. He was as bright as a bar. When he smiled at Maria, he revealed one golden tooth and many dazzling white ones.

"Beautiful!" The man clapped, and his golden bracelets chinked. "What a voice! Did you train in Mindao Opera House?"

"I'm not formally trained," Maria said. "These are songs we sang in our village while working in the paddies."

"Ah, a beautiful siren from the provinces!" The man in the purple suit bowed. "Wonderful. Wonderful!" He held out his hand, the fingers gleaming with rings. "I'm Rodrigo Reyes, but everyone calls me the Magic Man. Pleasure to make your acquaintance."

It was the most anyone in Mindao had said to her. He was the first person to treat her kindly, not just yell or threaten or catcall. Maria shook his hand. His skin was very smooth, almost like a child's hand, rubbed with scented oils.

"Pleasure," she said. "I'm Maria Imelda de la Cruz."

He laughed. "Ah, you're both talented and charming! And, might I add, quite beautiful." He admired her. "Smooth mocha skin. Long shimmering black hair like silk. A graceful form. You are a true princess, Maria."

She was surprised. Most men in Mindao just shouted at her to show her *dibdibs*, and many reached out to grab them. But the Magic Man did not touch her, did not speak crudely.

"Thank you, Magic Man," she said. "Would you like me to sing you a song for a coin?"

He seemed rich enough to afford several coins, but Maria wouldn't push her luck. Right now, her stomach grumbling, she'd sing an entire opera for a bowl of rice.

"I will pay you many coins," the Magic Man said. "My girls earn two hundred thousand pesos a month."

Maria gasped. That was over three thousand Earth dollars.

A fortune.

But then she frowned. "What kind of girls?"

"Girls like you, *Nini*." The Magic Man smiled warmly. "Girls with talent. With beauty. Girls who can sing and entertain my guests. Do you know the Go Go Cowgirl?"

Maria shook her head. "I don't go to bars."

"Me neither." The Magic Man wrinkled his nose. "Most bars are places of decay and despair. But the Go Go Cowgirl is a different sort of establishment. A place of magic. Of imagination. A place where true talent meets true appreciation. I own the Go Go Cowgirl, and I would be honored if you sang on my stage."

Maria shrank away. "I'm not a…" She lowered her voice. "A prostitute."

The Magic Man laughed. "Of course not! You're far too wholesome and virginal. None of my girls are prostitutes. They are… *princesses*. They are jewels. And you, *Nini*, will shine brightest of them all."

Nini. The word brought back such memories. It meant *little girl* in Tagalog. It was what her mother used to call her.

"I…" She hesitated. "I don't know."

The Magic Man lost his smile. Concern filled his eyes. "Oh, *Nini*, I worry about you. I've seen many young virgins from the provinces. They wash up in Mindao every day. So many live on the streets. They end up addicted to shabu, infected with syphilis, starving and filthy like the rats. It's only a question of what will kill them first: disease, drugs, or a thief's knife. I would hate to see such misfortune befall you. You're a rare talent, Maria de la Cruz. Don't hide in the mud. Let me polish you." He held out his hand. "Come, Maria. At the Go Go Cowgirl, a warm shower, hot meal, and soft bed await you. And most importantly—a stage to shine on."

Maria stared at the proffered hand. A soft hand, but one large and strong. A hand shining with jewels.

She looked up into the Magic Man's eyes. She saw kindness. She saw honestly.

She saw a life better than this.

She took his hand.

Chapter Thirty-Eight
Hilltop

The remains of the Lions platoon trudged through the jungle.

They were all silent. Dour. Staring ahead with dark eyes. Just yesterday, they had lost three friends. They knew that today, they might join them.

Everything hurt. Jon's leg was bandaged where a bullet had grazed him. His muscles cramped. His back ached under his heavy pack. The bugs kept biting him, and the heat kept pounding him.

But he trudged on. Climbing over boulders and coiling roots, pushing his way through curtains of vines. Seeking the enemy. Trapped in a dream.

"Hey, ballerina." Clay came walking toward Jon, a bandoleer across his chest. "Yeah, you."

Jon stared ahead at the jungle. "Get lost, Clay."

But the brute stepped closer, falling in line beside Jon. Grenades jangled across his belt like Christmas ornaments. He reeked of sweat and blood.

"You were on guard duty, weren't you?" Clay said. "When the slits raided our camp."

Jon said nothing. He climbed over a log and pushed vines aside.

"Hey, asshole!" Clay grabbed him. "I'm talking to you."

Jon shoved him aside. "Fuck off."

Hatred simmered in Clay's pale eyes. He sneered. "Yeah, it was you on guard duty. You let the slits sneak up on us. What happened? Your gun jammed? Or did you chicken out?"

"I don't report to you," Jon said, moving away. His heart pounded, but he refused to show fear.

"Three soldiers died because of you!" Clay grabbed Jon again, yanking him back. "Three good, brave warriors. They died because you failed to guard them."

Jon finally looked directly at Clay. He lost his breath.

Dear lord.

The soldier had gone savage. Clay had sawed off his battlesuit's sleeves, revealing muscular arms. He had painted Nazi runes on his helmet. They were red, perhaps painted with blood. And around his neck…

Jon felt sick.

"What the hell is that?" he said.

Clay laughed. "You like my necklace?"

Jon nearly gagged.

A necklace of severed ears hung around Clay's neck. Six ears. Human ears. Strung on a chain.

"That's right," Clay said. "Slit ears. I killed 'em myself. Back during the raid when you were busy pissing yourself. I earned these kills. Got myself a little souvenir."

Jon looked away. His stomach roiled.

"Don't you turn your back on me!" Clay said. "Or one day you're likely to get a bullet in it."

A muzzle poked Jon in the back.

And something snapped inside of him.

He spun around, shoving Clay's rifle aside.

The brute leaped at him, grabbed his collar. Clay raised a fist, and—

"Dammit, boys!" It was Corporal Bawden, a lanky soldier, so tall and thin he looked like a stick insect. He loped forward on stilt-like legs, scowling. "As your squad commander, I order you to calm your tits."

"Commander, the coward caused three Earthlings to die!"

Clay said. "Then he dared accuse me of—"

"Dammit, son, I don't give a damn." Bawden resumed walking down the trail. "I swear, these green privates with their petty bull—"

The ground opened up beneath him.

Bawden fell into a gaping pit.

His screams filled the forest—then died.

Jon ran forward, heart pounding, and leaned over the pit. He grimaced. Bawden was down there, impaled on spikes. One spike had driven through his skull, emerging from his mouth.

"Kennys in the trees!" somebody shouted.

And suddenly bullets were flying.

A soldier screamed, clutched his wounded chest, and collapsed.

Jon's hands shook so wildly he could barely cling to his gun. But somehow, he managed to open fire.

He even remembered to flick off the safety. Improvement.

He swept his gun from side to side, spraying the trees with bullets. Everyone else was firing with him, forming a ring of hell.

More bullets whistled.

A private crashed down dead at Jon's feet—a petite girl from Ontario with long blond hair.

Another soldier fell, his turban rolled off, and blood flowed down his beard. One of his eyes was blown away.

The raid only lasted a minute or two. And the Kennys vanished, leaving only echoes of their laughter.

For hours, the Earthlings swept the forest. They found two dead guerrillas, and Clay carved off their ears, adding them to his collection. Everyone knew there were more Kennys. That they had fled. That they would return.

Bloodied, down four more soldiers, the Lions platoon trudged on through the jungle.

* * * * *

They stood before it.

A hill rising in the heart of the jungle.

"Surigao Hill," Lieutenant Carter said. "Last known base of Ernesto Iron Santos."

Jon stood beside him, drenched in sweat. His wounded leg was aching badly. It was worse today. Scratches and bug bites covered the rest of him. One of the bites was festering, and little eggs quivered inside. The damn alien bugs were always laying eggs in the troops, and their medic could barely keep up.

The battlesuits only made things worse. The bugs got inside them and were impossible to crush. The armor trapped in body heat and sweat. These suits were leftovers from the Ganymede Uprising twenty years ago, and in the jungle, they became intolerable. Many troops had begun to rip off armored plates, to leave them in the forest. Some were topless now. That only invited the damn fangwood trees to reach out their hungry little leaves and bite. There was no relief in the jungle. If one thing wasn't trying to kill you, it was another.

Trying to forget the pain, Jon stared at Surigao Hill. Hill? It looked more like a mountain. It soared ahead, draped with rainforest, its steep slopes strewn with boulders. Jon could understand why the Kennys would make their base here.

"It'll be a tough climb," Jon said. "They have the higher ground, they know every tree, and if we try to climb, they'll butcher us. Sir, this is a job for the air force."

But the lieutenant shook his head. "No, private. I won't have bombs solve this problem. If we bomb this hill, we'll never know if we got him. We need to *see* him. We need to look Ernesto in the eyes. Then put a bullet in his brain."

"I understand, sir, but—"

"Don't you want to avenge your brother, Jon?"

Jon stiffened. "Of course. I just—"

"It'll be all right, Jon." Carter squeezed his shoulder. "We're going to do this. Together."

Jon stared into his officer's eyes, and he saw something that frightened him.

Not just determination. Obsession.

You're Captain Ahab, and Ernesto is your whale, Jon thought.

Jon licked his dry lips. "I've come this far. I won't turn back now. I'm with you, sir."

The platoon gathered around the lieutenant. Fifty had set out from Fort Miguel. Thirty-eight soldiers remained. Weary, wounded, haunted. But all stood tall, guns in hand.

Carter faced them. "Some of you have been fighting in the jungle for years. Others are on your first mission. You are all, every man and woman here, courageous warriors. The enemy has all the advantages in this fight. They know this land better than we do. They hide like ghosts in the trees, while we stumble like giants. But there is one advantage we Earthlings have. Our fighting spirit! The enemies we face are cruel, murderous, pitiless. Let's go kill 'em."

Sergeant Lizzy raised her rifle overhead. "For Earth!"

"For Earth!" they all repeated.

They began storming the hill.

Enemy fire greeted them.

Bullets streaked, slamming into trees and soldiers.

A mortar landed among the platoon, and an explosion rocked the hill, and severed limbs flew.

"For Earth!" Carter cried, charging uphill.

"For Earth!" Jon cried, running after his officer.

They ran, howling, firing at the unseen enemy. Fewer and fewer every moment. Roaring. Killing. Dying.

For Earth.

For you, Paul, Jon thought. *For a funeral on a cold rainy day. For a memory of a brother. For you, George. For you, Etty. For every son and daughter on Earth who is grieving.*

Jon did not know how this war had begun. Whether it was a just war. Whether Etty was right, claiming they were cruel conquerors, or whether he should believe Ensign Earth, believe they were heroes liberating a planet from alien claws. He did not know if Paul had died in vain. He did not know why his friends were dying in the mud. He did not know why he was killing. He did not know who he'd be when he returned home. If he returned home.

Private Jon Taylor did not know why he was on this hill, running into enemy fire.

But he knew that right now, his friends needed him.

That right now, his brother was watching him.

That right now, his officer, his sergeant, and his brothers and sisters in arms were running into hell. And he would not abandon them.

Maybe he was not a hero. But he was a soldier. He would complete his mission or die fighting.

"For Earth!" he cried, charging into the enemy fire.

For hours, they fought.

They climbed.

They killed and died.

Bullets flew. Mortars exploded. Jon kept climbing, shrapnel in his leg. Firing. A corpse fell before him.

"He's there!" Carter shouted. "On the hilltop! Ernesto is there! Onward, soldiers!"

The lieutenant led them forward.

The enemy was everywhere. A hatch opened in the ground, knocking back moss and grass, and a Kalayaan fighter opened fire. An Earthling fell. They climbed over his corpse, and another hatch opened. Another Kenny emerged from underground, firing, taking down more Earthlings.

Jon returned fire. The Bahayan fell. The soldiers ran toward the hatch, fired into the tunnel, and screams rose below.

"Fire in the hole!" Jon shouted and dropped a grenade into the tunnel.

An explosion rocked the hill. The screams below died.

They ran onward, fighting every step toward the hilltop. Through the mortar fire. Through the rain and storm. They were soldiers of Earth. They were boys and girls drafted into a war they did not understand. Perhaps they were heroes. Perhaps they were villains. But they did not turn back.

Another soldier fell.

And another.

They were like soldiers throughout history. Teenagers. From big cities. From sleepy little towns. Taken from their parents and trained to kill but never taught how to die. Their blood sank into foreign soil. Their bodies tore apart. They cried for their mothers as they died. They cried for their fallen.

But they did not turn back.

Because they were like soldiers throughout history. And they were brave.

They dropped grenades into tunnels, and they stumbled into traps, and the spikes tore them open. They pounded the trees with mortars, and they saw a severed hand fly, and a corporal crawled, his legs gone. They saw a burning man, a living flame, screaming, melting, still firing his gun, then kneeling, waiting, silently waiting to die. They saw the horrors of hell fill this planet of paradise.

But they did not turn back.

Engines rumbled above. Helicopters roared, angels of metal, and their guns pounded the hillside. Shell after shell exploded across Surigao Hill. Boulders cracked open. Trees burned. The enemy spilled from their burrows, charging in wave after wave, howling, on suicide missions of final glory. The hill became like a hive spilling furious hornets. The Kalayaan ran into Earth's lines, howling, strapped with bombs. And more of Earth's blood spilled. And the dead fell across the hillside.

So many fell.

So few remained.

And they did not turn back.

Finally, after a day and night of battle, the Lions platoon reached the summit.

A last Bahayan still stood, refusing to flee. He roared out, "Kalayaan para sa Bahay!" and charged at the Earthlings, holding nothing but a knife, and died fighting.

Kalayaan. The name of a guerrilla army. The Tagalog word for freedom.

The survivors of the Lions Platoon gathered on the hilltop. Of fifty who had left Fort Miguel, twenty-three remained.

Jon stood panting, blood dripping down his arms. George and Etty limped toward him, carrying a wounded comrade. Their faces were pale, their eyes haunted.

We won the hill, Jon thought. *We won nothing.*

"Where is he?" Carter barked, stomping across the hilltop. "Where is Ernesto?"

"He might have died on the hillside, sir," Jon said. "He—"

"Ernesto!" Carter roared, spinning from side to side. "You coward! Are you here? Come out and face me!"

Nobody answered.

The helicopter hovered above. A rope dangled. Captain Pete leaned from the cockpit, and his voice emerged from the platoon's radio.

"All aboard, boys and girls! Time to go home."

Lieutenant Carter ignored him.

"Ernesto!" he howled, then reeled back toward his

remaining troops. "Comb this hill. Every last tree and patch of moss. Bring every Bahayan corpse here. Then enter the tunnels and find him!"

They worked for long hours, seeking the dead on the forest hillside, dragging them to the hilltop.

Carter distributed photographs of Ernesto. A man with a cruel, angular face. A scar across the cheek. One eye blinded by a cataract.

There he is, Jon thought. *The man who killed my brother.*

They searched for Ernesto among the dead. But he was not there.

They entered the tunnels, and they found a labyrinth coiling inside the hill. There were warehouses for food and weapons. Bunks with bamboo cots. A little chapel—just an earthen burrow with bibles and a wooden cross. One corporal stepped into a false tunnel, and an explosion rocked the hill. The man never even had time to scream.

But the tunnels were lifeless.

If any enemy had survived the battle, they had fled.

They piled the enemy corpses and burned them. The helicopter returned, and Pete spoke again through the radio.

"Dammit, Carter, you have orders to return to base. This battle is over."

The lieutenant marched across the hilltop, stood on an outcrop of stone, and stared north. The two suns of Bahay framed him in searing yellow.

"He's out there," Carter said. "Ernesto must have escaped. Like the coward that he is. He's out in the jungle, and we'll find him. We'll keep going. We—"

"Sir," Jon said, "your soldiers are hurt, they—"

"They can keep going!" Carter said. "You can keep going, can't you, Private Taylor?" He clasped Jon's shoulder. "You'll go on with me, won't you? We'll find him. You and me. We'll catch that bastard, and—"

"Carter." A soft voice, draped with grief. "It's over."

Sergeant Lizzy came walking toward them. Her battlesuit was charred and bloody. One sleeve was blasted open, and her arm bled. Her braid had come undone during the battle, and golden hair spilled from under her helmet, caked with blood. Her eyes were damp with tears.

Jon had never seen his sergeant cry before. And he knew she wasn't crying only for the dead. But also for her lieutenant. For his soul. For a man she loved. A man consumed and lost.

Carter grabbed her arms.

"Lizzy, we have to keep going, to catch him," the lieutenant said. "It's why we came back. Why you and me came back to this godforsaken world. To find him. After what he did to you. God, Lizzy." And now a tear flowed down the lieutenant's face. "After the horrible things he did. We have to find him. We have to…"

Lizzy pulled the lieutenant into an embrace.

"Today is over, Carter," she whispered. "The battle is done. But not our war."

The two stood on the hilltop, the wind rustling ashes around their feet.

Jon could not imagine their pain. He did not know everything they had been through. But he recognized the loss. The trauma. The devastation of the soul. He had tasted of the same pain in this war. He had survived this battle. And he knew that his soul was forever changed.

Come back pure. Or come back dead.

He was neither.

He was victorious.

He was a killer.

Jon did not know how many enemies he had killed today. They had trained him to kill slits. He had not expected to find people. He looked at his bloody hands, and he lowered his head.

The surviving troops gathered in the helicopter. Fireteam Symphonica sat silently. George and Etty stared ten thousand miles into the distance, lost in memories of the horror.

Jon reached out and clasped his friends' hands. He held them all the way back to their base.

Chapter Thirty-Nine
The Daughters of Bahay

The Go Go Cowgirl was a large club, two stories tall. The concrete building was still under construction and already decaying. Smog and rust stained its walls, and plastic sheets stretched across the upper windows instead of glass. But at night, Maria knew, the crumbling top floor would vanish into darkness, and the neon lights would shine like beacons.

The neon sign was off now. It would only turn on at night. Yet even unlit, the sign was garish and colorful. It depicted a cowgirl riding a bull. Words appeared below her:

GO GO COWGIRL: HOT GIRLS COLD BEER

A poster was peeling on the wall:

SUNDAY NIGHT: MIDGET BOXING

The words were in English. This place, like thousands of other bars in Mindao, had sprung up to serve the invaders.

"This is your exquisite palace of the senses?" Maria said. "I'm underwhelmed. This is just another bar. Like a thousand others."

The Magic Man turned toward her. A flicker of anger passed across his eyes, and he curled his fists. But then he relaxed, and his smile returned, full of bright teeth.

"Ah, you're a saucy one! Has anyone ever told you that, *Nini*? You are a delight. Yes, this place looks underwhelming during the day. Ah, but when the sun sets! That's when the dreams come. That's when the Go Go Cowgirl transforms into a palace of pleasure."

They stepped toward the front door. Several orphans and stray cats lay on the cement patio, eating peels. The Magic Man began kicking them.

"Go, go, get lost!"

The cats hissed. The urchins blew him raspberries and fled.

They entered the bar, and Maria began to cough. The place stank of tobacco, shabu, and sex.

She found herself in a dusty common room, probably large enough for a hundred people, but quiet this morning. It must have been a good night last night. Several marines were passed out on the floor, empty beer bottles lying around them. A few still had bargirls in their arms—petite Bahayans with smudged makeup, their naked bodies covered with bruises, bite marks, and dollar bills. A stray cat hissed on the bar. A *unano*—a midget boxer—was snoring in the corner, one eye bruised shut. A few bargirls sat on a stage, wearing lacy lingerie, snorting shabu. Their eyes were sunken, set in sallow faces over dark bags.

Maria's eyes flicked toward an alien at a corner table. He reminded her of a spider. He had eight limbs, but they ended with hands. Disturbingly human hands. His head flared out like a hammerhead shark, each eye staring in a different direction. The alien was busy playing several games of solitaire at once, his many hands flipping and shuffling cards. When he turned one eye toward Maria, she looked away quickly, blushing.

Back in my village, the only alien I ever saw was Crisanto, she thought. *This will take some getting used to.*

Not that there were *many* aliens in Mindao. The city was almost entirely human. After all, if you had a spaceship, why would you visit this place? Probably the only aliens who came here were outlaws and renegades, hoping to vanish into the slums. Maria had heard that there were cities in space bustling with millions of aliens of every kind—countless species. Aliens made of liquid who swirled inside glass bulbs. Aliens like gaseous clouds. Aliens like living musical instruments whose songs would make grown men cry. Maria yearned to someday travel to space, to meet them, to explore the wonders of the cosmos. The sky was full of stars and life, and she was stuck here.

One of the bargirls took a deep snort of the drug. Then she bolted up, shuddered, and pulled a coat over her lingerie. She walked across the room, high heels clattering. She was in her early thirties, a little old for a bargirl, but Maria thought her very beautiful. She was slender, but her hips were curvy for a Bahayan girl, and her bob cut shimmered like black silk.

"I'm outta here!" the woman said, heading toward the door.

The Magic Man grabbed her wrist. "You wait one moment, Charlie. How much did you pull last night? You put my half in the register?"

Charlie wrenched her arm free. "Seven hundred pesos. Fuck! I told you last night, Rodrigo. It's in the cash register. Let me go. I gotta go feed my kids." She glanced at Maria, then back at the Magic Man. "Who's the new bitch?"

"Ah, isn't she a princess?" The Magic Man ran his fingers through Maria's hair. "Look at that silky hair! Those beautiful lips! And you should hear her voice."

The bargirl snorted. "She stinks. She's a fucking gutter rat." She grabbed Maria's crotch. "Probably has crabs."

"Hey, don't!" Maria stepped back, cheeks heating.

"Looks can be deceiving," said the Magic Man. "Our dear Princess Maria is a virgin. And only sixteen."

"Eighteen," Maria said. "Today's my birthday."

"Hush! I said you are sixteen!" The Magic Man put a finger on her lips, then looked at the other girls. "She'll fetch a high price tonight. More than seven hundred pesos. Much more."

Charlie sneered. She squeezed Maria's arm—painfully.

"Listen to me, you little bitch. I'm the queen of the Go Go Cowgirl. You got it? *I'm* the Cowgirl. Me! Charlie. You are nothing. You are a worm. You will never earn what I earn here. Do you understand?"

Charlie stood taller than Maria, and while slender, she was strong, her fingers digging like claws. Maria struggled to wrench herself free.

"Leave me alone!"

"Charlie, don't abuse my princess!" the Magic Man said. "Don't be so jealous. The girl isn't going to dethrone you." He stroked Charlie's cheek. "You will always be my special cowgirl. This new girl is a princess, but you are forever my queen."

Charlie seemed to melt. She released Maria and gave the Magic Man a half-hearted shove.

"Fuck you, Rodrigo. You always know how to woo me."

The Magic Man ran a hand through Charlie's gleaming bob. "Good. Now go wash the princess. And dress her. Something white and virginal. Tonight will be a big night."

"What?" Charlie took a step back. "Fuck you! I have to go, Rodrigo! My kids need me. I—"

The Magic Man hit her.

It happened so fast Maria jumped.

The back of his hand connected with Charlie's cheek, and the bargirl sprawled on the floor.

Maria gasped, dumbfounded for a second. Then she knelt by Charlie.

"Are you all right? You're bleeding!"

But Charlie shoved her away. "Don't touch me, bitch!" She stood up, wiped blood from her lip, and lowered her head. "I'm sorry, Magic Man. Whatever you say."

The bar owner kissed Charlie's cheek. "That's my lovely queen. Go, girls. Make me proud tonight."

He sent Charlie off with a solid slap on the bottom. The

bargirl headed across the common room, pulling Maria along.

They stepped over fallen beer bottles, overturned chairs, and sleeping Earthlings. One of the soldiers rose from his drunken stupor, smiled hazily, and reached toward Maria.

"Hey, I'll have a go with the virgin! Bring her here, Charlie."

The bargirl snorted. "Your ass is poor, Earthling. You don't have enough money for a virgin."

"Had enough to fuck your brains out last night," the Earthling said, then passed out again.

Maria winced.

She's a prostitute, she thought. *They all are here. All the girls. The Magic Man said I only need to sing, but the soldier said…*

"Charlie, I—"

"Shut up! Don't talk to me. Fuck! You're making me late."

Charlie pulled her upstairs. An Earthling soldier sat on the staircase, a boy of eighteen or nineteen, head in his hands. He was crying.

"Mom, he died…" The soldier shuddered. "I saw him die. In the forest. He had no arms. Oh god, Mom, oh god, I want to go home…"

Maria wanted to comfort him. But Charlie pulled her on. They climbed around the weeping soldier and reached a corridor.

The place stank of sweat and sex. Doorways lined the corridor. As they walked by, Maria glanced into the rooms. Soldiers lay snoring inside, a few with bargirls still in their arms, sleeping late into the morning. One soldier lay in a bed, two girls sleeping in his arms. He had no legs, just stumps wrapped in bandages. Probably not much money left now either, not with two girls and all those empty bottles around him.

He lost his legs, so he can go back to Earth soon, Maria thought. *But we're stuck here. We, the daughter of Bahay. We are the lost.*

They entered a bathroom. An Earthling soldier sat inside

the dry tub, holding a razor blade to his wrists. He looked up at the girls, eyes rimmed with red. Sunken eyes. Eyes staring ten thousand miles away.

"Oh, for fuck's sake!" Charlie blurted out. "Not again. Rick, get the fuck out of here! I told you a million times, if you wanna kill yourself, do it at your barracks."

He blinked at her, coming out of a trance. "But I want to die surrounded by beauty."

Charlie rolled her eyes. "Oh for fuck's sake." She pulled open her robe, letting him view her lingerie-clad body. "There. Take a mental photograph. Now get the fuck out of here."

The suicidal Earthling left the bathroom. Maria watched him go.

"Maybe we should talk to him?" she whispered.

Charlie snickered. "Oh, he's fine. He's been threatening suicide every day since coming back from the front. I swear he does it just to get a look at my *dibdibs*. Speaking of *dibdibs*." She tugged at Maria's rags. "Get this filthy shit off. Let me see what I've got to work with."

Maria recoiled. "I can wash myself."

Another scoff. "Oh, you need more than a scrub, princess. You came straight out of the gutter. You need the works. Charlie's Special Scouring Service. Now strip!"

The older woman scrubbed her roughly. Maria yelped and protested, but Charlie was stronger, and she nearly rubbed Maria's skin off, fighting layers of grime.

"My God, you sewer rats are filthy," Charlie said. "Do you swim in garbage or just sleep in it?"

I ate it too, Maria thought, but she said nothing. The memory shamed her. She remembered seeing the trash people, the community that lived on the landfill. Remembered seeing babies born there. Old women fishing through the garbage for anything half edible. Generations growing and dying there like flies, but they were humans with human souls.

But are the girls in this bar any different? she thought. *We're all broken, all ashamed, and all noble. We are the survivors. We are the daughters of war.*

They spent an extra-long time cleaning Maria's hair, shampooing, conditioning, then brushing over and over, trying to remove the tangles. A few tangles were too stubborn, and no patience could undo them.

Charlie pulled out scissors. She snipped the air twice. "Sit down, girl."

Maria winced. "Don't take off too much."

The scissors snipped, snipped, snipped. Locks of knotted hair fell onto the floor. Finally Maria was left with a bob cut. Her hair had once flowed down to her waist. It now barely tickled her chin. It stabbed her heart to lose her long hair, which she had once been rather vain of. But when she looked at Charlie, Maria felt comforted. Charlie was beautiful—perhaps the most beautiful woman Maria had ever seen—and she too wore a bob.

Maria smiled at the older woman. "Now we look the same!"

But Charlie did not return the smile. She sat on the bathtub rim, and she gazed at the wall, and like the suicidal soldier, she seemed to be looking ten thousand miles away.

"You shouldn't want to be me," Charlie said softly.

Maria hadn't exactly said that. But she just said, "Why not? You're very beautiful."

Charlie snorted. "And in my thirties. And a single mother." She sighed. "I remember my first day here. I was about your age. How old are you again?"

"Eighteen," Maria said. "Today's my birthday."

"Well, Happy Fucking Birthday. I was fifteen when the Magic Man fished me out of the gutter. I've been here most of my life. God fucking damn." She snorted. "Nobody wants to marry an aging whore with four little brats and half the diseases known to infect a crotch." She gripped Maria's chin and stared into her eyes. "Listen to me, girl. You grab a husband here, okay? An Earthling soldier. A kind one who doesn't hit you too much. You marry that son of a bitch, and when the war is over, you get him to take you home to Earth. Get the fuck off this planet, okay? Bahay is a trap. You don't want to end up an aging whore like me."

"I'm not a whore," Maria said. "The Magic Man said I'm just here to sing."

Charlie's eyes softened. She caressed Maria's cheek. "You're sweet. Too sweet for this world." She smiled. "My god, even at fifteen, I wasn't a fucking idiot like you."

"My mother said my head is too big and full of questions." Maria hung her head. "She died."

"All our families are dead, darling. And it's our job to fuck the men who killed them." She pulled a packet of powdered crystals from her coat, held it to her nose, sniffed deeply. "Shabu helps. But stay away from this shit. Trust me. It dims the pain. But it also dims the soul."

"Then why do you snort it?" Maria asked.

Charlie smiled thinly. "Because I'm a fucking idiot too. Now come, we'll get you some new clothes."

They entered a dressing room. Many outfits hung from hooks—lingerie, fishnet stockings, corsets, and scanty cowgirl costumes. Maria blushed. She could not imagine wearing such things.

But Charlie chose something different for Maria. It was a white dress. And not even scandalous. When Maria put it on it, it flowed down to her ankles.

"Ah, there you go." Charlie smoothed Maria's dress and fixed her hair. "You look like an angel. A virgin from the provinces. You'll find a husband this way, Maria. You can't wait too long."

Maria examined herself in a mirror.

She didn't recognize who she saw.

In some ways, she was the same Maria. The same round face, light brown skin, and dark eyes. The same smooth black hair, even if it was cut shorter now.

But she was not the same.

She was not the happy village girl anymore. She was perhaps dressed in virginal white, and a man had never touched her, but she was not innocent. Ghosts haunted her eyes. The death she had seen. The horror she had suffered through. The men she had killed. She looked like a precious doll, but that shell held a dark soul.

"I'll leave you without makeup," Charlie said. "You don't need it. You will at my age. Savor your youth while you can."

Maria looked at the older woman. "Charlie, you're very beautiful. Much more than me. I hope that you can meet a husband, and that he can take you to Earth, and that you can fulfill your dreams."

The bargirl wiped away a tear. "Charlie is my work name. I'm Dalisay Cortes from Smokey Mountain landfill. I was born a trash girl." She gave a bitter laugh. "I moved up in life." She stood up, eyes damp. "All right, enough! I have to go now. My kids are waiting at home. You have a few hours before a new crowd shows up. Try not to get filthy again by then."

The bargirl rushed out, leaving Maria in the dressing room.

Alone, fear filled Maria.

Fear of tonight.

Of a fresh group of drunken Earthlings spilling into the bar. Wanting her for… for…

Maria blushed. She knelt by her old dress, which was nothing but a tattered rag on the floor. She reached into the pocket and fished out Crisanto. The little Santelmo was so dim, barely glowing at all. He seemed to have shrunk from the size of a marble to a pea.

"Oh Crisanto," Maria whispered. "I want to run away. But I have nowhere else to go. The streets are full of hunger and filth, of rape and theft. The countryside is full of Mister Weird's poison, and the villages have burned. What should I do?"

But the Santelmo could not speak, only gave a weak flicker, then dimmed.

Maria went back downstairs. The soldiers were gone now, and a small child was mopping the floor, perhaps a bargirl's daughter.

"Where is the Magic Man?" Maria asked.

The child blushed, too shy to speak, but pointed at a door.

Maria walked around broken glass and a sleeping cat. Without knocking, she opened the door.

She found herself in a cluttered office. Centerfolds from dirty *banyaga* magazines hung on the walls, featuring naked Earthling women, blond and pouty and sporting huge silicon breasts. The Magic Man sat in a cracked leather armchair, counting bills. But when he saw Maria, he stood up, grinned, and approached her.

"Ah, my princess!" He stroked her hair. His golden chains chinked, and his purple polyester suit crinkled. "You are truly beautiful. You will make me a fortune!"

Maria stared him in the eyes. "You lied to me. You said I was only to sing. But this is a brothel. I know what you want me to do. I'm not so naive."

Well, I was until Charlie educated me, Maria thought. She left that part out. She remembered how the Magic Man had struck Charlie. She did not want the bargirl to suffer any more beatings.

The Magic Man's smile faltered. He lifted a stack of money from his desk.

"Do you see this, *Nini*?"

"Money," she said.

"Life!" The Magic Man shook the sweaty wad of bills. "Dignity! Freedom—from hunger, death, pain. For Charlie, for her brats, for you—for all the girls I take in. Do you want to return to Smokey Mountain, to live in trash and shit?"

"No," Maria said. "But—"

"Then you will dance, and you will sing, and you will sell drinks, and if an Earthling wants to fuck you, you will take him into your bed, and by God above, you will give him the best fuck of his life. For this!" He waved the money in her face, shouting now. "For life!"

"This isn't life," Maria whispered. "We're all already dead in here."

The Magic Man stared at her, then began to laugh. "Yes. We're the dead. But we're dreamers. Charlie dreams of a husband who'll take her to Earth. I dream of retiring with a fortune. What do you dream of, princess?"

"I have no more dreams," she said, and a tear flowed.

"Then step into the back alley and slit your wrists," the Magic Man said. "But if you stay here, you will do as the other girls do."

Maria lowered her eyes. Her tears flowed. "If they… if they have sex with me, it… it won't be me. It will only be my body, but not me. It'll be somebody else, and I'll be back home. I'll be back home in my village." She trembled. "It won't be me."

The Magic Man caressed her cheek and dried her tears. "That's a good girl. That's my sweet princess. Now go to the bar. Pour yourself a drink, anything you like, aside from the imported booze. For free. Tonight, the soldiers will come, and the cowgirls will dance. And you will shine brightest of all."

Maria left his office. And like Crisanto, the light inside her dimmed.

Chapter Forty
Go Go Cowgirl

They gave the platoon five days off.

For hell in the jungle. For losing more than half their platoon. For the deaths of their closest, dearest friends. For necklaces of severed ears. For bullet wounds and burns. For teenage boys and girls shipped into the gauntlet, terrified, taught to kill. For boys and girls with blood on their hands. For haunted eyes. For shattered souls.

Five days off.

A gift. A vacation before their return to the fire.

A bus picked them up from the Old Mig. Not even a military bus. A local Bahayan bus, painted with rainbows, flowers, and butterflies. The driver was an old Bahayan man with whiskey-colored skin, a grizzled goatee, and a mouth full of tobacco.

It seemed strange to Jon. Just yesterday, they had been busy killing Bahayans. Now one was driving them. But Etty, who always seemed to know too much for her own good, explained.

"He's South Bahayan," she told Jon. "It's the North Bahayans who hate Earth. Most South Bahayans like us. That is, aside from the Kalayaan."

"Wait a minute." George frowned. "I thought the Kennys were North Bahayans."

Etty snorted. "No, man. The North has a proper army. You know, the Luminous Army. The one the Red Cardinal leads. The Lumis got artillery and armored trucks and proper infantry units. We haven't met those bastards yet. The Kalayaan are the

South Bahayans who rebel against us."

"The Kalayaan are good for nothing alien-lovers!" the bus driver said, his Bahayan accent thick. "I love Earth. Go Earth! If I ever get a chance, I will punch the Red Cardinal right in his face." He turned toward the soldiers. "Hey, when you fly back to Earth, you take me with you, yes? I would make a good Earthling! Buy big Earth house, eat big Earth meals, kids go to good school. You take me, right? You—"

"Watch the road!" Etty said.

The driver looked, cursed, and swerved around a village girl herding pigs across the road.

They spent the rest of the drive in silence. Twenty-three soldiers. Survivors. Killers. The remains of Lizzy's Lions. They stared out the window at villages, rice paddies, and rolling hills draped with rainforest.

The jungle looks so peaceful from here, Jon thought. *But it contains such horrors.*

An hour later, they reached Mindao, the largest city on the planet, home to millions of Bahayans.

Jon watched the view with dark eyes and silent shock.

"Are you sure we should spend our free days here?" he said.

A few corporals and sergeants, having spent a year or two on Bahay, nodded emphatically.

"Best damn city in the galaxy!" one said.

"Lots of pretty girls."

"Hottest ass you've ever seen."

"Cold beer and hot chicks!"

"You're gonna enjoy this vacation, little privates, trust us. We've been coming here all war."

But Jon was doubtful. The view out the window depressed him. He had never seen so much poverty.

They were driving through a sprawling shantytown.

Countless shacks rose along rivers and train tracks, stacked three or four high like boxes. The lowest levels teetered on crooked struts to allow water and sewage to flow below. The shacks were built of plywood, corrugated iron, and tarpaulin. Everything wooden was rotting, and everything metal was rusting. Bundles of electric cables stretched between the shanties, tangled into crackling, buzzing webs, so thick in spots they blocked the sky.

Rickshaws, mopeds, and jeepneys clogged the narrow streets, plowing through trash. The garbage was everywhere, covering the streets, rotting around the struts of shanties, floating over the rivers, and rising into hills.

Just as shocking was the density. Jon had never seen so many people in one place. The city wasn't large, probably not much larger than Lindenville, his sleepy hometown back on Earth. But two million Bahayans crammed in here. At least, that was the official number. With all the refugees flooding the city, the actual population was probably triple that. The people crowded the shanties, lined the roadsides and train tracks, and rummaged through the garbage. Most were children. Naked. Filthy. Maybe close to dying.

"It's horrible," Etty whispered.

Jon's heart shattered. His mind leaped back to photos of Nazi death camps, Soviet gulags, and alien slaughterhouses. This seemed to him a humanitarian disaster on the same scale. Or at least close enough to send shivers down his spine.

"Many must be refugees," Jon said. "They fled the burning villages, seeking hope in the city. Looks like they found slow death." He frowned at the corporals and sergeants. "Tell me again, guys, why are we here?"

A grinning corporal slung an arm around Jon. "Trust me, my boy, once we're past the shantytown, and you behold the glittering inner city, you'll change your tune."

"Get ready for some slit-sluts, boys!" said another

corporal. He stood in the center of the bus and thrust his hips.

Jon groaned. "We could have spent our time back at the Old Mig, relaxing under a tree, drinking cold Cokes."

"No," George said, the first word he had uttered all day.

Jon looked at his friend. "George?"

"No, I don't want to spend my vacation days at Fort Miguel." The giant's voice got louder, shaking. "I don't want to be near that place! I don't want to go back. I don't want to do this anymore. I don't…"

The giant hung his head and said no more. Jon put a hand on his friend's back. They rode in silence.

The scenery gradually changed. Shanties gave way to concrete buildings, several stories tall. They were old and crumbling, stained with smog and rust from leaky, rattling air conditioners. The homeless lay outside upon beds of newspapers, cardboard, and paper cups. But as Sargas began to set in the east, lights turned on. Neon lights. Countless lights in every color and shape. And the decay faded into shadows.

Jon saw soldiers. Earthling soldiers. Thousands of them. They walked through the inner city, laughing, drinking. Many of them had Bahayan girls on their arms—not meek village girls like the one Jon had seen herding sheep. These girls wore miniskirts, high heels, and lots of makeup. Some soldiers walked with local boys, hand in hand, pausing to steal kisses in the shadows.

The sun vanished behind the horizon, and the neon lights shone even brighter. There must have been dozens—maybe hundreds—of bars here. They lined the roadsides, glittering, beckoning. Jon read some of the glowing signs.

BLUE PEARL GIRLS

SECRET PARADISE

BOYS NIGHT

HOT GIRLS COLD BEER

EARTHLING'S DELIGHT

The signs were in English. These were bars for Earthlings. They must have popped up like mushrooms after the rains of war.

"Drop us off here, my good man!" a corporal said and tossed a few bills at the driver.

The bus rolled to a stop, and the soldiers spilled out onto the street.

At once, the city accosted Jon.

A Bahayan man wearing a green leisure suit approached him, grinning. "You want a good time, soldier? Choose, choose your girlfriend!" He held out a photo album, each page showing several photographs of Bahayan girls.

An old man grabbed Jon by the shirt. "Please, Private, please, take me to Earth, I'll be a good Earthling, I can cut hair, cut grass, I can cook, if you take me to Earth, I can—"

Jon shook himself free. A Bahayan woman approached him, eyes sunken, arm poked full of needle holes. She carried a baby, and several young children gathered around her legs. She held out a grubby hand.

"Shabu, shabu?" she said. "Medicine?"

Mopeds and *tuk tuks* rumbled everywhere. Jon had to leap back to avoid being run over. A young girl sat on a curb, filthy, wasting away, only six or seven years old. She held out a grimy hand. A white-haired Earthling in a Hawaiian shirt strolled by, a rare civilian in this world of war. A Bahayan girl clung to each of his arms, both probably younger than Jon. A Bahayan man stood at a street corner, playing "Hey Jude" on guitar, trying to get the crowd to sing along—and hopefully toss him a few coins.

Jon even spotted an alien. The green giant lumbered down the street, ten feet tall, wearing a shaggy zoot suit. He held four beers in his four hands. He winked at Jon, stepped right over him like a man over a small dog, and continued down the street. It was an Altairian, Jon realized. He had read about these towering aliens, but Jon had never seen one. Hell, he had never seen *any* alien until now.

The lights, the people, the sounds—they all spun Jon's head. He could only stand there, stunned.

"Come on, boys!" The Lions' corporals strutted down the street. "Let's find a watering hole."

The corporals were soon whistling at girls, catcalling, and high-fiving one another. A gaggle of local girls gathered around them, chirping with seductive delight, their miniskirts barely covering a thing. Even in their high heels, they stood no taller than Jon's shoulders. In the jungle, the Bahayans had seemed like monsters, but here Jon could see how much smaller they were than Earthlings. The corporals hooted, slung arms around the girls, smacked their backsides, squeezed their breasts. The girls giggled. Their children crowded in the alleyways, peering with hungry eyes.

Jon knew that everyone here was scared. The hungry children, waiting for their mothers to return with Earth dollars. The prostitutes, so fragile next to these Earth giants. And the Earthlings themselves. The corporals—with all their posturing. They were so scared.

They were broken. They had fought in the jungle at Jon's side. They had lost friends. They had faced death. As the neon lights filled their eyes, Jon saw terror. They were like him. Just a year or two older. Boys who missed home. Boys who were so terrified.

A burly figure stomped toward Jon, interrupting his musings.

"What's a matter, asshole?" Clay smirked. "Scared of all the tits?"

Jon groaned. Unfortunately, Clay had survived this far, and he was here with them. Here was one Earthling soldier, at least, who had not shattered in the jungle. Clay's soul had broken long ago. If he ever had a soul.

"I need a drink," Jon said, turning away from his tormentor.

"Me too," said George.

"Me too!" said Etty.

They walked away from the others, heading down the street. On this block alone, a mere sliver of the electric boulevard, they encountered a dizzying array of options. Pool houses. Drug dens. Strip clubs. Fried chicken joints. And mostly—bars.

Etty pointed at one bar. The neon sign featured a cowgirl riding a bull. Words appeared below the luminous figure:

GO GO COWGIRL

A poster on the wall promised cold beer, spicy wings, midget boxing, and the prettiest girls on Bahay.

The flesh is cheap on Bahay, Jon mused. *They sell the girls like they sell chicken wings.*

"Let's try this one," Etty said.

Jon cringed. "I dunno, it looks pretty sleazy."

Etty raised an eyebrow. "You prefer Pussy Palace next door?"

"Go Go Cowgirl it is," Jon said.

They stepped inside. The rest of their platoon followed.

They found a bar already crammed full of Earthling soldiers and Bahayan girls. Local music filled the bar, a pop tune sung in Tagalog. It was far too loud. Soldiers were drinking and dancing with girls. Lights flashed and bottles rolled. Drugs and drinks flowed. Soldiers sat at tables, bouncing girls on their laps, faces flushed with booze. The place reeked of beer, sweat, and sex.

"There are barely any Bahayan men in the city," Jon said softly. "They're all fighting in the jungles. Or we killed them all."

A corporal slapped him on the back. "Relax, buddy. Now's the time to drink and be merry. Come on, I'll buy you a beer."

Jon glanced at his friends. Neither George nor Etty looked particularly merry. They were all new on Bahay, green privates. Jon wondered how long it took before death lost all meaning. Before he could become like these corporals, dead inside.

"Welcome, welcome to the Go Go Cowgirl, the best bar on Bahay!"

A man walked toward them, arms wide. Finally—a rare Bahayan man still in the city. He was middle-aged, maybe too old for fighting, but powerfully built. He sported a meticulous goatee, slicked-back hair, and a flashy purple suit. It looked like cheap polyester, but the man wore many rings, bracelets, and chains of gold, and those looked real enough.

"Hey, Magic Man!" a corporal said, slapping him on the back. Other corporals joined, shaking the Bahayan's hand, slapping his back, and mussing his oily hair.

"Howdy, partners!" the bar owner said, nervously laughing and fixing his hair. "Welcome back! And who's the fresh meat? Ah, privates from Earth! My God, and the redhead is a giant!" He turned toward Jon and his friends. "Welcome to Bahay, friends! I am Rodrigo Reyes, but my friends call me the Magic Man. Anything you want, I can get you. Like magic." He snapped his ringed fingers. "Beer? Shabu? Girls? Boys? Boys who look like girls? Whatever you want. I can make it magically appear."

The man grinned, revealing a golden tooth, and winked.

"Just beers," Jon said. "And a quiet table."

The Magic Man laughed. "You're in the wrong bar for quiet, friends! Ah, but the beer is as cold as the girls are hot. Come, come! Are you back from the jungle? You deserve a treat. I'll seat you at the best table in the house!"

Etty leaned toward Jon. "He seems friendly."

"This whole city seems friendly," Jon said. "At least if you have Earth dollars." He patted George on the back. "You okay, buddy?"

George was looking at a few girls dancing on the bar. They were topless, and George's cheeks were flushing.

"Um, yeah, I…" The giant loosened his collar. "I am now. I think. Sorry for my outburst before, I…" A girl in lingerie strutted by, pausing to rub against him, and George gulped. "Um, yes, a cold beer would be good."

"And maybe a cold shower," Etty suggested.

The group sat at a table.

The lights dimmed, and the music died.

The Magic Man hopped onto a stage and spread his arms open.

"Welcome, friends!" he announced, teeth sparkling, haloed in neon. "Welcome to the *Go Go Cowgirl*!"

The lights flared. The music pounded. The girls stepped onto the stage. And Jon's life changed forever.

Chapter Forty-One
Angels of Dust and Bruises

Maria was so scared.

The lights blinded her. The music deafened her. All around her, they were dancing, drinking, cheering. She cowered behind the bar and trembled. She wanted to run. Every instinct in her body cried to escape, to barge out the door or climb out the window, to vanish in the city. To return to the landfill. Or the train tracks. Or even the wilderness.

She didn't even have Crisanto with her. She wore her white silken dress, the fabric translucent, virginal yet dripping sensuality. There was no pocket for her friend.

"Welcome, welcome to the Go Go Cowgirl!" the Magic Man said, standing onstage nearby.

Across the bar, a hundred Earthlings cheered and raised mugs of beer.

"Take off your shirt!" a soldier shouted.

The Magic Man strutted across the stage, pulled open his jacket, pouted at the crowd—a mocking pantomime. Soldiers laughed and hooted. Somebody tossed a can of beer.

"Bring on the girls!"

Hiding behind the bar, Maria wrapped her arms around herself, wishing she could disappear. She was trapped. The exit lay across the crowd of Earthlings. She would never make it. There was no way out.

Oh God, she thought, clutching the cross that hung from her neck. *One of these men will buy me tonight. Will… will have sex with me*. She shivered.

"It's all right."

A soft voice spoke. A hand caressed her hair.

Maria looked up to see Charlie kneeling beside her. The bargirl wore red lingerie, high-heeled boots, and a cowboy hat—a ridiculous getup. But her eyes were soft and kind.

"I'm scared," Maria whispered to the older woman.

"I was scared my first time too," Charlie said. "Remember what I told you, Maria. You find a husband here. A good man. Somebody who doesn't just want to fuck you—but also love you. You find a man like that, and you marry him, okay? And you go with him to Earth. Don't wait until you have four kids like me. No Earthling will want you then."

"But they're horrible," Maria said. "Loud and drunk. Killers. They're the giants who bombed my village. Who killed so many of us."

Charlie stroked Maria's hair. "They're boys, Maria. Many are no older than you. They're boys who were fighting in the jungles. Who watched their friends die. Who come here to drink, to fuck, to forget. But sometimes, Maria, they fall in love. They take a girl home. Don't end up like me."

The Magic Man's voice boomed from the stage.

"May I introduce the first lovely lady of the night. Welcome, Charlie Wonder!"

The crowd cheered.

"Charlie!" the Magic Man said, gesturing at her. "Get your little ass up here. Here she comes, boys—Miss Charlie Wonder!"

Charlie gave Maria a sad look, and a tear rolled down her cheek. Then she snorted some shabu, spun on her heel, and strutted onto the stage.

"Hi boys!" She waved, leaned forward to showcase her cleavage, and blew the crowd a kiss.

The crowd howled and hooted. Charlie struck pose after

pose, each more seductive than the last. The Earthlings roared, rose onto the tabletops, and tossed dollar bills her way. The speakers played "Cat on a Roof," a popular Bahayan tune, while Charlie danced.

"Isn't she beautiful?" the Magic Man said. "Don't you want her to be your girlfriend tonight?"

A sergeant stood up and raised a bill. "Five dollars!"

From the stage, Charlie blew him a raspberry. The crowd laughed.

A corporal raised his wallet. "Ten dollars!"

Charlie pouted and trailed an imaginary tear down her cheek.

More soldiers rose and bid. Finally a mustached, pot-bellied sergeant won her for the night. He paid twenty-three dollars. With a beefy hand, the Earthling pulled Charlie back to his table. Soldiers howled and slapped him on the back. Charlie sat on the fat man's lap, tried to flirt. But the sergeant spun her around, shoved her onto the table, and unzipped his pants. He took her then and there. Charlie cried out, a pained imitation of pleasure, and soldiers cheered.

Maria watched from behind the bar, eyes wide, and her heart fluttered in her chest like a trapped bird.

"Now, please welcome our next lady of the night!" the Magic Man said. "Come onstage, Kitty LaRue!"

Another bargirl stepped onstage, strutted back and forth, and blew kisses to the crowd. Maria had spoken to her that morning. The slender woman had lost her daughter in the bombing. Her son lived above the bar. She had been a rice farmer once, but onstage, she was Kitty LaRue, seductress.

Men roared and raised wads of cash. A group of privates bought her, pulled her back to their table, and had their fun. One by one. In the open.

Another girl danced. A corporal began leading her

upstairs, found that he could not wait, and took her right on the stairway.

Girl after girl. Rice farmers. Fishermen's daughters. Refugees of the jungle and outcasts of the landfills. Bruised. Scratched. Haunted. Beautiful. Cheapest flesh in Mindao.

"Will one of you marry me?" Kitty LaRue was asking the privates who hired her. "Will you take me to Earth?"

A few privates laughed.

"Shut up, slit," one said.

Kitty stroked his cheek. "I'll cook for you. I'll love you. If you marry me and take me to Earth, I'll—"

The private struck her, knocking her down. His friend laughed.

I have to get out, Maria thought. *These are not good men. These are not frightened boys like Charlie said. They're cruel. They're killers.*

She began to crawl away, still hidden behind the bar. If she could crawl between everyone's feet, perhaps while a dancing girl distracted the crowd, she could reach the exit. She could flee into the streets. Even the landfills were better than this.

Hands grabbed her.

Somebody pulled her to her feet, spun her around.

Maria found herself facing the Magic Man.

He sneered at her, his fingers digging into her arms. A girl stepped onstage and began to dance. Others girls cavorted between the tables, wearing flimsy lingerie. Nobody was looking at Maria and her captor.

"Where do you think you're going?" the Magic Man hissed.

Maria struggled against him. "Let me go!"

He slapped her. Hard. Slamming her against the wall. Lights floated around her like little Santelmos. The Magic Man pulled her closer, and snarled in her face.

"Where would you go, girl? Back to the garbage heap to

live like a rat? To the poisoned villages where the air and soil deforms you? You're mine now, girl." He tightened his grip and shook her. "You belong to me, the Magic Man. Now get up there onstage! You will fetch the highest price tonight."

He dragged her onto the stage.

Maria stood there, dazed, her cheek still stinging.

She faced the crowd. A hundred soldiers or more, many drunk, many with girls on or under them. The lights spun Maria's head. Clouds of smoke invaded her nostrils. She nearly fainted. She stood there, still, not like the other girls. She did not dance, did not strut. She wore her white dress, and she saw the fields and mountains of San Luna, and a tear rolled down her cheek.

The men cheered and roared, already raising dollar bills.

The Magic Man's fingers dug into her arm.

"Allow me to introduce our newest cowgirl!" He spun Maria around. "Fresh from the provinces. Meet Holy Maria, a true virgin!"

The men roared and thrust their hips at her. The bidding began.

Maria closed her eyes, another tear fell, and she thought of home.

Chapter Forty-Two
Of Love and Lies

She was the most beautiful woman Jon had ever seen.

She stood onstage, dressed in white, virginal and innocent. A tear flowed down her cheek, and Jon's heart broke.

Holy Maria. An angel in hell.

"This is bullshit," Etty muttered, sitting at the table beside Jon. "I'm getting out of this bar."

George nodded. "Me too."

But Jon just sat there, looking at the girl onstage. She had silky black hair. Smooth olive-toned skin. A slender frame. And such sadness. Such purity. In the spotlight, she seemed to glow, a saint in the darkness.

"Holy Maria!" her pimp said, strutting across the stage. His bracelets jangled. "Who will bid on this beautiful virgin?"

George and Etty were already walking away. They looked back at Jon.

"Buddy, let's get out of here," George said.

But Jon could not tear his eyes away.

Men began to bid. Fifty dollars. Sixty. Soon a hundred dollars for the night—far more expensive than any other girl. Even soldiers who had already hired bargirls were bidding, ready for another round. And the bids kept climbing.

Clay Hagen climbed onto a table. He was still wearing his necklace of severed human ears.

"Two hundred dollars!" he cried and brandished the money.

Soldiers around him cursed and sat down, outbid.

Jon stared in horror.

"Two hundred dollars!" the Magic Man announced. "The highest price ever recorded in the Go Go Cowgirl! Congratulations, Holy Maria!"

Clay grinned and began unbuckling his belt. "She won't be so holy soon." He laughed. "Or so pretty. Not when I'm done with her."

Maria looked at him from the stage. She saw the severed ears, and she paled. She tried to flee, but the Magic Man held her fast. The girl trembled. Clay advanced toward her, licking his lips.

Jon stood up.

"Three hundred dollars!" he said.

His friends looked at him like he was crazy.

Clay spun toward him, a snarl replacing his grin.

"She's mine! I already bought her."

"You lost, Clay!" Jon said. "You were outbid."

They both turned toward the Magic Man, awaiting his judgment like peasants before a king. The pimp practically had dollar signs in his eyes. He took Maria's hand and raised it overhead.

"And the winner, for three hundred dollars, is…" He raised his eyebrows. "Your name, sir?"

"Private Jon Taylor!" Etty said, running up and pointing at Jon.

"Private Jon Taylor!" the Magic Man repeated. "Congratulation!"

The pimp began dragging Maria toward Jon, holding her tightly enough to leave bruises

But Clay was not going down without a fight. The brute kicked over a table, knocking over empty beer mugs and chicken bones, and roared. "This is bullshit!" He glared at Jon. "You don't have three hundred dollars, you piece of shit. No soldier does unless he's a fucking general."

Clay was right. Soldiers didn't earn much in the Human Defense Force. Just a few dollars a day, enough to buy supplies at the commissary, maybe enjoy a night out every few months. Jon opened his wallet and counted. He had ninety-three dollars. His entire life savings.

"See?" Clay said. "He can't pay up! The girl is mine."

He reached for Maria, pulled her toward him. His fingers tightened, looked ready to snap her arm. Maria cringed, turned away, and a tear fell. Clay pulled her closer and licked the tear off her cheek.

"Wait, Jon!" Etty opened her wallet. "Remember how you gave me money earlier? To hold onto so you don't overspend on beer?"

"No, I didn't—" Jon caught himself. "Um, yes! Of course. Can I have my money back now?"

Etty handed him all her own money, an act of kindness Jon vowed to never forget.

"You gave me some of your money too," George said, opening his wallet. "Here, have it back, Jon."

Jon wanted to hug his friends. It would have to wait.

He handed the money toward the Magic Man—a big sweaty wad of bills. "Here you go. The promised price. Maria is mine for the night."

Clay froze, teeth bared, still holding Maria. Everyone in the bar was watching.

The Magic Man counted the dollars. He looked up at Jon. "You're seventeen dollars short."

Clay laughed.

One of the bargirls ran up, wobbling on high heels. She wore red lingerie, a cowboy hat, and an assortment of bruises and teeth marks. Jon remembered her. The first girl to dance tonight. Charlie Wonder.

"Mister Jon!" the bargirl said. "You dropped something!"

Charlie pulled a twenty dollar bill from her bra and handed it to him.

Jon's eyes softened. How could he take this money from her? It was probably all her earnings tonight.

"Take it," Charlie whispered. "Be good to her."

Jon took the money. He handed it to the Magic Man.

The crowd cheered, and Clay roared and smashed a table.

"Sold!" the Magic Man said. "Congratulation, Private Jon Taylor, winner of Holy Maria!"

The pimp shoved the girl toward Jon. And then Maria was in his arms, trembling, his angel for the night.

* * * * *

The girl led Jon upstairs, eyes downcast, still trembling. But she clung to his hand like a drowning woman. Her hand was small, almost vanishing in his own, and Jon held it tightly.

They walked down a concrete corridor, navigating around rolling bottles, a sleeping sergeant, and a corporal with his pants around his ankles, thrusting into a bargirl right there on the floor.

Maria took Jon into a little room. There was no door, only a curtain, and she pulled it shut. Mold and cracks covered the walls, and dust drifted across the floor.

They were alone.

The girl stood before him, trembling, daring not meet his eyes. A tear dangled off her chin.

"I won't hurt you, Maria," Jon said. "I didn't want that other soldier to hurt you either. I'll keep you safe tonight."

She glanced into his eyes, then down again. She had beautiful eyes, Jon thought. Dark, intelligent, and haunted.

"Thank you, Sir Jon," she said. Her head was still lowered, and her hair framed her face.

Jon hesitated, then brushed back her hair. It was soft as silk. He tucked the strands behind her ear, revealing a bruise on her cheek.

"Who hurt you?" he said.

She looked down again. "I fell. I'm clumsy."

She began working at the straps of her dress, awkward, eyes downcast. The straps finally opened, and her dress puddled around her feet. She stood before him naked but for her cross pendant. Jon couldn't help but admire her body. She was slender, but in a graceful way, not the starving look many in this city had. Her skin was dark and smooth, her breasts small, and Jon felt his blood heating.

She's mine for the night, he thought. *And she's beautiful. She's the most beautiful woman I've ever seen. I can have her. All night long.*

But he looked away.

"You don't have to do this," he said.

Tears spiked her lashes. "I'm sorry, Sir Jon. I don't mean to cry. Or to be so awkward. I know my job is to pleasure men. But I'm a virgin."

Jon said something he would never dare confess to his fellow soldiers. "So am I."

Maria blinked, tilted her head, and then suddenly she was laughing. She was actually laughing! The girl who only moments ago was trembling and crying.

Jon shifted his weight uncomfortably. "Um, surely it's not *that* funny. I mean, I kissed a girl once. Her name is Kaelyn. Not that you want to hear about her now. I mean, not that I'm going to do anything. I mean, if you don't want me to. I mean, if you *did* want to… But you don't, so…" His cheeks were hot. "Oh boy, now I'm the awkward one."

She laughed harder. "You're funny, Sir Jon. You're not

like the other Earthlings."

"You can just call me Jon," he said. "Is Maria your real name? I noticed that the other girls have stripper names. Cookie, Amber, Kitty, that kind of thing."

She smiled. "Yes, my real name is Maria de la Cruz. It means Maria of the cross."

"I'm Jon Taylor. It means…" He thought for a moment. "Hell, I don't know. I guess it means that I'm just a dumb Earthling who probably has no business being here."

She blinked at him. "Being here?" She looked around at the room.

"No, I mean—being on Bahay," Jon said. "I like being in your room."

She lowered her eyelids shyly. "I like you too." She blushed and covered her cheeks. "You meant you like my *room*, not me! I'm sorry. I just talk so much sometimes. Like an idiot who can't stop ever talking. My mother said my head is too big, and that it's full of too many questions and nonsense, and she would always say: Maria, be quiet, and don't speak so much, because you just go on and on, and annoy everyone, and—" She covered her mouth. "And now I'm doing it again, and it's because I'm nervous, and—"

"Maria?" Jon said.

She blinked at him. "Yes?"

He held her hand. "I like you too."

Her blush deepened.

Jon looked around the room. It was austere. There was a cot. Concrete walls. A cracked dresser. That was about it. A small window revealed flashing lights outside. The din of rickshaws, mopeds, and drunken Earthlings spilled in from the night. The room seemed as depressing as a prison cell.

He looked back at Maria, a rose growing from concrete.

"Well, we have all night," Jon said. "Want to play cards?"

"I don't know how," Maria said.

He pulled a deck from his pocket. "I'll teach you. How about gin rummy?"

She blinked. "You would like me to get you a drink?"

He laughed, sat down on the bed, and patted the spot beside him. "Come, I'll teach you."

She pulled her dress back on, and they began to play. Within minutes, she had mastered the game. He beat her the first two times. Then she beat him, and she jumped for joy, laughed, and her eyes shone. There was true joy there. Still a lot of pain. Jon knew that she must have suffered great pain in this war. But also true joy, and it warmed his heart that he could make her laugh.

"Again, again!" Maria said, shuffling the deck.

"I let you win last time."

She shoved him playfully. "You liar! I'm clearly much better than you. Go on, your turn!"

They played again, and she won again, and her smile was huge and bright, and her eyes sparkled.

"You cheated!" Jon said.

She laughed and pushed him. "I did not."

"Sure you did."

She gasped. "How dare you accuse me! I'm going to tickle you to death."

She began tickling him, and Jon laughed and grabbed her wrists, and for a moment they struggled on the bed, laughing and wrestling, until they fell on their backs. They lay atop the cards, looking up at the ceiling, exhausted.

They were silent for a long moment.

Then Jon spoke.

"Maria, I'm sorry."

She frowned. "For what?"

His eyes dampened. "For doing this. For being here. I…

killed people, Maria. I don't know how many. I dropped grenades into tunnels, and I shot into the forest, and… I was told they're monsters. That they're evil. And I was scared of them, Maria. Of the Kalayaan. I was so scared." He looked at his hands, and his tears fell. "But my leaders lied to me. You're not evil. My brother died here for nothing, and I killed people here for nothing. The blood of Bahay is on my hands. And I'm so sorry. And I'm still so scared."

Maria held his hand. "I can't offer you absolution. But nor do I offer condemnation. You don't have to confess to me."

"I do," he said. "I have to tell someone. And there's nobody else I can tell. I have to talk about it. Maria, I grew up on Earth, a planet steeped in war. For generations, we fought. We fought Nazis and communists. We fought aliens. We fought robots. We fought war after war after war. And all those were wars of justice. Of good versus evil. I'm an Earthling. I was born for war, bred for war, trained for war. And I wanted to be like my heroes. Like Marco Emery, like Addy Linden, like Einav Ben-Ari, like the war heroes from the stories. Alien-killers. So I came here to be like them. And I found… people. Fellow humans. I found innocence. I found you." He caressed her cheek. "And I realized that I'm not a hero. In this war, *I* am the alien. *I* am the monster."

She put a hand on his cheek. "My village was bombed, Jon. They all died. My parents. My friends. All gone. I thought Earthlings were monsters too. But you're *not* a monster."

"I am—"

"You're not! Maybe your generals are. Maybe your president is. But you, Jon Taylor, are not a monster. You're a good man. Kind and funny and gentle. I can tell. I can feel it."

He embraced her. "Maria, I was taught to hate you. They broke me, Maria. They broke me so bad. And they taught me to come here, to kill your men, to fuck your women, to conquer and…" He could not speak for a moment, overcome, then brushed her hair and looked into her eyes. "You're so beautiful, Maria, and you're so sweet, and everything inside me is breaking right now, and I don't know how to ever put the pieces together."

They lay on the bed, holding each other for a long time. Her body was warm against his, her hair soft. She laid her hand on his chest.

"Jon?" she whispered.

"Maria?"

"I want you to make love to me," she said.

Jon shook his head. "Maria, you don't have to. I hired you for the night to protect you from Clay. Not to take advantage of you."

Her voice was soft. "Jon, I'm new here today, a virgin. But tomorrow night, another man will hire me. And the night after that. Maybe every night for years. That's who I am now. I don't want my first time to be with a cruel man. With somebody like those soldiers below. I don't want to lose my virginity tomorrow night to somebody like Clay. I choose you, Jon. I want you."

He caressed her cheek. "I'd still feel like you're forced. Like you have no choice."

"Bargirls don't kiss their clients. Charlie taught me that." Maria leaned forward and kissed Jon's lips. "You're not my client. You're a man I like. A man I choose. A kind man." She undressed again and lay naked beside him, the neon lights from outside dancing over her skin. "Be with me tonight."

He kissed her.

They kissed for a long time.

She closed her eyes, trembled for a moment, maybe still a little afraid. But when his hands explored her body, she kissed him again, and she whispered his name over and over as they made love.

Afterward, Jon lay on his back. He lay in silence. For a moment—in bliss.

The world burns, but here, for a moment, I feel true joy.

Maria curled up against him, her leg tossed over his leg, and laid her cheek upon his chest. She slept like that, nuzzling him, her breath soft on his skin. But he could not sleep for a long while. He stayed awake, stroking her hair, savoring her warmth. Her words echoed.

You're not a monster. You're a good man.

He held her in his arms.

I'm a good man who did horrible things. And I don't know if I can ever go home.

Chapter Forty-Three
The Earthling

He had four days of leave left, and Jon spent them with Maria.

Her value, the Magic Man said, dropped dramatically now that she was no longer a virgin. But hiring her for four days still cost a small fortune. Jon's friends helped. George sold his watch in a pawnshop. It fetched a good price.

"Don't worry about it, Jon," the giant said when Jon objected. "My dad gave me that watch, and he's a jerk."

Etty helped too, organizing a fundraiser in Cronus Company, to which the Lions platoon belonged. Many soldiers understood. Some had Bahayan girlfriends of their own. They gave a dollar here, a dollar there. And soon Etty returned with a bundle of cash.

It all went to the Magic Man.

And for four days, Maria was free.

On the first day, Jon hired a rickshaw, and they wandered through the city. They found a greasy joint that served fresh local food. There was *sinigang* stew, rich with chicken and tamarind; roast *lechon*, tender pork with crunchy skin; *lumpia* spring rolls they could not get enough of, and finally sticky rice cake for dessert. Maria was tiny, but she ate as much as Jon, and he ate a lot. Their bellies full, they found a vintage movie theater, at least a century old. They were showing classic movies from Earth. Maria and Jon sat holding hands, watching silly monster movies of giant reptiles destroying cities and battling robots. They laughed a lot.

On the second day, Jon hired two mopeds, and they

learned how to drive them. As they drove through the shantytown, they were both silent and sad. Outside the city, they traveled down a dirt road to a beach, and they spent all day walking along the sand. Every few moments, they heard booms from across the water. The war was still raging there. But here, on this side of the sea, they found peace and joy, and they collected seashells, chased each other, laughed, and kissed in the sunset.

On the third day it was Sunday, and Maria asked to go to church. Jon was not religious. But he went with her, and they prayed. After services ended, Jon asked around, and amazingly, he found a cafe with a piano. Here—on Bahay! In this city of poverty and war—an actual grand piano! The cafe owner let Jon play all day, hoping it would attract customers. Jon played for Maria. He played her all the songs from Symphonica, and he even taught her to sing "Falling Like the Rain." They were all sad songs, part of the concept album he was writing. Songs from the soul of a dead soldier. But then he played her the Beatles and Elton John, and everyone in the cafe, and even along the street, gathered around him and sang along. Maria sat beside Jon, singing too, and her eyes sparkled, and her smile was the dawn.

On the fourth day, they got married.

It wasn't a real wedding. Not with a priest or judge. They got married in the Go Go Cowgirl. Upstairs. With the other bargirls as bridesmaids.

"Are you sure you want to do this?" Jon asked her.

Maria smiled, holding his hands. "Let this be a symbol of our love. When you go back to war tomorrow, I want you to go as a husband. So that you have something to survive for. So that you come back to me."

Jon was not ready to get married. Neither was Maria, he knew. This was not a real wedding, just a symbol. A promise.

It was something good in a world falling apart. It was something to keep him together. It was love in a galaxy of hate.

The other girls brought bottles of champagne, and they cheered and wept, and Maria wore her white dress from the first night. Charlie donned a sheet as a robe and pretended to be a priest, speaking in a deep voice, even painting a mustache onto her face. Everyone laughed. But when she pronounced Jon and Maria husband and wife, everyone was solemn. And the couple kissed.

"Woo, now let's drink and get pissed!" Etty cried, cracking open a bottle of champagne.

More bottles popped, and fountains sprayed, and everyone laughed. Maria looked into Jon's eyes, her smile so bright, and he held her hands.

"Congratulations, Mrs. Taylor!" Charlie said, and kissed Maria's cheek, but she seemed so sad.

Maria hugged the older woman. "Thank you, Charlie. Are you okay?"

Charlie wiped her eyes and smiled. "I'm happy for you." She mussed Maria's hair. "Angel of Bahay."

"She's an angel of Earth!" Jon said. "You all came from Earth once, haven't you? The Bahayans. You came from the Philippines centuries ago. You're all Earthlings too."

Charlie raised her cup high. "To Maria the Earthling!"

The girls laughed. They raised their cups too. "To Maria the Earthling!"

Jon hugged her. This girl he had met in the slums. This daughter of a nation he was sent to destroy. His imaginary wife, maybe one he would someday marry for real. Maria. The only good thing he had found in this war.

* * * * *

That night, they went down to Go Go Cowgirl's common room, and they celebrated with food and drink. The whole platoon showed up. Even Sergeant Lizzy arrived to drink and laugh and dance with her soldiers. The ruthless sergeant, the woman who had tormented them so much at boot camp—drinking and dancing with them! She even danced with Jon, and her eyes shone.

"The whole platoon is talking!" Lizzy said, her hands on Jon's shoulders. "They say you're in love."

"Yeah, they've been busting my balls all week," Jon said.

Lizzy laughed and mussed his hair. "I'm happy for you. She's beautiful."

Jon grinned. "You know, Lizzy, you're a lot nicer when you're not whipping me."

She patted his cheek. "I might have to again. You're a horrible dancer." Playfully, she pushed him away. "Now stop dancing with your sergeant and go spend time with your wife."

Tomorrow, Jon and his friends were returning to war. Tomorrow, he would trudge through the jungle again, killing, maybe dying. But tonight he was here. Tonight he was with Maria. With his friends. With people he loved. They danced, laughed, and drank like it was their last night alive. And maybe it was.

It was midnight when the door banged open.

A man barged into the Go Go Cowgirl, eyes wild. One eye burning with dark fire. Another white with cataracts.

A man with a hard, angular face. With a pointy goatee. With a scar across his forehead.

"Ernesto!" Maria whispered, going pale.

Jon's heart dipped. He felt like he was back in Captain Pete's helicopter, plunging through turbulence.

Ernesto? Ernesto Santos? The man who killed my brother?

He had seen photos of the man. Carter had shown him on the hunt.

"It's him," Jon whispered.

The guerrilla stomped across the common room, his boots splattering mud. A bandoleer hung across his chest, and he held a flintlock pistol.

"Maria!" he cried, approaching her. "Maria, I found you. I finally found you!"

Jon stared, frozen. Maria cowered behind him.

"Jon, help," she whispered.

And everything seemed to happen at once.

Lizzy leaped to her feet. The sergeant was trembling. Of course she was trembling. Lizzy—the woman Ernesto had raped, tortured, mutilated.

The sergeant let out a howl. A great cry torn with anguish. She reached for her rifle, which leaned against the wall. She loaded. She aimed at Ernesto, and—

Ernesto fired his pistol.

A bullet tore through Lizzy's chest. Blood sprayed the wall behind her, and the sergeant crashed to the floor.

Jon grabbed his rifle, shielding Maria behind his back.

Pistol smoking, Ernesto was turning toward him.

For a second, the universe seemed to freeze. Images flashed before Jon. Rainforests burning. A dark labyrinth trapping him. A beautiful angel blessing him.

Ernesto aimed his gun at Jon, and Maria screamed.

Jon pulled his trigger.

Both guns fired at once, and blood painted the world.

The story continues in

Earthlings

Soldiers of Earthrise II

NOVELS BY DANIEL ARENSON

Earthrise:

Earth Alone

Earth Lost

Earth Rising

Earth Fire

Earth Shadows

Earth Valor

Earth Reborn

Earth Honor

Earth Eternal

Soldiers of Earthrise:

The Earthling

Earthlings

Earthling's War

I, Earthling

The Earthling's Daughter

We Are Earthlings

Children of Earthrise:

The Heirs of Earth

A Memory of Earth

An Echo of Earth

The War for Earth

The Song of Earth

The Legacy of Earth

The Moth Saga:

Moth

Empires of Moth

Secrets of Moth

Daughter of Moth

Shadows of Moth

Legacy of Moth

Dawn of Dragons:

Requiem's Song

Requiem's Hope

Requiem's Prayer

Song of Dragons:

Blood of Requiem

Tears of Requiem

Light of Requiem

Dragonlore:

A Dawn of Dragonfire

A Day of Dragon Blood

A Night of Dragon Wings

The Dragon War:

A Legacy of Light

A Birthright of Blood

A Memory of Fire

Requiem for Dragons:

Dragons Lost

Dragons Reborn

Dragons Rising

Flame of Requiem:

Forged in Dragonfire

Crown of Dragonfire

Pillars of Dragonfire

Misfit Heroes:

Eye of the Wizard

Wand of the Witch

Kingdoms of Sand:

Kings of Ruin

Crowns of Rust

Thrones of Ash

Temples of Dust

Halls of Shadow

Echoes of Light

Alien Hunters:

Alien Hunters

Alien Sky

Alien Shadows

Standalones:

Firefly Island

Flaming Dove

The Gods of Dream

Utopia 58

KEEP IN TOUCH

www.DanielArenson.com
Daniel@DanielArenson.com
Facebook.com/DanielArenson
Twitter.com/DanielArenson

Made in the USA
Coppell, TX
25 November 2019